Praise for
ICE COLD

"Gerritsen has outdone herself." —*Portsmouth Herald*

"Fantastic . . . will not disappoint."
—Fredericksburg *Free Lance-Star*

"[An] engrossing thriller . . . start-to-finish entertaining."
—*Kirkus Reviews*

"Colorful characters and an imaginative plot make this one of the must-reads of the summer." —*Tucson Citizen*

"[Gerritsen's] knowledge of medicine and crime gives her a unique talent for spinning complex, can't-put-down page-turners." —*Lincoln Journal Star*

"A good suspenseful mystery, building up the tension carefully to lead to its thrilling conclusion."
—*The Parkersburg News & Sentinel*

"Fans will be on the edge of their seats." —*Library Journal*

"There's a surprise around every corner, and that's the way her readers like it." —*Bangor Daily News*

"Gerritsen supplies plenty of depth in both plot and characters." —*Publishers Weekly*

"Compelling . . . a seamless melding of an Old West tale and a thoroughly modern thriller." —*BookPage*

"A solid entry in the series, with a compelling mystery and some good, old-fashioned shockers." —*Booklist*

"[Gerritsen] aims and reaches for the stars in *Ice Cold*."
—Bookreporter.com

"Excellent plot twists." —New Orleans *Times-Picayune*

ALSO BY TESS GERRITSEN

Harvest
Life Support
Bloodstream
Gravity
The Surgeon
The Apprentice
The Sinner
Body Double
Vanish
The Mephisto Club
The Bone Garden
The Keepsake
The Silent Girl

ICE COLD

A RIZZOLI & ISLES NOVEL

TESS GERRITSEN

BALLANTINE BOOKS • NEW YORK

2011 Ballantine Books Mass Market Edition

Copyright © 2010 by Tess Gerritsen
Excerpt from *The Silent Girl* copyright © 2011 by Tess Gerritsen

All rights reserved.

Published in the United States by Ballantine Books, an imprint of The Random House Publishing Group, a division of Random House, Inc., New York.

BALLANTINE and colophon are registered trademarks of Random House, Inc.

Originally published in hardcover in the United States by Ballantine Books, an imprint of The Random House Publishing Group, a division of Random House, Inc., in 2010.

This book contains an excerpt from the forthcoming book *The Silent Girl* by Tess Gerritsen. This excerpt has been set for this editon only and may not reflect the final content of the forthcoming edition.

ISBN 978-0-345-51549-0

Cover design: Jae Song
Cover images: Kwame Zikomo/Superstock

Printed in the United States of America

www.ballantinebooks.com

9 8 7 6 5 4 3 2 1

To Jack R. Winans
Kearny High School, San Diego

The lessons you taught me will last a lifetime.

ONE

PLAIN OF ANGELS, IDAHO

S HE WAS THE CHOSEN ONE.

For months, he had been studying the girl, ever since she and her family had moved into the compound. Her father was George Sheldon, a mediocre carpenter who worked with the construction crew. Her mother, a bland and forgettable woman, was assigned to the communal bakery. Both had been unemployed and desperate when they'd first wandered into his church in Idaho Falls, seeking solace and salvation. Jeremiah had looked into their eyes, and he saw what he needed to see: lost souls in search of an anchor, any anchor.

They had been ripe for the harvest.

Now the Sheldons and their daughter, Katie, lived in Cottage C, in the newly built Calvary cluster. Every Sabbath, they sat in their assigned pew in the fourteenth row. In their front yard they'd planted hollyhocks and sunflowers, the same cheery plants that adorned all the other front gardens. In so many ways, they blended in with the other sixty-four families in The Gathering, families who labored together, worshipped together, and, every Sabbath evening, broke bread together.

But in one important way, the Sheldons were unique. They had an extraordinarily beautiful daughter. The daughter whom he could not stop staring at.

From his window, Jeremiah could see her in the school yard. It was noon recess, and students milled about outside, enjoying the warm September day, the boys in their white shirts and black pants, the girls in their long pastel dresses. They all looked healthy and sun-kissed, as children ought to look. Even among those swanlike girls, Katie Sheldon stood out, with her irrepressible curls and her bell-like laughter. How quickly girls change, he thought. In a single year, she had transformed from a child into a willowy young woman. Her bright eyes, gleaming hair, and rosy cheeks were all signs of fertility.

She stood among a trio of girls in the shade of a bur oak tree. Their heads were bent together like the Three Graces whispering secrets. Around them swirled the energy of the school yard, where students chattered and played hopscotch and kicked around a soccer ball.

Suddenly he noticed a boy crossing toward the three girls, and he frowned. The boy was about fifteen, with a thatch of blond hair and long legs that had already outgrown his trousers. Halfway across the yard, the boy paused, as though gathering up the courage to continue. Then his head lifted and he walked directly toward the girls. Toward Katie.

Jeremiah pressed closer to the window.

As the boy approached, Katie looked up and smiled. It was a sweet and innocent smile, directed at a classmate who almost certainly had only one thing on his mind. Oh yes, Jeremiah could guess what was in that boy's head. *Sin. Filth.* They were speaking now, Katie and the boy, as the other two girls knowingly slipped away. He could not hear their conversation through the noise of the school yard, but he saw the attentive tilt of Katie's head, the coquettish way she flicked her hair off her shoulder. He saw the boy lean in, as though sniffing and savoring her scent. Was that the McKinnon brat? Adam or Alan or something. There were so many families now living in the compound, and so many children, that he could not remember all their names. He glared down at the two of them, gripping the window frame so tightly that his nails dug into the paint.

He pivoted and walked out of his office, thumping down the stairs. With every step, his jaw clenched tighter and acid burned a hole in his stomach. He banged out of the building, but outside the school yard gate he halted, wrestling for control.

This would not do. To show anger was unseen

The school bell clanged, calling the students in from recess. He stood calming himself, inhaling deeply. He focused on the fragrance of fresh-cut hay, of bread baking in the nearby communal kitchen. From across the compound, where the new worship hall was being built, came the whine of a saw and the echoes of a dozen hammers pounding nails. The virtuous sounds of honest labor, of a community working toward His greater glory. And I am their shepherd, he thought; I lead the way. Look how far they had already come! It took only a glance around the burgeoning village, at the dozen new homes under construction, to see that the congregation was thriving.

At last, he opened the gate and stepped into the school yard. He walked past the elementary classroom, where children were singing the alphabet song, and entered the classroom for the middle grades.

The teacher saw him and jumped up from her desk in surprise. "Prophet Goode, what an honor!" she gushed. "I didn't know you would be visiting us today."

He smiled, and the woman reddened, delighted by his attention. "Sister Janet, there's no need to make a fuss over me. I simply wanted to stop in and say hello to your class. And see if everyone is enjoying the new school year."

She beamed at her students. "Isn't it an *honor* to

have Prophet Goode himself visiting us? Everyone, please welcome him!"

"Welcome, Prophet Goode," the students answered in unison.

"Is the school year going well for all of you?" he asked.

"Yes, Prophet Goode." Again in unison, so perfect it sounded as if it had been rehearsed.

Katie Sheldon, he noticed, sat in the third row. He also noticed that the blond boy who'd flirted with her sat almost directly behind her. Slowly he began to pace the classroom, nodding and smiling as he surveyed the students' drawings and essays tacked on the walls. As if he really cared about them. His attention was only on Katie, who sat demurely at her desk, her gaze tipped downward like any properly modest girl.

"I don't mean to interrupt your lesson," he said. "Please, continue what you were doing. Pretend I'm not here."

"Um, yes." The teacher cleared her throat. "Students, if you could please open your math books to page two oh three. Complete exercises ten through sixteen. And when you're finished, we'll go over the answers."

As pencils scratched and papers rustled, Jeremiah wandered the classroom. The students were too intimidated to look at him, and they kept their eyes focused on their desktops. The subject was algebra, something that he had never bothered to master. He paused by the desk of the blond lad who had so clearly shown an interest in Katie, and, looking over the boy's shoulder, he saw the name written on the workbook. *Adam McKinnon*. A trouble-maker who would eventually have to be dealt with.

He moved on to Katie's desk, where he stopped and watched over her shoulder. Nervously she scribbled an answer, then erased it. A patch of bare neck showed through a parting of her long hair, and the skin flushed a deep red, as though seared by his gaze.

Leaning close, he inhaled her scent, and heat flooded his loins. There was nothing as delicious as the scent of a young girl's flesh, and this girl's was the sweetest of all. Through the fabric of her bodice, he could just make out the swell of newly budding breasts.

"Don't fret too much, dear," he whispered. "I was never very good at algebra, either."

She looked up, and the smile she gave him was so enchanting that he was struck speechless. *Yes. This girl is definitely the one.*

Flowers and ribbons draped the pews and cascaded from the soaring beams of the newly built worship hall. There were so many flowers that the room looked like the Garden of Eden itself, fragrant and shimmering. As the morning light beamed in through the ocular windows, two hundred joyous voices sang hymns of praise.

We are yours, O Lord. Fruitful is your flock and bountiful your harvest.

The voices faded, and the organ suddenly played a fanfare. The congregation turned to look at Katie Sheldon, who stood frozen in the doorway, blinking in confusion at all the eyes staring at her. She wore the lace-trimmed white dress that her mother had sewn, and her brand-new white satin slippers peeped out beneath the hem. On her head was a maiden's crown of white roses. The organ played on, and the congregation waited expectantly, but Katie could not move. She did not want to move.

It was her father who forced her to take the first step. He took her by the arm, his fingers digging into her flesh with an unmistakable command. *Don't you dare embarrass me.*

She began to walk, her feet numb in the pretty satin slippers as she moved toward the altar looming ahead. Toward the man whom God Himself had proclaimed would be her husband.

She caught glimpses of familiar faces in the pews: her teachers, her friends, her neighbors. There was Sister Diane who worked in the bakery with her mother, and Brother Raymond, who tended the cows whose soft flanks she loved to pet. And there was her mother, standing in the very first pew, where she had never stood before. It was a place of honor, a row where only the most favored congregants could sit. Her mother looked proud, oh so proud, and she stood as regal as a queen wearing her own crown of roses.

"Mommy," Katie whispered. "Mommy."

But the congregation had launched into a new hymn, and no one heard her through the singing.

At the altar, her father at last released her arm. "Be good," he muttered, and he stepped away to join her mother. She turned to follow him, but her escape was cut off.

Prophet Jeremiah Goode stood in her way. He took her hand.

How hot his fingers felt against her chilled skin. And how large his hand looked, wrapped around hers, as though she were trapped in the grip of a giant.

The congregation began to sing the wedding song. *Joyful union, blessed in heaven, bound forever in His eyes!*

Prophet Goode tugged her close beside him, and she gave a whimper of pain as his fingers pressed like claws into her skin. *You are mine now, bound to me by the will of God,* that squeeze told her. *You will obey.*

She turned to look at her father and mother. Silently she implored them to take her from this place, to bring her home where she belonged. They were both beaming as they sang. Scanning the hall, she searched for someone who would pluck her out of this nightmare, but all she saw was a vast sea of approving smiles and nodding heads. A room where sunlight glistened on flower petals, where two hundred voices swelled with song.

A room where no one heard, where no one wanted to hear, a thirteen-year-old girl's silent shrieks.

TWO

SIXTEEN YEARS LATER

THEY HAD COME TO THE END OF THE AFFAIR, but neither of them would admit it. Instead they talked about the rain-flooded roads and how bad the traffic was this morning, and the likelihood that her flight out of Logan Airport would be delayed. They did not speak of what weighed on both their minds, although Maura Isles could hear it in Daniel Brophy's voice, and in her own as well, so flat, so subdued. Both of them were struggling to pretend that nothing between them had changed. No, they were simply exhausted from staying up half the night, trapped in the same painful conversation that was their predictable coda to making love. The conversation that always left her feeling needy and demanding.

If only you could stay here with me every night. If only we could wake up together every morning.

You have me right here and now, Maura.

But not all of you. Not until you make a choice.

She looked out the window at cars splashing through the downpour. Daniel can't bring himself to choose, she thought. And even if he did choose me, even if he did leave the priesthood, leave his precious church, guilt would always be in the room with us, glaring at us like his invisible mistress. She watched windshield wipers beat away the sheeting water, and the somber light outside matched her mood.

"You'll be cutting it close," he said. "Did you check in online?"

"Yesterday. I have my boarding pass."

"Okay. That'll save you a few minutes."

"But I need to check in my suitcase. I couldn't fit my winter clothes in the carry-on."

"You'd think they'd choose someplace warm and sunny for a medical conference. Why Wyoming in November?"

"Jackson Hole's supposed to be beautiful."

"So is Bermuda."

She ventured a look at him. The gloom of the car hid the careworn lines of his face, but she could see the thickening silver in his hair. In just one year, how much older we've grown, she thought. Love has aged us both.

"When I get back, let's go someplace warm together," she said. "Just for a weekend." She gave a reckless laugh. "Hell, let's forget the world and go away for a whole month."

He was silent.

"Or is that too much to ask?" she said softly.

He gave a weary sigh. "As much as we might like to forget the world, it's always here. And we'd have to return to it."

"We don't *have* to do anything."

The look he gave her was infinitely sad. "You don't really believe that, Maura." He turned his gaze back to the road. "Neither do I."

No, she thought. We both believe in being so goddamn responsible. I go to work every day, pay my taxes right on schedule, and do what the world expects of me. I can babble all I want about running away with him and doing something wild and crazy, but I know I never will. And neither will Daniel.

He pulled up outside her departure terminal. For a moment they sat without looking at each other. Instead she focused on her fellow travelers waiting at curbside check-in, everyone bundled in raincoats, like a funeral gathering on a stormy November morning. She did not really want to step out of the warm car and join the dispirited throngs of travelers. Instead of boarding that flight, I could ask him to take me back home, she thought. If we had just a few more hours to talk about this, maybe we could find a way to make it work between us.

Knuckles rapped on the windshield, and she looked up to see an airport policeman glaring at them. "This is only for unloading," he barked. "You have to move the vehicle."

Daniel slid down the window. "I'm just dropping her off."

"Well, don't take all day."

"I'll get your luggage," Daniel said. He stepped out of the car.

For a moment they stood shivering together on the curb, silent amid the cacophony of rumbling buses and traffic whistles. If he were my husband, she thought, we would kiss each other goodbye right here. But for too long, they had scrupulously avoided any public displays of affection, and although he was not wearing his clerical collar this morning, even a hug felt dangerous.

"I don't have to go to this conference," she said. "We could spend the week together."

He sighed. "Maura, I can't just disappear for a week."

"When can you?"

"I need time to arrange a leave. We'll get away, I promise."

"It always has to be someplace else, though, doesn't it? Someplace where no one knows us. For once, I'd like to spend a week with you without having to go *away*."

He glanced at the policeman, who was moving back in their direction. "We'll talk about it when you get back next week."

"Hey, mister!" the cop yelled. "Move your car *now*."

"Of course we'll talk." She laughed. "We're good

at talking about it, aren't we? It's all we ever seem to do." She grabbed her suitcase.

He reached for her arm. "Maura, please. Let's not walk away from each other like this. You know I love you. I just need time to work this through."

She saw the pain carved on his face. All the months of deception, the indecision and guilt, had left their scars, had darkened whatever joy he'd found with her. She could have comforted him with just a smile, a reassuring squeeze of his arm, but at that moment she could not see past her own pain. All she could think of was retaliation.

"I think we've run out of time," she said, and walked away, into the terminal. The instant the glass doors whooshed shut behind her, she regretted her words. But when she stopped to look back through the window, he was already climbing into his car.

The man's legs were splayed apart, exposing ruptured testicles and the seared skin of buttocks and perineum. The morgue photo had flashed onto the screen without any advance warning from the lecturer, yet no one sitting in the darkened hotel conference room gave so much as a murmur of dismay. This audience was inured to the sight of ruined and broken bodies. For those who have seen and touched charred flesh, who are familiar with its stench, a sterile slide show holds few horrors. In fact, the white-haired man seated beside Maura had dozed off several times, and in the semi-darkness she could see his head bob as he struggled between sleep and wakefulness, impervious to the succession of gruesome photos glowing on the screen.

"What you see here are typical injuries sustained from a car bomb. The victim was a forty-five-year-old Russian businessman who climbed into his Mercedes one morning—a very nice Mercedes, I might add. When he turned the ignition key, he set off the booby trap of explosives that had been placed underneath his seat. As you can see from the X-rays . . ." The speaker clicked the computer mouse, and the next PowerPoint slide appeared on screen. It was a radiograph of a pelvis that was sheared apart at the pubis. Shards of bone and metal had been blasted throughout the soft tissues. "The force of the explosion blew car fragments straight up into his perineum, rupturing the scrotum and shearing off the ischial tuberosities. I'm sorry to say that we're becoming more and more familiar with explosive injuries like these, especially in this era of terrorist attacks. This was quite a small bomb, meant to kill only the driver. When you move into terrorism, you're talking about far more massive explosions with multiple casualties."

Again he clicked the mouse, and a photo of excised organs appeared, glistening like butcher shop offerings on a green surgical drape.

"Sometimes you may not find much evidence of external damage, even when the internal damage is fatal. This is the result of a suicide bombing in a

Jerusalem café. The fourteen-year-old female sustained massive concussive injuries to the lungs, as well as perforated abdominal viscera. Yet her face was untouched. Almost angelic."

The photo that next appeared drew the first audible reaction from the audience, murmurs of sadness and disbelief. The girl appeared serenely at rest, her flawless face unlined and unworried, dark eyes peering from beneath thick lashes. In the end, it was not gore that shocked that room of pathologists, but beauty. At fourteen, at the moment of her death, she would have been thinking about a school assignment, perhaps. Or a pretty dress. Or a boy she'd glimpsed on the street. She would not have imagined that her lungs and liver and spleen would soon be laid out on an autopsy table, or that a room of two hundred pathologists would one day be gawking at her image.

As the lights came up, the audience was still subdued. While the others filed out, Maura remained in her seat, staring down at the notes that she'd jotted on her pad about nail bombs and parcel bombs, car bombs and buried bombs. When it came to causing misery, man's ingenuity knew no limits. We are so good at killing each other, she thought. Yet we fail so miserably at love.

"Excuse me. You wouldn't happen to be Maura Isles?"

She looked up at the man who'd risen from his seat two rows ahead. He was about her age, tall and athletic, with a deep tan and sun-streaked blond hair that made her automatically think: California boy. His face seemed vaguely familiar, but she could not recall where she'd met him, which was surprising. His was a face that any woman would certainly remember.

"I knew it! It *is* you, isn't it?" He laughed. "I thought I spotted you as you came into the room."

She shook her head. "I'm sorry. This is really embarrassing, but I'm having trouble placing you."

"That's because it was a long time ago. And I no longer have my ponytail. Doug Comley, Stanford pre-med. It's been, what? Twenty years? I'm not surprised you've forgotten me. Hell, *I* would've forgotten me."

Suddenly a memory popped into her head, of a young man with long blond hair and protective goggles perched on his sunburned nose. He'd been far lankier then, a whippet in blue jeans. "Were we in a lab together?" she said.

"Quantitative analysis. Junior year."

"You remember that, even after twenty years? I'm amazed."

"I don't remember a damn thing about quant analysis. But I do remember *you*. You had the lab bench right across from me, and you got the highest score in class. Didn't you end up at UC San Francisco med school?"

"Yes, but I'm living in Boston now. What about you?"

"UC San Diego. I just couldn't bring myself to leave California. Addicted to sun and surf."

"Which sounds pretty good to me right now. Only November, and I'm already tired of the cold."

"I'm kind of digging this snow. It's been a lot of fun."

"Only because you don't have to live in it four months out of the year."

By now the conference room had emptied out, and hotel employees were packing up the chairs and wheeling out the sound equipment. Maura stuffed her notes into her tote bag and stood up. As she and Doug moved down parallel rows toward the exit, she asked him: "Will I see you at the cocktail party tonight?"

"Yeah, I think I'll be there. But dinner's on our own, right?"

"That's what the schedule says."

They walked out of the room together, into a hotel lobby crowded with other doctors wearing the same white name tags, carrying the same conference tote bags. Together they waited at the elevators, both of them struggling to keep the conversation flowing.

"So, are you here with your husband?" he asked.

"I'm not married."

"Didn't I see your wedding announcement in the alumni magazine?"

She looked at him in surprise. "You actually keep track of things like that?"

"I'm curious about where my classmates end up."

"In my case, divorced. Four years ago."

"Oh. I'm sorry."

She shrugged. "I'm not."

They rode the elevator to the third floor, where they both stepped off.

"See you at the cocktail party," she said with a goodbye wave, and pulled out her hotel keycard.

"Are you meeting anyone for dinner? Because I just happen to be free. If you want to join me, I'll hunt down a good restaurant. Just give me a call."

She turned to answer him, but he was already moving down the hallway, the tote bag slung over his shoulder. As she watched him walk away, another memory of Douglas Comley suddenly flashed into her head. An image of him in blue jeans, hobbling on crutches across the campus quadrangle.

"Didn't you break your leg that year?" she called out. "I think it was right before finals."

Laughing, he turned to her. "*That's* what you remember about me?"

"It's all starting to come back to me now. You had a skiing accident or something."

"Or something."

"It wasn't a skiing accident?"

"Oh man." He shook his head. "This is way too embarrassing to talk about."

"That's it. Now you have to tell me."

"If you'll have dinner with me."

She paused as the elevator opened and a man and

woman emerged. They walked up the hall, arms linked, clearly together and unafraid to show it. The way couples should act, she thought, as the pair stepped into a room and the door closed behind them.

She looked at Douglas. "I'd like to hear that story."

THREE

THEY FLED THE PATHOLOGISTS' COCKTAIL PARTY early and dined at the Four Seasons Resort in Teton Village. Eight straight hours of lectures about stabbings and bombings, bullets and blowflies, had left Maura overwhelmed by talk of death, and she was relieved to escape back to the normal world, where casual conversation didn't include talk of putrefaction, where the most serious issue of the evening was choosing between a red or a white wine.

"So how *did* you break your leg at Stanford?" she asked as Doug swirled Pinot Noir in his glass.

He winced. "I was hoping you'd forget about that subject."

"You promised to tell me. It's the reason I came to dinner."

"Not because of my scintillating wit? My boyish charm?"

She laughed. "Well, that, too. But mostly the tale behind the broken leg. I have a feeling it's going to be a doozy."

"Okay." He sighed. "The truth? I was fooling around on the rooftop of Wilbur Hall and I fell off."

She stared at him. "My God, that's a really long drop."

"As I found out."

"I assume alcohol was involved?"

"Of course."

"So it was just a typical dumb college stunt."

"Why do you sound so disappointed?"

"I expected something a little more, oh, unconventional."

"Well," he admitted, "I left out a few details."

"Such as?"

"The ninja outfit I was wearing. The black mask. The plastic sword." He gave an embarrassed shrug. "And the very humiliating ambulance ride to the hospital."

She regarded him with a calmly professional gaze. "And do you still like to dress up as a ninja these days?"

"You see?" He barked out a laugh. "*That's* what makes you so intimidating! Anyone else would have been laughing at me. But you respond with a very logical, very sober question."

"Is there a sober answer?"

"Not a single damn one." He lifted his glass in a toast. "Here's to stupid college pranks. May we never live them down."

She sipped and set down her wine. "What did you mean when you said that I'm intimidating?"

"You always have been. There I was, this goofy kid ambling my way through college. Partying too hard and sleeping too late. But you—you were so *focused,* Maura. You knew exactly what you wanted to be."

"And that made me intimidating?"

"Even a little scary. Because you had it all together, and I sure as hell didn't."

"I had no idea I had that effect on people."

"You still do."

She considered that statement. She thought about the police officers who always fell silent whenever she walked into a crime scene. She thought about the Christmas party where she'd so responsibly limited herself to a single flute of champagne while everyone else grew raucous. The public would never see Dr. Maura Isles drunk or loud or reckless. They would see only what she allowed them to see. A woman in control. *A woman who scares them.*

"It's not as if being focused is some sort of flaw," she said, in her own defense. "It's the only way anything gets accomplished in this world."

"Which is probably why it took me so long to accomplish anything."

"You made it to medical school."

"Eventually. After I spent two years bumming around, which drove my dad totally nuts. I worked as a bartender in Baja. Taught surfing in Malibu. Smoked too much pot and drank a lot of bad wine.

It was great." He grinned. "You, Dr. Isles, wouldn't have approved."

"It's not something I would have done." She took another sip of wine. "Not then, anyway."

His eyebrow tilted up. "Meaning you'd do it now?"

"People do change, Doug."

"Yeah, look at me! I never dreamed I'd one day end up a boring pathologist, trapped in the hospital basement."

"So how did that happen? What made you transform from a beach bum into a respectable doctor?"

Their conversation paused as the waiter brought their entrées. Roast duck for Maura, lamb chops for Doug. They sat through the obligatory grinding of the pepper, the refilling of their wineglasses. Only after the waiter left did Douglas answer her question.

"I got married," he said.

She had not noticed a wedding ring on his finger, and this was the first time he'd said anything about being in a relationship. The revelation made her glance up in surprise, but he was not looking at her; he was gazing at another table, at a family with two little girls.

"It was a bad match from the start," he admitted. "Met her at a party. Gorgeous blonde, blue eyes, legs up to *here*. She heard I was applying to med school and she had visions of being a rich doctor's wife. She didn't realize she'd end up spending weekends alone while I was working in the hospital. By the time I finished my pathology residency, she'd found someone else." He sliced into his lamb chop. "But I got to keep Grace."

"Grace?"

"My daughter. Thirteen years old and every bit as gorgeous as her mom. I'm just hoping to turn her in a more intellectual direction than her mom went."

"Where's your ex-wife now?"

"She got remarried, to a banker. They live in London, and we're lucky if we hear from her twice a year." He set down his knife and fork. "So that's how I became Mr. Mom. I've now got a daughter, a mortgage, and a job at the VA in San Diego. Who could ask for anything more?"

"And are you happy?"

He shrugged. "It's not the life I imagined when I was at Stanford, playing ninja on the rooftops. But I can't complain. Life happens, and you adjust." He smiled at her. "Lucky you, you're exactly what you envisioned. You always wanted to be a pathologist, and here you are."

"I also wanted to be married. I failed miserably at that."

He studied her. "I find it so hard to believe that there's no man in your life right now."

She pushed pieces of duck around on her plate, her appetite suddenly gone. "Actually, I am seeing someone."

He leaned in, focusing intently. "Tell me more."

"It's been about a year."

"That sounds serious."

"I'm not sure." His gaze made her uneasy, and she dropped her attention back to her meal. She could feel him studying her, trying to read what she wasn't telling him. What started as a lighthearted conversation had suddenly turned deeply personal. The dissection knives were out and secrets were spilling.

"Is it serious enough that there might be wedding bells?" he asked.

"No."

"Why not?"

She looked at him. "Because he's not available."

He leaned back, clearly surprised. "I never thought someone as levelheaded as you would fall for a married man."

She started to correct him, then stopped herself. Practically speaking, Daniel Brophy was indeed a married man, married to his church. There was no spouse more jealous, more demanding. She would have a better chance of claiming him if he'd been bound to merely another woman.

"I guess I'm not as levelheaded as you thought," she said.

He gave a surprised laugh. "You must have a wild streak I never knew about. How did I miss it back at Stanford?"

"That was a long time ago."

"Basic personalities don't really change much."

"You've changed."

"No. Beneath this Brooks Brothers blazer still beats the heart of a beach bum. Medicine's just my job, Maura. It pays the bills. It's not who I *am*."

"And what do you imagine I am?"

"The same person you were at Stanford. Competent. Professional. Not one to make mistakes."

"I wish that were true. I wish I didn't make mistakes."

"This man you're seeing, is he a mistake?"

"I'm not ready to admit that."

"Do you regret it?"

His question made her pause, not because she was unsure of the answer. She knew she was not happy. Yes, there were moments of bliss when she'd hear Daniel's car in the driveway or his knock on her door. But there were also the nights when she sat alone at her kitchen table, drinking too many glasses of wine. Nursing too many resentments.

"I don't know," she finally said.

"I've never regretted anything."

"Even your marriage?"

"Even my disaster of a marriage. I believe that every experience, every wrong decision, teaches us something. That's why we shouldn't be afraid to make mistakes. I jump into things with both feet, and sometimes it gets me into hot water. But in the end, everything has a way of working out."

"So you just trust in the universe?"

"I do. And I sleep very well at night. No doubts,

no closet full of anxieties. Life's too short for that. We should just sit back and enjoy the ride."

The waiter came to clear away the dishes. While she had finished only half her meal, Doug had cleaned his plate, devouring his lamb chops the way he seemed to devour life itself, with joyous abandon. He ordered cheesecake and coffee for dessert; Maura asked only for chamomile tea. When it all arrived, he slid the cheesecake halfway between them.

"Go on," he said. "I know you want some."

Laughing, she picked up her fork and took a generous bite. "You're a bad influence."

"If we were all well behaved, how boring would life be? Besides, cheesecake is only a minor sin."

"I'll have to repent when I get home."

"When are you headed back?"

"Not till Sunday afternoon. I thought I'd stay an extra day and take in some of the scenery. Jackson Hole's pretty spectacular."

"Are you touring around on your own?"

"Unless some gorgeous man volunteers to show me around."

He took a bite of cheesecake and chewed thoughtfully for a moment. "I don't know about coming up with a gorgeous man," he said. "But I could offer you an alternative. My daughter, Grace, is here with me. She's out tonight at the movies with two of my friends from San Diego. We were planning to drive to a cross-country ski lodge on Saturday and spend the night. We'd be back Sunday morning. There's room for you in the Suburban. And I'm sure there's room at the lodge, too, if you'd like to join us."

She shook her head. "I'd be a fifth wheel."

"Not at all. They'd love you. And I think you'd like them, too. Arlo's one of my best friends. By day, he's a boring accountant. But by night . . ." Doug's voice dropped to a sinister growl. "He turns into a celebrity known as the Mysterious Mr. Chops."

"Who?"

"Just one of the most popular food and wine bloggers on the Web. He's eaten at every Michelin-starred restaurant in America, and he's working his way through Europe. I just call him Jaws."

Maura laughed. "He sounds like fun. And the other friend?"

"Elaine. The gal he's been dating for years. She does something with interior design, I don't know what. I think you two would hit it off. Plus, you'd get to meet Grace."

She took another bite of cheesecake and took her time chewing. Considering.

"Hey, it's not like I'm proposing marriage," he teased. "It's just an overnight road trip, properly chaperoned by my thirteen-year-old daughter." He leaned in closer, his blue eyes focused intently. "Come on. My wild and crazy ideas almost always end up being fun."

"Almost always?"

"There's that unpredictability factor, that chance

that something completely unexpected—something amazing—could happen. That's what makes life an adventure. Sometimes you just have to jump in and trust in the universe."

At that moment, staring into his eyes, she felt that Doug Comley saw her the way few people did. That he was looking past her defensive armor to see the woman inside. A woman who'd always been afraid of where her heart might take her.

She looked down at the dessert plate. The cheesecake was gone; she didn't remember having finished it. "Let me give it some thought," she said.

"Of course." He laughed. "You wouldn't be Maura Isles if you didn't."

That night, back in her hotel room, she called Daniel.

By his tone of voice, she knew that he was not alone. He was polite but impersonal, as though speaking to any parishioner. In the background she could hear voices discussing the price of heating fuel, the cost of repairing the roof, the drop-off in donations. It was a church budget meeting.

"How is it out there?" he asked. Pleasant and neutral.

"A lot colder than Boston. There's already snow on the ground."

"It hasn't stopped raining here."

"I'll be landing Sunday night. Can you still pick me up at the airport?"

"I'll be there."

"And afterward? We can have a late supper at my house, if you'd like to stay the night."

A pause. "I'm not sure I can. Let me think about it."

It was almost the same answer she'd given Doug earlier that evening. And she remembered what he'd said. *Sometimes you just have to jump in and trust in the universe.*

"Can I call you back Saturday?" he said. "I'll know my schedule then."

"Okay. But if you can't reach me, don't worry. I may be out of cell phone range."

"Talk to you then."

There was no parting *I love you,* just a quiet goodbye and the conversation was over. The only intimacies they ever shared were behind closed doors. Every encounter was planned in advance, and afterward repeatedly analyzed. *Too much thinking,* Doug would have said. All that thinking hadn't brought her happiness.

She picked up the hotel phone and dialed the operator. "Can you connect me to the room of Douglas Comley, please?" she said.

It took four rings for him to answer. "Hello?"

"It's me," she said. "Does the invitation still stand?"

FOUR

THE ADVENTURE STARTED OFF WELL ENOUGH.
Friday night, the fellow travelers met for
drinks. When Maura walked into the hotel cocktail
lounge, she found Doug and his party already seated
at a table, waiting for her. Arlo Zielinski looked like
someone who had eaten his way through the Michelin guidebook—chubby and balding, a man with a
hearty appetite and just as hearty a laugh.

"The more the merrier, I always say! And now
we have an excuse to order *two* bottles of wine at
dinner," he said. "Stick with us, Maura, and I
guarantee a good time, especially when Doug's in
charge." He leaned in and whispered: "I can vouch
for his moral character. I've done his taxes for years,
and if anyone knows your most intimate secrets, it's
your accountant."

"What're you two whispering about?" asked
Doug.

Arlo looked up innocently. "Just saying that the

jury was *totally* rigged against you. They should never have convicted."

Maura burst out laughing. Yes, she liked this friend of Doug's.

But she wasn't as sure about Elaine Salinger. Though the woman had sat smiling during the conversation, it was a tight smile. Everything about Elaine somehow seemed tight, from her skin-hugging black ski pants to her eerily unlined face. She was about Maura's age and height, and model-thin, with a waistline to envy and the self-control to maintain it. While Doug, Maura, and Arlo split a bottle of wine, Elaine sipped only mineral water garnished with a slice of lime, and she virtuously shunned the bowl of nuts that Arlo was so enthusiastically digging into. Maura could not see what these two had in common; she certainly could not imagine them dating.

Doug's daughter, Grace, was yet another puzzle. He had described his ex-wife as a beauty, and her fortunate genes had clearly been passed on to the daughter. At thirteen, Grace was already stunning, a leggy blonde with arching brows and crystalline blue eyes. But it was a remote beauty, cool and uninviting. The girl had contributed scarcely a word to the conversation. Instead she'd sat with her iPod earpieces stubbornly in place. Now she gave a dramatic sigh and uncurled her lanky body from the chair.

"Dad, can I go back to my room now?"

"Come on, sweetie, hang around," urged Doug. "We can't be all that boring."

"I'm tired."

"You're only thirteen," Arlo teased. "At your age, you should be raring to rock-and-roll with us."

"It's not like you all need me here."

Doug frowned at her iPod, noticing it for the first time. "Turn that off, okay? Try joining the conversation."

The girl shot him a look of pure teenage disdain and slouched back in her chair.

". . . so I scoped out all the possible restaurants in the area, and there's nothing worth stopping for," Arlo said. He popped another handful of nuts into his mouth and wiped the salt from his pudgy hands. He took off his glasses and wiped them as well. "I think we should just go straight to the lodge and eat lunch there. At least they have steak on the menu. How hard is it to cook a decent steak?"

"We just had dinner, Arlo," said Elaine. "I can't believe you're already thinking about tomorrow's lunch."

"You know me, I'm a planner. Like to get my ducks all in a row."

"Especially if they're glazed with orange sauce."

"Dad," whined Grace. "I'm *really* tired. I'm going to bed, okay?"

"Oh, all right," Doug said. "But I want you up

by seven. I'd like to be loaded up and ready to leave by eight."

"I think we should be off to bed, too," said Arlo. He stood, brushing crumbs off his shirt. "Come on, Elaine."

"It's only nine thirty."

"Elaine," Arlo repeated, and tipped his head meaningfully at Maura and Doug.

"Oh." Elaine cast a speculative glance at Maura, then rose to her feet, lithe as a cheetah. "It's been nice getting to know you, Maura," she said. "See you in the morning."

Doug waited for the trio to leave, then said to Maura: "I'm sorry that Grace was such a pill."

"She's a beautiful girl, Doug."

"She's also got a good head on her shoulders. An IQ of a hundred thirty. Not that you could see it tonight. She's not usually this quiet."

"Maybe it's because I'm coming along. She may not be happy about it."

"Don't even think that, Maura. If she has a problem, she'll just have to deal with it."

"If my coming along feels awkward in any way—"

"Does it? To you?" His gaze was so probing, she felt compelled to tell the truth.

"A little," she admitted.

"She's thirteen. Everything about thirteen-year-olds is awkward. I refuse to let that dictate my life." He lifted his glass. "So here's to our adventure!"

She returned the toast, and they sipped, grinning at each other. In the flattering gloom of the cocktail lounge, he looked like that college student she remembered, the reckless young man who'd scaled rooftops and donned ninja outfits. She felt young again, too. Daring and fearless and ready for that adventure.

"I guarantee," he said. "We are going to have a great time."

During the night, it had started to snow, and by the time they loaded their luggage into the back of the Suburban, three inches of white fluff coated the cars in the parking lot, a pristine cloak that made the San Diego contingent ooh and ahh at the beauty of it. Doug and Arlo insisted on taking photos of the three ladies posed in front of the hotel entrance, everyone smiling and rosy-cheeked in their ski clothes. Snow was nothing new for Maura, but she saw it now the way these Californians did, with a sense of wonder at how clean and white it was, how softly it settled on her eyelashes, how silently it swirled from the sky. During Boston's long winters, snow meant tiresome shoveling and wet boots and slushy streets. It was merely a fact of life that had to be dealt with until spring. But this snow seemed different; it was vacation snow, and she smiled at the sky, feeling as giddy as her companions, enchanted by a world that suddenly looked new and bright.

"Folks, we are going to have an *amazing* time!" Doug declared as he fastened the rented cross-country skis onto the roof of the Suburban. "Fresh powder. Charming company. Dinner by a roaring fire." He gave the roof straps one last tug. "Okay, team. Let's go."

Grace climbed into the front passenger seat.

"Hey sweetheart," said Doug. "How about letting Maura sit next to me?"

"But this is always my seat."

"She's our guest. Give her the chance to ride shotgun."

"Doug, let her stay there," said Maura. "I'm perfectly fine sitting in back."

"Are you sure?"

"Absolutely." Maura climbed into a seat at the back of the Suburban. "I'm good right here."

"Okay. But maybe you two can switch later." Doug shot his daughter a disapproving glance, but Grace had already inserted her iPod earbuds and was staring out the window, ignoring him.

In fact, Maura didn't at all mind sitting alone in the third row, right behind Arlo and Elaine, where she had a view of Arlo's bald spot and Elaine's stylishly clipped dark hair. She was the last-minute add-on to the quartet, unfamiliar with their stories and their inside jokes, and she was content to merely be an observer as they headed out of Teton Village and drove south, into the ever-thickening snowfall. The windshield wipers swung back and forth, a metronome sweeping away showers of snowflakes. Maura leaned back and watched the scenery go by. She looked forward to lunch by the lodge fire, and then to an afternoon of skiing. Cross-country, not downhill, so no need to feel the least bit anxious, no fears of broken legs or fractured skulls or spectacularly embarrassing falls. Just a quiet glide through silent woods, the swoosh of her skis sliding across the powder, the pleasant burn of cold air in her lungs. During the pathology conference, she'd seen far too many images of damaged bodies. She was glad to be on a journey that had nothing to do with death.

"Snow's coming down pretty fast," said Arlo.

"We've got good tires on this baby," said Doug. "Hertz clerk said they can handle the weather."

"Speaking of the weather, did you check the forecast?"

"Yeah, snow. What a surprise."

"Just tell me we're gonna make it to the lodge in time for lunch."

"Lola says we'll arrive at eleven thirty-two. And Lola's never wrong."

Maura called out: "Who's Lola?"

Doug pointed to the portable GPS, which he'd mounted on the dashboard. "That's Lola."

"Why are GPSs always referred to as females?" asked Elaine.

Arlo laughed. "Because women are always telling

us men where to go. Since Lola says we'll be there before noon, we can have an early lunch."

Elaine sighed. "Do you ever stop thinking about eating?"

"The word is *dining*. In one lifetime, you can eat only so many meals, so you might as well—"

"—make each and every one worth it," Elaine finished for him. "Yes, Arlo, we know your philosophy of life."

Arlo turned in his seat to look at Maura. "My mom was a great cook. She taught me never to waste my appetite on mediocre food."

"That must be why you're so thin," said Elaine.

"Ouch," Arlo said. "You're in a weird mood today. I thought you were looking forward to this trip."

"I'm just tired. You snored half the night. I may have to insist on my own room."

"Aw, come on. I'll buy you some earplugs." Arlo slung an arm around Elaine and pulled her close against him. "Honeybun. Baby. Don't make me sleep alone."

Elaine extricated herself. "You're giving me a crick in the neck."

"Hey, people, will you look at this gorgeous snow!" said Doug. "It's a winter wonderland!"

An hour out of Jackson, they saw a sign: LAST CHANCE FOR FUEL. Doug pulled in to Grubb's Gas Station and General Store, and they all piled out of the vehicle to use the restrooms and cruise the narrow aisles, scanning the snacks and dusty magazines and windshield ice scrapers.

Arlo stood in front of a display of plastic-wrapped beef sticks and laughed. "Who eats these things, anyway? They're like ninety percent sodium nitrite, and the rest is red dye number two."

"They have Cadbury chocolates," said Elaine. "Shall we get some?"

"Probably ten years old. Oh, yuck, they've got licorice whips. I got sick on those when I was a kid. It's like we're back in the 1950s."

As Arlo and Elaine stood sniggering over the snack selection, Maura picked up a newspaper and headed to the cash register to pay for it.

"You know that's a week old, don't you?" said Grace.

Maura turned, surprised that the girl had spoken to her. For once, Grace wasn't wearing her earbuds, but her iPod was still playing, the music issuing out a tinny whine.

"It's last week's paper," Grace pointed out. "Everything in this store is expired. The potato chips are, like, a year old. I bet even the petrol is bad."

"Thanks for pointing it out. But I need something to read, and this will have to do." Maura pulled out her wallet, wondering how the word *petrol* ended up in an American teenager's vocabulary. But that was just one more detail about Grace that puzzled her.

The girl walked out the door, skinny hips swaying slightly in skintight jeans, oblivious to her effect on others. The old man standing behind the cash register gaped after her, as though he'd never seen such an exotic creature saunter through his store.

By the time Maura stepped outside again, Grace was already in the Suburban, but this time she was in the backseat. "The princess finally relinquished her throne," Doug whispered to Maura as he opened the door for her. "You get to sit up front with me."

"I didn't mind sitting in back."

"Well, I minded. I had a chat with her, and she's cool with it now."

Elaine and Arlo came out of the store, laughing, and climbed into their seats.

"That," said Arlo, "was like a time capsule. Did you see those Pez dispensers? They had to be twenty years old. And that old guy behind the counter was like some character out of *The Twilight Zone*."

"Yeah, he was strange," said Doug, starting the engine.

"*Creepy* is the word I'd use. He said he hoped we weren't headed to Kingdom Come."

"What's that supposed to mean?"

"You people are *sinners*!" Arlo boomed out in his best televangelist voice. "And you are on the road to *Hay-ell*!"

"Maybe he was just telling us to be careful," said Elaine. "With this snow and all."

"It seems to be slowing down." Doug leaned forward to peer up at the sky. "In fact, I think I can see a patch of blue up there."

"Always the optimist," said Arlo. "That's our Dougie."

"Positive thinking. It works every time."

"Just get us there in time for lunch."

Doug looked at the GPS. "Lola says ETA eleven forty-nine. You're not going to starve."

"I already am starving, and it's only ten thirty."

The GPS's female voice commanded: "Bear left at next fork."

Arlo burst out in song: *"Whatever Lola wants . . ."*

"Lola gets," Doug joined in, and he veered left at the fork.

Maura looked out her window, but she didn't spot any patch of blue sky. All she saw was low-hanging clouds and the white flanks of mountains in the distance.

"It's starting to snow again," said Elaine.

FIVE

WE MUST HAVE TAKEN A WRONG TURN," SAID Arlo.

The snow was swirling thicker than ever, and in between swipes of the windshield wipers, the glass instantly clouded over in a thick lattice of flakes. They'd been winding steadily up the mountain for nearly an hour now, and the road had long since vanished under an ever-deepening carpet of white. Doug drove with neck craned forward, straining to make out what lay ahead.

"Are you sure this is the right way?" said Arlo.

"Lola said so."

"Lola is a disembodied voice in a box."

"I programmed her for the most direct route. This is it."

"But is it the fastest route?"

"Hey, do you want to drive?"

"Whoa, man. I'm just asking."

Elaine said, "We haven't seen another car since

we turned onto this road. Not since that weirdo gas station. Why isn't anyone else here?"

"Do you have a map?" asked Maura.

"I think there's one in the glove compartment," said Doug. "It came with the rental car. But the GPS says we're right where we should be."

"Yeah. In the middle of nowhere," muttered Arlo.

Maura pulled out the map and unfolded it. It took her a moment to orient herself to the unfamiliar geography. "I don't see this road on here," she said.

"You sure you know where we are?"

"It's not here."

Doug snatched the map from her hands and propped it up on the steering wheel as he drove.

"Hey, a helpful suggestion from the backseat?" called Arlo. "How about keeping your eyes on the road?"

Doug shoved the map aside. "Piece of junk. It's not detailed enough."

"Maybe Lola's wrong," said Maura. *God, now I'm calling the gadget by that stupid name.*

"She's more up to date than that map," said Doug. "This could be a seasonal road. Or a private road."

"It didn't say private when we turned onto it."

"You know, I think we should turn around," said Arlo. "Seriously, man."

"It's thirty miles back to the fork. Do you want to make it there by lunch or not?"

"Dad?" Grace called from the back of the Suburban. "What's going on?"

"Nothing, honey. We're just having a discussion about which road to take."

"You mean you don't know?"

Doug heaved out a frustrated sigh. "I do know, and we're okay! We're fine! If everyone would just cool it, we can start having a good time."

"Let's turn around, Doug," said Arlo. "This road is getting seriously scary."

"Okay," said Doug, "I guess it's time for a vote. Everyone?"

"I vote we turn around," said Arlo.

"Elaine?"

"I think the driver should decide," she said. "I'll go with whatever you want, Doug."

"Thank you, Elaine." Doug glanced at Maura. "How do you vote?"

There was more to that question than what it seemed. She could see it in his eye, a look that said *Back me up. Believe in me.* A look that made her remember what he'd been like two decades ago as a college student, carefree and hang-loose in his faded aloha shirt. No worries, be happy. That was Douglas, the man who could survive falls off rooftops and broken legs without ever losing his optimism. He was asking her to trust him now, and she wanted to.

But she couldn't ignore her own instincts.

"I think we should turn around," she said, and her answer seemed to wound him as deeply as an insult.

"All right." He sighed. "I recognize a mutiny when I see one. When I find the right spot, we'll turn around. And retrace the thirty miles we just drove."

"I was on your side, Doug," said Elaine. "Don't forget that."

"Here, this looks wide enough."

"Wait," said Maura. She was about to add: *That could be a ditch there,* but Doug was already turning the wheel, sending the Suburban into a wide U-turn. Suddenly the snow collapsed beneath their right tire and the Suburban lurched sideways, sending Maura slamming against her door.

"Jesus!" yelled Arlo. "What the hell are you doing?"

They had jolted to a standstill, the Suburban tilted almost onto its side.

"Shit. Shit, *shit*!" said Doug. He floored the accelerator and the engine screamed, tires spinning in the snow. He shifted to reverse and tried to back up. The vehicle moved a few inches, then shuddered to a halt, the tires spinning again.

"Try rocking it back and forth," suggested Arlo.

"That's what I'm trying to do!" Doug shifted to the lowest gear and tried to roll forward. The wheels whined, but they didn't move.

"Daddy?" Grace's voice was thin with panic.

"It's okay, honey. Everything's going to be okay."

"What're we gonna do?" Grace wailed.

"We're gonna call for help, that's what. Get a tow truck to pull us out, and we'll be on our way." Doug reached for his cell phone. "We may miss lunch, but what the heck, it's all an adventure. You'll have something to talk about when you get back to school." He paused, frowning at his phone. "Is anyone getting a signal?"

"You mean you're not?" said Elaine.

"Could you all just check?"

Maura pulled her cell phone out of her purse. "I've got no bars."

"No signal here, either," said Elaine.

Arlo added: "Ditto."

"Grace?" Doug twisted around to look at his daughter.

She shook her head and whimpered: "Are we stuck here?"

"Let's all just relax. We can work this out." Doug took a deep breath. "If we can't call for help, we'll have to get ourselves out of this. We'll push the sucker back onto the road." Doug shifted into neutral. "Okay, everyone out. We can do it."

Maura's door was jammed tight against the snow, and she could not exit from her side. She crawled over the gearshift, into the driver's seat, and Doug helped her climb out through his door. She landed in calf-deep snow. Only then, standing beside the tipped vehicle, did she grasp the scope of their predicament. The Suburban had tumbled off the shoulder into a deep ditch. The wheels on the right were buried up to the chassis. The wheels on the left weren't even touching pavement. *There is no way we'll push this monster out.*

"We can do this," said Doug with a burst of enthusiasm. "Come on, folks. Let's work together."

"And do what, exactly?" said Arlo. "You need a tow truck to pull that sucker out of there."

"Well, I'm willing to give it a try," said Elaine.

"You're not the one with the bad back."

"Stop whining, Arlo. Let's pitch in."

"*Thank you,* Elaine," said Doug. He reached into his pocket for his gloves. "Grace, you get in the driver's seat. You'll need to steer it."

"I don't know how to drive!"

"You only have to steer it onto the road, sweetie."

"Can't someone else do it?"

"You're the smallest one here, and the rest of us need to push. Come on, I'll help you climb up."

Grace looked terrified, but she clambered up into the driver's seat.

"Good girl," said Doug. He waded down into the ditch, landing hip-deep in snow, and planted his gloved hands against the rear of the vehicle. "Well?" he asked, looking up at the other adults.

Elaine was the first to scramble into the ditch beside him. Maura followed next, and snow seeped up her pant legs and into her boots. Her gloves were still somewhere in the car, so she placed bare hands against steel so icy that it seemed to burn her skin.

"I'm gonna throw my back out," said Arlo.

"You have a choice," said Elaine. "It's that or freeze to death. Will you get down here?"

Arlo took his time pulling on gloves and a wool cap. Laboriously he wound a scarf around his neck. Only then, fully garbed against the cold, did he wade down into the ditch.

"Okay, all together," said Doug. "Push!"

Maura threw her weight against the Suburban, and her boots slid backward in the snow. She could hear Arlo grunting beside her, could feel the vehicle begin to rock forward.

"Steer, Gracie!" yelled Doug. "Turn left!"

The front end of the Suburban began to inch upward, toward the road. They kept pushing, Maura straining so hard now that her arms were trembling and her hamstrings ached. She closed her eyes, her breath locked in her throat, every ounce of effort focused on moving three tons of steel. She felt her heels slide. Suddenly the Suburban was sliding, too, rolling back against them.

"Watch out!" yelled Arlo.

Maura stumbled sideways just as the vehicle rolled backward and toppled onto its side in the ditch.

"Jesus!" yelled Arlo. "We could've been crushed!"

"Daddy! Daddy, I'm stuck in the seat belt!"

Doug scrambled up onto the vehicle. "Hold on, honey. I'll get you out." He pulled open the door and reached inside to haul out Grace. She dropped, gasping, into the snow.

"Oh man, we are so fucked," said Arlo.

They all climbed out of the ditch and stood on the road, staring at the Suburban. It was now lying on its side, half buried in the snow.

Arlo gave a laugh tinged with hysteria. "One thing's for sure. We're going to miss lunch."

"Let's think about this," said Doug.

"What's to think about? There's no way we'll get that tank out." Arlo tugged his scarf tighter. "And it's freezing out here."

"How much farther is the lodge?" asked Maura.

"According to Lola, it's another twenty-five miles," said Doug.

"It's been almost thirty miles since we left the gas station."

"Yeah. We're about smack-dab in the middle."

"Wow," said Arlo. "We couldn't have planned it better."

"Arlo," said Elaine, "shut up."

"But the thirty miles we just drove is mostly downhill from here," said Doug. "That makes it easier."

Arlo stared at him. "We're gonna walk thirty miles in a snowstorm?"

"No. You're going to stay here with the women. You can all climb back in the truck and stay warm. I'll pull my cross-country skis off the roof and ski out for help."

"It's too late," said Maura.

"I can do it."

"It's already noon. You have only a few hours of daylight, and you can't ski in the dark. You could fall right off the mountain."

"She's right," said Elaine. "You'd need a whole day, maybe two, to make it that far. And the snow's so deep, it'll slow you down."

"I got us into this. I'm going to get us out."

"Don't be an idiot. Stay with us, Doug."

But he was already wading back into the ditch to pull his skis off the roof rack.

"Man, I'll never say anything bad about meat sticks again," muttered Arlo. "I should've bought a few. At least it'd be protein."

"You can't go, Doug," said Elaine. "Not this late in the day."

"I'll stop when it gets dark. Build a snow cave or something."

"Do you know how to build a snow cave?"

"How hard can it be?"

"You're going to freeze to death out there."

"Daddy, don't." Grace stumbled down into the ditch and grabbed his arm, pulling him away from the skis. *"Please."*

Doug looked up at the adults standing in the road, and his voice rose to a shout of frustration. "I'm trying to *fix* things, okay? Don't you see that? I'm trying to get us out of here, and you're not making it any easier for me!"

His outburst startled them and they all fell silent,

shivering in the cold. The seriousness of their predicament was starting to sink in. *We could die out here.*

"Someone's going to come by, right?" said Elaine, glancing at her companions for reassurance. "I mean, this is a public road, so there'll be a snowplow or something. We can't be the only ones driving on it."

"Have you seen anyone?" said Arlo.

"It's not that far off the beaten track."

"Look at the snow. It's already a foot and a half deep and getting deeper. If they were going to plow it, they would have done it by now."

"What are you saying?"

"This must be a seasonal road," said Arlo. "That's why it isn't on the map. That damn GPS sent us on the shortest route, all right—straight over a mountain."

"Eventually someone's going to come by here."

"Yeah. In the spring. You remember that story a few years ago, about the family in Oregon who got stuck in the snow? They thought they were on a major road and ended up in the middle of nowhere. No one went looking for *them*. A week later, the man decides to walk out to save his family. And he freezes to death."

"Shut up, Arlo," said Doug. "You're scaring Grace."

"He's scaring *me*," said Elaine.

"Elaine, I'm just trying to impress upon you that

this is not something Dougie here can just blithely fix for us," said Arlo.

"I know that," said Elaine. "You think I don't know that?"

Wind gusted across the road, sending snowflakes whirling into their faces. Maura blinked against the sting. When she opened her eyes again, everyone was standing in exactly the same place, as though paralyzed by the cold, by despair. As a fresh gust blasted them, she turned to shield her face. Only then did she see the fleck of green, vivid against the relentless background of white.

She started toward it, wading up the road through snow that sucked at her boots, miring her in its grip.

"Maura, where are you going?" said Doug.

She kept walking, even as Doug continued to call out to her. As she moved closer, she saw that the patch of green was a sign, its face half obscured by clinging snow. She brushed away the flakes.

PRIVATE ROAD
RESIDENTS ONLY
AREA PATROLLED

So much snow had fallen that she could not see any pavement, only a narrow alley that cut into the trees and twisted away through the heavy screen of woods. A chain was draped across the entrance, the metal links encrusted in white fluff. "There's a road here!" she called out. As the others trudged toward her, she pointed at the sign. "It says *residents only.* That means there must be houses down this road."

"The chain's up," said Arlo. "I doubt anyone's there."

"But there'll be shelter. Right now, that's all we need."

Doug gave a laugh and threw his arms around Maura, crushing her against his down jacket. "I knew it was a good idea to bring you along! Sharp eyes, Dr. Isles! We would have missed this road completely."

As he released her, Maura noticed Elaine staring at them, and it unsettled her because it was not a friendly look. Suddenly it was gone, and Elaine turned back to the Suburban. "Let's get our things out of the car," she said.

They didn't know how far they would have to carry their belongings, so Doug suggested they take only what they needed for the night. Maura left her suitcase behind and grabbed her purse and a tote bag, which she filled with toiletries and an extra sweater.

"Elaine, you're not really going to bring your suitcase," said Arlo.

"It's just my carry-on. It has my jewelry and cosmetics."

"We're in the frigging wilderness."

"It's got other stuff, too."

"What stuff?"

"Other. *Stuff.*" She started toward the private

road, her roll-aboard plowing a trench in the snow behind her.

"I guess I'll have to carry that for you," Arlo said with a sigh, and he took the suitcase from her.

"Everyone got what they need?" called out Doug.

"Wait," said Maura. "We need to leave a note in case someone finds the Suburban." She pulled a pen and notepad from her purse and wrote: *Stranded, please call for help. We're down the private road.* She laid it in full view on the dashboard and shut the door. "Okay," she said, pulling on her gloves. "I'm ready."

They clambered over the chain and started down the road, Arlo huffing and puffing as he dragged Elaine's roll-aboard suitcase behind him.

"When we get back home, Doug," Arlo panted, "you owe me a major dinner. I'm talking *major*. Veuve Clicquot. Caviar. And a steak the size of Los Angeles."

"Stop it," said Elaine. "You're making us hungry."

"You're not already hungry?"

"It doesn't help to talk about it."

"It doesn't go away if we *don't* talk about it." Arlo trudged slowly, the suitcase scraping across the snow. "And now we're going to miss dinner, too."

"There's bound to be some food down there," said Doug. "Even if you close up your house for the winter, you usually leave stuff behind in the pantry. Peanut butter. Or macaroni."

"Now, *this* is desperation. When macaroni starts to sound good."

"It's an adventure, guys. Think of it as jumping out of a plane and trusting in the fates to get you safely on the ground."

"I'm not like you, Doug," said Arlo. "I don't jump out of planes."

"You don't know what you've missed."

"Lunch."

Every step was hard labor. Despite the dropping temperature, Maura was sweating inside her ski parka. Her throat ached with each searing breath of cold air. Too tired to break a path through fresh snow, she fell into step behind Doug, letting him plow the path first, planting her feet in the craters left behind by his boots. It was now a matter of stoically marching ahead, left–right–left, ignoring her sore muscles, the ache in her chest, the sodden hem of her pants.

As they slogged up a slight rise, Maura had her gaze focused downward on the trail of broken snow. When Doug suddenly halted, she almost bumped into him.

"Hey, everyone!" Doug called back to the others. "We're going to be okay!"

Maura moved beside him and stared down into a valley, at the rooftops of a dozen houses. No smoke curled up from any of the chimneys; the road leading down was covered in unbroken snow.

"I don't see any signs of life," she said.

"We may have to break into one of those buildings. But at least we'll have a place to stay tonight. It looks like maybe a two-mile walk down, so we'll make it before dark."

"Hey, look," said Arlo. "There's another sign here." He slogged farther down the road and brushed snow off the surface.

"What does it say?" asked Elaine.

For a moment Arlo was silent, staring at the sign as though it were written in a language he could not understand. "Now I know what that old man in the gas station meant," he said.

"What are you talking about?"

"It's the name of that village down there." Arlo moved aside, and Maura saw the words on the sign.

KINGDOM COME

SIX

I DON'T SEE ANY POWER LINES," SAID ARLO.

"You mean I can't recharge my iPod?" asked Grace.

"They could have underground lines," Doug suggested. "Or generators. It's the twenty-first century. Nobody lives without electricity." He adjusted his backpack. "Come on, it's a long walk. We want to get down there before dark."

They started down the slope, where the wind stung like icy nettles and the drifts made every step hard labor. Doug led the way, breaking a trail through deep virgin snow, with Grace, Elaine, and Arlo following in a line behind him. Maura brought up the rear. Though they were moving downhill, the ever-deepening snow made it an exhausting hike. No one was talking now; it took all their effort just to keep slogging ahead.

Nothing about this day had turned out the way Maura had expected. If only we'd ignored the GPS and followed the map, she thought. We'd be at that lodge right now, sipping wine in front of a fire. If only I'd turned down Doug's invitation in the first place, I wouldn't be stuck with these people at all. I'd be back in my own hotel, warm and safe for the night. *Safety* was the option she almost always chose. Safe investments, safe cars, safe travel. The only risks she'd ever taken had been with men, and every one of those had turned out badly. Daniel, and now Douglas. *Note to self: In future, avoid men whose names begin with D.* Aside from that, the two men were nothing alike. That had been Doug's charm, the fact that he was wild and a little reckless. He'd made her want to be reckless as well.

This is the result, she thought as she stumbled down the mountainside. I've let an impulsive man lead me into this mess. Worst of all, he refused to acknowledge how serious their predicament was, a predicament that only seemed to be worsening. In Doug's sunny world, everything was always going to turn out okay.

The light was starting to fade. They'd been walking at least a mile now, and her legs felt heavy as lead. If she dropped right here from exhaustion, the others might not even hear it. Once darkness fell, no one would be able to find her. By morning, she would be covered in snow. How easy it was to disappear out here. Get lost in a snowstorm, vanish beneath a drift, and the world would have no idea what became of you. She had told no one in Boston about this overnight jaunt. For once, she'd tried to be spontaneous, to jump aboard and enjoy the ride, as Doug had urged her. And it had been her chance to put Daniel out of her mind and declare her independence. Convince herself that she was still her own woman.

Her shoulder bag slipped off, sending her cell phone tumbling into the snow. She snatched it up, brushed away icy flakes, and checked the reception. Still zero bars. Useless piece of junk out here, she thought, and turned it off to conserve the battery. She wondered if Daniel had called. Would he become alarmed when she didn't return any of his voice mails? Or would he think she was purposefully ignoring him? Would he simply wait for her to break the silence?

If you wait too long, I could be dead.

Suddenly angry at Daniel, at Douglas, at the whole miserable, screwed-up day, she attacked the final drift and charged ahead like a bull through hip-deep snow. She staggered out of the drift and followed the others onto level ground, where they all halted to catch their breaths, gasping out frosty clouds. Snowflakes fluttered down like white moths and landed with soft *tick-tick*s.

In the deepening gloom, two rows of identical houses stood dark and silent. All the buildings had the same sloping rooflines, the same attached garages, the same porches, even the same porch swings. Right down to the number of windows, the houses were eerily perfect clones of one another.

"Hello?" Doug yelled. "Is anyone here?"

His voice echoed back from the surrounding mountains and faded to silence.

Arlo shouted: "We come in peace! And we bring credit cards!"

"This isn't funny," said Elaine. "We could freeze to death."

"Nobody's going to freeze to death," said Doug. He stomped up the steps to the covered porch of the nearest house and banged on the door. He waited a few seconds and banged again. The only sound was the creak of the porch swing, its seat frosted with windblown snow.

"Just break in," said Elaine. "This is an emergency."

Doug turned the knob, and the door swung open. He glanced back at the others. "Let's hope no one's waiting in there with a shotgun."

Inside the house, it was no warmer. They stood shivering in the gloom, exhaling steam like five fire-breathing dragons. The last gray light of day was fading in the window.

"Does anyone happen to have a flashlight?" asked Doug.

"I think I do," said Maura, hunting in her purse for the mini Maglite she always carried while on the job. "Damn it," she muttered. "I just remembered I left it at home. I didn't think I'd need it at a conference."

"Is there a light switch somewhere?"

"Nothing on this wall," said Elaine.

"I can't find any outlets at all," said Arlo. "There's nothing plugged in anywhere." He paused. "You know what? I don't think this place has any electricity."

For a moment they stood without speaking, too demoralized to say a word. They heard no clocks ticking, no refrigerators humming. Just the vacuum of dead space.

The sudden clang of metal made Maura jump.

"Sorry," said Arlo, standing near the hearth. "I knocked over one of the fireplace tools." He paused. "Hey, there are matches here."

They heard the *whick* of a match head being struck. In the flickering light of the flame they saw firewood stacked by the stone hearth. Then the match went out.

"Let's get a fire going," said Doug.

Maura remembered the newspaper she'd bought at the gas station and pulled it out of her purse. "You need some paper to get it started?"

"No, there's a pile right here."

In the darkness, they heard Doug rummage for kindling, crumpling newspapers. He struck another match and the paper caught fire.

"Let there be light," said Arlo.

And there was. And heat, too, blessed waves of it as the kindling lit. Doug added two logs to the fire and they all moved close, savoring the heat and the cheery glow.

They could see more of the room now. The furnishings were wood, plain and simply made. A large braided rug covered the wood floor near the hearth. The walls were bare, except for a framed poster of a man with coal-black eyes and a thick mane of dark hair, his gaze turned reverently toward the heavens.

"There's an oil lamp here," said Doug. He lit the wick and smiled as the room brightened. "We've got light and we've got a nice pile of wood. If we just keep that fire going, it should start to get warm in here."

Maura suddenly frowned at the hearth, which was still littered with old ashes. The fire was burning cleanly, the flames leaping up like jagged teeth. "We didn't open the flue," she said.

"It seems to be burning okay," said Doug. "There's no smoke."

"That's my point." Maura crouched down and looked up at the chimney. "The flue was already open. That's weird."

"Why?"

"When you close down your house for the winter, wouldn't you normally clean up the old ashes and close the flue?" She paused. "Wouldn't you lock your door?"

They were silent for a moment as the fire burned, consuming wood that hissed and popped. Maura saw the others glance nervously around at the shadows and knew that the same thought must be going through their heads. *Did the occupants ever leave?*

Doug rose to his feet and picked up the oil lamp. "I think I'll check out the rest of the house."

"I'm coming with you, Daddy," said Grace.

"Me, too," said Elaine.

Now they were all on their feet. No one wanted to be left behind.

Doug led the way down a hallway, and the oil lamp cast moving shadows on the walls. They entered a kitchen with pine floors and cabinets and a wood-burning cookstove. Over the soapstone sink was a hand pump for drawing well water. But what drew everyone's attention was the dining table.

On that table were four plates, four forks, and four glasses of frozen milk. Food had congealed on the plates—something dark and lumpy alongside concrete mounds of mashed potatoes, all of it coated in a fine layer of frost.

Arlo poked a fork at one of the dark lumps. "Looks like meatballs. So which plate do you suppose was Baby Bear's?"

No one laughed.

"They just left their dinner here," said Elaine. "They poured milk, set food on the table. And then . . ." Her voice faded and she looked at Doug.

In the gloom, the oil lamp suddenly flickered as a draft swept the kitchen. Doug crossed to the window, which had been left open, and slid it shut. "This is weird, too," he said, frowning down at a layer of snow that had accumulated in the sink. "Who leaves their windows open when it's freezing outside?"

"Hey, look. There's food in here!" Arlo had opened the pantry cabinet to reveal shelves stocked with supplies. "There's flour. Dried beans. And enough canned corn, peaches, and pickles to last us till Doomsday."

"Leave it to Arlo to find dinner," said Elaine.

"Just call me the ultimate hunter-gatherer. At least we're not going to starve."

"As if you'd ever let that happen."

"And if we light that woodstove," said Maura, "it will heat up the place faster."

Doug looked up toward the second floor. "Assuming they didn't leave any other windows open. We should check the rest of the house."

Again, no one wanted to be left behind. Doug poked his head into the empty garage, then moved to the foot of the staircase. He lifted his oil lamp, but the light revealed only shadowy steps rising into blackness. They started up, Maura in the rear, where it was darkest. In horror films, it was always the rear guard who got picked off first, the hapless character at the end of the column who caught the arrow in the back, the first blow of the ax. She glanced over her shoulder, but all she saw behind her was a well of shadows.

The first room Doug stopped at was a bedroom. They all crowded through the doorway and found a large sleigh bed neatly made up. At the foot was a pine hope chest over which a pair of blue jeans had been draped. A man's size thirty-six with a worn leather belt. Across the floor was a dusting of snow, blown in through yet another open window. Doug closed it.

Maura went to the dresser and picked up a photo with a simple tin frame. Four faces gazed back: a man and a woman, flanking two young girls of about nine or ten, their blond hair neatly bound into braids. The man had slicked-back hair and an unyielding gaze that seemed to dare anyone to challenge his authority. The woman was plain and pale, her blond hair braided, her features so colorless she seemed to recede into the background. Maura pictured that woman working in the kitchen, wisps of white-blond hair escaping her braid and feathering her face. Imagined her setting down plates and forks and dishing out food. Mounds of mashed potatoes, helpings of meat and gravy.

And then what had happened? What would make a family abandon their meal and leave it to harden to ice?

Elaine grabbed Doug's arm. "Did you hear that?" she whispered.

They all went dead-still. Only then did Maura hear the creaking, like footsteps moving across the floor.

Slowly, Doug moved into the hall and toward the second doorway. Holding his lamp high, he stepped into the room, revealing another bedroom.

All at once Elaine laughed. "God, we're idiots!" She pointed to the closet, where a door was creaking back and forth, propelled by gusts that blew in the open window. In relief, she sank onto one of the two twin beds. "An empty house, that's all this is! And we've managed to scare the hell out of ourselves."

"Speak for yourself," said Arlo.

"Oh right. Like you weren't freaking out."

Maura closed the window and stared out at the night. She saw no lights, no sign that anyone else in the world was alive except them. On the desk was a stack of school workbooks. *Independent Home Study Program. Level 4.* She flipped open the cover to a page of spelling exercises. The pupil's name had been printed on the inside cover: Abigail Stratton. One of the two girls in the photo, she thought. This is their room. But gazing around at the walls, she saw little to indicate that preteen girls lived here. There were no movie posters, no photos of teen idols. Only two twin beds, neatly made up, and those schoolbooks.

"I think we can now say this house is all ours," said Doug. "We've just got to sit tight until someone comes looking for us."

"What if no one does?" asked Elaine.

"Someone's bound to miss us. We had reservations at that lodge."

"They'll just think we stood them up. And we're not due back at work till after Thanksgiving. That's nine days from now."

Doug looked at Maura. "You're supposed to fly home tomorrow, right?"

"Yes, but no one knows I came with you, Doug. They won't know where to start looking."

"Why the hell would anyone look *here*?" Arlo pointed out. "This is the middle of nowhere! It'll be spring before the road clears, which means months could go by before they find us." Arlo sank on the twin bed, next to Elaine, and dropped his head in his hands. "Jesus, we are fucked."

Doug looked around at his dispirited companions. "Well, I'm not panicking. We have food and firewood, so we won't starve and we won't freeze." He gave Arlo a hearty slap on the back. "Come on, man. It's an adventure. It could be a lot worse."

"How much worse?" said Arlo.

No one answered. No one wanted to.

SEVEN

B Y THE TIME DETECTIVE JANE RIZZOLI ARRIVED at the scene, a group of bystanders had already gathered, attracted by the flashing lights of the Boston PD cruisers, and by the uncanny instinct that always seemed to draw crowds to places where bad things had happened. Violence gave off its version of pheromones, and these people had caught its scent and now stood pressed up against the U-Store-More chain-link fence, hoping for a glimpse of what had brought the police into their neighborhood.

Jane parked her car and stepped out, buttoning her coat against the cold. This morning the rain had stopped, but with clearing skies had come dropping temperatures, and she realized she hadn't brought any warm gloves, only the latex ones. She wasn't ready for winter yet, hadn't put the ice scraper and snow brush in her car. But tonight, winter was definitely blowing in.

She walked through the gate and onto the property, checking in with the patrolman who stood guard.

The bystanders were watching her, their camera phones out and snapping photos. *Hey, Ma, check out my shots of the crime scene.* Honestly, people, Jane thought. Get a life. She could feel those cameras trained on her as she walked across icy pavement, toward storage locker 22. Three well-bundled patrolmen stood outside the unit, hands buried in their pockets, caps pulled low against the cold.

"Hey, Detective," one of them called out.

"It's in there?"

"Yeah. Detective Frost is already inside with the manager." The cop reached down for the handle and yanked up the aluminum door. It rattled open, and in the cluttered space beyond, Jane saw her partner, Barry Frost, standing with a middle-aged woman. The woman wore a white down jacket that was so voluminous, she looked like she had pillows strapped to her chest.

Frost introduced them. "This is Dottie Dugan, manager of U-Store-More. And this is my partner, Detective Jane Rizzoli," he said.

They all kept their hands in their pockets; it was too cold for standard courtesies.

"You're the one who called it in?" Jane asked.

"Yes, ma'am. I was just telling Detective Frost here how shocked I was when I found out what was in here."

A gust of wind sent scraps of paper fluttering across the concrete floor. Jane said to the patrolman standing outside, "Can you close the door?"

They waited until the aluminum door rattled down, shutting them into a space that was just as frigid as outside, but at least shielded from the wind. A single bare lightbulb swung above them, and the harsh glow emphasized the bags under Dottie Dugan's eyes. Even Frost, who was only in his late thirties, looked strained and middle-aged in that light, his face anemically pale. Cluttering the space was a collection of shabby furniture. Jane saw a frayed couch covered with garishly floral fabric, a stained Naugahyde lounger, and various wooden chairs, none of them matching. There was so much furniture that it was stacked ten feet high along the walls.

"She always paid on time," said Dottie Dugan. "Every October, I'd get a check for the whole year's rent. And this is one of our bigger units, a ten-by-thirty. It's not exactly cheap."

"Who is the renter?" asked Jane.

"Betty Ann Baumeister," Frost answered. He flipped through his notes, reading the info he'd already jotted down. "She rented this unit for eleven years. Address was in Dorchester."

"Was?"

"She's dead," said Dottie Dugan. "I heard it was a heart attack. Happened awhile back, but I didn't find out about it until I tried collecting the rent. It's the first time she didn't send me a check, so I knew something was wrong. I tried to locate her relatives, but all I found was some senile old uncle down in

South Carolina. That's where she came from. Had a southern accent, really soft and pretty. Thought it was such a shame that she moved all the way up here to Boston, just to die alone. That's what I thought then, anyway." She gave a rueful laugh and shuddered inside her puffy jacket. "You just can never tell, can you? Sweet-looking southern lady like that. I felt really guilty about auctioning off her stuff, but I couldn't just let it sit here." She looked around. "Not that it's worth much."

"Where did you find it?" asked Jane.

"Against that wall back there. That's where the electrical outlet is." Dottie Dugan led them through the canyon of stacked chairs to a large chest freezer. "I figured she was storing expensive meats or something. I mean, why bother to keep this thing running all year round, unless you've got something worth freezing?" She paused and looked at Jane and Frost. "If you don't mind, I'd just as soon get out of your way. I don't really want to see it again." She turned and retreated toward the door.

Jane and Frost exchanged glances. It was Jane who lifted the lid. Cold mist rose from the freezer, obscuring what lay within. Then the mist cleared, and the contents came into view.

Shrouded in clear plastic, a man's face stared up at them, icy rime coating his brows and lashes. His nude body had been folded into a fetal position, his knees crammed up against his chest to better fit in the small space. Although his cheeks were parched with freezer burn, his skin was unwrinkled, his youthful flesh preserved like a good cut of meat, wrapped and frozen and put aside for later use.

"When she rented this unit, the one thing she insisted on was a reliable power outlet," said Dottie, her face averted to avoid seeing the occupant of the freezer. "Said she couldn't afford to have the electricity cut out on her. Now I know why."

"Do you know anything else about Ms. Baumeister?" asked Jane.

"Just what I already told Detective Frost here. Paid on time, and her checks were always good. My renters, they're mostly just in and out, don't necessarily want to chat much. A lot of them have sad stories. They lose their homes, and this is where their stuff ends up. Hardly ever anything worth auctioning off. Most of the time it's like this." She waved at the tired furniture stacked up against the walls. "Valuable only to the people who own it."

Jane slowly scanned the objects that Betty Ann Baumeister had felt were worth storing these past eleven years. At $250 a month, it would have cost her $3,000 a year, and over a decade that was $30,000 just to hold on to these possessions. There was enough here to furnish a four-bedroom house, though not in style. The dressers and bookshelves were made of warped particleboard. The yellowed lamp shades looked fragile enough to disintegrate at a touch. Worthless junk, to Jane's eye. But when Betty Ann looked at the frayed couch and the wobbly chairs, did she see treasures or trash?

And which category was the man in the freezer?

"Do you think she killed him?" asked Dottie Dugan.

Jane looked at her. "I don't know, ma'am. We don't even know who he is. We'll have to wait and see what the medical examiner says."

"If she didn't kill him, why did she stuff him in the freezer?"

"You'd be surprised what people do." Jane closed the freezer lid, glad to shut off her view of the frozen face, the ice-encrusted lashes. "Maybe she just didn't want to lose him."

"I guess you detectives see a lot of weird stuff."

"More than I care to think about." Jane sighed, exhaling steam. She did not look forward to combing for evidence in this miserably cold locker. At least time was not their enemy; neither the evidence nor the suspect was at risk of slipping away from them.

Her cell phone rang. "Excuse me," she said, moving a few paces away to answer it. "Detective Rizzoli."

"I'm sorry to bother you this late at night," said Father Daniel Brophy. "I just spoke to your husband, and he said you were working a scene."

She was not surprised to be hearing from Brophy. As the clergyman assigned to Boston PD, he was often called to crime scenes, to minister to the grieving. "We're okay here, Daniel," she said. "There don't seem to be any family members who'll need any counseling."

"I'm calling about Maura, actually." He paused. It was a subject he no doubt found difficult to broach, and no wonder. His affair with Maura was hardly a secret to Jane, and he had to know that she disapproved of it, even if she'd never said so to his face.

"She hasn't been answering her cell phone," he said. "I'm concerned."

"Maybe she's just not taking calls." *Your calls* was what she thought.

"I've left half a dozen voice mails. I just wondered if you've been able to reach her."

"I haven't tried."

"I want to be sure she's all right."

"She's attending a conference, isn't she? Maybe she turned off her phone."

"So you don't know where she is."

"I thought it was somewhere out in Wyoming."

"Yes, I know where she's supposed to be."

"Have you tried calling her hotel?"

"That's just it. She checked out this morning."

Jane turned as the storage unit door opened again and the medical examiner ducked inside. "I'm kind of busy at the moment," she said to Brophy.

"She wasn't supposed to check out until tomorrow."

"So she changed her mind. She made other plans."

"She didn't tell me. What worries me is that I can't reach her."

Jane waved at the ME, who squeezed through the mountains of furniture and joined Frost at the freezer. Impatient to get back to work, she said bluntly: "Maybe she doesn't want to be reached. Have you considered the possibility that she might need time alone?"

He was silent.

It had been a cruel question, and she was sorry she'd asked it. "You do know," she said more gently, "it's been hard for her this year."

"I know."

"You hold all the cards, Daniel. It's all about your decision, your choice."

"Do you think that makes it easier for me, knowing that I'm the one who has to choose?"

She heard his pain and thought: Why do people do this to themselves? How do two intelligent and decent human beings trap themselves in such misery? She'd predicted months ago that it would come to this, that after the hormones faded and the luster was off their shiny new affair, they'd be left with regret as their bitter companion.

"I just want to be sure she's all right," he said. "I wouldn't have bothered you if I wasn't worried."

"I don't keep track of her whereabouts."

"But could you check on her for me?"

"How?"

"Call her. Maybe you're right, maybe she's just

screening my calls. Our last conversation wasn't . . ." He paused. "It could have ended on a better note."

"You argued?"

"No. But I disappointed her. I know that."

"That could make her not return your calls."

"Still, it's not like her to be unreachable."

On that point he was right. Maura was too conscientious to be out of touch for long. "I'll give her a call," Jane said, and hung up, grateful that her own life was so settled. No tears, no drama, no crazy highs and lows. Just the happy assurance that at that moment, her husband and daughter were at home waiting for her. All around her, it seemed, romantic turmoil was destroying people's lives. Her father had left her mother for another woman. Barry Frost's marriage had recently collapsed. No one was behaving the way they used to, the way they should. As she dialed Maura's cell phone, she wondered: Am I the only one around here who's still sane?

It rang four times, then she heard the recording: "This is Dr. Isles. I'm not available right now, but if you leave a message, I'll return your call as soon as possible."

"Hey, Doc, we're wondering where you are," said Jane. "Give me a call, okay?" She disconnected and stared down at her cell phone, thinking of all the reasons why Maura hadn't answered. Out of range. Dead battery. Or maybe she was having too good a time in Wyoming, away from Daniel Brophy.

Away from her job, with all the reminders of death and decay.

"Everything okay?" Frost called out.

Jane slipped the phone in her pocket and looked at him. "Yeah," she said. "I'm sure it's fine."

EIGHT

"SO WHAT DO YOU THINK HAPPENED HERE?" SAID Elaine, her voice faintly slurred from drinking too much whiskey. "Where did this family go?"

They sat huddled around the fireplace, swaddled in blankets that they'd pulled from the cold upstairs bedrooms, the remains of their dinner littering the floor around them. They'd eaten canned pork and beans and macaroni and cheese, saltine crackers and peanut butter. A high-sodium feast, washed down with a bottle of cheap whiskey, which they'd found stashed at the very back of the pantry, hidden behind the sacks of flour and sugar.

It had to be *her* whiskey, Maura thought, remembering the woman in the photograph with the dull eyes and the blank expression. The pantry was where a woman would hoard a secret supply of liquor, a place where her husband would never bother to explore, not if he considered cooking to be a woman's job. Maura took a sip, and as the whiskey burned its way down her throat, she wondered what would drive a woman to secret drinking, what misery would make her seek liquor's numbing solace.

"Okay," said Arlo. "I can come up with one logical explanation for where these people went."

Elaine refreshed her glass and added only a splash of water. "Let's hear it."

"It's dinnertime. The wife with the bad hairdo puts food on the table, and they're all about to sit down and say grace, or whatever these people do. And the husband suddenly clutches his chest and says, 'I'm having a heart attack!' So they all pile into the car and rush off to the hospital."

"Leaving the front door unlocked?"

"Why bother to lock it? What's in here that anyone could possibly want to steal?" Arlo waved dismissively at the furniture. "Besides, there's no one around for miles who'd bother to break in here." He paused and raised his glass of whiskey in a wry toast. "Present company excepted."

"It looks to me like they've been gone for days. Why haven't they come back?"

"The roads," said Maura. She pulled out the newspaper that she had bought at Grubb's Gas Station and General Store earlier that day. A lifetime ago, it seemed. Spreading it flat, she slid it into the firelight so they could read the headline, which she'd noticed when she paid for the newspaper.

Cold Weather Returns

After a week of unseasonably warm weather, with temperatures peaking in the high 60s, a blast of wintry weather appears headed our way. Forecasters predict that two to four inches of snow could start falling Tuesday night. A far more powerful winter storm is right on its heels, with the potential of even heavier snowfall on Saturday.

"Maybe they couldn't get back here," said Maura. "Maybe they left before the Tuesday storm, while the road was still clear."

"It would explain why the windows were open," said Doug. "It's because the weather was still warm when they left. And then the storm came in." He tipped his head to Maura. "Didn't I tell you all that she was brilliant? Dr. Isles always comes up with a logical explanation."

"It means these people must be planning to return," said Arlo. "After the road gets cleared."

"Unless they change their minds," said Elaine. "They left the house unlocked and all their windows open. They've got to come back."

"To *this*? No electricity, no neighbors around? What woman in her right mind would put up with it? And where *are* all the neigbors, anyway?"

"This is a bad place," said Grace softly. "I wouldn't come back."

They all looked at her. The girl sat by herself,

wrapped so tightly in a blanket that she looked like a mummy in the shadows. She had been silent, lost in whatever music was playing on her iPod, but now the earbuds were out and she sat hugging herself, looking around the room with wide eyes.

"I looked in their closet," said Grace. "The room where the mom and dad slept. Do you know he has sixteen belts? Sixteen leather belts, each one hanging on its own hook. And there's rope there, too. Why would you keep rope in your closet?"

Arlo gave a nervous chuckle. "No G-rated purpose I can think of." Elaine gave him a light slap.

"I don't think he was a nice man." Grace stared at the darkness lurking beyond the firelight. "Maybe his wife and kids escaped. Maybe they saw a chance and ran." She paused. "If they were lucky. If he didn't kill them first."

Maura shivered inside her wool blanket. Even the whiskey could not dispel the chill that had suddenly settled over the room.

Arlo reached for the bottle. "Gee, if we're going to tell scary stories, we'd better get some sedation on board."

"You already have enough on board," said Elaine.

"Who else has a scary story for the campfire?" Arlo looked at Maura. "With your job, you must have a ton of them."

Maura glanced at Grace, who had retreated into silence. If I'm spooked by the situation, she thought, how frightening must it be for a mere thirteen-year-old girl? "I don't think this is the time to be telling any scary stories," she said.

"Well, how about funny stories then? Don't pathologists have a reputation for morgue humor?"

Maura knew he was merely hoping for entertainment to help pass the long and chilly night, but she was not in the mood to be amusing. "There's nothing funny about what I do," she said. "Trust me."

A long silence passed. Grace moved closer to the hearth and stared into the fire. "I wish we'd stayed at the hotel. I don't like this place."

"Well, I'm with you, sweetie," said Elaine. "This house gives me the creeps."

"Oh, I don't know," Doug said, as usual offering the sunny appraisal. "This is a good, solidly built house. It tells us what kind of people might live here."

Elaine gave a disparaging laugh. "People with really bad taste in furniture."

"Not to mention their taste in food," said Arlo, pointing at the empty can of pork and beans.

"You ate it fast enough."

"These are survival conditions, Elaine. One does what one must to stay alive."

"And did you see the clothes in the closets? Nothing but gingham and high collars. Pioneer dresses."

"Wait, wait. I'm getting a mental picture of these people." Arlo pressed his fingers to his temples and closed his eyes like a swami conjuring up visions. "I'm seeing . . ."

"American Gothic!" Doug tossed out.

"No, Beverly Hillbillies!" Elaine said.

"Hey, Ma," Arlo drawled, "pass me another helping of that there squirrel stew."

The trio of old friends burst out laughing, fueled
by whiskey and the potent joys of ridiculing people
whom they had never met. Maura did not join in.

"And what do you see, Maura?" asked Elaine.

"Come on," prodded Arlo. "Play the game with
us. Who do you think these people are?"

Maura looked around the room at walls devoid
of decorations except for that framed poster of the
dark-haired man with the hypnotic eyes and the
reverently upturned gaze. There were no curtains,
no knickknacks. The only books were how-to man-
uals. *Diesel Engine Repair. Basic Plumbing. Home
Veterinary Manual.* This was not a woman's house;
this was not a woman's world.

"He's in total control here," she said. "The husband."

The others watched, waiting for more.

"Do you see how everything in this room is cold
and practical? There's no hint of the wife in this
room. It's as if she doesn't exist, as if she's invisible.
A woman who doesn't matter, who's trapped and
can't find any way out except through a whiskey
bottle." She paused, suddenly thinking of Daniel,
and her gaze blurred with tears. *I'm trapped, too.
In love and unable to walk away. I might as well be*

shut up in a valley all my own. She blinked and as her vision cleared, she found them staring at her.

"Wow," said Arlo softly. "That's quite a psycho-analysis for a house."

"You asked me what I thought." She drank the last of her whiskey and set down the glass with a hard clunk. "I'm tired. I'm going to sleep."

"We all need some sleep," said Doug. "I'll stay awake for a while and keep the fire going. We can't let it go out, so we'll need to take shifts."

"I'll take the next shift," Elaine volunteered. She curled up on the rug and pulled her blanket around herself. "Wake me up when it's time."

The floor creaked as they all settled down, trying to get comfortable on the braided rug. Even with the fire burning in the hearth, the room was chilly. Beneath her blanket, Maura was still wearing her jacket. They had brought pillows down from the beds upstairs, and hers smelled like sweat and after-shave. The husband's pillow.

With his scent against her cheek she fell asleep and dreamed of a dark-haired man with stony eyes, a man who loomed over her and watched as she slept. She saw threat in his gaze, but she could not move, could not defend herself, her body paralyzed by sleep. With a gasp she woke up, eyes wide in ter-ror, heart banging in her chest.

No one stood above her. She stared up at empty shadows.

Her blanket had slid off, and the room was freezing. She looked at the fireplace and saw that the flames had died down to only a few glowing coals. Arlo sat snoring with his back propped up against the hearth, his head lolling forward. He had let the fire die down.

Shivering and stiff from the cold floor, Maura rose and placed another log on the hearth. The wood caught almost immediately, and flames soon crackled, throwing off delicious waves of heat. She looked in disgust at Arlo, who didn't even stir. Useless, she thought. I can't even count on them to keep a fire burning. What a mistake it had been to throw in her lot with these people. She was tired of Arlo's wisecracks and Grace's whining and Doug's annoyingly unflagging optimism. And Elaine made her uneasy, though she didn't know why. She remembered the way Elaine had stared when Doug had embraced Maura up on the road. I'm the interloper, the one who doesn't belong with this happy quartet, she thought. And Elaine resents me.

The fire was now burning hot and bright.

Maura glanced at her watch and saw it was four AM. It was almost time for her shift to watch the fire anyway, so she might as well stay awake until dawn. As she stood up to stretch, a reflected glimmer caught her eye on the periphery of the firelight. Moving closer, she saw that droplets of water had beaded on the wooden floor. Then she noticed, off in the shadows, a light dusting of white. Someone had opened the door, letting in a gust of snow.

She crossed toward the door, where the snow had not yet melted, and stared down at the fine powder. Pressed into that powder was a single shoe print.

She turned and quickly scanned the room, counting the sleeping forms. Everyone present and accounted for.

The door was unlocked; no one had bothered to latch it last night, and why would they? Whom would they be trying to lock out?

She slid the bolt shut and went to look out the window. Although the room was warming up again, she was shaking under her blanket. Wind moaned in the chimney, and she heard snow hiss across the glass. She could see nothing outside, only blackness. But anyone out there would be able to see *her*, backlit by the glow of firelight.

She retreated from the window and sat on the rug, shivering. The snow near the door melted, taking with it the last remnants of the shoe print. Maybe the door blew open during the night, and one of them got up to shut it, leaving the print. Maybe someone stepped out to check the weather or pee in the snow. Wide awake now, she sat and watched as night slowly gave way to dawn, as the blackness outside lifted to gray.

Her companions did not stir.

When she rose to feed the fire again, she saw that

they were down to their last few logs. There was plenty of wood outside in the shed, but it was probably damp. If she wanted it to dry out, someone would have to bring in an armload now. She looked at her sleeping companions and sighed. *That someone would be me.*

She pulled on her boots and gloves, wrapped her scarf around her face, and unlatched the front door. Bracing herself against the cold, she stepped outside, closing the door behind her. Wind swept the porch, its bite as sharp as needles. The swing creaked in protest. Glancing down, she saw no shoe prints, but the wind would have scoured anything away. A thermometer mounted on the wall read twelve degrees. It felt far colder.

The steps were buried in snow, and as she set her boot down on what she thought was the first step, her foot slid out and she fell. The impact shot straight up her spine and exploded in her skull. She sat for a moment, stunned and blinking in the dawn's brightness. Sun beamed down from a blue sky and glared on a world turned blinding. Wind blasted a puff of powder into her face and she sneezed, which only made her head hurt worse.

She got up and brushed off her pants. Squinted at snow glistening on rooftops. Between the two rows of houses was a swath of virgin white, inviting her to be the first to tread that perfect, untouched surface. She ignored the impulse and instead tramped around the corner of the house, struggling through knee-high snow to reach the woodshed. She tried to pull a split log from the top of the pile, but it was frozen in place. Bracing one foot against the pile, she tugged harder. With a loud crack, the frozen bark suddenly gave way and she stumbled backward. Her boot caught on something buried beneath the snow, and she sprawled to the ground.

Two falls in one day. And the morning was still young.

Her head ached and her eyes felt scorched by the sunlight. She was hungry and queasy at the same time, the result of too much whiskey last night. The prospect of pork and beans for breakfast wasn't making her feel any better. She struggled back to her feet and looked around for the log that she'd dropped. Kicking around in the snow, she bumped up against an obstruction. She dug in with gloved hands and felt a hard lump. Not the log, but something larger, something that was frozen to the ground. This was what she had caught her boot on.

She brushed away more snow and suddenly went still, staring down at what she'd uncovered. Repulsed, she backed away. Then turned and ran into the house.

NINE

THEY MUST HAVE LEFT HIM OUTSIDE, AND HE froze to death," said Elaine.

They stood in a solemn circle around the dead dog, like five mourners at a grave, buffeted by a wind with a bite as sharp as glass. Doug had used a shovel to widen the hole, and the dog now lay fully uncovered, its fur glistening with snow. A German shepherd.

"Who would leave a dog out in this weather?" said Arlo. "It's cruel."

Maura knelt down and pressed her gloved hand against the dog's flank. The body was frozen solid, the flesh hard as stone. "I don't see any injuries. And he's not a stray," she said. "He looks well fed, and he's wearing a collar." On the steel tag was engraved the unlikely name of LUCKY. "He's obviously someone's pet."

"He might have just wandered out of the house and his owners couldn't find him in time," said Doug.

Grace looked up with stricken eyes. "And then they just left him here, all alone?"

"Maybe they had to leave in a hurry."

"How can anyone do that? We'd never do that to a dog."

"We don't know what really happened here, honey."

"You're going to bury him, aren't you?"

"Grace, he's just a dog."

"You can't leave him out here."

Doug sighed. "Okay, I'll take care of it, I promise. Why don't you go inside and keep that fire going. I'll take care of everything."

They waited until Grace had retreated into the house. Then Elaine said, "You aren't really going to bother burying this dog, are you? The ground's frozen solid."

"You saw how freaked out she is."

"She's not the only one," said Arlo.

"I'll just cover it back up with snow. It's so deep, she won't know the dog's still here."

"Let's all go back in the house," said Elaine. "I'm freezing."

"I don't understand this," said Maura, still crouched over the dead animal. "Dogs aren't stupid, especially not German shepherds. He's well nourished and he has a thick winter coat." She rose to her feet and surveyed the landscape, her eyes narrowed against the glare of reflected sunlight. "This

is the north-facing wall. Why would he end up dying right here?"

"As opposed to where?" said Elaine.

"Maura raises a good point," said Doug.

"I'm not getting it," Elaine said, clearly annoyed
that no one was following her back into the house.

"Dogs have common sense," he said. "They know
enough to seek shelter from the cold. He could
have dug himself into the snow. Or crawled under
the porch. He could have found any number of
places where he'd be better protected against the
wind, but he didn't." He looked down at the dog.
"Instead he ended up here. Fully exposed to the
wind, as if he just keeled over and died."

They were silent as a gust whipped their clothes
and whistled between buildings, whirling white
glitter. Maura stared at deep drifts rippling the landscape like giant white waves, and she wondered:
What other surprises lie buried beneath the snow?

Doug turned to look at the other buildings.
"Maybe we should take a look at what's inside those
other houses," he said.

The four of them walked in single file toward the
next house, Doug leading the way as he always did,
breaking a path through deep snow. They mounted
the front steps. Like the house they'd slept in the
night before, this one had a porch with an identical
swing.

"You think maybe they got a volume discount?"

said Arlo. "*Buy eleven swings, we throw in the twelfth for free?*"

Maura thought of the glassy-eyed woman in the family photo. Imagined a whole village of pale and silent women sitting in these swings, mechanically rocking back and forth like windup dolls. Clone houses, clone people.

"This door's unlocked, too," said Doug, and he pushed it open.

Just inside lay a toppled chair.

For a moment, they paused on the threshold, puzzling over that fallen chair. Doug picked it up and set it upright. "Well, that's sort of weird."

"Look," said Arlo. He crossed toward the framed portrait hanging on the wall. "It's the same guy."

The morning light spilled down in a heavenly beam on the man's upward-gazing face, as though God Himself approved of his piety. Studying the portrait, Maura saw other details she hadn't noticed before. The backdrop of golden wheat behind him. The white peasant shirt, the sleeves rolled up to his elbows, as though he had been laboring in the fields. And his eyes, piercing and ebony black, staring into some distant eternity.

"*And he shall gather the righteous,*" said Arlo, reading the plaque mounted on the frame. "I wonder who this guy is, anyway? And why does everyone seem to have his portrait hanging in their house?"

Maura spotted what looked like a Bible lying open on the coffee table. She flipped it closed and saw the title, embossed in gold on the leather cover.

Words of Our Prophet
The Wisdom of The Gathering

"I think this is some sort of religious community," she said. "Maybe he's their spiritual leader."

"That would explain a few things," said Doug. "The lack of electricity. The simplicity of their lifestyle."

"The Amish in Wyoming?" said Arlo.

"A lot of people these days seem to crave a simpler life. And you could find that here, in this valley. Grow your own food, shut out the world. No TV, no temptations from the outside."

Elaine laughed. "If showers and electric lights are works of the devil, then sign me up for hell."

Doug turned. "Let's see the rest of the house."

They moved down the hall, into the kitchen, and found the same pine cabinets and wood-burning stove, the same hand pump for water that they'd seen in the first house. Here, too, the window was open, but a screen had kept out the snow, allowing in only the wind and a few sparkling motes. Elaine crossed the room to shut the window, and suddenly gasped.

"What?" Doug asked.

She backed away, pointing at the sink. "Something—there's something dead in there!"

As Maura moved closer, she saw the butcher knife, its blade smeared with blood. In the sink were frozen splatters of more blood and mounds of gray fur. "They're rabbits," she said, and pointed to a bowl of peeled potatoes sitting nearby. "I think someone was about to cook them."

Arlo laughed. "Good going, Salinger. Scare the bejesus out of us over someone's dinner."

"So what happened to the cook?" Elaine was still hanging back, as though the carcasses in the sink could reanimate into something dangerous. "She's about to skin the rabbits and then what? She just walks away and leaves them here?" Elaine looked around at their faces. "Someone answer that. Give me one logical explanation."

"Maybe she's dead," said a soft voice. "Maybe they're all dead."

They turned to see Grace standing in the doorway. They had not heard her come into the house. She stood hugging herself, shivering in the frigid kitchen.

"What if they're all lying under the snow, like that dog? And we just can't see them?"

"Grace, honey," said Doug gently. "Go back to the other house."

"I don't want to be alone."

"Elaine, can you walk her back?"

"What are you all going to do?" asked Elaine.

"Just *take* her, okay?" he snapped.

Elaine flinched at his tone. "All right, Doug," she said tightly. "I'll do whatever you say. Don't I always?" She took Grace's hand, and the two of them walked out of the kitchen.

Doug sighed. "Man, this keeps getting weirder."

"What if Grace is right?" said Arlo.

"Not you, too."

"Who knows what's under all this snow? There could be bodies."

"Shut up, Arlo." Doug turned toward the garage door.

"Why does that seem to be everyone's favorite phrase lately? *Shut up, Arlo.*"

"Let's just look through the rest of these houses. See if there's anything we can use. A radio, a generator." He stepped into the garage and halted. "I think I just found our way out of here," he said.

Inside was parked a Jeep Cherokee.

Doug ran to the driver's door and yanked it open. "The keys are in the ignition!"

"Doug, look!" said Maura, pointing to a mound of metal links on one of the shelves. "I think those are tire chains!"

Doug gave a laugh of relief. "If we can get this baby up to the main road, we might be able to drive it all the way down the mountain."

"Then why didn't *they*?" said Arlo. He stood staring at the Jeep, as though it were something alien, something that did not belong there. "The people who lived here. The people who were about to cook those rabbits, why did they leave this nice truck behind?"

"They probably had another car."

"It's a one-car garage, Doug."

"Then maybe they left with the people in the first house. There was no car in their garage."

"You're just guessing. It's an abandoned house with a nice new SUV, dead rabbits in the sink, and no people. Where is everyone?"

"It doesn't matter! What matters is that we've now got a way out of here. So let's get to work. If we go through the other garages, we should be able to find shovels. And maybe bolt cutters, to get through that chain at the top of the road." He went to the garage bay door and yanked up on the handle. The sudden glare of sunlight on snow made them all squint. "If you find anything you think we can use, just grab it. We'll settle up with these people later."

Arlo pulled his scarf tighter and waded across to the opposite house. Maura and Doug trudged to the house next door. Doug dug in the snow for the handle and yanked up the bay door. It squealed open and they both froze, staring into the garage.

A pickup truck was parked inside.

Maura turned and looked across the street, where Arlo had just opened another garage door. "Hey, there's a car in here!" Arlo yelled.

"What the hell is going on?" murmured Doug. He ran through knee-deep drifts toward the next house and hauled open the garage door. Took one look at what was inside then plunged ahead, toward the next house.

"Car in this garage, too!" Arlo called out.

The wind screamed as though in pain, and a squall

line raced toward them like white stallions kicking up snow. Maura blinked as the glittering cloud stung her face. Suddenly the wind fell still, leaving a strange, icy silence. She regarded the row of houses facing her, all their garage doors now gaping open.

There was a vehicle inside each one.

TEN

I DON'T KNOW HOW TO EXPLAIN IT," SAID DOUG as he scooped up a shovelful of snow and flung it aside, clearing the space behind the Jeep so he could lay out the tire chains. "All I care about now is getting out of here."

"Doesn't it bother you just a little? That we don't know what happened to these people?"

"Arlo, we have to *focus*." Doug straightened, his face florid from exertion, and glanced up at the sky. "I want to be on that main road before it gets dark."

They had all been shoveling, and now they paused to rest, their faces cloaked in the steam from their breath. Maura eyed the winding road out of the valley. There were deep drifts in their way, and even if they did make it up to where they'd abandoned the Suburban, they still had another thirty-mile drive down the mountain. Thirty miles during which they could get stranded again.

"We could also just stay right where we are," said Maura.

"And wait around to be rescued?" Doug snorted. "That's no way out. I refuse to sit back and be passive."

"I'm supposed to fly back to Boston tonight. When I don't show up, they'll know something's wrong. They'll start searching for me."

"You said no one knows you came with us."

"The point is, they *will* be searching. We've got food and shelter right here. We can hold out as long as we need to. Why take the risk?"

His face flushed an even deeper shade of red. "Maura, it's my fault that we got into this mess. Now I'm going to get us out. Just trust me."

"I'm not saying I don't trust you. I'm just pointing out the alternative to getting stuck on that road, where we may not find any shelter."

"The alternative? That we sit here and wait for God knows how long?"

"At least we're safe."

"Are we?" It was Arlo who asked the question. "I mean, I'm just throwing this out there for you all to think about, since I'm the only one who seems to be bothered by it. But this place. This *place* . . ." He looked around at the deserted houses and shuddered. "Something bad happened here. Something that I'm not sure is over with. I vote for getting the hell out, as soon as we can."

"So do I, Daddy," said Grace.

"Elaine?" said Doug.

"Whatever you decide, Doug. I trust you."

That's how we got into this mess in the first place, thought Maura. We all trusted Doug. But she was the outsider, overruled four to one, and nothing she could say would change the balance. And perhaps they were right. There *was* something wrong about this place; she could feel it. Old echoes of evil that seemed to whisper in the wind.

Maura lifted her shovel again.

With all of them working together, it took only a few more minutes to clear enough space behind the Jeep. Doug dragged over the clanking tire chains and laid them out behind the rear wheels.

"Those look pretty banged up," said Arlo, frowning at the rusted metal.

"This is all we've got," said Doug.

"Some of those cross links are broken. Those chains may not make it."

"They only have to hold out till we reach the gas station." Doug climbed into the Jeep and turned the ignition. The engine started up at the first crank. "Okay, we're good!" He grinned out the window. "Why don't you ladies pack up some supplies? Whatever you think we might need on the road. Arlo and I will work on the chains."

By the time Maura came out of the house with an armful of blankets, the chains were on, and Doug had the Jeep turned around and facing the road. Already it was past noon, and they scrambled to load in food and candles, shovels and the bolt cutter. When they finally all piled into the Jeep, they paused a moment in silence, as though simultaneously offering up prayers for success.

Doug took a breath and put the Jeep into gear. They began to roll, the chains clanking noisily against the chassis, and churned ahead through the snow.

"I think this is going to work," murmured Doug. Maura heard a note of wonder in his voice, as if even he had doubted their chances. "God, I think this is actually going to *work*!"

They left behind the houses and began to climb out of the valley, retracing the route that they had scrambled down on foot a day earlier. Fresh snow had covered their footprints, and they could not be certain where the edges of the road might be, but the Jeep kept barreling ahead, steadily ascending. From the backseat came Arlo's soft chant, one word repeated over and over.

Go. Go. Go.

Now Elaine and Grace joined in, their voices synchronized in time with the rhythm of the tire chains slapping the truck.

Go. Go. Go.

The chant was mixed with laughter now as they climbed ever higher, almost to the halfway point out of the valley. The road grew steeper, curving in hairpin turns, and they heard snow scraping the undercarriage.

Go. Go. Go.

Even Maura found herself murmuring the words now, not quite saying them aloud but thinking them. Daring to hope that yes, this was going to turn out fine. Yes, they would get out of this valley and roll down the main road, chains banging all the way, to Jackson. What a story they'd have to tell, just as Doug had promised them, a story that they could dine out on for years to come, about their adventure in a strange village called Kingdom Come.

Go. Go. Go . . .

Suddenly the Jeep lurched to a halt, snapping Maura forward against her seat belt. She glanced at Doug.

"Take it easy," he said, and shifted into reverse. "We'll just back up. Get a little running start." He pressed the accelerator. The engine whined, but the Jeep didn't budge.

"Is anyone getting a bad case of déjà vu?" said Arlo.

"Ah, but this time we have shovels!" Doug climbed out and looked at the front bumper. "We just hit a little deeper snow here. I think we can dig our way out of this drift. Come on, let's do it."

"I'm definitely feeling that déjà vu," muttered Arlo as he climbed out and grabbed a shovel.

As they began to dig, Maura realized that their problem was worse than Doug had advertised. They had veered off the road, and neither of the rear tires was in contact with solid ground. They cleared the snow away from the front bumper, but even then the Jeep would not move, the front wheels spinning on icy pavement.

Doug climbed out of the driver's seat again and stared in frustration at the suspended rear tires, girded in the rusting chains. "Maura, you take the wheel," he said. "Arlo and I are going to push."

"All the way back to Jackson?" said Arlo.

"You have a better idea?"

"If this is going to keep happening, we're sure not going to make it by sundown."

"So what do you want to do?"

"I'm just saying—"

"What, Arlo? You want us to go back to the house? Sit on our butts and wait for someone to rescue us?"

"Hey, man, take it easy." Arlo gave a nervous laugh. "It's not like I'm calling for a mutiny."

"Maybe you should. Maybe you'd like to make the tough decisions, instead of always leaving it up to me to figure out everything."

"I never asked you to take charge."

"No, it happens by default. Funny how it always seems to work out this way. I make the hard choices and you stand back and tell me what I'm doing wrong."

"Doug, come on."

"Isn't that how it usually goes?" Doug looked at Elaine. "Isn't it?"

"Why are you asking her? You know what she's going to say."

"What's that supposed to mean?" Elaine said.

"*Whatever you say, Doug,*" Arlo mimicked. "*I'm with you, Doug.*"

"Fuck you, Arlo," she snapped.

"It's Doug you'd rather be fucking!"

His outburst shocked them all into silence. They stared at one another as the wind swept the slope, pelleting their faces with blowing snow.

"I'll steer," Maura said quietly, and she climbed into the driver's seat, glad to escape the battle. Whatever history these three friends had together, she was not a part of it. She was merely the accidental observer, witness to a psychodrama that had begun long before she joined them.

When Doug finally spoke, his voice was quiet and in control. "Arlo, let's get behind this thing and push. Or we'll never get out of here."

The two men positioned themselves behind the Jeep, Arlo at the right rear bumper, Doug on the left. They were both grimly silent, as if Arlo's outburst had never happened. But Maura had seen the effect on Elaine's face, had watched it freeze in a mask of humiliation.

"Give it some juice, Maura," Doug called out.

Maura put the Jeep into first gear and lightly pressed the accelerator. She heard the wheels whine, loose chain links clanging against the chassis. The

Jeep inched forward, propelled by sheer muscle power as Doug and Arlo pitted their weight against the vehicle.

"Keep feeding it gas!" ordered Doug. "We're moving."

The Jeep rocked forward and rocked backward, gravity tugging it once again off the road's edge.

"Don't stop!" yelled Doug. "More gas!"

Maura caught a glimpse of Arlo's face in her rearview mirror, bright red from exertion as he strained against the car.

She goosed the accelerator. Heard the engine roar, the chains banging faster against the wheel well. The Jeep gave a sharp jerk and suddenly there was a different sound. A dull thumping that she felt more than heard, as though the Jeep had hit a log.

Then came the shrieks.

"Stop the engine!" Elaine banged on her door. "Oh my God, *stop it!*"

Maura instantly shut off the motor.

The shrieks were coming from Grace. Shrill, piercing wails that did not sound human. Maura turned to look at her, but didn't see why the girl was screaming. Grace stood at the side of the road, hands pressed to the sides of her face. Her eyelids were clenched shut, as though desperately blocking out something terrible.

Maura shoved open her door and scrambled out of the Jeep. Blood was splattered across the whiteness of snow in shockingly bright red ribbons.

"Hold him still!" Doug yelled. "Elaine, you've got to keep him still!"

Grace's shrieks faded to a choked sob.

Maura ran back to the rear of the Jeep, where the ground was awash in more blood, steaming on the churned-up snow. She could not see the source of it, because Doug and Elaine blocked her view as they knelt near the right rear tire. Only when she leaned over Doug's shoulder did she see Arlo, lying on his back, his jacket and trousers saturated. Elaine was holding down Arlo's shoulders as Doug applied pressure to the exposed groin. Maura caught sight of Arlo's left leg—what remained of it—and she reeled backward, nauseated.

"I need a tourniquet!" yelled Doug, struggling to keep his blood-slicked palms positioned over the femoral artery.

Maura quickly unbuckled her belt and yanked it free. Dropping to her knees in the bloody snow, she felt icy slush soak into her pants. Despite Doug's pressure on the artery, a steady stream of red was seeping into the snow. She slipped her belt under the thigh and blood smeared her jacket sleeve, a startling stripe across white nylon. As she looped the belt, she felt Arlo trembling, his body rapidly sinking into shock. She yanked the tourniquet tight, and the stream of blood slowed to a trickle. Only then, with the bleeding controlled, did Doug release his grip on the artery. He rocked back to stare at the torn flesh and protruding bone, at a limb so twisted that the foot jutted in one direction, the knee in another.

"Arlo?" Elaine said. *"Arlo?"* She shook him, but he had fallen limp and unresponsive.

Doug felt Arlo's neck. "He's got a pulse. And he's breathing. I think he just fainted."

"Oh my God." Elaine rose and stumbled away. They could hear her throwing up in the snow.

Doug looked down at his hands, and with a shudder he scooped up snow and frantically scrubbed away the blood. "The tire chain," he muttered, rubbing snow against his skin, as though he could somehow purify himself of the horror. "One of the broken links must have snagged his pants. Wrapped his leg around the axle . . ." Doug rolled back on his knees and released a breath that was half sigh, half sob. "We'll never get this Jeep out of here. The chain's broken all to hell."

"Doug, we have to get him back to the house."

"The house?" Doug looked at her. "What he needs is a fucking OR!"

"He can't stay out here in the cold. He's in shock." She rose to her feet and glanced around. Grace was huddled off by herself, her back turned to them. Elaine was crouched in the snow, as though too dizzy to stand straight. Neither of them would be any help.

"I'll be right back," said Maura. "Stay with him."

"Where are you going?"

"I saw a sled in one of the garages. We can drag him back on that." She left them and started running toward the village, her boots slipping and sliding in the ruts left by the Jeep's ascent. It was a relief to leave behind the bloody snow and her shell-shocked companions, a relief to focus on a concrete task that required only speed and muscle. She dreaded what came after they moved Arlo back into the house, when they'd be forced to confront what was left of his leg, now little more than mutilated flesh and splintered bones.

The sled. Where did I see that sled?

She finally found it in the third garage, hanging on wall pegs alongside a ladder and an array of tools. Whoever lived here had kept an organized household, and as she pulled down the sled, she imagined him hammering in these pegs, suspending his tools high enough that young hands couldn't reach them. The sled was made of birch and had no manufacturer's label. Handmade, it had been crafted with care, the runners sanded smooth and freshly polished in readiness for winter. All this she registered in a glance. Adrenaline had sharpened her vision and made her reflexes hum like high-voltage wires. She scanned the garage for anything else she might need. She found ski poles and rope, a pocketknife and a roll of duct tape.

The sled was heavy, and dragging it up the steep road soon had her sweating. But better to labor like a draft horse than to kneel helplessly by your friend's mangled body, agonizing over what to do next. She was panting now, struggling up the slippery road, wondering if Arlo would be alive when she got there. A stray thought slipped into her head, a thought that shocked her, but there it was nonetheless. A little voice whispering its cruel logic: *He might be better off dead.*

She yanked harder on the towline, pitting her weight against the drag of snow and gravity. Up the road she trudged, hands cramping around the rope as she curved up hairpin turns, past pine trees whose snow-heavy branches hid her view of the next stretch of road. Surely she should be there by now. Hadn't she been climbing long enough? But the Jeep tire tracks still curved ahead, and she saw the shoe prints she'd left when she'd run down this same road a short time earlier.

A scream pierced the trees, a pain-racked shriek that ended in a sob. Not only was Arlo still alive, he was now awake.

She rounded the curve and there they were, exactly where she'd left them. Grace was huddled by herself, hands clasped over her ears against Arlo's sobs. Elaine cringed back against the Jeep, hugging herself as though she were the one in pain. As Maura dragged the sled closer, Doug looked up with an expression of profound relief.

"Did you bring something to tie him to the sled?" he asked.

"I found rope and duct tape." She positioned the sled beside Arlo, whose sobs had faded to whimpers.

"You take the hips," said Doug. "I'll move his shoulders."

"We need to splint the leg first. That's why I brought the ski poles."

"Maura," he said softly. "There's nothing left to splint."

"We have to keep it rigid. We can't let it flop all the way down the mountain."

He stared down at Arlo's mutilated limb, but could not seem to move. He doesn't want to touch it, she thought.

Neither did she.

They were both physicians, pathologists accustomed to slicing into torsos and sawing open skulls. But living flesh was different. It was warm and it bled and it transmitted pain. At the mere touch of her hand against his leg, Arlo began to scream again.

"Stop! Please don't! *Don't!*"

As Doug held down the struggling Arlo, she insulated the leg with folded blankets, cloaking shattered bones and torn ligaments and exposed flesh that was already turning purple in the cold. The limb now cocooned, she taped it to the two ski poles. By the time she'd finished splinting the leg, Arlo was reduced to quiet sobs, his face streaked with glistening trails of drool and mucus. He did not resist as they slid him sideways onto the sled and taped him in place. After the agonies they had put him through, his face had paled to the waxy yellow of impending shock.

Doug took the towrope, and they all started back into the valley.

Back toward Kingdom Come.

ELEVEN

WHEN THEY BROUGHT ARLO INTO THE HOUSE, he had fallen unconscious again. It was a blessing, considering what they had to do next. With pocketknife and scissors, Maura and Doug sliced away what was left of Arlo's clothing. He had emptied his bladder, and they smelled the ammoniacal stench of urine that had soaked into his pants. Leaving only the tourniquet in place, they peeled off shredded and bloody scraps of fabric until he lay stripped, his genitals pitifully exposed. It was a view unsuitable for a thirteen-year-old girl, and Doug turned to his daughter.

"Grace, we need a lot more wood for the fire. Go out and get some. Grace, *go!*"

His sharp words snapped her back to attention. She gave a dazed nod and left the house, admitting a cold draft of wind as the door shut behind her.

"Jesus," murmured Doug, turning his full attention to Arlo's left leg. "Where do we start?"

Start? There was so little left to work with, just

twisted cartilage and torn muscles. The ankle had been rotated almost 180 degrees, but the foot itself was bizarrely intact, although it was a lifeless blue. It might have been mistaken for plastic were it not for the thick and all-too-real callus on the heel. It's dying, she thought. The limb, the tissue itself, was starved of circulation by the tourniquet. She did not have to touch the foot to know that it would be cold and pulseless.

"He's going to lose the leg," said Doug, echoing her thoughts. "We've got to loosen the tourniquet."

"Won't he start bleeding again?" asked Elaine. She remained at the other end of the room, her gaze averted.

"He'd want us to save his leg, Elaine."

"If you take off the tourniquet, how are you going to stop him from bleeding?"

"We'll have to ligate the artery."

"What does that mean?"

"Isolate the torn vessel and tie it off. It will interrupt some of the blood flow to the lower leg, but he still might have enough alternative circulation to keep the tissues alive." He stared down at the leg, thinking. "We'll need instruments. Suture. There's got to be a sewing box in this house. Tweezers, a sharp knife. Elaine, get some water boiling."

"Doug," Maura said. "He's probably ruptured multiple vessels. Even if we ligate one, he could bleed out through the others. We can't expose and ligate them all. Not without anesthesia."

"Then we might as well amputate it right now. Is that what you'd have us do? Just give up on it?"

"At least he'll still be alive."

"And missing his leg. That's not what I'd want if I were him."

"You're not him. You can't make this decision for him."

"Neither can you, Maura."

She looked down at Arlo and considered the prospect of slicing into the leg. Of digging through flesh that was still alive and sensate. She was not a surgeon. The subjects who ended up on her table did not spurt blood when she cut into them. They did not scream.

This could turn into one big, bloody mess.

"Look, we have two choices," said Doug. "Either we try to save the leg, or we leave it the way it is and let it necrose and turn gangrenous. Which could kill him anyway. I don't see that we have a lot of options here. We have to do *something*."

"*First do no harm*. Don't you think that applies here?"

"I think we'll regret *not* acting. It's our responsibility to at least make an attempt to save that leg."

They both looked down as Arlo sucked in a ragged breath and moaned.

Please don't wake up, she thought. Don't make us cut you while you're screaming.

But Arlo's eyes slowly opened, and although his gaze was cloudy with confusion, he was clearly conscious and trying to focus on her face. "Rather . . . rather be dead," he whispered. "Oh God, I can't stand it."

"Arlo," said Doug. "Hey, buddy, we're going to get you something for the pain, okay? We'll see what we can find."

"Please," Arlo whispered. "Please kill me." He was blubbering now, tears leaking from his eyes, his whole body quaking so hard that Maura thought he was convulsing. But his gaze remained fixed on them, pleading.

She draped a blanket over his exposed body. The fire in the hearth was burning brightly now, revived by a fresh load of wood, and with the rising warmth the smell of urine grew stronger.

"There's Advil in my purse," she said to Doug. "I left it back in the Jeep."

"Advil? That's not going to *touch* this."

"I have Valium," groaned Arlo. "In my backpack . . ."

"That's up in the Jeep, too." Doug stood. "I'll go get our stuff and bring it all back."

"And I'll search the houses," said Maura. "There's got to be something in this valley we can use."

"I'll go with you, Doug," said Elaine.

"No. You need to stay here with him," Doug said.

Reluctantly Elaine's gaze dropped to Arlo. Clearly this was the last place she wanted to be, trapped with a sobbing man.

"And boil some water," Doug said as he crossed the door. "We're going to need it."

Outside, the wind lashed Maura's face with stinging clouds of snow, but she was glad to be out of the house and breathing fresh air that did not stink of blood and urine. As she headed toward the next house, she heard footsteps crunching behind her, and she turned to see that Grace had followed her.

"I can help you look," said Grace.

Maura eyed her for a moment, thinking that Grace would probably be more of a hindrance. But at that moment, the girl looked lost, just a frightened kid whom they had ignored for far too long.

Maura nodded. "You could be a big help, Grace. Come with me."

They climbed the porch steps and pushed into the house.

"What kind of medicines are we looking for?" asked Grace as they headed up the stairs to the second floor.

"Anything. Don't waste any time reading the labels. Just take it all." Maura went into a bedroom and stripped off two pillowcases. She tossed one to Grace. "You search the dresser and nightstands. Look anyplace they might keep their pills."

In the bathroom, Maura scanned the contents of the medicine cabinet, tossing items into her pillowcase. She left behind the vitamins but took everything else. Laxatives. Aspirin. Hydrogen peroxide. Any one of those might be useful. She could hear Grace in the room next door, opening and slamming shut drawers.

They moved on to the next house, their pillowcases rattling with bottles. Maura was first through the front door, stepping into a home where silence hung as heavy as gloom. She had not set foot in this house before and she paused, glancing around the living room. At yet another copy of the now familiar portrait hanging on the wall.

"It's that man again," said Grace.

"Yeah. We can't seem to get away from him." Maura took a few steps across the room and suddenly halted. "Grace," she said quietly.

"What?"

"Take the pills back to Elaine. Arlo needs them."

"We haven't looked in this house yet."

"I'll do it. You just go back, okay?" She handed the girl her pillowcase of pill bottles and gave her a nudge toward the door. "Please, go now."

"But—"

"*Go.*"

Only after the girl had left the house did Maura cross the room. She stared at what Grace had not seen. The first thing she'd spotted was a birdcage, the dead canary lying on the bottom, just a tiny mound of yellow on the newsprint cage liner.

She turned and focused on the floor, on what had stopped her in her tracks: A smear of brown tracked across the pine planks. Following the drag mark, she moved into the hallway and came at last to the staircase.

There she halted, staring at a frozen puddle of blood at the bottom of the steps.

As her gaze lifted toward the second floor, she imagined a body tumbling down those steep stairs, could almost hear the crack of a skull as it bounced down the steps and smashed onto the floor near her feet. Someone fell here, she thought.

Or was pushed.

By the time she walked back into their house, Doug had already returned with their belongings from the Jeep. He unzipped Arlo's backpack and dumped the contents onto the coffee table. She saw sinus tablets and nose spray, sunscreen and ChapStick, plus a whole drugstore's supply of toiletries. Everything a man needed to stay well groomed, but nothing to help him stay alive. Only when Doug unzipped one of the side pockets did he find the pill bottle.

"*Valium, five milligrams. As needed for back spasms,*" he read. "It'll help him get through this."

"Doug," Maura said softly. "In one of the houses, I found—" She stopped as Grace and Elaine walked in the room.

"You found what?" Doug asked.

"I'll tell you later."

Doug spread out all the medications that they'd scavenged. "Tetracycline. Amoxicillin." He shook his head. "If his leg gets infected, he's going to need better antibiotics than these."

"At least we found some Percocet," said Maura, uncapping the bottle. "But there's only a dozen pills left. Do we have anything else?"

Elaine said, "I always have some codeine in my . . ." She stopped, frowning at what Doug had brought back from the Jeep. "Where's my purse?"

"I only found one purse." Doug pointed to it.

"That's Maura's. Where's mine?"

"Elaine, that's all I saw in the Jeep."

"Then you missed it. There's codeine in it."

"I'll go back for it later, okay?" He knelt down beside Arlo. "I'm going to give you some pills, buddy."

"Knock me out," whimpered Arlo. "Can't stand this pain."

"This should help." Doug gently lifted Arlo's head, slipped two Valiums and two Percocets into his mouth, and gave him a swallow of whiskey. "There you go. We'll give that medicine some time to work first."

"First?" Arlo coughed on the whiskey, and fresh tears leaked from his eyes. "What do you mean?"

"We need to work on your leg."

"No. No, don't touch it."

"Your circulation's been cut off by the tourniquet. If we don't loosen it, your leg's going to die."

"What are you going to do?"

"We're going to tie off the ruptured artery and control the bleeding that way. I think you've damaged either the posterior or anterior tibial artery. If one of them is still intact, it might be enough circulation to supply your leg with blood. And keep it alive."

"That means you're going to have to dig around in there."

"We need to isolate which artery is bleeding."

Arlo shook his head. "No way."

"If it's the anterior tibial, we only have to slide between a few muscles, just below the knee."

"Forget it. Don't touch me."

"I'm thinking of what's best for you. There'll be a little pain, but in the end you'll be glad I—"

"A little? A *little*?" Arlo croaked out a desperate laugh. "Stay the fuck away from me!"

"Listen, I know it hurts, but—"

"You don't know shit, Doug."

"Arlo."

"Stay away! Elaine, for God's sake, make him stay away!"

Doug rose to his feet. "We'll let you rest, okay? Grace, you stay here with him." He looked at Maura and Elaine. "Let's go in the other room."

They met in the kitchen. Elaine had left a pot of water to heat on the woodstove, and it was now simmering, ready to sterilize instruments. Through the steam-fogged window, Maura could see the sun was already dropping toward the horizon.

"You can't force him to go through this," said Maura.

"It's for his own good."

"Surgery without anesthesia? *Think* about it, Doug."

"Give the Valium some time to work. He'll calm down."

"But he won't be unconscious. He'll still be able to feel the incision."

"He'll thank us for it later. Trust me." Doug turned to Elaine. "You agree with me, don't you? We can't just give up on his leg."

Elaine hesitated, obviously torn between the two terrible options. "I don't know . . ."

"Ligating the artery is the only way we'll be able to remove that tourniquet. The only way we can restore some blood flow."

"Do you really think you can do it?"

"It's a straightforward procedure. Maura and I both know the anatomy."

"But he'll be moving around," said Maura. "There could be a lot more blood loss. I don't agree with this, Doug."

"The alternative is to sacrifice the limb."

"I think the limb is already a lost cause."

"Well, I don't." Doug turned back to Elaine. "We need to vote on this. Do we try to save his leg or not?"

Elaine took a breath and nodded. "I guess I'm with you."

Of course she would be. Arlo was right. She always sides with Doug.

"Maura?" he asked.

"You know what I think."

He glanced out the window. "We don't have a lot of time. We're losing our daylight and I'm not sure we'll be able to see enough with the kerosene lamp." He looked at Maura. "Elaine and I both vote to go ahead with this."

"You forgot a vote. There's Arlo's, and he made it pretty clear what he wants."

"He's not competent to make any decisions right now."

"It's *his* leg."

"And we can save it! But I need your help. Maura, I can't do it without you."

"Dad?" Grace was standing in the kitchen doorway. "He doesn't look so good."

"What do you mean?"

"He's not talking anymore. And he's snoring really loud."

Doug nodded. "The drugs must have kicked in. Let's get some instruments boiling. And we'll need needles. A spool of thread." He looked at Maura. "Are you with me or not?"

It doesn't matter what I say, she thought. *He's going to do it anyway.*

"I'll see what I can find," she said.

It took them an hour to collect and sterilize all the items they'd managed to scavenge. By then, the window admitted only a weak afternoon glow. They lit the kerosene lamp, and by the light of the hissing flame, Arlo's eyes were sunken in shadow, as though his soft tissues were collapsing, his body consuming itself. Doug peeled back the blanket, releasing the sharp smell of the urine-saturated rug.

The leg was as pale as a shank of cold meat.

No amount of scrubbing could cleanse all the bacteria from their hands, but Doug and Maura tried anyway, lathering and rinsing until their skin was raw. Only then did Doug reach for the blade. It was a paring knife, the most delicate one they could find, and they had sharpened it before sterilizing. As he knelt over the leg, the first hint of uncertainty flickered in his eyes. He glanced up at Maura.

"Ready to release the tourniquet?" he said.

"You haven't tied off the artery yet," said Elaine.

"We need to identify which artery it is. And the only way is to see where he's bleeding. You need to hold him still, Elaine. Because he's going to wake up." He glanced at Maura and nodded.

She barely loosened the tourniquet and a spurt of blood exploded from the wound, splattering Doug's cheek.

"It's the anterior tibial," said Doug. "I'm sure of it."

"Tighten the belt!" Elaine said, panicking. "He's bleeding too much!"

Maura refastened the tourniquet and looked at Doug. He took a breath and began to cut.

At the first slice of the knife, Arlo jolted awake with a scream.

"Hold him! Hold him still!" Doug yelled.

Arlo kept screaming, battling them away, the tendons on his neck so taut they looked ready to snap. Elaine wrestled his shoulders back to the floor, but she could not stop him from thrashing and kicking at his torturers. Maura tried to pin his thighs, but blood and sweat had made his bare skin slippery, so she threw her weight across his hips. Arlo's scream rose to a shriek that penetrated straight to her bones, a shriek so piercing it felt as if the sound were coming from her own body, as if she were screaming as well. Doug said something, but she couldn't hear him through that scream. Only when she glanced up did she see that he had set down the knife. He looked exhausted, his face gleaming with sweat even in that cold room.

"It's done," he said. Rocking back on his knees, he wiped his sleeve across his forehead. "I think I got it."

Arlo gave an agonized sob. "Fuck you, Doug. Fuck all of you."

"Arlo, we had to do it," said Doug. "Maura, loosen that tourniquet. Let's see if we got the bleeding controlled."

Slowly Maura released the belt, half expecting to see another gush of blood. But there was no trickle, not even a slow ooze.

Doug touched Arlo's foot. "The skin's still cool. But I think it's starting to pink up."

She shook her head. "I don't see any perfusion."

"No, look. It's definitely changing color." He pressed his palm against the flesh. "I think it's warming up."

Maura frowned at skin that looked every bit as dead and pale as it had before, but she said nothing. It made no difference what she thought; Doug had convinced himself that the operation was a success, that they'd done exactly what they should have. That everything was going to be fine. In Doug's world, everything always turned out fine. So be bold, jump out of planes, and let the universe take care of you.

At least the tourniquet was now off. At least he was no longer bleeding.

She rose to her feet, the sour stink of Arlo's sweat on her clothes. Exhausted by his ordeal, Arlo was now quiet and drifting to sleep. Massaging her aching neck, she went to the window and stared out, relieved to turn her attention to something else, anything else but their patient. "It's going to be dark in an hour," she said. "We can't get out of here now."

"Not in the Jeep," said Doug. "Not with that broken tire chain." She could hear him rattling through all the pill bottles. "We have enough Percocet to keep him comfortable for at least another day. Plus Elaine says she has codeine in her purse, if I can just find it."

Maura turned from the window. Everyone looked

as drained as she felt. Elaine sat slumped against the couch. Doug was staring listlessly at the array of pill bottles. And Grace—Grace had long ago fled the room.

"He needs to get to a hospital," said Maura.

"You said you're expected back in Boston tonight," said Elaine. "They'll be searching."

"The problem is, they won't know where to look."

"There was that old guy in the gas station. The one who sold you the newspaper. He'll remember us. When he hears you're missing, he'll call the police. Eventually *someone's* going to show up here."

Maura looked down at Arlo, who had sunk back into unconsciousness. *But not soon enough for him.*

TWELVE

"WHAT DID YOU WANT TO SHOW ME?" ASKED Doug.

"Just come with me," whispered Maura. Pausing at the door, she glanced back at the room, where the others had fallen asleep. Now was the time to slip away. She picked up the kerosene lamp and stepped outside, into the night.

A full moon had risen, and the sky was awash in stars. She did not need the lamp to see the way; the snow itself seemed to luminesce beneath their boots. The wind had died, and the only sound was their footsteps crunching through the icy glaze that coated the snow like meringue. She led the way up the row of silent houses.

"You want to give me a hint?" he asked.

"I didn't want to talk about it in front of Grace. But I found something."

"What?"

"It's in this house." She stopped before the porch and stared up at black windows that reflected no starlight, no moonlight, as if the darkness within could swallow up even the faintest glimmer of light. She walked up the steps and pushed open the door. The lamp cast a feeble pool of light around them as they crossed the living room. Beyond that pool, in the shadowy circumference, lurked the dark silhouettes of furniture and the reflected glint off the picture frame. The dark-haired man stared back from the portrait, his eyes almost alive in the shadows.

"That's what I noticed first," she said, pointing to the birdcage in the corner.

Doug moved closer and peered into the cage at the canary lying on the bottom. "Another dead pet."

"Like the dog."

"Who leaves a pet canary behind to starve?"

"This bird didn't starve," said Maura.

"What?"

"Look, there's plenty of seed." She brought the lamp up to the cage to show him that the feeder was filled with birdseed, and ice had frozen in the water dispenser. "The windows were left open in this house, too," she said.

"It froze to death."

"There's more." She moved up the hallway and pointed at the streak across the pine floorboards, as though someone had swiped a paintbrush. In the dim candlelight, the stain looked more black than brown.

Doug stared at the drag mark, and he didn't try to explain it. He didn't say anything at all. In silence he followed the smear as it grew broader, until it led him to the staircase. There he stopped, staring down at the dried pool of blood at his feet.

Maura raised the lamp and the light revealed dark spatters on the steps. "The splash marks start about halfway up," she said. "Someone fell down those stairs, hitting the steps on the way down. And landed here." She lowered the lamp, illuminating the dried pool at the bottom of the stairs. Something gleamed in that blood, a silvery thread that she had missed earlier that afternoon. She crouched down and saw that it was a long blond hair, partially trapped in dried blood. *A woman.* A woman who had lain here while her heart continued to pump, at least for a few minutes. Long enough for a lake of blood to pour from her body.

"An accident?" said Doug.

"Or a homicide."

In the dim light, she saw his mouth twitch in a half smile. "That's a medical examiner talking. What I see here isn't necessarily a crime scene. Just blood."

"A lot of it."

"But no body. Nothing to tell us one way or another how it happened."

"The missing body is what bothers me."

"I'd be a lot more bothered if it was still here."

"Where is it? Who took it?"

"The family? Maybe they brought her to the hospital. That would explain why the canary was forgotten."

"They would *carry* an injured woman, Doug. They wouldn't drag her across the floor like a carcass. But if they were trying to get rid of a body . . ."

His gaze followed the drag marks until they vanished into the shadows of the hallway. "They never came back to clean up the blood."

"Maybe they were planning to," she said. "Maybe they couldn't get back into the valley."

He looked at her. "The snowstorm kept them away."

She nodded. The flame in the lamp shuddered, as though buffeted by a ghostly breath. "Arlo was right. Something terrible happened in this village, Doug. Something that left bloodstains and dead pets and empty houses." She looked at the floor. "And evidence. Evidence that tells a story. We keep hoping that someone will come back here and find us." She looked at him. "But what if they're not here to save us?"

Doug gave himself a shake, as though trying to snap out of the dark spell she'd spun around him. "We're talking about a whole community that's missing, Maura," he said. "Twelve houses, twelve families. If something happened to this many people, there'd be no way to hide it."

"In this valley, you could. You could hide a lot of things." She looked at the shadows surrounding them, thought of what might be hidden beyond the glow of the lantern, and drew her jacket tighter. "We can't stay in this place."

"You're the one who thought we should wait to be rescued. You said it this morning."

"Since this morning, things have gone from bad to worse."

"I'm trying to get us out of here. I'm doing my best."

"I didn't say you weren't."

"But that's what you're thinking, isn't it? That everything's my fault. That's what you're all thinking." He gave a loud sigh and turned. "I promise, I'll find a way to get us out of here."

"I'm not blaming you."

He shook his head in the darkness. "You should."

"Everything's just gone wrong, things that no one could predict."

"And now we're trapped, and Arlo's probably going to lose his leg. If not worse." His back was still turned to her, as if he couldn't bear to meet her gaze. "I'm sorry I ever talked you into this. It sure as hell isn't the trip I was hoping for, not with you along. Especially not with you along." He turned to look at her, and the lamplight deepened every hollow of his face. This wasn't the same man whose eyes had twinkled at her in the restaurant, not the same man who'd spoken so breezily about trusting in the universe.

"I needed you today, Maura," he said. "It may be selfish of me, but for my sake, and Arlo's, I'm glad you're here."

She managed a smile. "I can't say I share the sentiment."

"No, I'm pretty sure you'd rather be just about anywhere else right now. Like on that plane headed for home."

To Daniel. By now her flight would have landed, and he'd know she wasn't on it. Was he frantic? Or did he think this was her way of punishing him for all the heartache he'd caused her? *You know me better than that. If you love me, you'll know I'm in trouble.*

They left the bloodstained hallway, walked back through the shadowy front room, and stepped outside, into a landscape lit by the moon and stars. They could see firelight glowing in the house where the others now slept.

"I'm tired of being in charge," he said, gazing at that window. "Tired of always having to lead the way. But they expect it. When things don't go right, Arlo whines about it, yet he never steps up to take the lead. He'd rather just stay on the sidelines and complain."

"And Elaine?"

"You've seen how she is. It's always: *You decide, Doug.*"

"That's because she's in love with you."

He shook his head. "I never saw it. We've been friends, that's all."

"It's never been more than that?"

"Not on my part."

"She feels differently. And Arlo knows it."

"I never encouraged her, Maura. I'd never do that to him." He turned to her, his features sharper, starker, in the lantern light. "You're the one I wanted." He reached out to touch her arm. It was no more than a brush of his glove across her sleeve, a silent invitation that told her the next move was hers.

She pulled away, pointedly moving out of his reach. "We should get back to Arlo."

"Then there's nothing between us, is there?"

"There never was."

"Why did you accept my invitation? Why did you come with us?"

"You caught me at a moment in time, Doug. A moment when I needed to do something wild, something impulsive." She blinked away tears that blurred the lantern light into a golden haze. "It was a mistake."

"So it wasn't about me at all."

"It was about someone else."

"The man you spoke of at dinner. The man you can't have."

"Yes."

"That situation hasn't changed, Maura."

"But I have," she said, and walked away.

When she stepped inside, she found that everyone was still asleep and the fire had calmed to glowing embers. She added a log and stood before the hearth as flames sprang to life, hissing and snapping. She heard Doug walk in behind her and close the door, and the sudden whoosh of fresh air made the flames shudder.

Arlo opened his eyes and whispered, "Water. Please, water."

"Sure thing, buddy," said Doug. He knelt down and held Arlo's head as he pressed the cup to his lips. Arlo took greedy gulps, spilling half the water down his chin. Satisfied, he slumped back onto his pillow.

"What else can I get you? Are you hungry?" asked Doug.

"Cold. It's so cold."

Doug took a blanket from the couch and gently draped it over him. "We'll build up that fire. You'll feel better."

"Been having dreams," Arlo murmured. "Such weird dreams. All these people were in here, looking at me. Standing around, watching. Waiting for something."

"Narcotics will give you bad dreams."

"They're not bad, really. Just strange. Maybe they're angels. Angels in funny clothes, like the man in that picture." He turned his sunken eyes to Maura, but he did not seem to be looking at her. He was focused past her shoulder, as if a presence lurked right behind her. "Or maybe they're ghosts," he whispered.

Who is he looking at? She swung around and

stared at empty air. Saw the portrait of the man with the coal-dark eyes staring back at her. The same portrait that hung in every house in Kingdom Come. His face glowed with reflected firelight, as though sacred flames burned within him.

"And he shall gather the righteous," Arlo said, quoting from the plaque on the portrait's frame. "What if it's true?"

"What's true?" asked Doug.

"Maybe that's where they all went. He gathered them up and led the way."

"Out of the valley, you mean?"

"No. To heaven."

Wood snapped in the hearth, startling as a gunshot. Maura thought of the cross-stitched sampler she had seen hanging in one of the bedrooms. PREPARE FOR ETERNITY.

"It's strange, don't you think?" said Arlo. "How none of the car radios work here. All we get is static. No stations at all. And we can't get a cell phone signal. Nothing."

"We're in the middle of nowhere," said Doug. "And we're in a valley. There's no reception."

"Are you sure that's all it is?"

"What else would it be?"

"What if something really bad happened out in the world? Being stuck here, we wouldn't hear about it."

"Like what? A nuclear war?"

"Doug, no one's come looking for us. Don't you think that's strange?"

"They haven't noticed we're missing yet."

"Or maybe it's because there's no one left out there. They're all gone." Arlo's sunken eyes slowly took in the room where shadows flickered. "I think I know who these people were, Doug. The people who lived here. I think I'm seeing their ghosts. They were waiting for the end of the world. For the Rapture. Maybe it came, and we just don't know it yet."

Doug laughed. "Trust me, Arlo. The Rapture is not what happened to these people."

"Dad?" Grace asked softly from the corner. She sat up, pulling the blanket close around her. "What's he talking about?"

"The pills are confusing him, that's all."

"What's the Rapture?"

Doug and Maura looked at each other, and he sighed. "It's just a superstition, honey. A crazy belief that the world as we know it is doomed to end with Armageddon. And when it does, God's chosen people will be sucked straight up to heaven."

"What happens to everyone else?"

"Everyone else is trapped on earth."

"And slaughtered," whispered Arlo. "All the sinners left behind will be slaughtered."

"What?" Grace looked at her father with frightened eyes.

"Honey, it's nonsense. Forget it."

"But some people really believe it? They believe the end of the world is coming?"

"Some people also believe in alien abductions. Use

your noggin, Grace! Do you really think people are going to be magically transported to heaven?"

The window rattled, as though something were clawing at the glass, trying to get in. A draft of air moaned down the chimney, scattering flames and sending a gust of smoke into the room.

Grace hugged her knees to her chest. Staring up at the wavering shadows, she whispered: "Then where did all these people go?"

THIRTEEN

THE GIRL WAS TWENTY-THREE POUNDS OF *NO!
No, bed! No, sleep!
No, no, no!*

Jane and Gabriel slumped bleary-eyed on the sofa and watched their daughter, Regina, spin around and around like a pygmy dervish.

"How long can she possibly stay awake?" asked Jane.

"Longer than we can."

"You'd think she'd get sick and throw up."

"You would think," said Gabriel.

"Someone has to take control here."

"Yeah."

"Someone has to be the parent."

"I absolutely agree." He looked at Jane.

"What?"

"It's your turn to play bad cop."

"Why me?"

"Because you're so good at it. Besides, I put her

to bed the last three times. She just doesn't listen to me."

"Because she figured out that Mr. FBI is a total marshmallow."

He looked at his watch. "Jane, it's midnight."

Their daughter only whirled faster. When I was her age, was I just as exhausting? Jane wondered. This must be what the term *poetic justice* meant. Someday, you'll have a daughter just like you, her mother used to complain.

And here she is.

Groaning, Jane shoved herself off the sofa, the bad cop at last springing into action. "Time for bed, Regina," she said.

"No."

"Yes it is."

"*No!*" The imp scampered away, black curls bouncing. Jane corralled her in the kitchen and scooped her up. It was like trying to hold on to a flopping fish, every muscle and sinew fighting her.

"No *go!* No *go!*"

"Yes, go," said Jane, carrying her daughter toward the nursery as little arms and legs flailed at her. She set Regina in the crib, turned off the light, and shut the door. That only made her cries more piercing. Not wails of distress but of sheer fury.

The phone rang. *Oh hell, it's the neighbors, calling to complain again.*

"Tell them that giving her Valium is not an option!" Jane said as Gabriel went into the kitchen to answer the phone.

"We're the ones who need the Valium," he told her, then picked up the receiver. "Hello?"

Too weary to stand straight, she slumped in the kitchen doorway, imagining the diatribe now pouring from that receiver. It had to be those Windsor-Millers, the thirty-somethings who'd moved into the building only a month ago. Already they'd called to complain at least a dozen times. *Your child keeps us awake all night. We both have demanding jobs, you know. Can't you control her?* The Windsor-Millers had no kids of their own, so it wouldn't occur to them that an eighteen-month-old couldn't be turned on and off like a TV set. Jane had once caught a glimpse inside their apartment, and it was spotless. White sofa, white carpet, white walls. The apartment of a couple who'd freak out at the thought of sticky little hands getting anywhere near their precious furniture.

"It's for you," said Gabriel, holding out the receiver.

"The neighbors?"

"Daniel Brophy."

She glanced at the kitchen clock. Calling at midnight? Something had to be wrong. She took the phone. "Daniel?"

"She wasn't on the plane."

"What?"

"I've just left the airport. Maura wasn't on the flight she booked. And she never called me. I don't know what—" He paused, and Jane heard the sound of a car horn blaring.

"Where are you?" she asked.

"I'm driving into the Sumner Tunnel right now. I'm going to lose you any second."

"Why don't you come over to our place?" said Jane.

"You mean right now?"

"Gabriel and I are both awake. We should talk about this. Hello? Hello?"

The tunnel had cut off their connection. She hung up and looked at her husband. "It sounds like we've got a problem."

Half an hour later, Father Daniel Brophy arrived. By then Regina had finally cried herself to sleep; the apartment was quiet when he walked in. Jane had seen this man at work under the most trying of circumstances, at crime scenes where wailing relatives reached out to him for comfort. He had always radiated quiet strength, and just by his touch or a few soft words, he could soothe even the most distraught. Tonight it was Brophy himself who looked distraught. He removed his black winter coat, and Jane saw that he was not wearing his clerical collar but a blue sweater and oxford shirt. Civilian clothes that made him appear more vulnerable.

"She never showed up at the airport," he said. "I waited around for nearly two hours. I know her flight landed, and all the baggage was claimed. But she wasn't there."

"Maybe you missed each other," said Jane. "Maybe she got off the plane and couldn't find you."

"She would have called me."

"You tried calling her?"

"Repeatedly. No answer. I haven't been able to reach her all weekend. Not since I spoke to you."

And I brushed off his concerns, she thought, feeling a twinge of guilt.

"I'll make some coffee," she said. "I think we're going to need it."

They sat in the living room, Jane and Gabriel on the sofa, Brophy in the armchair. The warmth of the apartment had not brought any color to Brophy's cheeks; he was still sallow, and both his hands were curled into fists on his knees.

"So your last conversation with Maura wasn't exactly a happy one," said Jane.

"No. I . . . I had to cut it off abruptly," Brophy admitted.

"Why?"

His face snapped even tighter. "We need to talk about Maura, not me."

"We are talking about her. I'm trying to understand her state of mind. Do you think she felt snubbed when you cut the call short?"

He looked down. "Probably."

"Did you call her back?" asked Gabriel, using his *just-the-facts* voice.

"Not that night. It was late. I didn't try calling her until Saturday."

"And she didn't answer."

"No."

"Maybe she's just annoyed with you," said Jane. "You know, it's been tough on her this past year. Having to hide what's going on between you."

"Jane," cut in Gabriel. "This isn't helping."

Brophy gave a sigh. "But I deserve it," he said softly.

Yes you do. You broke your vows, and now you're breaking her heart.

"Do you think Maura's state of mind could explain this?" Gabriel asked, again in his matter-of-fact law enforcement voice. Of the three of them, he was the only one who seemed to be approaching this logically. She had seen him react to other tense situations in just this way, had watched her husband grow calmer and more focused as everything and everyone around him melted down. Hand him a crisis, and Gabriel Dean could instantly transform from an exhausted father into the Bureau man she sometimes forgot he was. He was watching Brophy with eyes that gave away nothing, but noticed everything.

"Was she upset enough to do something rash?" Gabriel asked. "Hurt herself? Maybe worse?"

Brophy shook his head. "Not Maura."

"People do surprising things under stress."

"*She* wouldn't! Come on, Gabriel, you know her.

You both do." Brophy looked at Jane, then back at Gabriel. "Do you really think she's that immature? That she'd drop out of sight just to punish me?"

"She's done the unexpected before," said Jane. "She fell in love with you."

He flushed, color at last suffusing his cheeks. "But she wouldn't do something irresponsible. Disappear like this."

"Disappear? Or just stay away from you?"

"She had a reservation on that flight. She asked me to pick her up at the airport. When Maura says she'll do something, she does it. And if she can't follow through, she'll call. No matter how upset she might be with me, she wouldn't stoop to something like this. You know that about her, Jane. We both do."

"But if she were distraught enough?" said Gabriel. "People do drastic things."

Jane frowned at him. "You're talking what? Suicide?"

Gabriel kept his gaze on Brophy. "Exactly what's happened between you two recently?"

Brophy's head drooped. "I think we've both come to realize that . . . something has to change."

"Did you tell her you were going to end it?"

"No." Brophy looked up. "She knows I love her."

But that's not enough, thought Jane. Not enough to build a life.

"She wouldn't hurt herself." Brophy straightened in the chair, his face hardening in a look of certainty.

"She wouldn't play games. Something is wrong, and I can't believe you're not taking this seriously."

"We are," said Gabriel calmly. "That's why we're asking these questions, Daniel. Because these are the same questions the police will ask in Wyoming. About her state of mind. About whether she might have chosen to disappear. I just want to be sure *you* know the answers."

"Which hotel was she staying at?" asked Jane.

"It's in Teton Village. The Mountain Lodge. I've already called them, and they said she checked out Saturday morning. A day early."

"Do they know where she went?"

"No."

"Could she have flown home earlier? Maybe she's already back in Boston."

"I called her home phone. I even drove by her house. She's not there."

"Do you know anything else about her travel arrangements?" Gabriel asked.

"I have her flight numbers. I know she rented a car in Jackson. She was planning to drive around the area after the conference was over."

"Which rental agency?"

"Hertz."

"Do you know if she's spoken to anyone besides you? Her colleagues at the ME's office, maybe? Her secretary?"

"I called Louise on Saturday, and she hadn't heard anything, either. I didn't follow up on it because I assumed . . ." He looked at Jane. "I thought you would check on her."

There was no note of accusation in his voice, but there might as well have been. Jane felt a guilty flush in her cheeks. He *had* called her, and she'd dropped the ball because her mind had been on other things. Bodies in freezers. Uncooperative toddlers. She had not really believed that anything was wrong, had thought it was merely a lovers' spat followed by silent treatment. This sort of thing happened all the time, didn't it? Plus, there was the fact that Maura had checked out of her hotel a day early. That didn't sound like an abduction, but a deliberate change in plans. None of it absolved Jane of the fact that she'd done nothing beyond placing that call to Maura's cell phone. Now almost two days had passed, the golden forty-eight, that window of opportunity when you're most likely to find a missing person and identify a perp.

Gabriel stood. "I think it's time to make some calls," he said, and went into the kitchen. She and Brophy sat silent, listening to him speak in the other room. Using his FBI voice, as Jane liked to call it, the quiet and authoritative tone he adopted for official business. Hearing it now, she found it hard to believe that that voice belonged to the same man who'd been so easily defeated by a stubborn toddler. I should be the one making the calls, she thought. I'm the cop who failed to follow up. But she knew that just hearing those letters *FBI* would make whoever was on the other end of the line snap to attention. When your husband's a fibbie, you might as well take advantage of it.

". . . female, age forty-two, I think. Black hair. Five foot six, around a hundred twenty pounds . . ."

"Why would she check out of the hotel a day early?" Brophy said softly. He was sitting rigid in the armchair, staring straight ahead. "That's what I haven't figured out yet, why she did that. Where was she going, another town, another hotel? Why suddenly change her plans?"

Maybe she met someone. A man. Jane didn't want to say it, but that was the first thought that occurred to her, the first thought that would occur to any cop. A lonely woman on a business trip. A woman whose lover has just disappointed her. Along comes an attractive stranger who suggests a little drive out of town. Ditch the old plans and have a little adventure.

Maybe she had an adventure with the wrong man.

Gabriel came back into the living room, carrying the portable phone. "He'll call us right back."

"Who?" asked Brophy.

"The detective in Jackson. He said they've had no traffic fatalities over the weekend, and he's not aware of any hospitalized patients who remain unidentified."

"What about . . ." Brophy paused.

"Or bodies, either."

Brophy swallowed and slumped back into the chair. "So we know that much, at least. She's not lying in some hospital."

Or the morgue. It was an image Jane tried to block out, but there it was: Maura stretched out on the table like so many other corpses that Jane had stared down at. Anyone who'd ever stood in an autopsy room and watched a postmortem had surely imagined the nightmarish scene of someone they knew or loved lying on the table. No doubt it was the same image that was now tormenting Daniel Brophy.

Jane brewed another pot of coffee. Out in Wyoming, it would be eleven PM. The phone remained ominously silent as they watched the clock.

"You never know, she may surprise us." Jane laughed, jittery from too much caffeine and sugar. "She may turn up at work tomorrow, right on time. Tell us that she lost her cell phone or something." It was a lame explanation, and neither man bothered to respond.

The ringing phone made them all snap straight. Gabriel picked up the receiver. He did not say much; nor did his face reveal what information he was hearing. But when he hung up and looked at Jane, she knew the news was not good.

"She never returned the rental car."

"They checked with Hertz?"

Gabriel nodded. "She picked it up Tuesday at the airport, and was supposed to return it this morning."

"So the car's missing as well."

"That's right."

Jane did not look at Brophy; she didn't want to see his face.

"I guess that settles it," said Gabriel. "There's only one thing we can do."

Jane nodded. "I'll call my mom in the morning. I'm sure she'll be happy to watch Regina. We can drop her off on the way to the airport."

"You're flying to Jackson?" asked Brophy.

"If we can find two seats on a flight tomorrow," said Jane.

"Make it three," Brophy said. "I'm coming, too."

FOURTEEN

Maura awakened to the sound of Arlo's chattering teeth. Opening her eyes, she saw it was still dark, but sensed that dawn was near, that the blackness of night was just starting to lift to gray. In the glow from the hearth, she could count the sleeping bodies: Grace curled up on the sofa; Doug and Elaine sleeping close together, almost touching. Always almost touching. She could guess who had migrated toward whom in the night. It was so obvious, now that she was aware of it: the way Elaine looked at Doug, the way she so frequently touched him, her eager acquiescence to everything he suggested. Arlo lay alone beside the hearth, the blanket molding his body like a shroud. His teeth clattered together as a fresh chill gripped his body.

She rose, her back stiff from the floor, and placed more wood in the fireplace. Crouching close, she warmed herself as the fire crackled to life, bright and fierce. Turning, she looked at Arlo, whose face was now illuminated by the flames.

His hair was greasy and stiff with sweat. His skin had taken on the yellowish cast of a corpse. If not for his chattering teeth, she might have thought him already dead.

"Arlo," she said softly.

Slowly, his eyelids lifted. His gaze seemed to come from some deep and shadowy pit, as though he had fallen far beyond all reach of help. "So . . . cold," he whispered.

"I've built up the fire again. It'll be warmer in here soon." She touched his forehead, and the heat of his skin was so startling that she felt as if her hand were seared. At once she went to the coffee table, where they had lined up all the medicines, and struggled to read the labels in the dark. She found the bottles of amoxicillin and Tylenol, and shook out capsules into her hand. "Here. Take these."

"What is it?" Arlo grunted as she lifted his head to help him swallow the pills.

"You have a fever. That's why you're shivering. These should make you feel better."

He swallowed the pills and slumped back, seized by another chill so violent that she thought he might be convulsing. But his eyes were open and aware. She surrendered her own blanket to him, draping yet another layer of wool over his body. She knew that she should check the condition of his leg, but the room was still too dark, and she didn't want to light the kerosene lamp yet, not while everyone else was still asleep. Already the window had brightened.

In another hour or so, it would be dawn, and she could examine his limb. But she already knew what she would find. The fever meant his leg was almost certainly infected, and bacteria had invaded his bloodstream. She also knew that the amoxicillin was not a powerful enough antibiotic to save him.

They had only twenty tablets left, anyway.

She glanced at Doug, tempted to wake him so that he could share this burden, but Doug was still deeply asleep. So she alone sat beside Arlo, holding his hand, stroking his arm through the blankets. Though his forehead was hot, his hand was alarmingly chilled, more like dead flesh than living.

And I know what dead flesh feels like.

Since her days as a medical student, it was the autopsy room, and not the patient's bedside, where she'd felt most comfortable. The dead don't expect you to make small talk or listen to their endless complaints or watch while they writhe in pain. The dead are beyond pain, and they don't expect you to perform miracles you are incapable of. They wait patiently and uncomplainingly as long as it takes for you to finish your job.

Looking down at Arlo's racked face, she thought: It's not the dead who make me uneasy, but the living.

Yet she remained at his side, holding his hand as dawn broke, as his chills gradually ebbed. He was breathing more easily now, and beads of sweat glistened on his face.

"Do you believe in ghosts?" he asked softly, watching her with eyes that were feverishly bright.

"Why do you ask?"

"Your job. If anyone ever saw a ghost, it would be you."

She shook her head. "I've never seen one."

"So you don't believe."

"No."

He stared beyond her, focused on something that she could not see. "But they're here, in this room. Watching us."

She touched his forehead. His skin was already cooler to the touch, his fever fading. Yet he was clearly delirious, his eyes tracking the room as though following the progress of phantoms gliding past.

It was light enough now for her to look at his leg.

He did not protest as she lifted the blanket. He was nude from the waist down, his penis shriveled and almost lost in the nest of brown pubic hair. In the night he had wet himself, and the towels they had placed under him were soaked. She peeled off layers of gauze from his wound, and the gasp was out of her throat before she could suppress it. She'd last examined the wound only six hours ago, by the light of the kerosene lamp. Now, in the unforgiving glare of brightening daylight, she could see the blackened edges of skin, the bloated tissues. And she caught the foul whiff of decaying meat.

"Tell me the truth," said Arlo. "I want to know. Am I going to die?"

She struggled for reassuring words, for an answer she did not truly believe. Before she could say a word, a hand suddenly settled on her shoulder and she turned in surprise.

"Of course you're not going to die," said Doug, standing right behind her. "Because I'm not going to let you, Arlo. No matter how much damn trouble you give me."

Arlo managed a weak smile. "You've always been full of shit, man," he whispered and closed his eyes.

Doug knelt down and stared at the leg. He didn't have to say it; Maura could read in his face the same thing she was now thinking. *His leg is rotting before our eyes.*

"Let's go in the other room," Doug said.

They stepped into the kitchen, out of earshot of the others. Dawn had given way to a blindingly bright morning, and the glare through the window washed out Doug's face, made every gray hair stand out in his stubbly beard.

"I gave him amoxicillin this morning," she said. "For all the good it'll do."

"What he needs is surgery."

"I agree. You want to be the one to cut off his leg?"

"Jesus." He began to pace the kitchen in agitation. "Ligating an artery is one thing. But to do an amputation . . ."

"Even if we *could* do the amputation, it wouldn't be enough. He's already septic. He needs massive doses of IV antibiotics."

Doug turned to the window and squinted at the brilliant reflection of sunlight on ice-encrusted snow. "I've got a full eight, maybe nine hours of daylight. If I leave right now, I might make it down the mountain by dark."

"You're going to ski out?"

"Unless you have a better idea."

She thought of Arlo, sweating and shaking in the other room as his leg bloated and his wound slowly putrefied. She thought of bacteria swarming through his blood, invading every organ. And she thought of a corpse she'd once dissected, of a woman who had died of septic shock, and remembered the patchy hemorrhages in the skin, the heart, the lungs. Shock caused multiple system failure, shutting down heart, kidneys, and brain. Already Arlo was showing signs of delirium. He was seeing people who did not exist, ghosts hovering around him. But at least he was still producing urine; as long as his kidneys did not fail, he had a chance of survival.

"I'll pack you some food," she said. "And you'll need a sleeping bag, in case you don't make it out by dark."

"I'll go as far as I can tonight," said Doug. He glanced toward the front room, where Arlo lay dying. "I'm afraid I'm going to have to leave him in your hands."

* * *

Grace did not want her father to go. She clung to his jacket as he stood outside on the porch, pleading with him not to leave them, whining that he was her father, and how could he leave her behind, just as her mother had? What kind of father would do that?

"Arlo's really sick, honey," said Doug, peeling her hands away from his sleeve. "If I don't get help, he could die."

"If you leave, *I'm* the one who could die!" she said.

"You're not alone. Elaine and Maura will take care of you."

"Why do *you* have to go? Why can't *she* go?" Grace pointed at Maura, a gesture so aggressive it felt like an accusation.

"Stop it, Grace. Stop it." He grabbed his daughter's shoulders and gave her a hard shake. "I'm the strongest. I'll have the best chance of making it. And Arlo is *my* friend."

"But you're my *father*," Grace shot back.

"I need you to grow up right now. You have to realize that you're not the center of the universe." He strapped on his backpack. "We'll talk about this when I get back. Now give me a kiss, okay?"

Grace backed away. "No wonder Mom left you," she said and walked into the house, slamming the door behind her.

Doug stood stunned, staring in disbelief at the closed door. But the outburst should hardly have surprised him. Maura had seen how hungrily Grace vied for her father's attention, and how skillfully the girl used guilt as a weapon to control him. Now Doug seemed ready to pursue his daughter into the house, which was just what Grace wanted, and no doubt expected.

"Don't worry about her," said Maura. "I promise I'll look after her. She'll be perfectly all right."

"With you in charge, I know she will." He took her into his arms for a farewell hug. "I'm sorry, Maura," he murmured. "Sorry for everything that's gone wrong." He pulled away and looked at her. "Back when you knew me at Stanford, I'm sure you thought I was a fuckup. I guess I haven't done too good a job of changing your mind."

"You get us out of here, Doug, and I'll rethink that opinion."

"You can count on it." He tightened the chest strap of his backpack. "Hold the fort, Dr. Isles. I promise I'll be back with the cavalry."

She watched from the porch as he headed up the road. The day had already warmed into the twenties, and not a cloud was visible in the sky. If he was going to attempt the journey, today was the day to do it.

The door suddenly opened and Elaine came flying out of the house. She had already said her goodbye to Doug moments earlier, but here she was again, running to catch up with him, running as though her life depended on it. Maura could not hear their conversation, but she saw Elaine pull off the cashmere scarf she always wore and gently drape it around Doug's neck as a parting gift. They embraced, a hug that seemed to last forever. Then Doug was on his way, climbing up the rutted road that led out of the valley. Only when he'd rounded the bend and vanished behind the trees did Elaine finally turn back to the house. She climbed the porch steps to where Maura was standing but didn't say a word, just brushed past her and walked inside, shutting the door behind her.

FIFTEEN

EVEN BEFORE DETECTIVE QUEENAN INTRODUCED himself, Jane would have pegged him as a cop. He stood beside a snow-covered Toyota in the parking lot of the Mountain Lodge, conversing with a man and a woman. As Jane and her party climbed out of their rental car and approached the Toyota, it was Queenan who turned to look at them, watching with the alert gaze that characterized a man whose job was all about observation. In every other way he seemed ordinary—balding, overweight, his mustache streaked with the first hints of gray.

"Are you Detective Queenan?" said Gabriel.

The man nodded. "You must be Agent Dean."

"And I'm Detective Rizzoli," said Jane.

Queenan frowned at her. "Boston PD?"

"Homicide unit," she said.

"Homicide? Aren't you folks kind of jumping the gun here? We don't know that any crime's been committed."

"Dr. Isles is a friend of ours," said Jane. "She's a reliable professional, and she wouldn't go missing on a whim. We're all concerned about her welfare."

Queenan turned to look at Brophy. "And are you with Boston PD, too?"

"No, sir," said Brophy. "I'm a priest."

At that, Queenan gave a startled laugh. "A fibbie, a cop, and a priest. Now, that's a team I haven't seen before."

"What have you got so far?" Jane asked.

"Well, we have this," Queenan said, and he pointed at the parked Toyota where two people stood, watching the conversation. The man was named Finch, and he worked as a security guard for the lodge. The woman was an employee with the Hertz rental car agency.

"This Toyota's been parked here since at least Friday night," said Finch. "Hasn't been moved."

"You confirmed that on surveillance video?" asked Jane.

"Uh, no, ma'am. Cameras don't cover this lot."

"Then how do you know it's been here that long?"

"Look at the snow piled up on it. We had a big storm on Saturday that dumped almost two feet, which is about what I see on this car."

"This is Maura's car?"

The Hertz lady said, "The rental contract for this vehicle was made out to a Dr. Maura Isles. It was booked online three weeks ago, and she picked it up last Tuesday. Paid for it with an AmEx card. It was supposed to be returned to our airport lot yesterday morning."

"She didn't call to extend the rental?" asked Gabriel.

"No, sir." The woman pulled a key ring out of her pocket and looked at Queenan. "Here's that spare key you wanted, Detective."

Queenan pulled on a set of latex gloves and unlocked the front passenger door. Gingerly he leaned inside and opened the glove compartment, where he found the rental contract. "Maura Isles," he confirmed, scanning the papers. He peered at the odometer. "Looks like she put in about ninety miles. Not much driving for a six-day rental."

"She was here for a medical conference," said Jane. "And she was staying at this hotel. She probably didn't get much of a chance for sightseeing." Jane peered through the window, careful not to touch the glass. Except for a folded *USA Today* lying on the front passenger seat, the interior looked spotless. Of course it would be; Maura was a neatness freak, and Jane had never spied so much as a stray Kleenex in her Lexus. "What's the date on that newspaper?" she asked.

Queenan unfolded the *USA Today*. "It's last Tuesday's."

"The day she flew here," said Brophy. "She must have picked it up at the airport."

Queenan straightened. "Let's take a look in the

trunk," he said. He circled to the rear, brushed off the snow, and pressed the unlock button on the remote. They all gathered around to watch, and Jane noticed Queenan hesitate before reaching down with a gloved hand to lift open the trunk. The same thought was probably going through all their heads at that moment. *A missing woman. An abandoned vehicle.* Too many surprises had been found in car trunks, too many horrors folded like embryos inside steel wombs. In these freezing temperatures, there would be no odors to alert anyone, no olfactory clues of what might lie inside. As Queenan lifted the trunk, Jane felt her breath catch in her throat. She stared into the now revealed space.

"Empty and clean as a whistle," said Queenan, and she heard relief in his voice. He looked at Gabriel. "So we have a rental car that looks to be in good shape, and no luggage. Wherever your friend went, she took her stuff with her. That sounds like a planned jaunt to me."

"Then where is she?" said Jane. "Why isn't she answering her cell phone?"

Queenan looked at her as though she were merely an irritating distraction. "I don't know your friend. Maybe you have a better handle on that answer than I do."

The Hertz lady said, "When can we get this vehicle back? It's part of our fleet."

"We'll need to hold on to it for a while," said Queenan.

"How long?"

"Until we decide if a crime has actually been committed. At the moment, I'm not sure."

"Then how do you explain her disappearance?" said Jane.

Once again, that flicker of irritation passed through his eyes when he looked at her. "I said I'm not sure. I'm keeping an open mind, ma'am. How about we all try doing that?"

"I can't say I really remember this particular guest," said Michelle, a desk clerk at the Mountain Lodge. "But then, we had two hundred doctors, plus their families, staying here last week. There's no way I could have kept track of everyone."

They had crowded into the manager's office, which was barely large enough to hold them all. The manager stood near the door with his arms crossed as he watched the interview. It was his presence, more than the questions, that seemed to make Michelle nervous, and she kept glancing toward her boss, as if afraid he'd disapprove of her answers.

"Then you don't recognize her picture?" Queenan asked, tapping on the official photo that Jane had printed off the Massachusetts medical examiner's website. It was an image of a somber professional. Maura gazed directly at the camera, her mouth neutral and unsmiling—appropriate for the line of work she was in. When one's job involved slicing open the dead, a broad grin would be unsettling.

Michelle studied the photo again with self-conscious diligence. She was young, in her midtwenties, and having so many people watching would make it difficult for anyone to concentrate. Especially when one of those people was your boss.

Jane said to the manager, "Would you mind stepping out, sir?"

"This is my office."

"We only need to borrow it for a short time."

"Since this business involves my hotel, I think I should know exactly what's going on." He looked at the clerk. "Do you remember her or not, Michelle?"

The young woman gave a helpless shrug. "I can't be sure. Are there any other pictures?"

After a silence, Brophy said quietly: "I have one." From the inside pocket of his jacket, he produced the photo. It was a casual snapshot of Maura seated at her kitchen table, a glass of red wine in front of her. Compared with the somber photo from the ME's office, this looked like a different woman entirely, her face flushed with alcohol and laughter. The photo was worn around the edges from repeated handling; it was something that he probably always carried with him, to be brought out and gazed at in lonely moments. For Daniel Brophy, there must be many such moments, torn between duty and longing, between God and Maura.

"Does she look familiar?" Queenan asked Michelle.

The young woman frowned. "This is the same woman? She looks so different in this picture."

Happier. In love.

Michelle looked up. "You know, I think I do remember her. Was she here with her husband?"

"She's not married," said Jane.

"Oh. Well, maybe I'm thinking of the wrong woman, then."

"Tell us about the woman you do remember."

"She was with this guy. A really cute guy with blond hair."

Jane avoided looking at Brophy; she didn't want to see his reaction. "What else do you remember about them?"

"They were going out to dinner together. I remember they stopped at the desk, and he asked for directions to the restaurant. I just assumed they were married."

"Why?"

"Because he was laughing and said something like, 'You see? I *have* learned to ask for directions.' I mean, that's something a guy would say to his wife, right?"

"When did you see this couple?"

"It would have been Thursday night. Because I was off duty on Friday."

"And Saturday, the day she checked out? Were you working that morning?"

"Yes, but a lot of us were on duty. That's when

the conference ended and we had all those guests checking out. I don't remember seeing her then."

"Someone at the desk must have helped her check out."

"Actually, no," the manager said. He held up a computer printout. "You said you wanted her room bill, so I ran off a copy. Looks like she used the in-room checkout feature on her TV. She didn't have to stop at the desk at all when she left."

Queenan took the printout. Flipping through the pages, he read aloud all the charges. "Room tax. Restaurant. Internet. Restaurant. I don't see anything out of the ordinary here."

"If it was an in-room checkout," Jane said, "how do we know she actually did it herself?"

Queenan didn't even bother to suppress a snort. "Are you suggesting that someone broke into her room? Packed up her stuff and checked out *for* her?"

"I'm just pointing out that we don't have proof she was actually here on Saturday morning, the day she supposedly left."

"What kind of proof do you need?"

Jane turned to the manager. "You have a security camera mounted over the reception desk. How long do you keep the recordings?"

"We'd still have the video from last week. But you're talking about hours and hours of recordings. Hundreds of people walking through the lobby. You'd be here all week watching those."

"What time did she check out, according to the bill?"

Queenan looked at the printout. "It was seven fifty-four AM."

"Then let's start there. If she walked out of this hotel on her own two feet, we should be able to spot her."

There was nothing in life so mind numbing as reviewing a surveillance video. After only thirty minutes, Jane's neck and shoulders were sore from craning forward, trying to catch every passing figure on the monitor. It did not help matters that Queenan kept sighing and fidgeting in his chair, making it clear to everyone else in the room that he thought this was a fool's errand. And maybe it is, thought Jane as she watched figures twitch across the screen, groups gathering and dispersing. As the time stamp moved toward eight AM, and dozens of hotel guests converged on the reception desk for checkout, her attention was pulled in too many directions at once.

It was Daniel who spotted her. "There!" he said.

Gabriel froze the recording. Jane counted at least two dozen people captured in that freeze-frame of the lobby, most of them standing near the desk. Others were caught in the background, clustered near the lobby chairs. Two men stood talking on their cell phones, and both were simultaneously looking at their watches. Welcome to the era of the compulsive multitasker.

Queenan said: "I don't see her."

"Go back," said Daniel. "I'm sure it was her."

Gabriel reversed the sequence, frame by frame. They watched as people walked backward, as groups broke apart and new clusters formed. One of the cell phone talkers twitched this way and that, as though dancing to some erratic beat coming through his receiver.

"That's her," Daniel said softly.

The dark-haired woman was at the very edge of the screen, her face caught in profile. No wonder Jane had missed seeing it the first time: Maura was weaving through the lobby with half a dozen people standing between her and the camera. Only at that instant, as she walked past a gap in the crowd, did the lens capture her image.

"Not a very clear shot," said Queenan.

"I know it's her," said Daniel, staring at Maura with undisguised yearning. "It's her face, her haircut. And I recognize the parka."

"Let's see if we can get any other views," said Gabriel. He moved the recording forward, frame by frame. Maura's dark hair reappeared, bobbing in and out of view as she moved past. Only at the very edge of the screen did she emerge again from the crowd. She was wearing dark pants and a white ski parka with a furred hood. Gabriel advanced one more image, and Maura's head moved beyond the frame, but half her torso was still visible.

"Well, look at that," said Queenan, pointing.

"She's wheeling a suitcase." He looked at Jane. "I think that settles the issue, doesn't it? She packed her own bag and checked out. She wasn't dragged from the building. As of Saturday, eight oh five, she was alive and well and leaving the hotel on her own steam." He glanced at his watch and stood. "Call me if you see anything else worth noting."

"You're not staying?"

"Ma'am, we've sent her photo to every newspaper and TV station in the state of Wyoming. We're fielding every call that comes in. The problem is, she—or someone who looks like her—has been sighted just about everywhere."

"Where, exactly?" asked Jane.

"You name it, she's been seen there. The Dinosaur Museum in Thermopolis. Grubb's General Store in Sublette County. Eating dinner at the Irma Hotel in Cody. A dozen different places, all around the state. At the moment, I'm not sure what more I can do. Now, I don't know your missing friend here. I don't know what kind of woman she is. But I'm thinking that she met some guy, maybe one of those other doctors here. She packs her suitcase, checks out a day early, and they decide to drive off somewhere together. Don't you agree that's the most likely explanation? That she's holed up in some hotel room with this guy, and they're having such hot sex that she's lost track of the calendar?"

Painfully aware that Daniel was standing beside her, Jane said: "She wouldn't do that."

"I can't count the number of times people have said that to me, or some variation on those words. *He's a good husband. He'd never do that.* Or: *She'd never leave her kids.* The point is, people surprise you. They do something crazy, and suddenly you realize you never really knew them. You must've dealt with that situation yourself, Detective."

Jane could not deny it; were their roles reversed, she would probably be giving the same little speech. How people are not who you think they are, not even people you've loved all your life. She thought of her own parents, whose thirty-five-year marriage had disintegrated after her father's affair with another woman. She thought of her mother's startling transformation from dowdy housewife into a lusty divorcée in low-cut dresses. No, people are too often not who you think they are. Sometimes they do foolish and inexplicable things.

Sometimes, they fall in love with Catholic priests.

"The point is, we haven't seen evidence of a crime yet," said Queenan, pulling on his winter jacket. "No blood, nothing to suggest that anyone forced her to do anything."

"There was that man. The one the hotel clerk saw with Maura."

"What about him?"

"If Maura went off with this guy, I'd like to know who he is. Shouldn't we at least check the videos from Thursday night?"

Queenan stood scowling as he debated whether

to pull off his jacket again. At last he sighed. "Okay. Let's look at Thursday night. The clerk said they were headed out to dinner, so we can start the recording around five PM."

This time, it was easier to spot their target. According to Michelle, the couple had come up to the reception desk to ask for directions to the restaurant. They fast-forwarded through the video, pausing only when someone approached the desk. Passersby jittered back and forth across the screen. The time stamp advanced toward six PM and the crowd grew larger as guests headed toward dinner, the women now adorned in earrings and necklaces, the men in coats and ties.

At six fifteen, a blond man appeared, facing across the desk.

"There," said Jane.

For a moment, there was silence as everyone focused on the dark-haired woman standing beside the man. There was no doubt about her identity.

It was Maura, and she was smiling.

"That's your gal, I take it?" asked Queenan.

"Yes," said Jane softly.

"She doesn't seem particularly distressed. That looks like a woman who's headed out to a nice restaurant, wouldn't you say?"

Jane stared at the image of Maura and the nameless man. Queenan's right, she thought. Maura looked happy. She could not remember the last time she'd seen such a smile on her friend's face. Over the past months, Maura had grown wan and increasingly private, as though, by avoiding Jane's questions, she could also avoid confronting the truth: that love had made her unhappier than ever.

And the reason for that unhappiness now stood beside Jane, staring at the video of that smiling pair. They were a startlingly attractive couple. The man was tall and lean, with boyishly tousled blond hair. Even though it was not a high-resolution image, Jane imagined she could see a twinkle in his eye, and she knew why the clerk would remember this encounter. Whoever the man was, he knew how to attract a woman's attention.

Abruptly Daniel walked out of the room.

That sudden departure made Queenan stare after him thoughtfully. "Was it something I said?" he asked.

"He's taking it hard," said Jane. "We were all hoping for answers."

"I think this video may be your answer." Once again, Queenan stood and reached for his jacket. "We'll continue to field any calls that come in. And hope that your friend decides to surface on her own."

"I want to know who that man is," said Jane, pointing to the monitor.

"Good-looking fella. No wonder your friend's got a big smile on her face."

"If he's a hotel guest," said Gabriel, "we could winnow down the names."

"We had a full house last week," the manager said. "We're talking about two hundred and forty rooms."

"We eliminate the females. Focus on men who booked singles."

"It was a medical conference. There were a lot of men who booked singles."

"Then we'd better get started now, don't you think?" Gabriel said. "We'll need names, addresses, phone numbers."

The manager looked at Queenan. "Don't these people need a warrant? We've got privacy issues here, Detective."

Jane pointed to Maura's face on the monitor. "You've also got a missing woman who was last seen in this hotel. In the company of one of *your* guests."

The manager gave a disbelieving laugh. "It was a bunch of doctors! You really think one of them—"

"If she was abducted," said Jane, "we have only a short time to work with." She moved toward the manager, close enough to make him retreat against the doorway. Close enough see his pupils dilate. "Don't make us waste a single minute."

The ringing of Queenan's cell phone cut the silence. "Detective Queenan," he answered. "What? Where?"

The tone of his voice made them all turn to watch

the conversation. His face was grim as he disconnected.

"What's going on?" Jane asked. Afraid to hear
the answer.

"You folks need to drive down to Sublette County.
The Circle B Guest Ranch. It's not my jurisdiction,
so you'll have to talk to Sheriff Fahey when you get
there."

"Why?"

"They've just found two bodies," said Queenan.
"A man and a woman."

SIXTEEN

IN ALL HER YEARS AS A HOMICIDE DETECTIVE, Jane Rizzoli had never felt so reluctant to walk into a death scene. She and Gabriel sat in their rental car across from the Circle B Guest Ranch, watching as yet another Sublette County Sheriff's Department vehicle pulled up, joining the cluster of official cars and trucks parked in front of the guest reception cottage. In the driveway, a woman with a microphone stood talking to a news camera, her blond hair hopelessly tangled in the wind. It looked like the usual scrum of cops and reporters that Jane was accustomed to wading through at every crime scene, but this time she viewed that gauntlet with dread. *Thank God we convinced Daniel to stay at the hotel. This is not an ordeal he should have to face.*

"I can't imagine Maura ever checking into a place like this," said Gabriel.

Jane stared across the road at the sign advertising SUPER SAVER WEEKLY AND MONTHLY RATES AVAILABLE! INQUIRE INSIDE! There was desperation in that sign, a last-ditch appeal to stay in business. No, she could not imagine Maura checking into one of those tired-looking cabins.

Gabriel took her arm as they crossed the icy road. He seemed eerily calm, and that was exactly what she needed from him at this moment. This was the Gabriel she'd met two summers ago, when they'd worked their first homicide together, a man whose cool efficiency had made him seem remote and heartless. It was merely the persona he adopted when situations turned grim. She glanced up at her husband, and his resoluteness steadied her own nerves.

They approached a sheriff's deputy, who stood arguing with a young woman.

"I need to talk with Fahey," the woman insisted. "We need more information or we can't do our jobs."

"Sheriff's kind of busy right now, Cathy."

"We're responsible for her welfare. At least tell me their names. Who's the next of kin?"

"You'll know when we know."

"The couple's from Plain of Angels, aren't they?"

The deputy frowned at her. "How'd you hear that?"

"I keep track of those people. I make it my business to know when they show up in town."

"Maybe you should mind your own business for a change and leave those folks alone."

She snorted. "Maybe you should try doing your

job, Bobby. At least *pretend* to follow up on my complaints."

"Leave. Now."

"You tell Sheriff Fahey I'll be calling him." The woman huffed out a breath so fierce that steam clouded her face as she spun around. She halted in surprise to find Jane and Gabriel standing right behind her. "Hope you have better luck with these people," she muttered, and stalked off down the driveway.

"Was that a reporter?" Gabriel asked, with the sympathy of a fellow lawman.

"Naw, county social worker. Those bleeding hearts are a real pain in the ass." The deputy looked Gabriel up and down. "Can I help you, sir?"

"Sheriff Fahey is expecting us. Detective Queenan called to let him know we were coming."

"You the folks from Boston?"

"Yes, sir. Agent Dean and Detective Rizzoli." Gabriel struck just the right note of respect to emphasize that he knew whose jurisdiction they were in. And who was in charge.

The deputy, who looked no older than his midtwenties, was young enough to be flattered by Gabriel's approach. "Come with me, sir. Ma'am."

They followed him to the Circle B check-in cottage. Inside, a wood fire crackled in the hearth, and low pine beams overhead made the space feel as claustrophobic as a dark cave. The cold wind outside had numbed Jane's face, and she stood near the fire as the heat slowly brought sensation back to her cheeks. The room was a time capsule from the 1960s, the wall adorned with bullwhips and spurs and muddy-colored paintings of cowboys. She heard voices talking in the back room—two men, she thought, until she peered through the doorway and saw that one of them was a blond woman with weather-beaten skin and a smoker's hacking cough.

". . . never did lay eyes on the wife," the woman said. "He's the one who checked in."

"Why didn't you ask for his ID?"

"He paid cash and signed in. This ain't Russia, you know. Last I checked, folks are free to come and go in this country. Besides, he looked like good people."

"You could tell?"

"Polite and respectful. Drove in during that snowstorm Saturday, and said they needed a place to stay while they waited for the roads to be cleared. Sounded reasonable to me."

"Sheriff?" the deputy called out. "Those people from Boston are here."

Fahey waved at them through the doorway. "Hold on," he said, and continued his conversation with the manager. "They checked in two days ago, Marge. When was the last time you cleaned their cabin?"

"Never got the chance. They had the DO NOT DISTURB sign hanging on the knob Saturday and Sunday. Figured they wanted their privacy so I left 'em alone. Then this morning, I noticed it wasn't hanging there anymore. So I went into the room around two o'clock to clean it. That's when I found 'em."

"So the last time you saw that man alive was when he checked in?"

"They couldn't have been dead all that time. They took the DO NOT DISTURB sign off the door, didn't they? Or someone did."

"Okay." Fahey sighed and zipped up his jacket. "DCI's coming in to assist, so they'll be talking to you, too."

"Yeah?" The woman hacked a watery cough. "Maybe they'll need rooms for the night. I got vacancies."

Fahey came out of the office and nodded at the new arrivals. He was a beefy man in his fifties, and like his younger deputy he sported a military buzz cut. His stony gaze went right past Jane and fixed on Gabriel. "You're the folks who reported that missing woman?"

"We're hoping this isn't her," said Gabriel.

"She went missing Saturday, right?"

"Yes. From Teton Village."

"Well, the timing's right. These people checked in on Saturday. Why don't you come with me?"

He led them up a path of trampled snow, past other cabins that stood dark and clearly unoccupied. Except for guest reception, there was only one other building that had its lights on, and it stood at the outer edge of the property. When they reached cabin eight, the sheriff paused to hand them latex gloves and paper shoe covers, the must-wear fashion at any crime scene.

"Before you walk in, I need to warn you," Fahey said. "It's not going to be pleasant."

"Never is," said Gabriel.

"What I mean is, they're gonna be hard to identify."

"There's disfigurement?" Gabriel asked it so calmly that the sheriff frowned at him.

"Yeah, you could say that," Fahey finally answered, and opened the door.

Jane stared across the threshold into cabin eight. Even from the doorway, she could see the blood, alarming splatters of it arcing across the wall. Wordlessly she stepped into the room, and as the unmade bed came into view she saw the source of all that blood.

The body lying beside the bed was faceup on the bare pine floor. He was balding and at least fifty pounds overweight, clad in black pants, white shirt, and white cotton socks. But it was his face—or the lack of one—that drew Jane's horrified gaze. It had been obliterated.

"An attack fueled by sheer rage. If you ask me, that's what you're looking at," said a silver-haired man who had just emerged from the bathroom. He was dressed in civilian clothes, and he looked shaken by the horrors that surrounded them. "Why else would you take a hammer to someone's face? Smash every bone, every tooth? It's nothing but pulp now. Cartilage, skin, bones, all pounded down to one bloody mess." Sighing, he lifted a blood-smeared glove in greeting. "I'm Dr. Draper."

"Medical examiner?" asked Gabriel.

Draper shook his head. "No, sir, just the county coroner. We don't have an ME in the state of Wyoming. A forensic pathologist will be driving in from Colorado."

"They're here to identify the female," Sheriff Fahey said.

Dr. Draper cocked his head toward the bathroom. "She's in there."

Jane stared at the doorway but could not bring herself to take the first step. It was Gabriel who crossed to the bathroom. For a long time, he stood gazing into the next room, saying nothing, and Jane could feel dread twisting her stomach. Slowly, she approached, and she was startled to catch sight of her own reflection staring back from the bathroom mirror, her face pale and tight. Gabriel moved aside, and she stared into the shower stall.

The dead woman was slumped with her back propped up against mildewed tiles. Her bare legs were splayed apart, her modesty protected only by the plastic shower curtain that had fallen across her body. Her head lolled forward, her chin almost resting on her chest, her face hidden by her hair. Black hair, matted with blood and brains. *Too long to be Maura's.*

Jane registered other details. The gold wedding band on the left hand. The heavy thighs, dimpled with cellulite. The large black mole on the forearm.

"It's not her," said Jane.

"You're sure about that?" asked Fahey.

Jane crouched down to stare at the face. Unlike the man's, this victim's features were not obliterated. The blow had landed on the side of her skull, caving it in, but that killing blow had not been followed by mutilation. She released a deep breath, and as she exhaled, all the tension suddenly left her body. "This isn't Maura Isles." She stood and looked through the doorway at the male victim. "And that's definitely not the man we saw on the hotel surveillance video."

"Which means your friend is still missing."

That's a hell of a lot better than dead. Only now, as all her fears dissipated, could Jane begin to focus on the crime scene with a cop's eyes. Suddenly she noticed details that she'd missed earlier. The lingering odor of cigarette smoke. The puddles of melted snow and multiple boot prints tracking across the floor, left by law enforcement personnel. And something that she should have spotted as soon as she'd entered the cabin: the small portable crib, tucked into the far corner.

She looked at Fahey. "Was there a child in here?"

He nodded. "Baby girl. Around eight, nine months old according to the county social worker. They took her into protective custody."

Jane remembered the woman they'd just met outside. Now she knew why a social worker had been on the scene. "So the child was alive," she said.

"Yeah. Killer didn't touch her. She was found in that crib over there. Diaper was soaked, but otherwise she was in good shape."

"After being left unfed for a day, two days?"

"There were four empty baby bottles in the crib. Kid never had a chance to get dehydrated."

"The baby must have been screaming," said Gabriel. "No one heard her?"

"They were the only guests staying at the Circle B. And as you noticed, this cabin's off by itself. Well insulated, windows shut. Outside, you might not hear a thing."

Jane approached the dead man again. Stood looking down at a face so destroyed it was hard to tell it had ever been human. "He didn't fight back," she said.

"Killer probably took him by surprise."

"The woman, I can see. She was in the shower, so she might not hear someone coming in. But the man?" She looked at Fahey. "Was the door forced?"

"No. Windows were all latched. Either the victims left the door unlocked, or they let the killer in themselves."

"And this victim's so surprised that he doesn't defend himself? Even while his head's being bashed in?"

"That bothered me, too," said Dr. Draper. "No

obvious defense wounds. He just let the killer in, turned his back, and he got whacked."

The knock on the door made them all turn. The deputy stuck his head into the cabin. "We just got confirmation on those plates. Car registration matches up with the victim's ID. Name is John Pomeroy. Plain of Angels, Idaho."

There was a silence.

"Oh my," Dr. Draper said. "Those people."

"What people?" asked Jane.

"They call themselves The Gathering. Some kind of religious commune out in Idaho. Lately they've been moving into Sublette County." The coroner looked at Fahey. "These two must have been headed up to that new settlement."

"That's not where they were going," said the deputy.

Dr. Draper looked at him. "You sound pretty sure of yourself, Deputy Martineau."

"Because I was up there just last week. The valley's completely deserted. They've all packed up and left for the winter."

Fahey frowned at the dead man. "Then why were these two people in town?"

"I can tell you they weren't going to Kingdom Come," said Deputy Martineau. "That road's been closed since Saturday. And it won't be open again till spring."

SEVENTEEN

H YDRATE, *HYDRATE, HYDRATE*. THAT WAS THE mantra that kept going through Maura's head as she coaxed Arlo to drink water, ever more water. She mixed a pinch of salt and a tablespoon of sugar into every cup—a poor man's version of Gatorade. By forcing the fluids into him, she'd keep up his blood pressure and flush his kidneys. It meant repeatedly changing his towels as they got saturated with urine, but urine was a good thing. If he stopped producing it, it meant he was going into shock, and he was doomed.

He may be doomed anyway, she thought as she watched him swallow the last two antibiotic capsules. Against the infection now raging in his leg, amoxicillin was little more than a magical charm. Already she could smell the impending gangrene, could see the creeping edge of necrotic tissue in his calf. Another day, perhaps two at the most, and she would be left with no choice, if she wanted to save him.

The leg would have to come off.

Can I really bring myself to do it? To amputate that leg without anesthesia? She was familiar with the anatomy. She could hunt down the necessary instruments from kitchens and garages. All she really needed were sharp knives and a sterilized saw. It was not the mechanics of amputation that made her hands sweat and her stomach clench at the prospect. It was the screaming. She thought of relentlessly sawing through bone while her patient shrieked and writhed. She thought of knives slippery with blood. And through it all, she would have to rely on Elaine and Grace to hold him down.

You have to bring help soon, Doug. Because I don't think I can do it. I can't torture this man.

"Hurts so bad," Arlo whispered. "Need more pills."

She knelt down beside him. "I'm afraid we've run out of Percocet, Arlo," she said. "But I have Tylenol."

"Doesn't help."

"There's codeine coming. Elaine's gone up the road to look for her purse. She says she has a bottle of it, enough to last you until help comes."

"When?"

"Soon. Maybe even tonight." She glanced at the window and saw that it was now afternoon. Doug had left yesterday morning. By now, he was surely down the mountain. "You know him. He'll probably swoop back up here in style, with TV cameras and everything."

Arlo gave a tired laugh. "Yeah, that's our Doug. Born under a lucky star. Always manages to skate through life with hardly a scratch, whereas I . . ." He sighed. "I swear, if I live through this, I'm never going to leave my house again."

The front door flew open and cold air swept in as Elaine came stomping back into the house. "Where's Grace?" she said.

"She went outside," said Maura.

Elaine spotted Grace's backpack in the corner. She knelt down and unzipped the pack.

"What are you doing, Elaine?"

"I can't find my purse."

"You said you left it up in the Jeep."

"That's where I thought it was, but Doug said he never saw it. I've been looking all up and down the road, in case it got dropped somewhere in the snow." She began digging through the backpack, scattering the contents on the floor. Out came Grace's iPod, sunglasses, a sweatshirt, a cell phone. In frustration, she turned the backpack upside down, and loose change clattered onto the floor. "Where the hell is my purse?"

"You really think Grace would take it?"

"I can't find it anywhere. It had to be her."

"Why would she?"

"She's a teenager. Can anyone explain teenagers?"

"Are you sure you didn't leave it somewhere in the house?"

"I'm sure." In frustration, Elaine threw down the empty backpack. "I know I had it with me in the Jeep when were driving up the road. But after the accident, we were all panicking. I was just focused on Arlo. The last time I remember seeing it, it was on the backseat, next to Grace." She scanned the room, searching for any hiding place where the purse might be concealed. "She's the only one who had the chance to take it. You ran down the hill to get the sled. Doug and I were trying to stop the bleeding. But no one was watching Grace."

"It could have fallen out of the Jeep."

"I told you, I looked all up and down the road."

"Maybe it got buried in the snow."

"It hasn't snowed for two days, and everything's crusted over in ice." Elaine suddenly jerked straight as the front door opened. She was caught in an unmistakably guilty pose, kneeling beside the empty backpack, the contents strewn on the floor.

"What are you doing?" said Grace. She slammed the door shut. "That's *my* stuff."

"Where's my purse, Grace?" said Elaine.

"Why are you looking in my backpack?"

"It has my pills. The bottle of codeine. Arlo needs it."

"And you thought you'd find it in my stuff?"

"Just tell me where it is."

"How would I know?" Grace snatched up the backpack and began thrusting her belongings back into it. "How do you know *she* didn't take it?" The girl didn't have to name names; they all knew she was referring to Maura.

"Grace, I'm just asking you a simple question."

"You didn't even stop to think it could be anyone else. You just assumed it's *me*."

Elaine sighed. "I'm too tired to have this fight. Just tell me if you know where it is."

"Why should I tell you anything? You wouldn't believe me anyway." Grace zipped up the pack and threw it over her shoulder as she headed toward the door. "There are eleven other houses here. I don't see why I have to stay in this one."

"Grace, we need to stick together," said Maura. "I promised your father I'd look after you. Please stay here."

"Why should I? I came to tell you what I found, and the first thing I hear when I come in the door is, *You're a thief.*"

"I didn't say that!" Elaine protested.

Maura rose and calmly approached the girl. "What did you find, Grace?"

"As if you're interested."

"I am. I want to know what you found."

The girl paused, torn between injured pride and her eagerness to share her news. "It's outside," she finally said. "Near the woods."

Maura pulled on her jacket and gloves and followed Grace outside. The snow, earlier churned up by all their comings and goings, had crusted over into knobby ice, and Maura navigated carefully over the slippery surface as she and Grace circled to the rear of the house and started across the field of snow, toward the trees.

"This is what I saw first," the girl said, pointing to the snow. "These tracks."

They were animal footprints. A coyote, thought Maura, or perhaps a wolf. Although blowing snow had obscured the prints in places, it was obvious that they moved in a direct line toward their house.

"It must have left these prints last night," said Grace. "Or maybe the night before. Because they're all frozen over now." She turned toward the woods. "And there's something else I want to show you."

Grace headed across the field, following the tracks toward a snow-covered mound. It was just a white hillock, its features blending into the vast landscape of snow, where everything was white, where bush and boulder were indistinguishable beneath their thick winter blankets. Only as they drew closer to the mound did Maura see the streak of yellow peeking through, where Grace had swiped away the snow to reveal what was underneath.

A bulldozer.

"It's just sitting out here in the open," said Grace. "Like they were in the middle of digging up something and they just . . . stopped."

Maura pulled open the door and looked into the driver's cab. There was no key in the ignition. If they could somehow get it started, they might be able to plow their way up to the road. She looked at Grace. "You wouldn't know how to hot-wire an engine, would you?"

"If we had Google, we could look it up."

"If we had Google, we'd be long gone from this place." With a sigh, Maura swung the door shut.

"See these tracks?" said Grace. "They go right past here and head toward the woods."

"We're in the wild. You'd expect to find animal tracks."

"It knows we're here." Grace looked around uneasily. "It's been sniffing around us."

"Then we'll just stay inside at night, okay?" Maura gave her arm a reassuring squeeze. It felt so thin, so fragile through the jacket sleeve, a reminder that this girl was, after all, only thirteen. A child with neither her mother nor her father to comfort her. "I promise, I'll fight off any wolf that comes to the door," said Maura.

"There can't be just one wolf," Grace pointed out. "They're pack animals. If they all attacked, you couldn't fight them off."

"Grace, don't worry about it. Wolves rarely attack people. They're probably more scared of us."

The girl didn't look convinced. To prove she wasn't afraid, Maura followed the tracks toward the trees, into snow that was deeper, so deep that she suddenly plunged in over her knees. This was why deer so easily fell prey in the winter: Heavy an-

imals sank deeply into the snow, and could not outrun the lighter and nimbler wolves.

"I didn't do it, you know!" Grace called out after
her. "I didn't take her stupid purse. Like I'd even
want it."

Suddenly Maura spotted a new set of impressions,
and she paused at the edge of the trees, staring. These
prints had not been left by wolves. When she realized what she was looking at, a sudden chill lifted
the hairs on the back of her neck.

Snowshoes.

"What would I want with her purse, anyway?"
said Grace, still standing by the bulldozer. "You believe me, don't you? At least *you* treat me like a
grown-up."

Maura peered into the woods, straining to make
out what lurked in the shelter of those pines. But the
trees were too dense, and all she saw were drooping
branches and tangled underbrush, a curtain so thick
that any number of eyes could be watching her at
that moment, and she would not be able to see them.

"Elaine acts all sweet and concerned about me,
but that's only when Dad's around," Grace said.
"She makes me want to barf."

Slowly, Maura backed away from the woods.
Every step seemed alarmingly loud and clumsy. Her
boots cracked through the snow crust and snapped
dead twigs. And behind her, Grace continued.

"She's only nice to me because of *him*. Women

always start off being nice to me. Then they can't wait to get rid of me."

"Let's go back to the house, Grace," Maura said quietly.

"It's just an act, and Dad's too blind to see it." Grace paused as she suddenly saw Maura's face. "What's the matter?"

"Nothing." Maura took the girl's arm. "It's getting cold. Let's go inside."

"Are you pissed at me, or what?"

"No, Grace, I'm not."

"Then why are you squeezing me so hard?"

Maura instantly released the girl's arm. "I think we should get in before it's dark. Before the wolves come back."

"But you just said they don't attack people."

"I promised your dad I'd look after you, and that's what I'm trying to do." She managed a smile. "Come on, I'll make us some hot chocolate."

Maura did not want to make the girl any more fearful than she already was. So she said nothing to Grace about what she had just seen in the woods. Elaine, though, would have to be told. They needed to be prepared, now that she knew the truth.

They were not alone in this valley.

EIGHTEEN

"IF SOMEONE'S OUT THERE, WHY HAVEN'T WE SEEN him?" asked Elaine.

They sat awake late in the night, alert to every creak, every rustle. On the sofa, Grace slept deeply, unaware of their tense whispers, their anxious speculation. When Maura barred the door and propped a chair against it, Grace had assumed it was to keep out the wolves. But tonight it wasn't four-legged predators that Maura and Elaine were afraid of.

"The prints are recent," said Maura. "Any older than a day or two, and the wind and blowing snow would have covered them."

"Why haven't we seen any other prints?"

"Maybe he's managed to erase them. Or he's watching us from a distance."

"Which means he doesn't want us to know he's out there."

Maura nodded. "It would mean that."

Elaine shivered and looked at the hearth. "Well,

he'd certainly know *we're* here. He could probably spot our light from a mile away."

Maura glanced at the window, at the darkness outside. "He could be watching us now."

"You could be all wrong. Maybe it wasn't a snowshoe."

"It was, Elaine."

"Well, I wasn't there to see it." She gave a sudden, hysteria-tinged laugh. "It's like you're making up some crazy campfire story, just to freak me out."

"I wouldn't do that."

"*She* would." Elaine pointed at Grace, who slept on, unaware. "And she'd get a kick out of it. Was this her idea, to play a practical joke on me? Because I don't think it's very funny."

"I told you, she doesn't know about it. I didn't want to scare her."

"If there *is* someone out there, why doesn't he just come up and introduce himself? Why's he hiding out in the woods?" Her eyes narrowed. "You know, Maura, we're all going a little crazy out here. Arlo's seeing ghosts. I can't find my purse. You're not immune. Maybe your eyes are playing tricks on you, and those weren't snowshoe tracks. There's no watcher in the woods."

"Someone else is in this valley. Someone who's known about us since we arrived."

"You only found those tracks today."

"There's something else I haven't told you about.

It happened the first night we got here." Maura glanced at Grace again, to confirm that the girl was still asleep. She lowered her voice to a whisper. "I woke up in the middle of the night and there was snow scattered on the floor. And a footprint. Obviously, someone opened the door, letting in the wind. But all of you were sound asleep. So who opened that door, Elaine? Who came into this house?"

"You never mentioned this before. Why are you only telling me about it now?"

"At the time, I assumed that one of you had stepped outside during the night. By the next morning, the footprint was gone, and there was no evidence left. I thought maybe I'd dreamed the whole thing."

"You probably did. You've built up this paranoid fantasy over nothing. And now you're freaking *me* out because of some footprint you *thought* you saw in the woods."

"I'm telling you this because we both need to be alert. We need to watch for other signs."

"We're in the middle of nowhere. Who else could possibly be out here, the abominable snowman?"

"I don't know."

"If he's been inside this house, if he's been skulking around watching us, why haven't any of us seen him?"

"I have," a soft voice said. "I've seen him."

Maura had not noticed that Arlo was awake. She

turned and saw that he was watching them, his eyes dull and sunken. She moved closer to him, to speak in a whisper. "What did you see?" she asked.

"I told you yesterday. Think it was yesterday . . ." He swallowed, wincing with the effort. "God, I don't know anymore how long it's been."

"I don't remember you saying anything," said Elaine.

"It was dark. Face looking in."

"Oh." Elaine sighed. "He's talking about those ghosts again. All those people he keeps seeing in the room." She knelt beside Arlo and tucked in his blanket. "You're just having bad dreams. The fever's making you see things that aren't here."

"Didn't imagine him."

"No one else sees him. It's those pain pills. Honey, you're confused."

Again, Arlo tried to swallow, but his mouth was dry and he couldn't quite manage it. "He was there," he whispered. "Saw him."

"You need to drink some more," said Maura. She filled a cup and tilted it to his lips. He managed to swallow only a few sips before he started coughing, and the water dribbled down the sides of his mouth. Weakly he pushed the cup away and collapsed back with a groan. "Enough."

Maura set the cup down and studied him. He had not urinated in hours, and the sound of his breathing had changed. It was coarse and rattling, a sign that he was aspirating fluid into his lungs. If he grew much weaker, it would be dangerous to force him to drink, but the alternative was to let him sink into dehydration and shock. Either way, she thought, we are losing him.

"Tell me again," she said. "What you saw."

"Faces."

"People in the room?"

He took in another rattling breath. "And in the window."

Is someone there now?

An icy breath whispered up her spine, and Maura spun around to look at the window. All she saw beyond the glass was darkness. No ghostly face, no demonic eyes stared back at her.

Elaine burst out in scornful laughter. "You see? Now both of you are losing it! I'm beginning to think I'm the only sane person left in this house."

Maura crossed to the window. Outside, the night was as thick as a velvet drape, concealing whatever secrets lurked in the valley. But her imagination filled in the details she could not see, painting with splashes of blood and horror. Something had caused the previous occupants of this settlement to flee, leaving doors unlocked, windows open, and meals uneaten. Something so terrible it had caused them to abandon cherished pets to cold and starvation. Was it still here, the thing that drove them from this place? Or was there nothing at all out there except her own dark fantasies, born of fear and isolation?

It's this place. It's playing with our minds, stealing our sanity.

She thought of the relentless sequence of catastrophes that had stranded them here. The snowstorm, the wrong road. The Suburban's slide into the ditch. It was as if they were fated to end up here, lured like innocent prey into the trap of Kingdom Come, and any attempt to flee would meet only with more misfortune. Hadn't Arlo's accident proven the folly of trying to escape? And where was Doug? Nearly two mornings ago, he had walked out of the valley. By now, help should have arrived.

Which meant he had not made it. Kingdom Come had not allowed him to escape, either.

She gave herself a shake and turned from the window, suddenly disgusted with herself for entertaining thoughts of the supernatural. This was what stress did to even the most logical minds: It created monsters who didn't exist.

But I know I saw that print in the snow. And Arlo saw a face in the window.

She went to the door, pulled away the chair she'd propped there, and slid open the bolt.

"What are you doing?" said Elaine.

"I want to find out if I am imagining things." Maura pulled on her jacket and zipped it up.

"You're going *outside*?"

"Why not? You're the one who thinks I'm going insane. You keep insisting there's nothing out there."

"What are you going to do?"

"Arlo saw a face at the window. It hasn't snowed in three days. If someone was standing outside, their prints might still be there."

"Will you just stay inside, please? You don't have to prove anything to me."

"I'm proving this to myself." Maura picked up the kerosene lamp and reached for the door. Even as she grasped the knob, she had to beat back the fear that was screaming at her: *Don't go out! Lock the bolt!* But such fears were illogical. No one had tried to harm them; they themselves had brought on all their misfortunes, through a series of bad decisions.

She opened the door and stepped outside.

The night was still and silent. No wind blew, no trees rustled. The loudest sound was her own heart, pounding in her chest. The door suddenly opened again and Elaine emerged, wearing her jacket.

"I'm coming, too."

"You don't have to."

"If you find any more footprints, I want to see them for myself."

Together they circled around to the side of the house where the window faced. They had not tramped this way before, and as Maura scanned the snow by the light of the kerosene lamp, she saw no footprints, only unbroken snow. But when they reached the window she stopped, staring down at the unmistakable evidence revealed by the lamplight.

Now Elaine saw it, too, and she sucked in a breath. "Those look like wolf tracks."

As if in answer, a distant howl pierced the night, followed by an answering chorus of yips and wails that sent shivers racing across Maura's skin. "These are right under the window," she said.

Elaine suddenly burst out laughing. "Well, that explains the face that Arlo saw, doesn't it?"

"How?"

"Isn't it obvious?" Elaine turned toward the woods, and her laughter was as wild and uncontrollable as the wails coming from the forest. "Werewolves!"

Abruptly, the howls ceased. The silence that followed was so complete, so unexplainable, that Maura felt her skin prickling. "Back inside," she whispered. "*Now.*"

They ran through crusted snow, back to the porch and into the house. Maura slid the bolt home and dragged the chair against it. For a moment, they stood panting, saying nothing. In the hearth, a log collapsed into the bed of glowing ashes, and sparks flew up.

Elaine and Maura suddenly stiffened and looked at each other as they both heard the sound, echoing through the valley. It was the wolves, howling again.

NINETEEN

BEFORE THE SUN ROSE THE NEXT DAY, MAURA knew that Arlo was dying. She could hear it in his breathing, in the wet gurgle in his throat, as though he were struggling to draw air through a water-clogged snorkel. His lungs were drowning in fluid.

She awakened to the sound and turned to look at him. In the firelight, she saw that Elaine was bending over him, gently wiping his face with a washcloth.

"Today's the day, Arlo," Elaine murmured. "They'll be coming to rescue us, I know it. As soon as it gets light."

Arlo inhaled a tortured breath. "Doug . . ."

"Yes, I'm sure he's made it by now. You know how he is. *Never give up, never surrender.* That's our Doug. You just have to hang on, okay? A few more hours. Look, it's already starting to get light."

"Doug. You." Arlo took in a ragged breath. "I never had a chance. Did I?"

"What do you mean?"

"Always knew." Arlo choked out a sob. "Always knew you'd choose him."

"Oh, Arlo. No, it's not what you're thinking."

"Time to be honest. Please."

"Nothing ever happened between Doug and me. I swear it, honey."

"But you wanted it to."

The silence that followed was an answer more honest than anything Elaine could have said. Maura remained silent and still, an uncomfortable witness to this painful confession. Arlo had to know his time was running out. This would be his last chance to hear the truth.

"Doesn't matter." He sighed. "Not now."

"But it *does* matter," said Elaine.

"Still love you." Arlo closed his eyes. "Want you . . . to know that."

Elaine put her hand over her mouth to smother her sob. The first light of dawn lit the window, washing her in its glow as she knelt beside him, racked by grief and guilt. She took in a shuddering breath and straightened. Only then did she notice that Maura was awake and watching them, and she turned away, embarrassed.

For a moment, the two women did not speak. The only sound was Arlo's hoarse breathing, in and out, in and out, through rattling clots of phlegm. Even from across the room, Maura could see that his face had changed, his eyes more sunken, his skin now tinged with a sickly green cast. She did not want to look at his leg, but there was enough light now to examine it, and she knew she should. This was her responsibility, a responsibility that she wanted no part of, but she was the doctor. Yet all her medical training had turned out to be useless without modern drugs and clean surgical instruments and the icy determination to do what was necessary: to cut off a screaming man's leg. Because that was what needed to be done. She knew it even before she exposed the limb, before she smelled the stink of what festered beneath the blanket.

"Oh God," Elaine groaned, and stumbled away. Maura heard the front door swing shut as Elaine escaped the fetid room in search of fresh air.

It has to be done today, thought Maura, staring down at the putrefying leg. But she couldn't do it alone; she needed Elaine and Grace to hold him down, or she'd never be able to control the bleeding. She glanced at the girl, who was still sound asleep on the sofa. Could she count on Grace? Did Elaine have the fortitude to hold firm despite the screaming and the pitiless rasp of the saw? If they buckled, Maura could end up killing him.

She pulled on her jacket and gloves and stepped outside. She found Elaine standing on the porch, drawing in deep breaths of cold air, as though to wash the stink of Arlo's rotting body from her lungs.

"How long do you think he has?" Elaine asked softly.

"I don't want to talk about countdowns, Elaine."

"But he's dying. Isn't he?"

"If nothing is done."

"You and Doug already *did* something. It didn't help."

"So we have to take the next step."

"What?"

"Amputation."

Elaine turned and stared at her. "You can't be serious."

"We're left with no other choice. We've gone through all the antibiotics. If that leg stays on, he'll die of septic shock."

"You were the one who didn't want to do surgery before! Doug had to talk you into it."

"Things have gotten a lot worse. Now it's not his leg we want to save. It's his life. I need you to hold him down."

"I can't do it by myself!"

"Grace will have to help."

"*Grace?*" Elaine snorted. "You think you can trust that spoiled brat to be useful for anything?"

"If we explain it to her. If we tell her how important this is."

"I know her better than you do, Maura. She's got Doug completely under her control, and he'll do anything for his little princess. It's all about keeping *her* happy, about making up for the fact her mother walked out."

"You don't give her enough credit. She may be

just a kid, but she's smart. She'll understand what's at stake here."

"She doesn't care. Don't you get that about her? She *doesn't fucking care* about anyone but herself." Elaine shook her head. "Don't count on Grace."

Maura released a breath. "If you're the only one who'll help me, then we'll need rope. Something to tie him down on the table."

"You really plan to go through with it?"

"What would you have me do? Stand by and watch him die?"

"They could come for us today. They could be here in just a few hours."

"Elaine, we need to be realistic."

"Another day won't make a difference, will it? If they show up tomorrow, it will be soon enough."

"Doug's been gone for two days. Something's gone wrong." She paused, reluctant to admit the obvious. "I don't think he made it," she said quietly. "I think we're on our own."

Elaine's eyes suddenly glistened with tears, and she turned and stared at the snow. "And if you do it? If you cut off his leg, what are the chances he'll die anyway?"

"Without antibiotics, I'm afraid his chances aren't good. No matter what we do."

"Then why put him through it? If he's going to die no matter what, why torture him?"

"Because I don't have any other tricks in my bag, Elaine. It's down to this, or just give up."

"Doug could still send help—"

"It should've come already."

"You need to give him time."

"How long do we have to wait before you accept the obvious? *Help isn't coming.*"

"I don't care how long it takes! Jesus Christ, do you even hear what you're saying? Are you serious, cut off his fucking *leg*?" Elaine suddenly sagged against the porch post, as though too weary to support her own weight. "I won't help you do it," she said softly. "I'm sorry."

Maura turned and looked at the road leading out of the valley. It was another brilliantly clear day, and she squinted at the glare of the morning sunlight on the snow. We have one last option, she thought. If she didn't take it, Arlo would die. Maybe not today, maybe not even tomorrow, but in that room, she could smell the inevitability of what was to come, unless she acted.

"You have to keep him hydrated," she said. "As long as he's awake enough to drink, keep feeding him sips of sugar water. And food, if he's able. All we've got left for the pain is Tylenol, but we've got plenty of that."

Elaine frowned at her. "Why are you telling me this?"

"Because you're now in charge. Just keep him comfortable; that's the best you can do."

"What about you?"

"My cross-country skis are still up on the Suburban. I'll pack some overnight gear in case I don't make it out before dark."

"You're going to try skiing down the mountain?"

"Would you rather be the one to do it?"

"If Doug couldn't make it—"

"He may have had an accident. He may be lying somewhere with a broken leg. In which case, it's even more important that I get started now, while I've still got a full day ahead."

"What if you don't come back, either?" Elaine asked, desperation in her voice.

"You have plenty of food and firewood. You and Grace could hang on here for months." She turned.

"Wait. I need to tell you something."

Maura paused on the porch and looked back. "Yes?"

"Doug and I, we were never together."

"I heard you tell Arlo."

"It's the truth."

"Why does it matter?"

"I thought you'd want to know."

"To be honest, Elaine, what happened or didn't happen between you and Doug makes absolutely no difference to me." Maura turned toward the house. "All I care about right now is getting all of us out of this place alive."

It took her an hour to fill a backpack. She stuffed it with food and extra socks and gloves and a sweater. From the garage, she was able to scavenge a tarp and sleeping bag, items she hoped she wouldn't need. With any luck, she could be down the mountain by nightfall. Her cell phone battery had drained to nothing, so she left it in Elaine's care, along with her purse, and packed only cash and ID. On a thirty-mile journey, there was no room for even one unnecessary ounce.

Even so, the pack weighed heavily on her shoulders as she started up the valley road. Every step took her past reminders of their earlier ill-fated attempt to leave. Here were the rutted tracks left by the Jeep as it had struggled to climb through the snow. Here were the footprints they'd left after they'd abandoned the stranded vehicle and walked back down, dragging Arlo on the sled. Another hundred yards, another few hairpin turns, and she began spotting Arlo's blood on the snow, tracked down the road on their boots. Another turn of the road, and there was the stranded Jeep with the broken tire chain. And more blood.

She paused to catch her breath and stared down at the churned snow, stained in different shades of red and pink, like the icy confections you slurped up on a hot summer's day. It brought back the screams and the panic, and her heart pounded as much from that terrible memory as it did from her trudge up the hill.

She left the Jeep behind and kept walking. Here the snow was broken only by Doug's footprints. Over the past three days, they had partially melted in the sun, and had hardened into icy crusts. She continued her climb, unsettled by the thought that she was following in Doug's footsteps, that every step she took he, too, had taken two mornings ago. How far down the mountain would she be able to follow this trail? Would there be a point when it suddenly stopped, when she would discover what had become of him?

Am I bound for the same fate?

The road grew steeper, and she was sweating in her heavy clothes. She unzipped the jacket, pulled off her gloves and hat. This climb would be the most strenuous part of her journey. Once she reached the main road, it would be a mostly downhill glide on skis. That, at least, was the theory. Yet Doug had failed to complete it. Now she was beginning to wonder if she was being reckless, attempting a feat that Doug, so fit and athletic, had been unable to complete.

She could still change her mind. She could turn around and head back to the house, where they had enough food to last them until spring. She reached a viewpoint from which she could see the settlement far below, where smoke was curling from the chimney of their house. She was not even at the main road yet, and already she was exhausted, her legs aching and wobbly. Had Doug felt as weary when he'd reached this point in the climb? Had he paused at this very spot, looked down at the valley, and debated the wisdom of continuing?

She knew what he chose; his footprints left the record of his decision. They continued up the road.

So, too, did she. This is for Arlo, she thought. His name became her silent chant as she walked. *Save Arlo. Save Arlo.*

Pine trees soon blocked her view, and the valley disappeared behind her. The backpack seemed to grow heavier with every step, and she considered dumping some of the contents. Did she really need those three tins of sardines? Wouldn't the half jar of peanut butter provide enough energy to get her down the mountain? She debated the issue as she huffed up the road, the cans clanking in her pack. It was a bad sign that she was already considering such a move, less than two hours into her journey.

The road leveled out and she spotted the sign ahead, marking the viewpoint where they had caught their very first glimpse of Kingdom Come five days ago. The valley was so far below her now that the settlement looked like a toy landscape, decorated with artificial forests and flocked with fake snow. But the chimney smoke was real, and so were the people in that house, and one of them was dying.

She turned to continue the trek, took two steps, and came to a sudden halt. Staring down at the snow, she saw Doug's footprints marking the route ahead of her.

Another set of prints trailed behind his. Snowshoes.

She knew they'd been left after Doug came this way, because they overlaid the impression of his boots. But how soon after? Hours later, a day later?

Or had Doug's pursuer been right behind him, moving ever closer?

Is he now right behind me?

She spun around, heart hammering as she scanned her surroundings. The trees seemed closer, as though they had somehow crept in on the road when she wasn't looking. The sun's glare left her half blind to the gloom under those heavy branches, and her gaze could penetrate only a few feet into the woods before the shadows veiled her view. She heard nothing on that silent trail. No wind, no footfalls, only the sound of her own frantic breathing.

Get the skis. Get down this mountain.

She began to run, following the trail of Doug's footprints. He had not been running. His stride continued as it had before, steady and even, his soles leaving deep impressions in the snow. At this point, he had not realized he was being followed. He was probably thinking only about the task ahead. About getting on his skis and starting his glide down the mountain. It would never occur to him that he was being followed.

Her chest ached and her throat burned from the cold air. Every step she took seemed deafeningly loud as her boots cracked through the icy glaze. Anyone nearby would think that an elephant was lumbering through. A wheezing, clumsy elephant.

At last she spotted the chain strung across the entrance to the private road. Almost there. She followed Doug's boot prints the last few dozen yards, past the chain, past the RESIDENTS ONLY sign, and saw the Suburban, still tipped on its side in the ditch. One pair of cross-country skis was missing from the roof rack.

So Doug had made it this far. She saw the parallel tracks left by his skis as he'd glided away down the road.

She waded into the ditch, sinking thigh-deep in snow, and unlatched the second set of skis from the rack. Retrieving the ski shoes would take longer. They were inside the Suburban, and with the vehicle lying on its side, it was a struggle to lift the heavy door. When at last she managed to swing it open, she was out of breath and panting hard.

Suddenly she heard a distant rumble. She went still, listening through the pounding of her own heart, afraid that she'd only imagined it. No, there it was—the sound of an engine.

A snowplow was coming up the mountain.

He made it. Doug made it, and now we're going to be saved.

She gave a shout of joy and let the Suburban's door slam shut. She could not yet see the plow, but the noise was louder, closer, and she was laughing and crying at the same time. Back to civilization, she thought. Back to hot showers and electric lights and telephones. Most important, back to hospitals.

Arlo was going to live.

She scrambled onto the road and stood waiting for her rescuers. Feeling the sun on her face, the joy coursing through her veins. Here is where it all turns out right, she thought. Here is where the nightmare ends.

Then, through the approaching rumble of the plow, she heard the soft crunch of weight settling onto snow. The sound came from just behind her. She sucked in a startled breath, and it rushed into her lungs like a cold wind. Only then did she see the shadow moving in to engulf hers.

The watcher in the woods. He's here.

TWENTY

JANE FOUND DANIEL BROPHY HUNCHED IN A booth in the hotel's empty cocktail lounge. He did not look up at her, but kept his gaze on the table, clearly signaling that he wanted to be alone.

She sat down anyway. "We missed you at lunch," she said. "Did you get something to eat?"

"I'm not hungry."

"I'm still waiting to hear back from Queenan. But I don't think he has anything new to tell us today."

He nodded, still not looking at her. Still giving off signals of *Go away. I don't want to talk.* Even in the forgiving gloom of the lounge, he looked visibly older. Weary and beaten down.

"Daniel," she said. "I'm not going to give up. And neither should you."

"We've driven through five counties," he said. "Talked on the air with six radio stations. Watched every minute of those surveillance videos."

"There could be something we missed. Something we'll spot if we watch them again."

"She looked happy in those videos. Didn't she?" He raised his head and she saw torment in his eyes. "She looked happy with that man."

After a silence, Jane admitted: "Yeah. She did."

The surveillance cameras had caught several glimpses of Maura and the blond man in the lobby. But the views had been fleeting, each time only a few seconds at the most, and then she'd slipped out of sight. It was like watching a ghost, viewing those images on the monitor. A phantom reliving her last moments on earth again and again.

"We don't know what any of it means," Jane said. "He could be an old acquaintance."

"Someone who made her smile."

"This was a medical conference. A bunch of pathologists who probably knew each other. Maybe he had nothing to do with why she went missing."

"Or maybe Queenan's right. And they're holed up together in some hotel right now, having hot, crazy . . ." He stopped.

"At least it would mean she's alive."

"Yes. It would mean that."

They both fell silent. It was only three PM, too early for cocktails. Except for a bartender stacking glasses behind the counter, they were the only ones in the gloomy lounge.

"If she did go off with another man," said Jane quietly, "you can understand why it might happen."

"I blame myself," he said. "For not being that man. And I can't help wondering . . ."

"What?"

"If she flew out here with plans to meet him."

"Do you have any reason to think that?"

"Look at the way they smiled at each other. How comfortable they seemed."

"*They might be old friends.*" *Or old lovers* was what she didn't say. She didn't need to; that thought must be tormenting him as well. "These are just theories, based on nothing," she said. "All we have is the video of her going out to dinner with him. Meeting him in the lobby."

"And smiling." Pain darkened his eyes. "I couldn't do that for her. I couldn't give her what she needed."

"What she needs now is for us not to give up hope. To keep looking for her. I'm not going to give up."

"Tell me the truth." He met her gaze. "You've been a homicide cop long enough to know. What do your instincts tell you?"

"Instincts can be wrong."

"If she weren't a friend, if this was just another missing persons case, what would you be thinking right now?"

She hesitated, and the only sound in the lounge was the clink of glassware as the bartender tidied up behind the counter, prepping for the upcoming cocktail hour.

"After this much time?" She shook her head. "I'd be forced to consider the worst."

He didn't seem surprised by her answer. By now he would have reached the same conclusion.

Her cell phone rang and they both froze. She glanced at the number. Queenan. As soon as she heard his voice on the line, she knew this was not a call that he wanted to be making. Nor a call that she wanted to receive.

"I'm sorry to have to break the news," he said.

"What is it?"

"You should head over to Saint John's Medical Center in Jackson. Dr. Draper will meet you there."

"Dr. Draper? You mean the Sublette County Coroner?"

"Yes. Because that's where it happened, in Sublette County." There was a long and agonizing pause. "I'm afraid they found your friend."

"I think it's best that you not see her," Dr. Draper said, somberly facing Maura's three friends across the conference table. "You should remember her the way she was. I'm sure she would want it that way as well."

St. John's was built to serve the living, not the dead, and through the closed door of the conference room they could hear the sounds of a normal day in a hospital: ringing phones, the chime of an elevator, the far-off wails of an infant in the ER. The sounds reminded Jane that, in the aftermath of tragedy, life still went on.

"The vehicle was discovered only this morning, off a backcountry road," said Draper. "We can't be certain how long it was lying in that ravine. There was a lot of damage from the fire. And afterward, from animal . . ." He paused. "It's a wilderness area."

He didn't need to elaborate. Jane knew what he was leaving out. In the natural world, creatures always lurked in Death's shadow, waiting to feed with beaks and claws and sharp teeth. Even in Boston's suburban parks, a corpse would attract dogs and raccoons, rats and turkey vultures. In the rugged mountains of western Wyoming, there would be an even larger host of scavengers waiting to feast, scavengers that could gnaw off a face and detach a hand and scatter limbs. Jane thought of Maura's ivory skin and regal cheekbones, and she wondered what remained of those features. *No, I don't want to see her. I don't want to know what has become of her face.*

"If the remains were so badly damaged, how did you make the identification?" asked Gabriel. He, at least, was still thinking like an investigator, still able to focus on what needed to be asked.

"There was sufficient evidence at the crash site to make an ID."

"Evidence?"

"When the vehicle went into the ravine, a number of items were ejected from it. Several suitcases and other personal belongings that survived the fire." He reached for the large cardboard box that he'd brought into the room. The smell of scorched plastic escaped as he lifted the lid. Although the items inside were sealed in evidence bags, the stench of fire and smoke was potent enough to penetrate even a ziplock bag. He paused for a moment, staring into the box, as though suddenly wondering if it might be a mistake to share the contents. But it was too late now to close it, to deny them the proof that he had promised. He pulled out the first evidence bag and set it on the desk.

Through the clear plastic, they could see a leather luggage tag. Flipping it over, Draper revealed the name written in neat block letters.

MAURA ISLES, MD.

"I take it that's her correct address on the tag?" he asked.

Jane swallowed. "Yes," she murmured. She did not dare glance at Daniel, who was sitting beside her. She didn't want to see the devastation on his face.

"That was attached to one of the suitcases that was thrown from the vehicle," said Draper. "You can examine the suitcase itself if you'd like. It's in the custody of the Sublette County Sheriff's Department, along with the larger items." Reaching into the box, he pulled out other evidence bags and laid them on the table. There were two cell phones, one of them scorched. Another luggage tag, this one with the name Douglas Comley, MD. A man's toilet case. A prescription bottle of lovastatin for a patient named Arlo Zielinski.

"The Suburban was rented by a Dr. Douglas Comley from San Diego," said Draper. "He'd reserved it for ten days. We assume it was Dr. Comley who was behind the wheel when the vehicle went off the edge. The road makes a sharp curve there, and if it was nighttime, or snow was falling, visibility would have been poor. An icy road could have been a contributing factor as well."

"Then you assume it was an accident," said Gabriel.

Draper frowned. "As opposed to what?"

"There are always other possibilities to consider."

The coroner sighed. "Given your line of work, Agent Dean, I suppose it's natural that you'd be thinking of those other possibilities. But Sheriff Fahey concluded that this was an accident. I've already looked at the X-rays. The bodies have multiple fractures, which is what you'd expect. There are no bullet fragments, nothing to indicate anything other than what seems to have happened. The vehicle simply veered off a mountain road. It plunged fifty feet into a ravine, where it caught fire. I doubt any of the passengers survived the initial crash, so I think it's safe to assume that your friend died on impact."

"There was a snowstorm last Saturday, wasn't there?" asked Gabriel.

"Yes. Why?"

"If there's heavy snow on the vehicle, it might tell us when this happened."

"I saw only a light dusting," said Draper. "But then, the fire would have melted any snow cover."

"Or the accident happened more recently."

"But that still begs the question of where your friend has been for the last seven days. Time of death is going to be almost impossible to determine. I'm inclined to go by when the victims were last seen alive, which would make it Saturday." He looked around the table at their troubled faces. "I realize this leaves many questions unanswered. But at least now you know what happened, and you can go home with a feeling of closure. You know her death was quick, and she probably didn't suffer." He sighed. "I'm so sorry it turned out this way."

Draper rose to his feet, looking older and wearier than he had just half an hour earlier, when they'd first walked in. Even when the grief is not your own, merely being in its vicinity can drain the soul, and Draper had probably seen many lifetimes' worth of it. "Let me walk you out."

"May we view the remains?" asked Gabriel.

Draper frowned at him. "I wouldn't recommend it."

"But I think it needs to be done."

Jane almost hoped that Draper would refuse, would spare her from the ordeal. She knew what Maura had looked like alive; once she viewed what Maura had become, there'd be no erasing that image, no turning back the clock on the horror. Looking at her husband, she wondered how he could stay so calm.

"Let me show you the X-rays," said Draper.

"Maybe that will be enough to convince you of my findings."

Gabriel said to Brophy: "It's better if you wait here."

Daniel nodded and remained where he was, his head bowed, alone with his grief.

As Jane and Gabriel followed Draper to the elevator, she felt dread bubbling like acid in her stomach. I don't want to see this, she thought. I don't need to see this. But Gabriel kept striding ahead purposefully, and she was too proud not to follow him. When they stepped into the morgue, she was relieved to see that the autopsy table was empty, the cadavers safely stored out of sight.

Draper shuffled through a bundle of X-rays and clipped several films onto the viewing box. He flipped a switch, and skeletal images appeared against the glow.

"As you can see, there's ample evidence of trauma," said Draper. "Fractures of the skull, multiple ribs. Impaction of the left femur into the hip joint. Because of the fire, the limbs have contracted into a pugilistic posture." His voice assumed the matter-of-fact drone of a professional conveying data to colleagues. As if, by the act of entering this room and seeing the cool gleam of stainless steel, he had stepped into the uniform of a coroner. "I e-mailed these images to our forensic pathologist in Colorado. He concluded that this is a female between thirty and forty-five. Her estimated height is five foot five or five foot six. And judging by the sacroiliac joint, she was nulliparous. She never gave birth." He paused and looked at Jane. "Would that describe your friend?"

Numbly, Jane nodded. "Yes," she whispered.

"And she's had very good dental care. There's a crown here on the lower right molar. Several fillings." Again, he looked at Jane, as though she was the one with all the answers.

Jane stared at the jaw glowing on the light box. *How would I know?* She hadn't studied Maura's mouth, hadn't counted her crowns and fillings. Maura was her colleague and her friend. Not a collection of teeth and bones.

"I'm sorry," said Draper. "That was probably too much information for you to deal with. I just wanted you to feel confident about the identification."

"Then there won't be an autopsy," said Jane softly.

Draper shook his head. "There's no reason for one. The pathologist in Colorado is satisfied with the ID. We have her luggage tag, and the X-rays match a woman of her age and height. These injuries are consistent with what you'd find in an unrestrained passenger subjected to high-speed deceleration."

It took a few seconds for Jane to register what he'd said. She blinked away tears and the X-ray hanging on the light box suddenly came back into focus. "An unrestrained passenger?" she said.

"Yes."

"Are you saying she wasn't wearing a seat belt?"

"That's correct. None of the deceased was wearing a seat belt."

"That can't be right. Maura would never forget to buckle her seat belt. That's the kind of person she was."

"I'm afraid this time, she neglected to do so. At any rate, wearing a seat belt probably wouldn't have saved her. Not in an accident this traumatic."

"That's not the point. The point is, something's wrong here," said Jane. "It's completely out of character for her."

Draper sighed and flipped off the viewing light. "Detective, I know it must be hard to accept the death of a close friend. Whether she was belted in or not, it doesn't change the fact that she is dead."

"But how did it happen? Why?"

"Does it really make a difference?" Draper said quietly.

"Yes." Again, she felt tears prickle her eyes. "It doesn't make sense to me. I need to understand."

"Jane," said Gabriel. "It may never make sense. We'll just have to accept it." Gently he took her arm. "I think we've seen enough. Let's go back to the hotel."

"Not yet." She pulled away from him. "There's something else I need to see."

"If you insist on viewing the remains," said Draper, "I can show them to you. But you won't be able to recognize anything. There's not much except charred flesh and bone." He paused and said softly: "Trust me. You're better off not seeing her. Just take her home."

"He's right," said Gabriel. "We don't need to look at the body."

"Not the body." She took a breath and straightened. "I want to see the crash site. I want to see where it happened."

TWENTY-ONE

A LIGHT SNOW WAS FALLING THE NEXT MORNING when Gabriel and Jane stepped out of their car and walked to the edge of the road. There they stood in silence, staring down into the ravine where the burned hulk of the Suburban was still lodged. A path of trampled snow marked the winding trail that the recovery team had hiked down the day before to retrieve the bodies. It would have been an exhausting climb back up to the road, carrying the stretchers up switchbacks, boots sliding on icy rocks.

"I want to get closer," she said, starting down the trail.

"There's nothing down there to look at."

"I owe it to her. I need to see where she died." She kept walking, her gaze focused on the slippery path. Beneath the fresh dusting of powder, the snow was icy and treacherous, and she had to move slowly. Her thighs soon ached from the steep descent, and melting snowflakes, mingled with her sweat, trickled down her cheeks. She began to spot debris from the crash, scattered down the slope: a fragment of twisted metal, a lone tennis shoe, a scrap of blue cloth, all of it starting to vanish now beneath fresh powder. By the time she finally reached the blackened vehicle, it was covered by a light coating of snow. The scent of fire still hung in that cold and pristine air, and she could see the scars left by the fire: the charred bushes and the scorched pine branches. She thought of the Suburban's terrifying trajectory as it plummeted off the cliff. Imagined the shrieks as the last split seconds of life flashed before Maura's eyes.

She halted, releasing a shaken breath as she watched falling snow slowly erase the ugly evidence of death. Footsteps crunched closer, and Gabriel came to a stop beside her.

"It's so hard to believe," Jane said. "You wake up in the morning, thinking it'll just be another day. You get in a car with some friends. And suddenly it's over. Everything you knew and thought and felt, in an instant, it's all gone."

He drew her close beside him. "That's why we have to enjoy every minute."

She brushed snow off the vehicle, revealing a streak of blackened metal. "You never know, do you? Which little decision will end up changing your life. If she hadn't come to this conference, she wouldn't have met Doug Comley. She wouldn't have climbed into his truck." Abruptly she lifted her hand from the Suburban, as though the touch of it burned her. Staring at the ruined truck, she imagined the last days in Maura's life. They now knew it was Comley whom they'd seen with Maura on the surveillance tape. They'd viewed his photograph on the staff physician website of the San Diego hospital where he'd worked as a pathologist. Forty-two years old, a divorced single father, he'd been an attendee at the same medical conference. Attractive man spots equally attractive woman, and nature takes its course. Dinner, conversation, all sorts of possibilities swirling in their heads. Any woman would be tempted, even a woman as levelheaded as Maura. What kind of future, after all, could Daniel Brophy promise her, except a lifetime of furtive meetings and disappointments and regrets? If Daniel had given her what she needed, Maura wouldn't have strayed. She wouldn't have joined Douglas Comley on his doomed excursion.

She would be alive.

Daniel was no doubt tormented by those same thoughts. They had left him at the hotel without telling him where they were going. This was not a visit he should make. Now, standing in the gently falling snow, she was not sure that she should have come, either. What purpose did it serve, to see this blackened hulk, to visualize the vehicle's plunge through the air, the flying glass, the explosion of flames? But now I've seen it, she thought. And I can go home.

She and Gabriel turned and headed back up the

trail. The wind had picked up, and fine snow swirled into her face, stinging her eyes. She sneezed, and when she opened her eyes again, something blue fluttered past. She picked it up and saw that it was a torn airline ticket envelope, the edges blackened by fire. A scrap of the boarding pass was still inside, but only the five last letters of the name were visible.

inger.

She looked at Gabriel. "What was the name of the other man in the car?" she asked.

"Zielinski."

"That's what I thought."

He frowned at the scrap of boarding pass. "They identified all four bodies. Comley and his daughter, Zielinski, and Maura."

"So who does this ticket belong to?" she asked.

"Maybe it's leftover litter from an earlier rental car customer."

"It's one more thing that doesn't fit. This and the seat belt."

"It could be totally unrelated."

"Why isn't this bothering you, Gabriel? I can't believe you're just accepting it!"

He sighed. "You're only making this harder on yourself."

"I need you to support me on this."

"I'm trying to."

"By ignoring what I'm saying?"

"Oh, Jane." He wrapped his arms around her, but she remained stiff and unresponsive in his embrace.

"We've done what we could. Now we need to go home. We need to get on with our lives."

While Maura can't. She was suddenly, achingly aware of all the sensations that Maura would never again experience. The cold air rushing in and out of her lungs. The warmth of a man's arms around her. *I may be ready to go home,* she thought. *But I'm not finished asking questions.*

"Hey!" a voice shouted from above. "What are you people doing down there?"

They both looked up to see a man standing on the road above.

Gabriel waved and called back: "We're coming up!"

The climb was far harder than the descent. The new accumulation of powder masked treacherous ice, and the wind kept puffing snow into their faces. Gabriel was first to reach the road and Jane scrambled up after him, breathing hard.

A battered pickup truck was parked at the side of the road. Beside it stood a silver-haired man holding a rifle, the barrel pointed to the ground. His face was deeply weathered, as though he'd spent a lifetime in the harsh outdoors, and his boots and ranch coat looked equally well worn. Although he appeared to be in his seventies, he stood as straight and unyielding as a pine tree.

"That's an accident scene down there," the man said. "Not a place for tourists."

"We're aware of that, sir," said Gabriel.

"It's also private property. My property." The man's grip tightened around the rifle. Although he kept it pointed at the ground, his stance made it clear that he was prepared to bring it up at an instant's notice. "I've called the police."

"Oh, for God's sake," said Jane. "This is ridiculous."

The man turned his unsmiling gaze on her. "You've got no business scavenging down there."

"We weren't scavenging."

"Chased a buncha teenagers out of that ravine last night. They were hunting for souvenirs."

"We're law enforcement," said Jane.

The man shot a dubious glance at their rental car. "From out of town?"

"One of the victims was our friend. She died in that ravine."

That seemed to take him aback. He stared at her for a long time, as though trying to decide whether to believe her. He kept his gaze on them, even as a Sublette County Sheriff's Department vehicle rounded the curve and pulled to a stop behind the pickup truck.

A familiar police officer stepped out of the vehicle. It was Deputy Martineau, whom they'd met at the double homicide a few nights earlier. "Hey, Monty," he called out. "So what's going on here?"

"Caught these people trespassing, Bobby. They claim they're law enforcement."

Martineau glanced at Jane and Gabriel. "Uh, actually, they are."

"What?"

He gave a polite nod to Jane and Gabriel. "It's Agent Dean, right? And hello, ma'am. Sorry about the misunderstanding, but Mr. Loftus here's been a little jumpy about trespassers. Especially after those kids came by last night."

"How do you know these people?" Loftus demanded, clearly not convinced.

"Monty, they're okay. I saw them over at the Circle B, when they came by to talk to Fahey." He turned to Jane and Gabriel, and his voice softened. "I'm really sorry about what happened to your friend."

"Thank you, Deputy," said Gabriel.

Loftus gave a conciliatory grunt. "Then I guess I owe you folks an apology." He extended his hand.

Gabriel shook it. "No apologies needed, sir."

"It's just that I spotted your car and thought we had more of those souvenir hunters down there. Crazy kids, all into that death and vampire nonsense." Loftus looked down at the charred Suburban in the ravine. "Not like it used to be when I was growing up here. When folks respected property rights. Now anyone thinks they can come hunting on my land. Leave my gates wide open."

Jane could read the look that flickered across Martineau's face: *I've heard him say this a thousand times before.*

"And you never show up in time to do anything, Bobby," Loftus added.

"I'm here now, ain't I?" protested Martineau.

"You come by my place later, and I'll show you what they did to my gates. Something has to be done."

"Okay."

"I mean *today*, Bobby." Loftus climbed into his pickup truck, and the engine rattled to life. With a gruff wave, he called out, grudgingly, "Sorry again, folks," and drove away.

"Who is that guy?" asked Jane.

Martineau laughed. "Montgomery Loftus. His family used to own like, a gazillion acres around here. Double L Ranch."

"He was pretty pissed at us. I thought he was going to blast us with that rifle."

"He's pissed about everything these days. You know how it is with some old folks. Always complaining it ain't the way it used to be."

It never is, thought Jane as she watched Martineau climb back into his vehicle. And it won't be the same in Boston, either. Not with Maura gone.

As they drove back to the hotel, Jane stared out the window, thinking about the last conversation she'd had with Maura. It was in the morgue, and they'd been standing at the autopsy table as Maura sliced into a cadaver. She'd talked about her upcoming trip to Wyoming. How she'd never been there, how she looked forward to seeing elk and buffalo and maybe even a wolf or two. They'd talked about Jane's mother, and Barry Frost's divorce, and how life always kept surprising you. You just never know, Maura had said, what lies around the corner.

No, you never do. You had no idea you'd be coming home from Wyoming in a coffin.

They pulled into the hotel parking lot, and Gabriel shut off the engine. For a moment they sat without speaking. There is still so much to do, she thought. Make phone calls. Sign papers. Arrange for the coffin's transportation. The thought of it all exhausted her. But at least they'd be going home, now. To Regina.

"I know it's only noon," said Gabriel. "But I think we could both use a drink."

She nodded. "I second that." She pushed open her door and stepped out, into the softly falling snow. They held on to each other as they walked across the parking lot, their arms wrapped tightly around each other's waists. How much harder this day would have been without him here, she thought. Poor Maura has lost everything, while I am still blessed with this man. Blessed with a future.

They stepped into the hotel bar, where the light was so subdued that at first she didn't spot Brophy sitting in one of the booths. Only as her eyes adjusted to the gloom did she see him.

He was not alone.

Seated with him at the table was a man who now rose to his feet, a tall and forbidding figure in black. Anthony Sansone was notoriously reclusive, and so paranoid about his privacy that he seldom ventured out in public. Yet here he was, standing in their hotel bar, his grief in full view.

"You should have called me, Detective," said Sansone. "You should have asked for my help."

"I'm sorry," said Jane. "I didn't think about it."

"Maura was my friend, too. If I'd known she was missing, I would have flown back from Italy in a heartbeat."

"There's nothing you could have done. Nothing any of us could have done." She glanced at Brophy, who was stone-faced and silent. These two men had never liked each other, yet here they were, a truce declared between them in Maura's memory.

"My jet's waiting at the airport," said Sansone. "As soon as they release her body, we can all fly home together."

"It should be this afternoon."

"Then I'll let my pilot know." His sigh was heavy with sadness. "Call me when it's time to make the transfer. And we'll bring Maura home."

In the comfortable cocoon of Anthony Sansone's jet, the four passengers were quiet as they flew east, into the night. Perhaps they were all thinking, as Jane was, of their unseen companion who rode below in cargo, boxed in a coffin, stored in the dark and frigid hold. This was the first time Jane had ever flown on a private jet. Were it for any other occasion, she would have taken delight in the soft leather seats, the spacious legroom, the myriad comforts that supremely wealthy travelers are accustomed to. But she scarcely registered the taste of the perfectly pink roast beef sandwich that the steward had presented to her on a china plate. Although she'd missed both lunch and dinner, she ate without enjoyment, fueling up only because her body needed it.

Daniel Brophy did not eat at all. His sandwich sat untouched as he stared out at the night, his shoulders sagging under the weight of grief. And guilt, too, surely. The guilt of knowing what could have been, had he chosen love above duty, Maura above God. Now the woman he cared about was charred flesh, locked in the hold beneath their feet.

"When we get back to Boston," said Gabriel, "we have decisions to make."

Jane looked at her husband and wondered how he managed to stay focused on necessary tasks. In times like these, she was reminded that she'd married a marine.

"Decisions?" she said.

"Funeral arrangements. Notifications. There must be relatives who need to be called."

"She has no family," said Brophy. "There's only her mo—" He stopped, not finishing the word *mother*. Nor did he say the name they were all thinking: *Amalthea Lank*. Two years ago, Maura had sought out her birth mother, whose identity had been a mystery to her. The search had eventually brought her to a women's prison in Framingham. To a woman guilty of unspeakable crimes. Amalthea was not a mother anyone would want to claim, and Maura never spoke of her.

Daniel said again, more firmly: "She has no family."

She had only us, thought Jane. Her friends. While Jane had a husband and daughter, parents and brothers, Maura had few intimate connections. She had a lover whom she saw only in secret, and friends who did not really know her. It was a truth that Jane now had to acknowledge: *I did not really know her.*

"What about her ex-husband?" Sansone asked. "I believe he still lives in California."

"Victor?" Brophy gave a disgusted laugh. "Maura despised him. She wouldn't want him anywhere near her funeral."

"Do we know what she did want? What her final wishes were? She wasn't religious, so I assume she'd want a secular service."

Jane glanced at Brophy, who had suddenly stiffened. She did not think Sansone's comment was meant as a barb at the priest, but the air between the two men suddenly felt charged.

Brophy said, tightly: "Even though she fell away from the Church, she still respected it."

"She was a committed scientist, Father Brophy. The fact that she respected the Church doesn't mean she believed in it. It would probably strike her as odd to have a religious service at her funeral. And as a nonbeliever, wouldn't she be denied a Catholic funeral, anyway?"

Brophy looked away. "Yes," he conceded. "That is official policy."

"There's also the question of whether she would have wanted burial or cremation. Do we know what Maura wanted? Did she ever broach the subject with you?"

"Why would she? She was *young*!" Brophy's voice suddenly broke. "When you're only forty-two, you don't think about how you want your body disposed of! You don't think of who should and shouldn't be invited to the funeral. You're too busy being *alive*." He took a deep breath and looked away.

No one spoke for a long time. The only sound was the steady whine of the jet engines.

"So we have to make those decisions for her," Sansone finally said.

"*We?*" asked Brophy.

"I'm only trying to offer my help. And the necessary funds, whatever it may cost."

"Not everything can be bought and paid for."

"Is that what you think I'm trying to do?"

"It's why you're here, isn't it? Why you've swooped in with your private jet and taken control? Because you *can*?"

Jane reached out to touch Brophy's arm. "Daniel. Hey, relax."

"I'm here because I cared about Maura, too," said Sansone.

"As you made so abundantly obvious to both of us."

"Father Brophy, it was always clear to me where Maura's affections lay. Nothing I could do, nothing I could offer her, would have changed the fact that she loved you."

"Yet you were always waiting in the shadows. Hoping for a chance."

"A chance to offer my help if she ever needed it. Help that she never asked for while she was alive." Sansone sighed. "If only she had. I might have . . ."

"Saved her?"

"I can't rewrite history. But we both know things could have been different." He looked straight at Brophy. "She could have been happier."

Brophy's face flushed a deep red. Sansone had just delivered the cruelest of truths, but it was a truth obvious to anyone who knew Maura, anyone who'd watched her over the past few months and seen how her already slender frame had become thinner, how sadness had dimmed her smile. She was not alone in her pain: Jane had seen the same sadness reflected in Daniel Brophy's eyes, compounded by guilt. He loved Maura, yet he'd made her miserable, a fact that was all the harder for him to bear because it was Sansone pointing it out.

Brophy half rose from his seat, his hands clenched

into fists, and she reached for his arm. "Stop it," she said. "Both of you! Why are you two doing this? It's not some contest to decide who loved her the most. We all cared about her. It doesn't matter now who would have made her happier. She's dead and there's no way to change history."

Brophy sank back in his seat, the rage draining from his body. "She deserved better," he said. "Better than me." Turning, he stared out the window, retreating into his own misery.

She started to reach out to him again, but Gabriel stopped her. "Give him some space," he whispered.

So she did. She left Brophy to his silence and his regrets, and she joined her husband on the other side of the aisle. Sansone rose and moved as well, to the rear of the plane, retreating into his own thoughts. For the remainder of the flight they sat separate and silent, as the plane with Maura's body soared eastward, toward Boston.

TWENTY-TWO

O *H MAURA, IF ONLY YOU WERE HERE TO SEE THIS.*
Jane stood outside the entrance to Emmanuel Episcopal Church and watched as a steady stream of mourners arrived to pay their last respects to Dr. Maura Isles. Maura would be surprised by all this fuss. Impressed and maybe a little embarrassed, too: She never did enjoy being the center of attention. Jane recognized many of these people because they came from the same world that she and Maura both inhabited, a world that revolved around death. She spotted Drs. Bristol and Costas from the ME's office, and quietly greeted Maura's secretary, Louise, and Maura's morgue assistant, Yoshima. There were cops, too—Jane's partner, Barry Frost, as well as most of the homicide unit, all of whom were well acquainted with the woman they privately referred to as the Queen of the Dead. A queen who herself had now entered that realm.

But the one man whom Maura loved above all was not here, and Jane understood why. A deeply grieving Daniel Brophy was now in seclusion, and would not be attending the services. He had said his private goodbyes to Maura; to bare his pain in public was more than anyone should ask of him.

"We'd better take our seats," Gabriel said gently. "They're about to begin."

She followed her husband up the aisle to the front pew. The closed coffin loomed right in front of her, framed by massive vases of lilies. Anthony Sansone had spared no expense, and the coffin's mahogany surface was polished to such a bright gloss that she could see her own reflection.

The officiating priest entered—not Brophy, but the Reverend Gail Harriman of the Episcopal Church. Maura would have appreciated the fact that a woman was performing her memorial service. She would have liked this church as well, known for its open policy of welcoming all into its fold. She hadn't believed in God, but she had believed in fellowship, and she would have approved.

As the Reverend Harriman began to speak, Gabriel took Jane's hand. She felt her throat close up and fought back humiliating tears. Through the forty minutes of homilies and hymns and words of remembrance, she struggled to stay in control, her teeth clenched, her back pressed rigidly against the pew. When at last the service ended, she was still dry-eyed, but all her muscles ached as though she had just staggered off the battlefield.

The six pallbearers rose, Gabriel and Sansone

among them, and they shepherded the casket in its slow progression up the aisle, toward the hearse that waited outside. As the other mourners filed from the building, Jane did not move. She remained in her seat, imagining Maura's final journey. The solemn drive to the crematorium. The slide into the flames. The final rendering of bone into ashes.

I can't believe I will never see you again.

She felt her cell phone go off. During the memorial service, she had turned off the ringer, and the sudden vibration against her belt was a startling reminder that duty still demanded her attention.

The call was from a Wyoming area code. "Detective Rizzoli," she answered quietly.

It was Queenan's voice on the line. "Does the name Elaine Salinger mean anything to you?" he asked.

"Should it?"

"So you've never heard that name before."

She sighed. "I just sat through Maura's memorial service. I'm afraid I'm not really focusing on the point of this call."

"A woman named Elaine Salinger has just been reported missing. She was due back at her job in San Diego yesterday, but it seems she never returned from vacation. And she never caught her flight home from Jackson Hole."

San Diego. Douglas Comley was from San Diego, too.

"It turns out they knew one another," Queenan continued. "Elaine Salinger and Arlo Zielinski and

Douglas Comley. They were friends, and they were all booked to fly back on the same day."

Jane heard her own heartbeat whooshing in her ears. An image suddenly came back to her, of a torn airline boarding pass that she'd picked up in the ravine. The scrap of paper with the fragment of the passenger's name: *inger*.

Salinger.

"What did this woman look like?" she asked. "How old, how tall?"

"That's what I just spent the last hour finding out. Elaine Salinger is thirty-nine years old. Five foot six, a hundred twenty pounds. And a brunette."

Jane shot to her feet. The church had not yet emptied out, and she had to push past stragglers as she ran up the aisle, toward the exit. She made it to the door just in time to see the hearse pull away.

"Stop it!" she yelled.

Gabriel turned to her. "Jane?"

"What's the name of the mortuary? Does anyone know?"

Sansone looked up at her in puzzlement. "I made the arrangements. What's the problem, Detective?"

"Call them, *now.* Tell them the body can't be cremated."

"Why not?"

"It needs to go to the medical examiner's office."

Dr. Abe Bristol stared down at the draped cadaver, but he made no attempt to uncover it. For a man who spent his workdays cutting open dead bodies, he looked shaken by the prospect of peeling back the sheet. Most of the people in the room were veterans of multiple death scenes, yet they all quailed from what lay beneath the drape. Only Yoshima had so far laid eyes on the body, when he had taken the X-rays after its arrival. Now he hung back from the table, as though so traumatized, he wanted nothing more to do with it.

"This is one postmortem I really don't want to do," said Bristol.

"Someone has to look at this body. Someone has to give us a definitive answer."

"The problem is, I'm not sure the answer is going to be any more to our liking."

"You haven't even looked at her yet."

"But I can see the X-rays." He pointed to the films of the skull, spine, and pelvis that Yoshima had clipped onto the light box. "I can tell you they're completely consistent with a woman of Maura's height and age. And those fractures are exactly what you'd find from injuries sustained by an unrestrained passenger."

"Maura always wore her seat belt," said Jane. "She was compulsive about it. You know how she was." *Was. I can't stop using the past tense. I can't quite believe this exam will change anything.*

"True," Bristol said. "Not wearing a seat belt isn't like her at all." He pulled on gloves and reluctantly peeled back the sheet.

Even before she saw the body, Jane flinched away, her hand lifted over her nose against the smell of burned flesh. Gagging, she turned and saw Gabriel's face. He at least seemed to be holding his own, but there was no mistaking the appalled look in his eyes. She forced herself to turn back to the table. To see the body they had believed was Maura's.

It was not the first time Jane had seen charred remains. Once she had watched postmortems on three arson victims, two young children and their mother. She remembered those three cadavers lying on the tables, their limbs bent, their arms thrust forward like boxers spoiling for a fight. The woman she saw now was frozen in the same pugilistic pose, her tendons contracted by intense heat.

Jane took another step closer and stared down at what should have been a face. She tried to see something—anything—familiar, but all she saw was an unrecognizable mask of charred flesh.

Someone gave a startled gasp behind her, and she turned to see Maura's secretary, Louise, standing in the doorway. Louise seldom ventured into the autopsy room, and Jane was surprised to see her there, and so late in the day. The woman was wearing her winter coat, and her windblown gray hair sparkled with melting snowflakes.

"You probably don't want to come any closer, Louise," said Bristol.

But it was too late. Louise had already glimpsed

the corpse and she stood frozen, too horrified to take another step into the room. "Dr.—Dr. Bristol—"

"What is it?"

"You asked about her dentist. The one Dr. Isles went to. I suddenly remembered that she'd asked me to make an appointment for her, so I went back over the calendar. It was about six months ago."

"You found her dentist's name?"

"Even better." Louise held out a brown envelope. "I have her X-rays. When I explained to him why we needed them, he told me I should drive right over and pick them up."

Bristol crossed the room in a few swift steps and snatched the envelope from Louise's hand. Yoshima was already pulling down the skull X-rays from the light box, the unwieldy films twanging as he hastily yanked them from the clips to make room.

Bristol pulled the dental films from the envelope. These were not morgue panograms, but small bite-wing X-rays that looked dwarfed by Bristol's meaty hands. As he clipped them onto the box, Jane spotted the patient's name on the label.

ISLES, MAURA.

"These films were all taken within the last three years," Bristol noted. "And we've got plenty here for ID purposes. Gold crowns on the lower left and right molars. An old root canal here . . ."

"I did panograms on this body," said Yoshima. He shuffled through the X-rays he'd taken of the burned cadaver. "Here." He slid the films onto the box, right beside Maura's bitewing X-rays.

Everyone crowded closer. For a moment no one said a word as gazes flicked back and forth between the sets of films.

Then Bristol said: "I think it's pretty clear." He turned to Jane. "The body on that table isn't Maura's."

The breath whooshed out of Jane's lungs. Yoshima sagged against a countertop, as though suddenly too weak to support himself.

"If this body is Elaine Salinger's," said Gabriel, "then we're still left with the same question we had before. Where's Maura?"

Jane took out her cell phone and dialed.

After three rings, a voice answered: "Detective Queenan."

"Maura Isles is still missing," she said. "We're coming back to Wyoming."

TWENTY-THREE

MAURA AWAKENED TO THE CRACKLE OF BURN-ing wood. Firelight danced across her closed eyelids, and she smelled the sweetness of molasses and bacon, the scent of pork and beans bubbling over the campfire. Although she lay perfectly still, her captor sensed that she was no longer asleep. His boots scraped closer, and his shadow blocked out the firelight as he bent over her.

"Better eat," he grunted, and shoved a spoonful of beans in her direction.

She turned away, nauseated by the smell. "Why are you doing this?" she whispered.

"Trying to keep you alive."

"There's a man, in the village. He needs to be in the hospital. You have to let me help him."

"You can't."

"Untie me. *Please.*"

"You'll just run away." He gave up trying to force the food on her and slipped the spoon in his own mouth instead. She looked at the face staring down at her. Backlit by the fire, his features were invisible. All she saw was the outline of his head, frighteningly enormous in the fur-lined hood. Somewhere in the shadows a dog whined and claws scratched. The animal moved closer and she smelled his hot breath, felt the lick of a tongue across her face. He was a huge dog, his silhouette shaggy and wolflike, and although he seemed friendly, she recoiled from his attentions.

"Bear likes you. Doesn't like most people."

"Maybe he's telling you I'm okay," she said. "And you should let me go."

"Too soon." He turned and moved closer to the fire. Scooping up beans from the pot, he shoveled spoonfuls into his mouth with feral hunger. Veiled in smoke, he looked like some primitive creature squatting in the light of an ancient campfire.

"What do you mean, it's too soon?" she asked.

He just kept eating, noisily slurping from the spoon, his concentration completely focused on filling his belly. He was an animal, stinking of sweat and smoke, no more civilized than the dog. Her wrists were raw from the rope bindings, and her hair was matted and infested with fleas. For days she had been wheezing and coughing in the smoke that hung thick in their shelter. She was suffocating in here, while that filthy creature sat calmly stuffing food into his mouth, not caring if she lived or died.

"Goddamn you," she said. "Let. Me. *Go*."

The dog gave a low growl and moved beside his master.

The figure squatting by the fire slowly turned to her, and in the featureless shadow that was his face, she imagined evils that were all the more frightening because she could not see them. In silence, he reached into his backpack. When she saw what he brought out, she froze. The firelight's reflection gleamed in the blade and cast ripples of shadow along the serrations. A hunter's knife. She had seen, at the autopsy table, what such a knife could do to human flesh. She had probed incised skin, used a ruler to measure the wounds that split apart muscle and tendon and sometimes even bone. She stared at the blade poised above her, and cringed as he brought the knife down.

With a sharp flick, he cut the rope binding her wrists, then freed her ankles. Blood rushed into her hands. She scrabbled away, retreating into a shadowy corner. There she huddled, breathing hard, her heart pounding from the unaccustomed exertion. For days she had been restrained, allowed up only when she needed to use the bucket. Now she felt light-headed and weak, and the shelter seemed to rock like a ship on the high seas.

He moved closer, until he was right in front of her and she could smell the stink of damp wool. Up till now his face had been obscured by shadow. Now she could make out thin cheeks smeared with soot, a beardless jaw. Hungry, deep-set eyes. Maura stared at that gaunt face and came to a stunning realization: He was just a boy, sixteen at the oldest. But a boy with the size and strength to cut her down with one stroke of his knife.

The dog moved close beside its master, and was rewarded with a pat on the head. Boy and dog both stared at her, contemplating the strange creature that they had captured on the road.

"You have to let me go," said Maura. "They'll be looking for me."

"Not anymore." The boy slid the knife into his belt and went back to the fire. It was dying, and already the chill had started to penetrate their shelter. He threw on another log, and the flames danced to life in the ring of stones. As the fire brightened, she could make out more details of the hovel in which she had been imprisoned. *How many days have I been here?* She didn't know. There were no windows, and she could not see whether it was day or night outside. The walls were rough-hewn logs sealed with dried mud. A pallet of twigs covered with blankets served as his bed. By the fire was a single cooking pot and cans of food, stacked into a neat pyramid. She spotted a familiar-looking jar of peanut butter; it was the same jar that she had been carrying in her backpack.

"Why are you doing this?" she asked. "What do you want from me?"

"I'm trying to help you."

"By dragging me here? Keeping me a prisoner?" She could not hold back a disdainful laugh. "Are you *insane*?"

His gaze narrowed, a look so dark, so intent, that she wondered if she had just pushed him too far. "I saved your life," he said.

"People will look for me. And they'll keep searching, for as long as it takes. If you don't let me go—"

"No one's looking for you, ma'am. Because you're dead."

His words, spoken so calmly, chilled her to the marrow. *You're dead.* For one wild, disorienting moment she thought that maybe it was true, that she *was* dead. That this was her hell, her punishment, trapped forever in a dark and frigid wilderness of her own creation with this strange companion who was half boy, half man. He watched her confusion with an eerie stillness, saying nothing.

"What do you mean?" she whispered.

"They found your body."

"But I'm right here. I'm *alive*."

"That's not what the radio said." He threw another log on the fire and the flames leaped up, filling the shelter with smoke that made her eyes water, her throat burn. Then he went to the corner where he crouched over a dark jumble of clothes and backpacks. Rummaging through the pile, he produced a small radio. He clicked it on and tinny music played, shot through with static. A country-western song, sung by a woman wailing about love and betrayal. He held out the radio to her. "Wait for the news."

But her gaze was focused instead on the pile of belongings in the corner. She saw her own backpack, the one she'd been wearing on her last hike out of the valley. And she spotted something else that startled her.

"You took Elaine's purse," she said. "You're a thief."

"Wanted to know who was in the valley."

"Those were your snowshoe tracks. You were watching us."

"Been waiting for someone to come back. I saw your fire."

"Why didn't you just come talk to us? Why sneak around?"

"I didn't know if you were one of his people. One of them."

"Who?"

"The Gathering," he said softly.

She remembered the words that had been stamped in gold on the leather-bound Bible. *Words of Our Prophet. The Wisdom of The Gathering.* And she remembered, too, the portrait that hung in every house. One of his people, the boy had said. The prophet.

The country-western song faded. They both turned to the radio as the DJ's voice came on.

"More details are coming out about that fiery

crash up on Skyview Road. Four tourists were killed last week when their rented Suburban veered over the edge and plummeted fifty feet into a ravine. The names of the victims have now been identified, and they are Arlo Zielinski and Dr. Douglas Comley of San Diego, as well as Dr. Comley's thirteen-year-old daughter, Grace. The fourth victim was Dr. Maura Isles from Boston. Drs. Isles and Comley were both in town to attend a medical conference. Icy roads and poor visibility during last Saturday's snowstorm may have been a factor."

The boy shut off the radio. "That's you, isn't it? You're the doctor from Boston." He reached into her backpack and took out her wallet. "I found your driver's license."

"I don't understand," she murmured. "There's been a terrible mistake. They aren't dead. They were alive when I left them. Grace and Elaine and Arlo, they were *alive*."

"They think she's you." He pointed to Elaine's purse.

"There was never any crash! And Doug skied out days ago!"

"He never made it."

"How do you know?"

"You heard what the radio said. They caught him before he got down the mountain. No one made it out alive, except for you. And that's only because you weren't there when they came."

"But they were coming to *rescue* us! There was a

snowplow. I heard it, coming up the road. Just before you . . ." Suddenly dizzy, she dropped her head between her knees. *This is wrong, all wrong.* The boy was lying to her. Confusing her, scaring her, so that she would stay with him. But how could the radio be wrong, too? A crashed Suburban with four people dead, the news report had said.

One of the victims was Dr. Maura Isles from Boston.

Her head was throbbing, an aftermath of the blow the boy had landed on her skull to silence her. The last memory she had before that blow was his hand clamped over her mouth as she'd flailed and kicked, as he'd hauled her away from the road, away from the brightness of sunlight and into the gloom of the trees.

There, in the woods, the memory abruptly ended.

She pressed her hands to her temples, trying to think through the ache, trying to understand everything she had heard. I must be hallucinating, she thought. Maybe he hit me hard enough to rupture a vessel. Maybe my brain is slowly being crushed by hemorrhaging blood. That's why none of this makes sense. I have to concentrate. I have to focus on what I *do* know, what I'm absolutely certain is true. I know that I'm alive. I know that Elaine and Grace did not die in a car crash. The radio is wrong. The boy is lying.

Slowly she struggled to stand. The boy and dog watched as she rose to her feet, wobbly as a new-born calf. It was only a few paces to the rough-hewn door, but after days of confinement, her legs felt weak and unsteady. If she tried to flee, she knew she could not outrun them.

"You don't really want to leave," he said.

"You can't keep me a prisoner."

"If you go, they'll find you."

"But you're not going to stop me?"

He sighed. "I can't, ma'am. If you don't want to be saved." He looked down at the dog, as though seeking his comfort. Sensing his owner's distress, the dog whined and licked the boy's hand.

She inched toward the door, half expecting the boy to yank her back. The boy remained motionless as she swung open the door, as she stepped outside into a pitch-black night. She stumbled into thigh-deep snow. Staggering back to her feet, she found herself facing the utter blackness of woods. Behind her, the fire glowed invitingly through the open doorway. Glancing back, she saw the boy standing there watching her, the firelight silhouetting his shoulders. She looked ahead again, at the trees, took two steps forward, and stopped. *I don't know where I am or where I'm going. I don't know what waits for me in those woods.* She saw no road, no vehicle, nothing but the claustrophobic trees surrounding that miserable little hovel. Surely Kingdom Come must be within walking distance. How far could one malnourished boy have dragged her unconscious body?

"It's thirty miles to the nearest town," he said.

"I'm going back to the valley. That's where they'll look for me."

"You'll get lost before you get there."

"I have to find my friends."

"In the dark?"

She glanced around at trees and darkness. "Where the hell am I?" she blurted in frustration.

"Safe, ma'am."

She faced him. Steadier now, she moved toward him, reminding herself that this was just a boy, not a man. It made him seem less threatening. "Who are you?" she asked.

The boy was silent.

"You won't even tell me your name."

"It doesn't matter."

"What are you doing out here by yourself? Don't you have a family?"

He took in a breath and it came out in a heavy sigh. "I wish I knew where they were."

Maura blinked as wind swirled snow into her eyes. She looked up as flakes began to fall, as fine as dust. The snow landed on her face like cold needle pricks. The dog emerged from the hovel and waded across to lick Maura's bare hand. His tongue left slick trails that cooled and chilled her skin. He seemed to be asking to be petted, and she laid her hand on his thick fur.

"If you want to freeze to death out here," the boy said, "I can't stop you. But I'm going in." He looked at the dog. "Come on, Bear."

The dog went stock-still. Maura felt the fur on the back of his neck suddenly bristle as every muscle in his body seemed to tense. Turning toward the trees, Bear gave a low growl that sent a chill whispering up Maura's back.

"Bear?" the boy said.

"What is it?" she asked. "Why's he doing that?"

"I don't know."

They both stared into the night, trying to see what had alarmed the animal. They heard the wind, the rustle of the trees, but nothing else.

The boy began to strap on a pair of snowshoes. "Go inside," he said. Then he and the dog walked off into the woods.

Maura hesitated only a few heartbeats. Much longer, and she would have been left too far behind to locate them in the dark. Heart thumping, she followed.

At first she could not see them, but she could hear the creak of the snowshoes and the thrashing of the dog through the underbrush. As she moved deeper into the woods, as her eyes adjusted to the darkness, she began to make out more details. The looming trunks of pines. And the two figures moving ahead, the boy striding purposefully, the dog leaping to clear deep snow. Through the trees ahead, she saw something else: a faint glow that was gauzy orange through the falling snowflakes.

She smelled smoke.

Her legs were wobbly from the effort to keep up,

but she kept struggling ahead, afraid to be left behind, wandering and lost. The boy and dog seemed tireless and they kept moving, covering what seemed like endless ground as she fell farther behind. But she would not lose them now, because she saw where they were headed. They were all being drawn to that ever-brightening glow.

When at last she caught up, the boy was standing very still, his back turned to her, his gaze focused down on the valley.

Far below them, the village of Kingdom Come was ablaze in flames.

"Oh my God," whispered Maura. "What happened?"

"They came back. I knew they would."

She stared down at the twin rows of flames, as orderly and regular as military campfires. This was no accident, she thought. Those flames did not spread from rooftop to rooftop. Someone had deliberately set the houses on fire.

The boy moved to the edge of the cliff, so close to the drop-off that for a panicked moment she thought he was about to leap off. He stared down, hypnotized by the destruction of Kingdom Come. The seductive power of fire trapped her gaze as well. She imagined the flames licking at the walls of the house where she had sheltered, turning all to ash. Snowflakes fell, melting on her cheeks to mingle with her tears. Tears for Doug and Arlo, for Elaine and Grace. Only now, as she watched the fires burn, did she truly believe they were dead.

"Why kill them?" she whispered. "Grace was only thirteen—just a girl. *Why?*"

"They do whatever he wants."

"Whatever *who* wants?"

"Jeremiah. The Prophet." On the boy's lips, the name sounded more like a curse than a name.

"The man in the painting," she said.

"And he shall gather the righteous. And lead them all to *hell*." He shoved the fur-trimmed hood off his head, and she could see his profile in the gloom, his jaw squared in anger.

"Whose houses were those?" she asked. "Who lived in Kingdom Come?"

"My mother. My sister." His voice broke and he lowered his head in mourning for a village that was now engulfed in flames. "The chosen ones."

TWENTY-FOUR

WHEN JANE, GABRIEL, AND SANSONE PULLED up at the accident site, they found the search team already waiting for them at the side of the road. Jane recognized Sheriff Fahey and Deputy Martineau, as well as that old crank Montgomery Loftus, who owned the land and greeted the new arrivals with a grudging nod. At least this time, he wasn't brandishing a rifle.

"Did you bring the items?" asked Fahey.

Jane held up a satchel. "We took a number of things out of her house. There are pillowcases and some clothes from her laundry hamper. It should be enough to give them the scent."

"We can hold on to these?"

"Keep them. As long as it takes to find her."

"This is the logical place to start." Fahey handed off the satchel to Deputy Martineau. "If she managed to survive the crash and wandered away, they may be able to pick up her scent down there."

Jane and Gabriel moved to the edge of the road

and looked down at the ravine. The wrecked Suburban was still wedged there, its charred surface
now covered with snow. She did not see how anyone
could have survived this accident, much less walked
away from it. But Maura's luggage had been in that
vehicle, so it was only logical to assume that Maura
herself had been riding in the ill-fated SUV when it
plunged off the cliff. Jane tried to imagine how that
miraculous survival could have happened. Perhaps
Maura was thrown from the vehicle early and
landed on soft snow, saving her from incineration.
Perhaps she'd wandered away from the wreckage,
dazed and amnesiac. Jane scanned the rugged terrain
and felt little optimism that they would find Maura
alive. This was why she had not informed Daniel
Brophy about their return to Wyoming. Even had
she been able to penetrate the wall of seclusion that
now cloaked him, she could offer him no hope of a
different outcome, no possibility that this search
would change the ultimate answer. If Maura had
been in that Suburban, she was now almost certainly
dead. And all they were here to do was find the
body.

The dogs and searchers began their hike down to
the wreckage, pausing every few yards as the dogs
sniffed the area, seeking the scent they'd now been
primed to follow. Sansone moved down with them,
but he stood apart, as though aware the team considered him an outsider. And no wonder they did. He
was a man of few smiles, a dark and unapproachable

figure to whom past tragedies seemed to cling like a cloak.

"Is that guy another priest?"

Jane turned to see Loftus standing beside her, scowling down at the invaders on his property. "No, he's just a friend," she said.

"Deputy Martineau told me you came with a priest last time. And now this fella. Huh," Loftus grunted. "Interesting friends she had."

"Maura was an interesting person."

"So I gather. But we all end up the same way." He yanked down the brim of his hat, gave them a nod, and started back to his pickup truck, leaving Jane and Gabriel alone at the edge of the road.

"He's going to take it hard when they find her body," said Gabriel, staring down at Sansone.

"You think she's down there."

"We have to be prepared for the inevitable." He watched as Sansone moved steadily down the ravine. "He's in love with her, isn't he?"

She gave a sad laugh. "You think?"

"Whatever his reasons for being here, I'm glad he came. He's made things a lot easier."

"Money usually does." Sansone's private jet had whisked them straight from Boston to Jackson Hole, sparing them the ordeal of scrambling for flight reservations, waiting in security lines, and filing the paperwork to pack their weapons. Yes, money did make things easier. But it doesn't make you happier, she thought, looking down at Sansone, who appeared as somber as a mourner as he stood beside the wrecked Suburban.

The searchers were now moving around the vehicle in ever-widening circles, clearly not picking up any scent. When at last Martineau and Fahey started hiking back up the trail, carrying the satchel with Maura's belongings, Jane knew they'd given up.

"They didn't pick up anything?" Gabriel asked as the two men emerged onto the road, both breathing hard.

"Not a whiff." Martineau tossed the satchel into his vehicle and slammed the door.

"You think too much time has gone by?" asked Jane. "Maybe her scent's dissipated."

"One of those dogs is trained to find cadavers, and he's not signaling anything, either. The handler thinks the real problem is the fire. The smell of gasoline and smoke is overwhelming their noses. And then there's the heavy snowfall." He looked down at the search team, which was starting to head up toward them. "If she's down there, I don't think we're going to find her until spring."

"You're giving up?" said Jane.

"What else can we do? The dogs aren't finding anything."

"So we just leave her body down there? Where scavengers can get it?"

Fahey reacted to her dismay with a tired sigh. "Where do you suggest we start digging, ma'am? Point out the spot, and we'll do it. But you have to accept the fact this is now a recovery, not a rescue. Even if she survived the crash, she wouldn't have survived the exposure. Not after all this time."

Searchers clambered back onto the road, and Jane saw flushed faces, downcast expressions. The dogs seemed just as discouraged, tails no longer wagging.

The last one up the trail was Sansone, and he looked the grimmest of all. "They didn't give it enough time," he said.

"Even if the dogs did find her," Fahey quietly pointed out, "it won't change the outcome."

"But at least we'd know. We'd have a body to bury," said Sansone.

"I know it's a hard thing to accept, that you don't have closure. But out here, sir, that's the way it sometimes is. Hunters have heart attacks. Hikers get lost. Small planes go down. Sometimes we don't find the remains for months, even years. Mother Nature chooses when to give them up." Fahey glanced up as snow began to fall again, as dry and powdery as talc. "And she's not ready to give up this body. Not today."

He was sixteen years old, born and raised in Wyoming, and his name was Julian Henry Perkins. But only grown-ups—his teachers, his foster parents, and his caseworker—ever called him that. At school, on a good day, his classmates called him Julie-Ann. On a bad day, they called him Fuckface Annie. He hated his name, but it was what his mom had chosen for him after she'd seen some movie with a hero named Julian. That was just like his mom, always doing something loopy like calling her son a name no one else had. Or dumping Julian and his sister with their grandfather while she ran off with a drummer. Or, ten years later, suddenly showing up to reclaim her kids after she'd discovered the true meaning of life, with a prophet named Jeremiah Goode.

The boy told all this to Maura as they slowly made their way down the slope, the dog panting after them. A day had passed since they'd watched the fires burning in Kingdom Come; only now did the boy feel it was safe for them to descend into the valley. On her boots, he had strapped a pair of makeshift snowshoes, which he'd crafted using tools scavenged from conveniently unlocked houses in the town of Pinedale. She thought of pointing out to him that this was theft, not scavenging, but she did not think he'd appreciate the difference.

"So what do you want to be called, since you don't like the name Julian?" Maura asked as they tramped toward Kingdom Come.

"I don't care."

"Most people care what they're called."

"I don't see why people need names at all."

"Is that why you keep calling me *ma'am*?"

"Animals don't use names and they get along fine. Better than most people."

"But I can't keep saying *hey you*."

They walked on for a while, snowshoes creaking, the boy leading the way. He cut a ragged figure, moving across that white landscape, the dog huffing at his heels. And here she was, willingly following those two wild and filthy creatures. Maybe it was Stockholm syndrome; for whatever reason, she'd given up any thoughts of fleeing from the boy. She relied on him for food and shelter, and except for the initial blow on the head that first day, when he'd been frantic to keep her quiet, he had not hurt her. In fact, he'd made no move to even touch her. So she had settled into the wary role of part prisoner, part guest, and in that role she followed him into the valley.

"Rat," he suddenly said over his shoulder.

"What?"

"That's what my sister, Carrie, calls me."

"That's not a very nice name."

"It's okay. It's from that movie, about the rat who cooks."

"You mean *Ratatouille*?"

"Yeah. Our grandpa took us to see it. I liked that movie."

"I did, too," said Maura.

"Anyway, she started calling me Rat, because sometimes I'd cook her breakfast in the morning. But she's the only one ever calls me that. It's my secret name."

"So I guess I'm not allowed to use it."

He walked on for a moment, snowshoes swishing

down the slope. After a long silence, he stopped and looked back at her, as if, after much thought, he'd finally come to a decision. "I guess you can, too," he said, then continued walking. "But you can't tell anyone."

A boy named Rat and a dog named Bear. Right.

She was starting to get into the rhythm of walking on snowshoes, moving more easily, but still struggling to keep up with the boy and dog.

"So your mom and sister were living here, in the valley. What about your father?" she asked.

"He's dead."

"Oh. I'm sorry."

"Died when I was four."

"And where's your grandpa?"

"He died last year."

"I'm sorry," she repeated automatically.

He stopped and looked back. "You don't need to keep saying that."

But I am sorry, she thought, looking at his lonely figure standing against the vast background of white. I'm sorry that the men who loved you are gone. I'm sorry that your mother seems to drop in and out of your life whenever it suits her. I'm sorry that the only one you seem able to count on, the only one who stands by you, has four legs and a tail.

They descended deeper into the valley, entering the zone of destruction. Coming down the ridge, they had caught whiffs of the stench from the burned buildings. With every step they took, the damage appeared more horrifying. Every house had been reduced to blackened ruins, the village devastated as completely as if conquerors had swept through, intent on erasing it from the face of the earth. Except for the creak of their snowshoes, the sound of their breathing, the world was silent.

They came to a halt next to the remains of the house where Maura and her companions had sheltered. Tears suddenly clouded her vision as she stared at charred wood and shattered glass. Rat and Bear moved on down the line of burned homes, but Maura remained where she was, and in that silence she felt the presence of ghosts. Grace and Elaine, Arlo and Douglas, people whom she had not particularly liked, but with whom she had bonded nevertheless. Here they still lingered, whispering warnings from the ruins. *Leave this place. While you can.* Looking down, she saw tire tracks. This was the proof of arson. While the fires were raging, melting the snow, a truck had left a record of its passage pressed into the now frozen mud.

She heard an anguished cry and turned in alarm. Rat dropped to his knees beside one of the burned houses. As she moved toward him, she saw that he was clutching something in both hands, like a rosary.

"She wouldn't have left this!"

"What is it, Rat?"

"Carrie's. Grandpa gave it to her and she *never* took it off." Slowly he opened his hands and revealed a heart-shaped pendant, still attached to a strand of broken gold chain.

"This is your sister's?"

"Something's wrong. It's all *wrong*." He rose to his feet, agitated, and began digging into the charred remains of the house.

"What are you doing?" asked Maura.

"This was our house. Mom's and Carrie's." He pawed through the ashes, and his gloves were soon black with soot.

"This pendant doesn't look like it was in the fire, Rat."

"I found it on the road. Like she dropped it there." He pulled up a burned timber and with a desperate grunt heaved it aside, scattering ashes.

She looked at the ground, which was now down to bare mud after the heat of the fire had melted the snow cover. The pendant might have been lying here for days, she thought. What else had the snow hidden from them? As the boy continued to attack the ruins of his family's house, tearing at charred boards, searching for scraps of his lost mother and sister, Maura stared at Carrie's pendant, trying to understand how something that was cherished could end up abandoned under the snow. She remembered what they'd found inside these houses. The untouched meals, the dead canary.

And the blood. The pool of it at the bottom of the stairs, left to congeal and freeze on the floorboards after the body had been removed. These families didn't just walk away, she thought. They were forced from their homes with such haste that meals were left behind and a child could not pause to retrieve a treasured necklace. This is why the fires were set, she thought. To hide what happened to the families of Kingdom Come.

Bear gave a soft growl. She looked down at him and saw that he was crouched with teeth bared, his ears laid back. He was looking up toward the valley road.

"Rat," she said.

The boy wasn't listening. His attention was focused on digging into the remains of the house where his mother and Carrie had lived.

The dog gave another growl, deeper, more insistent, and the scruff of his neck stood up. Something was coming down that road. Something that scared him.

"*Rat.*"

At last the boy looked up, filthy with soot. He saw the dog, and his gaze snapped up toward the road. Only then did they hear the faint growl of an approaching vehicle, making its way into the valley.

"They're coming back," he said. He grabbed her arm and pulled her toward the cover of trees.

"Wait." She yanked free. "What if it's the police, looking for me?"

"You don't want to be found here. *Run,* lady!"

He turned and sprang away, moving faster than she thought possible on snowshoes. The approaching

vehicle had cut off their easiest route out of Kingdom Come, and any trail up the slope would leave
them fully exposed to view. The boy was fleeing in
the only direction left to them, into the woods.

For a moment she hesitated; so did the dog. Nervously, Bear glanced at his departing master, then
looked at Maura as if to say *What are you waiting
for?* If I follow the boy, she thought, I could be running away from my own rescuers. Am I so thoroughly brainwashed that I'd willingly stick with my
kidnapper?

*What if the boy is right? What if Death is coming
down that road for me?*

Bear suddenly took off running after his master.

That was what made her finally choose. When
even a dog had the sense to flee, she knew it was time
to follow.

She chased after them, her snowshoes clacking
across the frozen mud. Beyond the last burned
house, the mud gave way to deep snow again. Rat
was far ahead and moving into the woods. She labored to catch up, already out of breath as she frantically kicked up powder. Just as she reached the
trees, she heard the sound of a dog barking. A different dog, not Bear. She ducked behind a pine and
looked back at Kingdom Come.

A black SUV pulled to a stop among the ruins, and
a large dog jumped out. Two men emerged, carrying
rifles, and they stood scanning the burned village.
Although they were too far away for Maura to make

out their faces, they clearly seemed to be searching for something.

A paw suddenly landed on her back. With a gasp, she turned and came face-to-face with Bear, his pink tongue lolling out.

"Now do you believe me?" whispered Rat, who was crouched right behind her.

"They could be hunters."

"I know dogs. That's a bloodhound they got there."

One of the men reached into the SUV and pulled out a satchel. Crouching beside the hound, he let it sniff the contents.

"He's giving it the scent," said Rat.

"Who are they tracking?"

The hound was moving now, wandering among the ruins, nose to the ground. But the smell of the fire seemed to confuse it, and it paused beside the blackened timbers where Maura and Julian had earlier lingered. As the men waited, the dog circled, trying to catch a whiff of its quarry while the two men fanned out, searching the area.

"Hey," one man yelled, and pointed to the ground. "Snowshoe prints!"

"They've spotted our tracks," said Rat. "Don't need a dog to find us now." He backed away. "Let's go."

"Where?"

He was already moving deeper into the woods, not looking back to see whether she was behind him, not caring that his snowshoes were clattering through underbrush. The hound began baying, pulling in their direction.

Maura chased after the boy. He moved like a panicked deer, shoving through branches, scattering snow in his wake. She could hear the men in pursuit behind them, shouting to each other, and the bloodhound's excited howling. But even as she scrambled through the woods, the debate still raged in her head. *Am I running from my own rescuers?*

The rifle shot answered her question. A chunk of wood exploded off the tree near her head, and she heard the bloodhound baying closer. Terror blasted new energy into her bloodstream. Suddenly her muscles were pumping wildly, legs thrashing ahead through the woods.

Another rifle shot exploded. Another chunk of bark splintered off a tree. Then she heard a curse, and the next shot went wild.

"Fucking snow!" one of the men yelled. Without snowshoes, they were sinking, mired in the drifts.

"Let the dog loose! He'll bring her down!"

"Go, boy. *Get her.*"

Fresh panic sent Maura plunging ahead, but she could hear the bloodhound gaining on her. On snowshoes, she could outpace her human pursuers, but she could not outrun a dog. In desperation, she scanned the trees for a glimpse of Rat. How had he gotten so far ahead? She was on her own now, isolated prey, and the hound was closing in. The snowshoes made her clumsy, and the undergrowth was too thick here, clawing at the frames.

Ahead, she saw a break in the trees.

She burst through a tangle of branches, into a broad clearing. In a glance she took in the skeletal beams of three new houses, frozen in mid-construction. At the far edge of the clearing, an excavator was parked, its cab almost buried beneath snow. Beside it stood Rat, frantically waving at her.

She started toward him. But halfway across, she knew she would not outrun the bloodhound. She heard it crash through the underbrush behind her. It landed like an anvil against her shoulders and she pitched forward. She put out her hands to break her fall and her arms sank in elbow-deep snow. As she landed, she heard a strangely metallic clunk beneath her, felt something slice right through her glove and into her hand. Sputtering, her face coated in icy powder, she struggled to push herself up, but debris shifted away beneath her weight, and she floundered, as helpless as if trapped in quicksand.

The bloodhound wheeled around and leaped at her again. Weakly she raised an arm to protect her throat and waited to feel teeth sink into her flesh.

A flash of gray suddenly soared past, and Bear collided in midair with the bloodhound. The yelp was as startling as a human shriek. The two dogs thrashed and rolled, ripping at fur, their growls so savage that Maura could only huddle in terror. Red spatters stained the snow, shockingly bright. The hound tried to pull away, but Bear gave him no chance to retreat, and again dove straight at him. Both dogs tumbled, plowing a blood-smeared trench through the snow.

"Bear, stop!" commanded Rat. He came into the clearing, clutching a branch, ready to swing it. But the bloodhound had had enough, and the instant Bear released him, the hound fled back toward the truck, crashing through underbrush in his panic to escape.

"You're bleeding," said Rat.

She tore off her soaked glove and stared at her lacerated palm. The slice was clean and deep, made by something razor-sharp. In the churned-up snow, she saw scraps of sheet metal and a jumble of dull gray canisters, dredged up by the dogs when they'd thrashed and rolled. All around her were snow-covered hummocks, and she realized she was kneeling in a field of construction debris. She looked down at her bleeding hand. *Just the place to pick up tetanus.*

A rifle blast jolted her straight. The men had not yet given up the chase.

Rat pulled her to her feet and they plunged back into the cover of woods. Though their tracks would be easy to follow, the men pursuing them would not be able to keep up in deep snow. Bear led the way, his bloodstained fur like a scarlet flag waving ahead of them as he trotted deeper into the valley. Blood continued to stream from Maura's sliced palm, and she pressed her already saturated glove against the wound as she obsessed irrationally about bacteria and gangrene.

"Once we lose them," said Rat, "we have to get back up the ridge."

"They'll track us back to your shelter."

"We can't stay there. We'll pack as much food as we can carry and keep moving."

"Who were those men?"

"I don't know."

"Were they from The Gathering?"

"I don't know."

"Goddamn it, Rat. What *do* you know?"

He glanced back at her. "How to stay alive."

They were climbing now, moving steadily up the ridge, and every step was a labor. She did not know how he could cover ground so quickly.

"You have to get me to a telephone," she said. "Let me call the police."

"He owns them. They just do what he wants."

"Are you talking about Jeremiah?"

"No one goes against the Prophet. No one ever fights back, not even my mom. Not even when they—" He stopped talking and suddenly focused his energy on attacking the ridge.

She halted on the slope, out of breath. "What did they do to your mom?"

He just kept climbing, his anger driving him at a killing pace.

"Rat." She scrambled to catch up. "Listen to me.

I have friends, people I trust. Just get me to a telephone."

He paused, his breath clouding the air like a steam engine. "Who are you going to call?"

Daniel was her first thought. But she remembered all the times when she could not reach him, all the awkward phone conversations when others were listening in, and he had been forced to speak in code. Now, when she needed him most, she did not know if she could count on him.

Maybe I never could.

"Who is this friend?" Rat persisted.

"Her name is Jane Rizzoli."

TWENTY-FIVE

S HERIFF FAHEY DID NOT LOOK HAPPY TO SEE Jane again. Even from across the room, she could read his face through the glass partition, a look of dismay, as if he expected her to issue some new demand. He rose from his desk and resignedly stood waiting in his doorway as she crossed toward him, past law enforcement personnel who were now familiar with the three visitors from Boston. Before she could ask the expected question, he headed her off with the same answer he'd given her for two days in a row.

"There are no new developments," he said.

"I didn't come in expecting any," said Jane.

"Trust me, I'll call you if anything changes. There's really no need for you folks to keep dropping in." He glanced past her shoulder. "So where are your two gentlemen today?"

"They're back at the hotel, packing. I thought I'd come by to thank you before we head to the airport."

"You're leaving?"

"We're flying back to Boston this afternoon."

"I hear rumors there's a private jet involved. Must be nice."

"It's not my jet."

"His, huh? The guy in black. He's a strange fella."

"Sansone's a good man."

"Sometimes it's hard to know. We see a lot of folks around here who are loaded with money. Hollywood types, big-shot politicians. Buy themselves a few hundred acres, call themselves ranchers, and then they think they got a right to tell us how to do our jobs." Although he was talking about nameless others, his words were really directed at her, at the Boston outsiders who'd swooped into his county and sucked up his attention.

"She was our friend," said Jane. "You can understand why we'd want to do everything possible to find her."

"Quite a group of friends she collected. Cops. A priest. A rich guy. Must've been quite a woman."

"She was." She looked down as her cell phone rang and saw a Wyoming area code, but she did not recognize the number. "Excuse me," she said to Fahey and answered the call. "Detective Rizzoli."

"Jane?" The voice was close to a sob. "Thank God you answered!"

For a moment Jane could not utter a sound. She stood mute and paralyzed, the cell phone pressed to her ear, the noise of the sheriff's office drowned out by the pounding of her own pulse. *I am talking to a ghost.*

"I thought you were dead!" Jane blurted.

"I'm alive. I'm okay!"

"Jesus, Maura, we had your memorial service!" Tears suddenly stung Jane's eyes, and she wiped them away with an impatient swipe of her sleeve. "Where the hell are you? Do you have any idea what—"

"Listen. *Listen to me.*"

Jane sucked in a breath. "I'm right here."

"I need you to come to Wyoming. Please come and get me."

"We're already here."

"What?"

"We've been working with the police to find your body."

"Which police?"

"The Sublette County sheriff. I'm standing in his office right now." She turned to find that Fahey was right beside her, his eyes full of questions. "Just tell us where you are and we'll come get you."

There was no answer.

"Maura? Maura?"

The line had gone dead. She hung up and stared at the number on her call history. "I need an address!" she yelled, and recited the phone number. "It's a Wyoming area code!"

"That was *her*?" Fahey asked.

"She's alive!" Jane gave a joyous laugh as she dialed the number. It rang and rang unanswered. She disconnected and redialed. Again, there was no answer. She stared at her cell phone, willing it to ring again.

Fahey went back to his desk and tried calling from his phone. By now everyone in the office was riveted to the conversation, and they watched as he punched in the number. He stood drumming his fingers on the desk and finally hung up.

"I'm not getting an answer, either," he said.

"But she just called me from that number."

"What did she say?"

"She asked me to come get her."

"Did she give you any idea where she is? What happened to her?"

"She never got the chance. We were cut off." Jane looked down at her silent cell phone, as if it had betrayed her.

"Got the address!" a deputy called out. "The phone's listed to a Norma Jacqueline Brindell, up on Doyle Mountain."

"Where's that?" said Jane.

Fahey said, "That's a good five miles west of the accident scene. How the hell'd she end up out there?"

"Show me on the map."

They crossed to the county map displayed on the wall, and he tapped a finger on a remote corner. "There's nothing but a few seasonal cabins. I doubt anyone's living there this time of year."

She looked at the deputy who'd given them the address. "Are you sure about that location?"

"That's where the call came from, ma'am."

"Keep calling it. See if anyone answers," said Fahey. He looked at the dispatcher. "Check and see who we've got in that area right now."

Jane looked at the map again and saw wide expanses with few roads and rugged elevations. How had Maura ended up there, so far from the wrecked Suburban? She scanned the map, her gaze moving back and forth between the accident site and Doyle Mountain. Five miles due west. She pictured snowbound valleys and towering crags. Scenic country, to be sure, but no villages, no restaurants, nothing to attract an East Coast tourist.

The dispatcher called out: "Deputy Martineau just radioed in. Says he'll handle the call. He's heading to Doyle Mountain now."

The phone in the kitchen would not stop ringing.

"Let me answer it," said Maura.

"We have to leave." The boy was emptying out pantry cabinets and throwing food into his backpack. "I saw a shovel on the back porch. Get it."

"That's my friend trying to reach me."

"The police will be coming."

"It's okay, Rat. You can trust her."

"But you can't trust *them*."

The phone was ringing again. She turned to answer

it, but the boy snatched the cord and wrenched it from the wall. "Do you *want* to die?" he yelled.

Maura dropped the dead receiver and backed away. In his panic, the boy looked frightening, even dangerous. She glanced at the cord dangling from his fist, a fist that was powerful enough to batter a face, to crush a trachea.

He threw down the cord and took a breath. "If you want to come with me, we need to leave now."

"I'm sorry, Rat," she said quietly. "But I'm not going with you. I'm going to wait here for my friend."

What she saw in his eyes wasn't anger, but sorrow. In silence he strapped on his backpack and took her snowshoes, which she would no longer need. Without a backward look, without even a goodbye, he turned to the door. "Let's go, Bear," he said.

The dog hesitated, glancing back and forth between them, as though trying to understand these crazy humans.

"Bear."

"Wait," said Maura. "Stay with me. We'll go back to town together."

"I don't belong in town, ma'am. I never did."

"You can't wander alone out there."

"I'm not wandering. I know where I'm going." Again, he looked at his dog, and this time Bear followed him.

Maura watched the boy walk out the back door, the dog at his heels. Through the broken kitchen window, she saw them trudge across the snow toward the woods. The wild child and his companion, returning to the mountains. A moment later they vanished among the trees, and she wondered if they had existed at all. If, in her fear and isolation, she had conjured up imaginary saviors. But no, she could see their prints tracking through the snow. The boy was real.

Just as real as Jane's voice had been on the phone. The outside world had not vanished after all. Beyond those mountains, there were still cities, still people going about their normal business. People who did not skulk in the woods like hunted animals. For too long, she'd been trapped in the boy's company, had almost started to believe, as he did, that the wilderness was the only safe place.

It was time to go back to that real world. Her world.

She examined the telephone and saw that the cord was too badly damaged to reconnect, but she had no doubt that Jane would nevertheless be able to track her location. Now all I have to do is wait, she thought. Jane knows I'm alive. Someone will come for me.

She went into the living room and sat down on the sofa. The cabin was unheated, and wind blew in through the broken kitchen window, so she kept her jacket zipped. She felt guilty about that window, which Rat had smashed so they could get into the house. Then there was the ruined phone cord and the ransacked pantry, all damage that she would pay for, of course. She'd mail a check with a sincere apology. Sitting in this stranger's house, a house in which she was trespassing, she stared at the photos on the bookshelves. She saw pictures of three young children in various settings, and a gray-haired woman, proudly holding up an impressive trout. The books in the library were summer entertainment fare. Mary Higgins Clark and Danielle Steel, the collection of a woman with traditional tastes, who liked romance novels and ceramic kittens. A woman she would probably never meet face-to-face, but to whom she'd always be grateful. *Your telephone saved my life.*

Someone pounded on the front door.

She jolted to her feet. She had not heard the vehicle pull up to the house, but through the living room window, she saw a Sublette County Sheriff's Department SUV. *At last my nightmare is over,* she thought as she opened the front door. *I'm going home.*

A young deputy with the name tag MARTINEAU stood on the porch. He had close-cropped hair and the stern bearing of a man who took his job seriously. "Ma'am?" he said. "Are you the one who made the phone call?"

"Yes! Yes, yes, *yes.*" Maura wanted to throw her arms around him, but he did not look like a cop who welcomed hugs. "You have no idea how glad I am to see you!"

"Can I have your name, please?"

"I'm Dr. Maura Isles. I believe there've been premature rumors of my death." Her laugh sounded wild, almost unhinged. "Obviously, it's not true!"

He peered past her, into the house. "How did you get into this residence? Did someone let you in?"

She felt her face flush with guilt. "I'm afraid we had to break a window to get in. And there's some other damage. But I promise, I'll pay for it."

"We?"

She paused, suddenly afraid that she'd get the boy into trouble. "I didn't have a choice," she said. "I needed to get to a telephone. So I broke into the house. I hope that's not a hanging offense around here."

At last he smiled, but something was wrong about that smile. It didn't quite reach his eyes. "Let's get you back to town," he said. "You can tell us all about it."

Even as she climbed into his backseat, even as he swung the door shut, she was trying to understand what bothered her about this young deputy. The SUV was a sheriff's department vehicle, and a metal grate isolated her in the backseat, trapping her in a cage meant to hold prisoners.

As the deputy slid in behind the steering wheel, his radio crackled to life. "Bobby, this is Dispatch," a woman's voice said. "You make it up to Doyle Mountain yet?"

"Ten four, Jan. Just checked out the whole house," Deputy Martineau answered.

"You find her there? 'Cause this Boston cop's on our backs."

"Sorry, I didn't."

"Anyone there at all?"

"Must've been a hoax, 'cause no one's here. Leaving the scene now, ten seventeen."

Maura stared through the grate and suddenly met the deputy's gaze in the rearview mirror. The look he gave her froze her blood. *I saw it in his smile. I knew there was something wrong.*

"I'm here!" Maura screamed. "Help me! I'm *here*!"

Deputy Martineau had already switched off the radio.

She reached for the door handle, but there was nothing to grab. *Cop car. No way out.* Frantically she pounded on the windows, shrieking, oblivious to the pain of her fists slamming against the glass. He started the engine. What came next, a drive to a lonely spot and an execution? Her body left to the mercy of scavengers? Panic made her claw at the prisoner grate, but flesh and bone were no match for steel.

He turned the SUV around in the driveway, and abruptly slammed on the brake. "Shit," he muttered. "Where did *you* come from?"

The dog stood in the road, blocking the vehicle.

Deputy Martineau leaned on his horn. "Get the fuck out of the way!" he yelled.

Instead of retreating, Bear rose up on his hind legs, planted two paws on the hood, and began barking.

For a moment the deputy stared at the animal, debating whether to simply hit the accelerator and run over him. "Shit. No point getting blood all over the bumper," he muttered, and stepped out of the SUV.

Bear dropped to all fours and inched toward him, growling.

The deputy raised his weapon and took aim. So intent was he on hitting his target, he didn't notice the shovel swinging at the back of his head. It slammed into his skull and he staggered against the vehicle, his weapon flying into the snow.

"Nobody shoots my dog," said Rat. He yanked open Maura's door. "Time to go, lady."

"Wait, the radio! Let me call for help!"

"Are you *ever* going to listen to me?"

As she scrambled out of the SUV, she saw that the deputy was on his knees and had retrieved his weapon. Just as he lifted it, the boy flew at him. The two went sprawling. Rolled over and over in the snow, wrestling for the gun.

The explosion seemed to freeze time.

In the sudden silence, even the dog went completely still. Slowly Rat rolled away and staggered to his feet. The front of his jacket was splattered with red. But it was not his blood.

Maura dropped to her knees beside the deputy. He was still alive, his eyes open and wild with panic, blood fountaining from his neck. She pressed against the wound to stop the arterial gush, but already his blood soaked the snow. Already, the light was fading from his eyes.

"Get on the radio," she yelled at the boy. "Call for help."

"Didn't mean to," the boy whispered. "It went off by itself . . ."

Gurgling sounds came from the deputy's throat. As his last breath fled his body, so, too, did his soul. She watched his eyes darken, saw the muscles in his neck go slack. The blood that had been surging from the wound slowed to a trickle. Too stunned to move, she knelt in the trampled snow and did not hear the approaching vehicle.

But Rat did. He yanked her up by the arm with such force that she was wrenched straight to her feet. Only then did she glimpse the pickup truck turning into the driveway.

Rat snatched up the deputy's weapon, just as the rifle blast slammed into the SUV.

A second rifle blast blew out the SUV's window, and pellets of glass stung Maura's scalp.

Those aren't warning shots; he's aiming to kill.

Rat took off for the trees, and she was right behind him. By the time the pickup pulled up behind the deputy's vehicle, they were already scrambling into the woods. Maura heard a third blast of the rifle, but she did not look back. She kept her focus on Rat, who was leading them deeper into cover, loaded down with the ungainly backpack. He paused only to hand her the snowshoes. In seconds she had them strapped on.

Then they were moving again, the boy leading the way as they headed into the wild.

TWENTY-SIX

JANE STARED DOWN AT THE SPOT WHERE THE deputy's body had been found, and she tried to read the snow. The corpse had already been removed. Personnel from both the county sheriff's office and the Wyoming Department of Criminal Investigations had searched the site, trampling the snow, and she could distinguish at least half a dozen different shoe impressions. What caught her attention, and the attention of the other investigators, were the snowshoe tracks. They led away from the dead deputy's SUV and headed toward the woods. Moving in that same direction were a dog's paw prints, as well as a set of boot prints—a woman's size seven, possibly Maura's. The trio of prints led into the woods, where the boot tracks later stopped. There a second pair of snowshoe tracks began.

Maura paused among those trees to strap on the snowshoes. And then she kept running.

Jane tried to picture the scenario that would explain these prints. Her initial theory was that whoever had killed Martineau had then taken the deputy's weapon and forced Maura into the woods with him. But these tracks didn't fit the theory. Staring down at the snow, Jane spotted a boot impression that overlaid the snowshoe track. Which meant that Maura had been trailing *behind* her presumed captor, not pushed in front of him. Jane stood mulling over this puzzle, trying to match what she saw here with what made sense. Why would Maura willingly follow a cop-killer into the woods? Why did she make that phone call in the first place? Had she been forced to lure a deputy into this trap?

"They've picked up fingerprints everywhere," said Gabriel.

She turned to her husband, who'd just come out of the house. "Where?"

"On the broken window, the kitchen cabinets. The phone."

"Where she made the call."

Gabriel nodded. "The cord was wrenched out of the wall. Obviously someone wanted to cut off the conversation." He nodded at the slain deputy's vehicle. "They lifted prints off the car door as well. There's a good chance we'll know who we're dealing with."

"She sure as hell didn't act like a hostage," a voice insisted. "I'm telling you, she ran for those trees. No one was dragging her."

Jane turned to watch the conversation between the Wyoming DCI detective and Montgomery Loftus, who had reported the slaying. The old rancher's voice had risen in agitation, drawing everyone's attention.

"I saw them here, bending over his body like two vultures. Man and a woman. The man, he picks up the gun and turns toward me. I figure he's gonna try to blast my truck, so I got off a shot."

"More than one shot, it looks like to me," said the detective.

"Yeah. Well, might've been three or four." Loftus eyed the SUV's shattered window. "Afraid that there's my fault. But what the hell'd you expect me to do? Not defend myself? Soon as I got off the first few shots, they both took off for the woods."

"Independently? Or was the woman forced?"

"Forced?" Loftus snorted. "She ran after him. No one was making her do it."

No one except a pissed-off old rancher shooting at her. Jane did not like the way this story was being spun, as if Maura was one half of Bonnie and Clyde. Yet she couldn't contradict what the footprints in the snow were telling her. Maura hadn't been dragged into the woods; she had fled.

Sansone said, "How is it you happened to be on this property, Mr. Loftus?" Everyone turned to look at him. He had been silent up till then, an unapproachable figure who had drawn curious glances from DCI personnel, but no one had dared to challenge his presence at the crime scene.

Though Sansone's question had been asked in a

respectful tone, Loftus bristled. "You implying something, mister?"

"This seems like a rather out-of-the-way place to just show up. I wondered why you happened to be here."

"Because Bobby called me."

"Deputy Martineau?"

"He said he was up on Doyle Mountain, and he thought he might have a problem. I live just east of here, so I offered to come by in case he needed a hand."

"Is this normal procedure, for a law enforcement officer to call a civilian when he needs assistance?"

"I don't know what it's like in Boston, mister. But out here, when someone gets in a jam, folks are quick to step in and help. Especially when it's a lawman."

Sheriff Fahey added, "I'm sure Mr. Loftus was just trying to be a good citizen, Mr. Sansone. We've got a big county to cover, a lot of territory. When your closest backup is twenty miles away, we're lucky to have folks like him to call on."

"I didn't mean to question Mr. Loftus's motives."

"But that's what you were doing," said Loftus. "Hell, I know where this is going. Next you'll ask if I'm the one who killed Bobby." He strode over to his pickup and pulled out his rifle. "Here, Detective Pasternak!" He handed the weapon to the DCI detective. "Feel free to confiscate it. Run it though your fancy lab."

"Come on, Monty." Fahey sighed. "No one thinks you killed Bobby."

"These folks from Boston don't believe me."

Jane stepped into the conversation. "Mr. Loftus, it's not like that at all. We're just trying to understand what went down here."

"I told you what I saw. They left Bobby Martineau bleeding to death. And they ran."

"Maura wouldn't do that."

"You weren't here. You didn't see her take off into those woods. Sure as hell acted like she did something wrong."

"Then you misinterpreted it."

"I saw what I saw."

Gabriel said, "A lot of these questions might be answered by the dash camera." He looked at Sheriff Fahey. "We should take a look at the deputy's video."

Fahey suddenly looked uncomfortable. "I'm afraid there's a problem with that."

"A problem?"

"The camera in Deputy Martineau's vehicle wasn't recording."

Jane stared at the sheriff in disbelief. "How did that happen?"

"We don't know how it happened. It was turned off."

"Why would Martineau shut it down? You must have regulations against that."

"Maybe he didn't do it," Fahey said. "Maybe someone else turned off the dash cam."

"Don't tell me," she muttered. "You're going to blame this on Maura, too."

Fahey flushed. "You keep reminding us that she works with law enforcement. She'd know about dash cameras."

"Excuse me," cut in Detective Pasternak from the state's Department of Criminal Investigations. "I'm just getting up to speed on who Dr. Isles is. I'd like to know more about her."

Although he'd introduced himself earlier, this was the first time Jane had focused fully on Pasternak. Wan and sniffling, his storklike neck exposed to the cold, he looked like a man longing to be in a warm office, not shivering on this windswept driveway.

"I can tell you about her," said Jane.

"How well do you know her?"

"We're colleagues. We've been through a lot together."

"You think you can paint a full picture for me?"

Jane thought about how easy it would be to skew this man's impression of Maura in one way or another. It was all in which details she chose to reveal. Emphasize Maura's professionalism, and he'd see a scientist, reliable and law abiding. But divulge different details, and the portrait became murkier, the features obscured by shadows. Her dark and blood-splattered family history. Her illicit affair with Daniel Brophy. That was a different woman, prone to reckless impulses and destructive passions. If I'm not careful, Jane thought, I could give Pasternak all the reasons he needs to treat Maura as a suspect.

"I want to know everything about her," said Pasternak. "Any information that can help the search team before they start off tomorrow. They'll need to be briefed, when we convene back in town."

"I can tell you this much," she said. "Maura's no outdoorswoman. If you don't find her soon, she's not going to survive out there."

"It's been almost two weeks since she went missing. She's managed to stay alive this long."

"I don't know how."

"Maybe it's because of the man she's traveling with," said Sheriff Fahey.

Jane looked at the mountain, where ravines were already darkening into shadow. In just the last few moments, as the sunlight had dipped below the peak, the temperature had plunged. Shivering in the cold, Jane wrapped her arms around herself and thought of a night spent unsheltered on that mountain, where the forest had claws, and the wind could always find you. A night with a man they knew nothing about.

What happens next may all depend on him.

"His fingerprints aren't new to us," said Sheriff Fahey, addressing the law enforcement officers and volunteers who filled the seats in the Pinedale Town

Hall. "The state of Wyoming already has the prints on record. The perp's name is Julian Henry Perkins, and he's compiled quite a rap sheet." Fahey read from his notes. "Auto theft. Breaking and entering. Vagrancy. Multiple charges of misdemeanor theft." He looked around at his audience. "That's who we're dealing with. And we know he's now armed and dangerous."

Jane shook her head. "Maybe I'm a little jaded," she called out from her seat in the third row. "But that doesn't sound like much of a rap sheet for a cop-killer."

"It is when you're only sixteen years old."

"This perp is a juvenile?"

Detective Pasternak said: "His fingerprints were all over the kitchen cabinets, as well as on the door of Deputy Martineau's vehicle. We have to assume he was the individual whom Mr. Loftus saw on the scene."

"Our office is familiar with the Perkins boy," said Fahey. "We've picked him up numerous times for various infractions. What we can't figure out is his connection to the woman."

"His connection?" said Jane. "Maura's his hostage!"

In the front row, Montgomery Loftus gave a snort. "Not what I saw."

"What you *thought* you saw," Jane countered.

The man turned and gave the three visitors from Boston a cold stare. "You people weren't there."

Fahey said, "Ma'am, we've known Monty all our lives. He's not going to go making stuff up."

Then maybe he needs glasses, Jane wanted to say, but she swallowed the retort. The three Boston visitors were outnumbered in this town hall, where dozens of locals had assembled for the briefing. The murder of a deputy had shocked the community, and volunteers had streamed in, eager to bring the killer to justice. Volunteers with guns and grim faces and righteous anger. Jane looked around at those faces and felt a premonitory chill. They're spoiling for a kill, she thought. And it doesn't matter that their quarry is a sixteen-year-old kid.

A woman suddenly called out from the back row. "Julian Perkins is just a boy! You can't be serious about sending an armed posse after him."

"He killed a deputy, Cathy," said Fahey. "He's not *just* a boy."

"I know Julian better than any of you do. I have a hard time believing that he'd kill anyone."

"Excuse me," said Detective Pasternak. "I'm not from this county. Maybe you could introduce yourself, ma'am?"

The young woman stood, and Jane immediately recognized her. It was the social worker they'd met at the scene of the Circle B double homicide. "I'm Cathy Weiss, Sublette County Child Protective Services. I've been Julian's caseworker for the past year."

"And you don't believe he could have killed Deputy Martineau?" said Pasternak.

"No, sir."

"Cathy, look at his rap sheet," said Fahey. "The kid's no angel."

"But he's no monster. Julian is a victim. He's a sixteen-year-old kid just trying to survive, in a world where nobody wants him."

"Most kids manage to survive just fine without breaking into homes and stealing cars."

"Most kids aren't used and abused by cults."

Fahey rolled his eyes. "Here we go again with that stuff."

"I've warned you about The Gathering for years. Ever since they moved into this county and built their perfect little Stepford village. Now you're seeing the result. This is what happens when you ignore the danger signs. When you look the other way while pedophiles operate right under your noses."

"You have absolutely no proof. We've looked into the allegations. Bobby went up there three times, and all he found were hardworking families who just want to be left alone."

"Left alone to abuse their children."

"Can we get back to the business at hand?" a man shouted from the audience.

"Yeah, you're wasting our time!"

"This *is* the business at hand," said Cathy, looking around the town hall. "This is the boy you're all so eager to hunt down. A kid who's been crying out for help. And no one's been listening."

"Ms. Weiss," said Detective Pasternak, "the search

team needs all the information they can get before they set off tomorrow. You say you know Julian Perkins. Tell us what to expect from this boy. He's out there on a bitterly cold night, with a woman who may be a hostage. Is he even capable of surviving?"

"Absolutely," she said.

"You're that sure of it?"

"Because he's the grandson of Absolem Perkins."

There was a murmur of recognition in the room, and Detective Pasternak looked around, puzzled. "I'm sorry. Is that significant?"

"You'd know the name if you grew up in Sublette County," said Montgomery Loftus. "Backwoods man. Built his own cabin, lived up in the Bridger-Teton Mountains. I used to catch him hunting near my property."

"Julian spent most of his childhood up there," said Cathy. "With a grandfather who taught him how to forage. How to stay alive in the wilderness with only an ax and his wits. So yes, he could survive."

"What's he doing up in the mountains, anyway?" asked Jane. "Why isn't he in school?" She didn't think it was a stupid question, but she heard laughter ripple through the hall.

"The Perkins kid, in school?" Fahey shook his head. "That's like trying to teach higher mathematics to a mule."

"I'm afraid Julian had a hard time living here in

town," said Cathy. "He was picked on a lot in school. Got into quite a few fights. He kept running away from his foster home, eight times in thirteen months. The last time he vanished was a few weeks ago, when the weather turned warm. Before he left, he emptied out his foster mother's pantry, so he's got enough food to last awhile out there."

"We have copies of his photo," said Fahey, and he handed a stack of papers up the aisle. "So you can all see who we're looking for."

The photos were passed around the audience, and for the first time Jane saw the face of Julian Perkins. It looked like a school photo, with a standard bland background. The boy had clearly made an effort to dress up for the occasion, but he looked painfully ill at ease in a long-sleeved white shirt and a tie. His black hair had been parted and combed, but a few rebellious strands of a cowlick refused to be slicked down. His dark eyes looked directly at the camera, eyes that made Jane think of a dog gazing out of an animal shelter cage. Wary. Untrusting.

"This photo was taken from last year's school yearbook," Fahey said. "It's the most recent one we could find of him. Since then, he's probably grown a few inches and put on some muscle."

"And he's got Bobby's gun," Loftus added.

Fahey looked around at the gathering. "The search team assembles at first light. I want every volunteer equipped with overnight winter gear. This isn't going to be a picnic, so I want only the fittest men out there." He paused, his gaze settling on Loftus, who caught the meaning of that look.

"You trying to tell me I shouldn't go?" said Loftus.

"I didn't say anything, Monty."

"I can outlast the whole lot of you. And I know that terrain better than anybody. It's my own backyard." Loftus rose to his feet. Although his hair was silver and his face deeply creased from decades in the outdoors, he looked as sturdy as any man in the room. "Let's make quick work of this. Before someone else gets killed." He shoved his hat on his head and walked out.

As the others began to file out as well, Jane spotted the social worker rising to her feet, and she called out: "Ms. Weiss?"

The woman turned as Jane approached. "Yes?"

"We haven't actually been introduced. I'm Detective Rizzoli."

"I know. You're the folks from Boston." Cathy glanced at Gabriel and Sansone, who were still pulling on their coats. "You people have made quite an impression on this town."

"Can we go someplace and talk? About Julian Perkins."

"You mean right now?"

"Before they use him and our friend for target practice."

Cathy looked at her watch and nodded. "There's

a coffee shop right down the block. I'll meet you there in ten minutes."

It was more like twenty minutes. When Cathy finally swept into the coffee shop, her hair wild and wind-blown, she brought in the smell of tobacco on her wrinkled, smoke-permeated clothes, and Jane knew she had been sneaking a quick cigarette in her car. Now the woman looked jittery as she slid into the booth where Jane was waiting.

"So where are your two guys?" asked Cathy, glancing at the empty seats.

"They went to buy camping gear."

"They're joining the search party tomorrow?"

"I can't talk them out of it."

Cathy gave her a long and thoughtful look. "You people have no idea what you're dealing with."

"I was hoping you could tell me."

The waitress came by with the coffeepot. "Fill it up, Cathy?" she asked.

"Good and strong, I hope."

"Always is."

Cathy waited for the waitress to leave before she spoke again. "The situation is complicated."

"They made it sound simple in that meeting. Send out the posse, hunt down a cop-killer."

"Right. Because people always prefer things simple. Black and white, right and wrong. Julian as the evil kid." Cathy drank her coffee straight, gulping down the bitter brew without a wince. "That's not what he is."

"What is he, then?"

Cathy fixed her intense gaze on Jane. "Have you ever heard of the Lost Boys?"

"I'm not sure what you're referring to."

"They're young men, mostly teenagers, who've been cast out of their homes and families. They end up abandoned on the streets. Not because they've done anything wrong, but simply because they're *boys*. In their communities, that alone makes them fatally flawed."

"Because boys cause trouble?"

"No. Because they're competition, and the older men don't want them around. They want all the girls for themselves."

Suddenly Jane understood. "You're talking about polygamous communities."

"Exactly. These are groups that have nothing at all to do with the official Mormon Church. They're breakaway sects that form around charismatic leaders. You'll find them in a number of states. Colorado and Arizona, Utah and Idaho. And right here in Sublette County, Wyoming."

"The Gathering?"

Cathy nodded. "It's a sect led by a so-called prophet named Jeremiah Goode. Twenty years ago, he started attracting followers in Idaho. They built a compound called Plain of Angels, northwest of

Idaho Falls. Eventually it grew into a community of nearly six hundred people. They're completely self-sufficient, grow their own food, raise their own livestock. No visitors are allowed in, so it's impossible to know what's really happening behind their gates."

"They sound like prisoners."

"They might as well be. The Prophet controls every aspect of their lives, and they adore him for it. That's the way cults operate. You start with a man like Jeremiah, someone who attracts the weak-minded and the needy, people who desperately want someone to accept them. To give them love and attention, to fix their pitiful broken lives. That's what he offers them—at first. That's how all cults start, from the Moonies to the Manson Family."

"You're equating Jeremiah Goode with Charles Manson?"

"Yes." Cathy's face tightened. "That's exactly what I'm doing. It's the same psychology, the same social dynamics. Once a follower drinks the Kool-Aid, they're his. They give Jeremiah all their property, all their assets, and move into his compound. There he exerts total control. He uses their free labor to maintain a number of highly profitable businesses, from construction to furniture making to mail-order jams and jellies. To an outsider, it looks like a utopian community where everyone contributes. In return, everyone is taken care of. That's what Bobby Martineau probably thought he saw when he visited Kingdom Come."

"What should he have seen instead?"

"A dictatorship. It's all about Jeremiah and what he wants."

"And what's that?"

Cathy's gaze hardened to steel. "Young flesh. That's what The Gathering is all about, Detective. Owning, controlling, and fucking young girls."

A woman in the next booth turned and glared at them, offended by the language.

Cathy took a moment to regain her composure. "That's why Jeremiah can't afford to keep too many boys around," she said. "So he gets rid of them. He orders families to shun their own teenage sons. The boys are driven to the nearest town and abandoned. In Idaho, they were dumped in Idaho Falls. Here, they're dumped in Jackson or Pinedale."

"And these families actually cooperate?"

"The women are obedient little robots. The men are rewarded for their loyalty with young brides of their own. *Spiritual brides,* they're called, to avoid being prosecuted for polygamy. Men can have as many as they want, and it's all biblically sanctioned."

Jane gave an appalled laugh. "Yeah? Which Bible?"

"The Old Testament. Think about Abraham and Jacob, David and Solomon. The old biblical patriarchs who had multiple wives or concubines."

"And his followers buy in to it?"

"Because it satisfies some burning need inside them. The women, maybe they yearn for security, for a life where they don't have to make hard choices. The men—well, it's obvious what the men get out of it. They get to take a fourteen-year-old to bed. *And* get into heaven."

"And Julian Perkins was part of all that?"

"He has a mother and a fourteen-year-old sister who still live in Kingdom Come. Julian's father died when he was only four. The mother, I'm sorry to say, is a total flake. Sharon dropped out of her kids' lives to go *find herself*, or whatever bullshit you want to call it, and she dumped them on their grandfather, Absolem."

"The mountain man."

"Right. A decent guy who took good care of them. But ten years later, Sharon reappears, and woo-hoo! She's got a new man, plus she's discovered religion! The religion of Jeremiah Goode. She takes her kids back, and they move into Kingdom Come, the new settlement that The Gathering is building here in Wyoming. A few months later, Absolem dies, and Sharon's the only adult left in Julian's life." Cathy's voice took on a razor-sharp edge. "And she betrays him."

"She threw him out?"

"Like a piece of trash. Because the Prophet demanded it."

The two women stared at each other, a gaze of shared rage that was broken only when the waitress returned with the coffeepot. In silence they both sipped, and the hot brew only worsened the angry burn in Jane's stomach.

"So why isn't Jeremiah Goode in jail?" Jane asked.

"You think I haven't tried? You saw how they reacted to me at that meeting. I'm just the town scold, the annoying feminist who won't stop talking about abused girls. And they don't want to listen anymore." She paused. "Or they're getting paid not to listen."

"Jeremiah's bought them off?"

"That's how it worked in Idaho. Cops, judges. The Gathering has loads of cash to buy them all. His settlements are cut off from outside communication— no phones, no radios. Even if a girl wanted to call for help, she wouldn't be able to." Cathy set down her coffee cup. "There's nothing I want more than to see him, and the men who follow him, in shackles. But I don't think it's ever going to happen."

"Does Julian Perkins feel the same way?"

"He hates them all. He told me so."

"Enough to kill?"

Cathy frowned. "What do you mean?"

"You were at the double homicide at the Circle B lodge. That dead couple belonged to The Gathering."

"You aren't thinking Julian did it."

"Maybe that's why he went on the run. Why he had to kill the deputy."

Cathy gave a vehement shake of the head. "I've

spent time with that boy. He hangs out with this stray dog, and you've never seen anyone so gentle with an animal. He doesn't have violence in him."

"I think we all have it in us," said Jane quietly. "If we're pushed hard enough."

"Well, if he did do it," Cathy said, "he had justice on his side."

TWENTY-SEVEN

THE SNOW CAVE WAS RIPE WITH THE ODOR OF wet dog and mildewed clothes and the sweat of two filthy bodies. Maura had not bathed in weeks, and the boy had probably gone far longer. But the shelter was cozy as a wolf den, just large enough for them to stretch out on the pine-branch floor, and the fire that Rat built was now bright and crackling. In the light from the flames, Maura surveyed her down jacket, once white, but now soiled with soot and blood. She imagined the horror that would greet her in a mirror. I'm turning into a wild animal, like these two, she thought. An animal hiding in a cave. She remembered accounts that she'd read of children raised by wolves. Brought back to civilization, they remained feral and impossible to tame. Now she could feel her own transformation beginning. Sleeping and eating on hard ground, living for days in the same clothes, curling up every night beside Bear's furry warmth. Soon no one would recognize her.

I might not recognize myself.

Rat threw a bundle of twigs into the fire. Smoke swirled in the snow cave, stinging their eyes and throat. Without this boy, I would not survive one night out here, she thought. I would already be dead and frozen, my body vanishing under the blowing snow. But the wilderness was a world Rat seemed to feel comfortable in. Within an hour, he had dug out this cave, choosing a spot on the lee side of a hill and tunneling upward to hollow out the cavity. Together they'd gathered firewood and pine boughs, racing the darkness and the killing chill of night.

Now, huddled in surprising comfort beside the fire, she listened to the wind moan outside their pine-branch door, and watched him root around in his backpack. Out came powdered dairy creamer and a box of dried dog kibble. He shook out a handful of kibble and tossed it to Bear. Then he held out the box to Maura.

"Dog food?" she asked.

"It's good enough for him." Rat nodded at the dog, who was happily devouring his meal. "Better than an empty stomach."

But not by much, she thought as she bit resignedly into a chunk. For a moment, the only sound in the cave was three pairs of jaws crunching away. She stared across the guttering flames at the boy.

"We have to find a way to surrender," she said.

He kept chewing, his attention ferociously focused on filling his belly.

"Rat, you know as well as I do that they're going to come after us. We can't survive out here."

"I'll take care of you. We'll do okay."

"Living on dog food? Hiding in snow caves?"

"I know a place, up in the mountains. We can stay there all winter, if we have to." He held out packets of powdered dairy creamer. "Here. Dessert."

"They won't give up. Not when the victim is a cop." She looked at the bundle containing the dead deputy's weapon, which Rat had wrapped in a rag and shoved into a shadowy corner, as though it were a corpse he didn't want to look at. She thought of an autopsy she'd performed on a cop-killer who'd died in police custody. *He went nuts on us, must've been PCP* was what the officers claimed. But the bruises she saw on the torso, the lacerations on the face and scalp, told a different story. *Kill a cop and you'll pay for it* was the lesson she'd learned from that. She looked at the boy and suddenly had a vision of him lying on an autopsy table, battered and bloodied by vengeful fists.

"It's the only way we'll have a chance of convincing them," she said. "If we surrender together. Otherwise, they'll assume we murdered that man with his own gun."

The blunt assessment seemed to shake him, and the kibble suddenly fell from his hand as he lowered his head. She could not see his face, but she saw him shaking in the firelight and knew that he was crying.

"It was an accident," she said. "I'll tell them that. I'll tell them you were only trying to protect me."

He shook harder, pulling his arms around himself as though to stifle the sobs. Bear moved closer, whining, and laid his huge head on the boy's knee.

She reached out to touch his arm. "If we don't surrender, we look guilty. You see that, don't you?"

He shook his head.

"I'll make them believe me. I swear, I won't let them blame you for this." She gave him a shake. "Rat, trust me on this."

He pulled away from her. "Don't."

"I'm only thinking of what's best for *you*."

"Don't tell me what to do."

"Somebody has to."

"You're not my mother!"

"Well, you could use a mother right now!"

"I *have* one!" he cried. His head came up, and his face glistened with tears. "What good did it do me?"

For that she had no good answer. In silence she watched as he ashamedly wiped away the tears, leaving streaks on his soot-stained face. For days, he'd struggled so hard to be a man. The tears reminded her that he was just a boy, a boy who was now too proud to meet her gaze, to show her how frightened he felt. Instead he focused his attention on the packets of powdered creamer, which he ripped open and emptied in his mouth.

She tore open her own packets. Some of the contents spilled onto her hand, and she let Bear lap the powder off her skin. When he'd licked it clean, he gave her face a few licks as well, and she laughed. She noticed that Rat was watching them.

"How long has Bear been with you?" she asked, stroking the dog's thick winter fur.

"Few months."

"Where did you find him?"

"He's the one who found me." He held out his hand and smiled as Bear moved back to him. "I walked out of school one day, and he just came right up to me. Followed me home."

She smiled, too. "I guess he needed a friend."

"Or he knew I needed one." Finally he looked up at her. "Do you have a dog?"

"No."

"Kids?"

She paused. "No."

"Didn't you want any?"

"It just didn't happen." She sighed. "My life is . . . complicated."

"Must be. If you can't even keep a dog."

She laughed. "Yeah. I'll definitely have to sort out my priorities."

Another silence passed. Rat lifted Bear's head and rubbed their faces together. As she sat by the sputtering fire, watching the boy commune silently with his dog, he suddenly seemed much younger than his sixteen years. A child in a man's body.

"Rat?" she asked quietly. "Do you know what happened to your mother and sister?"

He stopped stroking the dog, and his hand went still. "He took them away."

"The Prophet?"

"He decides everything."

"But you didn't see it? You weren't there when it happened?"

He shook his head.

"Did you go into the other houses? Did you see . . ." She hesitated. "The blood?" she asked quietly.

"I saw it." His gaze lifted to hers, and she saw that the blood's significance had not been lost on him. This is why I'm still alive, she thought. Because he knew what the blood meant. He knew what would happen to me if I stayed in Kingdom Come.

Rat hugged the dog, as though only in Bear would he find the solace he needed. "She's only fourteen. She needs me to look out for her."

"Your sister?"

"When they took me away, Carrie tried to stop them. She screamed and screamed, but my mom just kept holding on to her. Telling her I had to leave. I had to be shunned." His hand tightened to a fist in the dog's fur. "That's why I went back. For her. For Carrie." He looked up. "But she wasn't there. No one was there."

"We'll find her." Maura reached out and held his arm, the way he was now holding Bear. They were joined, the three of them, woman, boy, and dog. An unlikely union forged by hardship into something close to love. Maybe even stronger than love. I couldn't help Grace, she thought. But I'll do whatever it takes to save this boy. "We'll find her, Rat," she said. "Somehow this will turn out all right. I swear it will."

Bear gave a loud whine and closed his eyes.

"He doesn't believe you, either," said Rat.

TWENTY-EIGHT

JANE WATCHED HER HUSBAND METHODICALLY pack an internal-frame backpack, cramming every nook with necessities. In went the sleeping bag and Therm-a-Rest, the one-man tent, winter camping stove, and freeze-dried meals. In smaller pockets he stuffed a compass and knife and headlamp, parachute cord and first-aid kit. No space was wasted, no ounce of weight unnecessary. He and Sansone had bought the equipment earlier that evening and now Gabriel's items were organized on the hotel bed, small items clustered into stuff sacks, the water bottles wrapped with ever-useful duct tape. He had done this many times before, as a young backcountry hiker, and later as a marine. The weapon now strapped to his hip was an unnerving reminder that this was not merely a winter camping trip.

"I should be going with you two," said Jane.

"No you shouldn't. You need to stay behind and monitor phone calls."

"What if something goes wrong out there?"

"If it does, I'll feel a lot better knowing you're here and safe."

"Gabriel, I always thought we were a team."

He set down the backpack and shot her a wry smile. "And which member of this team is allergic to camping in any way, shape, or form?"

"I'll do it if I have to."

"You have no winter camping experience."

"Sansone doesn't, either."

"But he's fit and strong. I don't think you can even lift that pack. Go ahead. Try."

She grabbed the backpack and hefted it off the bed. Through gritted teeth she said, "I can do it."

"Now imagine that much weight on your back as you climb a mountain. Imagine carrying that pack for hours, for days, and at altitude. Imagine trying to keep up with men who have about fifty pounds more muscle than you have. Jane, we both know that's not realistic."

She released the pack and it thudded onto the floor. "You don't know this terrain."

"We'll be traveling with people who do."

"Can you trust their judgment?"

"We'll find out soon enough." He closed the backpack and set it in the corner. "The important thing is that we're out there with them. They may be too quick to pull the trigger, and Maura's in the line of fire."

Jane dropped onto the bed and sighed. "What the hell's she doing out there, anyway? Her actions don't make any sense!"

"That's why you have to stay available on the phone. She called you once. She may try to reach you again."

"And how will I reach *you*?"

"Sansone's bringing a satellite phone. It's not as if we're dropping off the face of the earth."

But it feels that way, she thought as she lay in bed beside him that night. He was about to hike into the wild, yet he slept soundly, untroubled by fears. She was the one who lay awake, fretting that she was neither strong enough nor experienced enough to join him. She thought of herself as any man's equal, but this time she had to acknowledge the sorry truth. She could not carry that backpack. She could not keep up with Gabriel. After a few miles, she'd probably collapse in the snow, screwing up the expedition and embarrassing herself.

So how will Maura manage to survive?

That question took on more urgency when she woke up before dawn and looked out the window at wind-whipped snow flying across the hotel parking lot. She imagined that wind stinging her eyes, flash-freezing her skin. It was a brutal day to launch a search.

The sun had not yet risen when she, Gabriel, and Sansone drove up to the staging point. A dozen other members of the search team had already arrived, along with the tracking dogs, and the men stood around in the predawn gloom, sipping steaming coffee. Jane could hear the excitement in their voices, could feel the electricity in the air. They were like any cops just before a raid, oozing testosterone and twitching for action.

As Gabriel and Sansone pulled on their backpacks, she heard Sheriff Fahey ask: "Where do you two think you're going with those packs?"

Gabriel turned to him. "You did ask for search-and-rescue volunteers."

"We didn't request a federal agent for the team."

"I'm a trained hostage negotiator," said Gabriel. "And I know Maura Isles. She'll trust me."

"This is rugged terrain. You have to know what you're doing."

"Eight years in the Marine Corps. Winter mountain operations training. Anything else you'd like to know?"

Unable to argue with those qualifications, Fahey turned to Sansone, but the man's stony expression stopped Fahey cold from even trying to challenge him. With a grunt, Fahey stalked off. "Where's Monty Loftus?" he yelled. "We can't wait around for him much longer!"

"Told me he's not coming," someone answered.

"After the fuss he threw last night? I thought he'd be here for sure."

"Maybe he looked in the mirror and remembered he's seventy-one."

Amid the laughter that followed, one of the handlers called out: "Dogs have got the scent!"

The search team started into the woods, and Gabriel turned to Jane. They shared a last kiss, an embrace, and then he was on his way. So many times before, she had admired his easy athleticism, the confidence in his gait. Even the heavy backpack did not slow him down. As she stood at the edge of the trees watching him, she could still see the young marine he once was.

"This is not going to come out well," a voice said.

Jane turned and saw Cathy Weiss shaking her head.

"They're going to hunt him down like an animal," said Cathy.

"It's Maura Isles I'm worried about," said Jane. "And my husband."

They stood side by side as the departing search team threaded its way into the woods. Slowly the driveway emptied out as vehicles began to leave, but the two women remained, watching until the men finally vanished among the trees.

"At least he seems like a levelheaded man," said Cathy.

Jane nodded. "That would describe Gabriel."

"But the rest of those guys, they're ready to shoot first and ask questions later. Hell, Bobby could have slipped on the ice and shot *himself*." Cathy huffed out a sigh of frustration. "How does anyone know what really happened? No one saw it."

And there was no video of the shooting, thought Jane. That detail alone deeply bothered her. Martineau's dash camera had been in perfect working order. It had simply been turned off, in violation of sheriff's department regulations. The last footage recorded was while Martineau was en route to Doyle Mountain. Moments before he arrived at the house, he had deliberately shut off the camera.

She turned to Cathy. "How well did you know Deputy Martineau?"

"I've had dealings with him." By the tone of her voice, those dealings did not sound cordial.

"Did you ever have any reason not to trust him?"

For a moment Cathy stared at her in the bone-chilling dawn, and the steam from their breaths mingled, coalescing into a vaporous union.

"I was wondering when someone would finally get up the nerve to ask that question," she said.

"Bobby Martineau is now considered a hero. And we're not supposed to speak ill of dead heroes. Even if they deserve it," said Cathy.

"So you weren't a fan of his."

"Between you and me, Bobby was an abusive control freak." Cathy kept her gaze on the road as she spoke, driving with care on pavement coated in snow and ice. Jane was glad she wasn't the one navigating these unfamiliar roads, even more glad that they were traveling in Cathy's rugged four-wheel-drive SUV. "In my line of work," said Cathy, "you find out pretty quick which families in the county are in trouble. Who's getting divorced, whose kids are missing too much school. And whose wives are showing up at work with black eyes."

"Bobby's?"

"She's his ex-wife now. It took her long enough to wake up and get out. Two years ago, Patsy finally left him and moved to Oregon. I only wish she'd hung around here to press charges, because guys like Bobby shouldn't be wearing badges."

"He beat up his wife, and he was still in uniform?"

"It probably happens in Boston, too, right? People refuse to believe that a fine, upstanding citizen like Bobby would clock his wife." Cathy snorted. "If the boy really did shoot him, maybe Bobby deserved it."

"You don't really mean that, do you?"

Cathy looked at her. "Maybe I do. Just a little. I work with victims. I know what years of abuse can do to a kid. To a woman."

"This is starting to sound personal for you."

"You see too much of it, and yeah. It becomes personal. No matter how hard you try not to let it."

"So Bobby was a jerk who beat up his wife. It doesn't explain why he shut off his dash camera. What was he trying to hide up on Doyle Mountain?"

"I don't know the answer to that one."

"Did he know Julian Perkins?"

"Oh sure. The kid's been picked up by just about every deputy in the county for one offense or another."

"So they have a history, the two of them."

Cathy thought about this as she guided her SUV up a road where the houses had become few and far between. "Julian didn't like the police, but that's a typical teenage boy for you. Cops are the enemy. Still, I don't think that would explain it. And let's not forget." She glanced at Jane. "Bobby shut off the dash camera *before* he got to Doyle Mountain. Before he knew the kid was up there. Whatever his reason, it had something to do with your friend Maura Isles."

Whose actions remained the biggest mystery of all.

"Here it is," said Cathy, and she pulled the SUV to the side of the road. "You wanted to know about Bobby. Well, that's where he lived."

Jane looked at the modest house across the road. Great mounds of snow had piled up on either side of the plowed driveway, and the building seemed to be in hiding, its windows peeking over the snow as though to catch a furtive glimpse of passersby. There were no nearby homes, no neighbors easily available for her to interview.

"He lived alone?" asked Jane.

"As far as I know. Doesn't look like anyone's at home."

Jane zipped up her jacket and stepped out of the car. Heard the rattle of wind in the trees, and felt its sting on her cheeks. Was that why she suddenly felt a chill sweep through her? Or was it this house, the house of a dead man, its windows peering darkly above the snowbank? Cathy was already walking toward the front porch, boots crunching over compacted snow, but Jane paused by the car. They had no search warrant. They had no reason to be here, except that Deputy Martineau was a puzzle to her, and any good homicide investigation included a victimology analysis. Why was this particular man attacked? What actions did he take that led to his death in the windswept driveway on Doyle Mountain? So far, all the attention had been focused on the alleged shooter, Julian Perkins. It was time to focus on Bobby Martineau.

She followed Cathy up the driveway, her boots finding traction on the gritty sand scattered across the ice. Cathy was already knocking on the front door.

As expected, no one answered.

Jane noted the rotten windowsills, the peeling paint. Firewood had been carelessly piled up at one end of the porch, against a railing that looked dangerously close to collapse. Peering through the front window, she saw a sparsely furnished living room. A pizza box and two beer cans were on the coffee table. She saw nothing that surprised her, nothing she wouldn't expect to see in the home of a bachelor living alone on a deputy's salary.

"Boy, this is a dump," said Cathy, looking at the detached garage, which seemed to sag under the weight of snow on its roof.

"Do you know about any of his friends? Anyone who might know him well?"

"Probably in the sheriff's office, but good luck getting them to say anything negative. Like I said, a dead cop is always a hero."

"Depending on how the cop ended up dead." Jane tried the doorknob and found it locked. She turned her focus to the detached garage. The driveway leading to the bay door was plowed clear, and she spotted tire tracks—wide ones, from a truck. Gingerly she made her way down the slippery porch steps. At the garage bay door she hesitated, knowing that, by opening that door, she was about to cross an ethical line. She had no warrant, and this wasn't even her own jurisdiction. But Bobby Martineau was dead so he could hardly complain about it. And in the end, this was all about justice, wasn't it? Justice for Bobby himself, as well as for the boy accused of killing him.

She reached down for the bay door handle, but the tracks had iced over and she couldn't make it budge. Cathy pitched in and together they strained to lift the door. Suddenly it jerked free, and they slid it up. They stood, staring in astonishment.

A massive black behemoth gleamed inside.

"Will you look at that," murmured Cathy. "It's so new, it's still got the dealer plates on it."

Admiringly, Jane stroked the flawless finish as she walked around the truck. It was a Ford F-450

XLT. "This baby's gotta cost at least fifty thousand bucks," she said.

"How could Bobby afford this?"

Jane circled to the front bumper and halted. "An even better question is, how could he afford *that*?"

"What is it?"

Jane pointed at the Harley. It was a black V-Rod Muscle model, and like the truck, it looked brand new. She didn't know how much a bike like this cost, but it certainly didn't come cheap. "Looks like Deputy Martineau recently came into some money," she said softly. She turned to Cathy, who stared openmouthed at the Harley. "He didn't have a rich uncle somewhere, did he?"

Cathy gave a baffled shake of the head. "From what I heard, he couldn't even keep up with his alimony payments."

"Then how did he pay for this bike? For the truck?" Jane looked around at the shabby garage with its sagging timbers. "Obviously, we have a disconnect here. It makes you question everything we've been told about Martineau."

"He was a cop. Maybe someone was paying him to look the other way."

Jane again focused on the Harley, trying to understand how it connected with Martineau's death. It was clear to her now that he had purposefully shut off his dash camera to hide his actions. Dispatch had just told him that Maura Isles was waiting there, a lone woman, in need of rescue. After taking the call, Martineau had shut off the camera and proceeded to drive up Doyle Mountain.

Then what happened? Where did the boy come in? *Maybe it all comes down to the boy.*

She looked at Cathy. "How far is Kingdom Come?"

"It's about thirty, forty miles from here. Middle of nowhere."

"Maybe we should drive out there and talk to Julian's mother."

"I don't think anyone's living there right now. I heard the residents have left for the winter."

"You do remember who reported that piece of information? The same deputy who visited Kingdom Come again and again. And never saw anything wrong there."

Cathy said, softly: "Bobby Martineau."

Jane nodded at the Harley. "Based on what we've found here, I don't think we can trust anything Martineau said. Someone's been paying him off. Someone who has plenty of money to do it."

Neither one of them had to say the name aloud. *Jeremiah Goode.*

"Let's pay a visit to Kingdom Come," said Jane. "I'd like to find out what we're not supposed to see."

TWENTY-NINE

THROUGH THE CAR WINDOW, JANE SPOTTED brown humps dotting a vast field of white. They were bison, huddled together against the wind, their great shaggy coats dusted with snow. Wild animals, belonging to no one. That was a novelty for a girl from the big city, where all pets were leashed and tagged and registered. But pets were fed and sheltered, not left to fend for themselves in the brutal elements. Here is the consequence of freedom, she thought, staring at the bison, a consequence that Julian Perkins had accepted when he fled his foster home with only a backpack of food. How could a sixteen-year-old boy survive in that unforgiving world?

How could Maura?

As if reading her thoughts, Cathy said: "If anyone can keep her alive out there, it'd be Julian. He grew up with a grandfather who knew every trick of living off the land. Absolem Perkins is a legend around here. Built his own cabin by hand, up in the Bridger-Teton Mountains."

"Where's that?"

"It's that mountain range over there." Cathy pointed.

Through the swirling dust of snow kicked up by the tires, Jane saw impossibly rugged peaks. "*That's* where Julian grew up?"

"It's national forest now. But if you go hiking up there, you'll come across a few old homesteads just like Absolem's. Most of them are down to nothing but foundations, but they remind you how hard it was just to stay alive back then. I can't imagine going a day without flush toilets and a hot shower."

"Hell. I can't imagine a day without cable."

They were climbing into foothills now, through terrain where the trees grew thicker and buildings vanished. They passed Grubb's General Store, and Jane spotted the ominous sign: LAST CHANCE FOR FUEL. She couldn't help an anxious glance at Cathy's fuel gauge, and was relieved to see that they had three-quarters of a tank.

It was almost a mile farther down the road before that name suddenly struck her as familiar. Grubb's General Store. She remembered what Queenan had told her about the many sightings of Maura. That people had reported seeing her all over the state, at the Dinosaur Museum in Thermopolis, in the Irma

Hotel in Cody. And at Grubb's General Store in Sublette County.

She pulled out her cell phone to call Queenan. Zero bars, no reception. She put her phone back in her purse.

"Well, this is interesting," Cathy said as they turned off the highway onto a much narrower road.

"What?"

"It's been plowed."

"Is this the road to Kingdom Come?"

"Yes. If Bobby told the truth, and the valley's deserted, why would anyone bother to clear the road?"

"Have you been up this way before?"

"The one time I drove up here was last summer," said Cathy as she steered around a hairpin turn that made Jane instinctively reach for the armrest. "I'd just become Julian's caseworker. The police caught him in Pinedale, where he'd broken into someone's house and was raiding the kitchen for food."

"After he got kicked out of The Gathering?"

Cathy nodded. "Another one of their Lost Boys. I drove up here, hoping to interview his mother. And I was worried about his sister, Carrie. Julian told me she was only fourteen, and I know that's the age when the men begin to . . ." Cathy paused and took a deep breath. "Anyway, I never made it to Kingdom Come."

"What happened?"

"I turned onto their private road and was just heading down into the valley when a truck came roaring up and intercepted me. They must have some sort of warning system that tells them when someone's entered their property. Two men with walkie-talkies demanded to know the purpose of my visit. As soon as they found out I was a social worker, they ordered me to leave and never return. I got only a glimpse of the settlement from the road. They'd built ten houses, and there were two more under construction, with bulldozers and tractors rumbling around. Obviously, they've got plans to expand. This is going to be their next Plain of Angels."

"So you never spoke to Julian's mother."

"No. And she never once tried to contact anyone about his welfare." She shook her head in disgust. "How's that for parental love? You're given the choice between your cult and your own child, and you toss out the child. I don't get it, do you?"

Jane thought of her own daughter, thought of what she would sacrifice to keep Regina safe. *I'd die for her, and I wouldn't think twice about it.* "No, I don't get it, either."

"Imagine what it was like for poor Julian. Knowing his mom thinks he's disposable. Knowing that she just looked the other way when the men dragged him out of the house."

"My God, is that how it happened?"

"That's how Julian described it. He was sobbing and screaming. His sister was screaming. And their mother let it all happen, without a peep of protest."

"What a worthless piece of shit."

"But remember, she's a victim, too."

"That's no excuse. A mother fights for her kids."

"In The Gathering, mothers never do. In Plain of Angels, dozens of mothers willingly surrendered their sons, letting them be dragged off and dumped in the nearest town. The boys end up so broken, so damaged, that a lot of them turn to drugs. Or they're exploited by predators. They're desperate for someone, anyone, to love them."

"How did Julian cope?"

"He just wanted to go back to his family. He's like some beaten dog, trying to return to his abusive master. Last July, he stole a car and actually made it all the way back to the valley to see his sister. Managed to hide out in the area for three weeks before The Gathering caught him and dumped him back in Pinedale."

"So he might head back there this time as well." She looked at Cathy. "How far are we from Doyle Mountain? Where Martineau was shot?"

"As the crow flies, it's not far. It's right on the other side of those hills. A lot farther if you go by road."

"So he could hike it."

"If he really wanted to."

"He just killed a deputy. He's scared and he's on the run. He might seek shelter in Kingdom Come."

Cathy thought about it, her frown deepening. "If he's there now . . ."

"He's armed."

"He wouldn't hurt me. He knows me."

"I'm just saying, we have to be cautious. We can't predict what he'll do next." *And he has Maura.*

They had been steadily ascending for nearly an hour, and had seen no other vehicles, no buildings, no evidence at all that anyone resided on this mountain. Only as Cathy slowed to a stop did Jane spot the sign, its post half buried in deep snow.

PRIVATE ROAD

RESIDENTS ONLY

AREA PATROLLED

"Makes you feel welcome, doesn't it?" said Cathy.

"It also makes me wonder why they're so afraid of visitors."

"Interesting. The chain's down, and this road's been plowed as well."

They started down the private road, Cathy's SUV rolling slowly over pavement coated with an inch of recent snow. The pines were thick here, casting the road in claustrophobic gloom, and Jane could see little beyond the evergreen curtain. She stared ahead, muscles tensed, not certain what to expect. A hostile interception by The Gathering? A burst of gunfire from a frightened boy? Suddenly the trees parted and she blinked at the view of open sky, cold and bright.

Cathy pulled onto an overlook and braked to a stop. Both women stared down in shock at what was once the settlement of Kingdom Come.

"Dear God," Cathy whispered. "What happened here?"

Black ruins dotted the valley. Charred foundations marked where houses had once stood, the two rows forming a strangely orderly record of destruction. Among the ruins, something was moving, something that trotted arrogantly between the burned-out houses, as though this valley now belonged to him and he was merely surveying his domain.

"Coyote," said Cathy.

"This doesn't look like an accident," said Jane. "I think someone came in and torched those buildings." She paused, struck by the obvious. "Julian."

"Why would he?"

"Rage against The Gathering? Revenge for throwing him out?"

"You're pretty quick to blame him for everything, aren't you?" said Cathy.

"He wouldn't be the first kid who's torched a house."

"And destroy his only available shelter for miles?" Cathy heaved out an agitated breath and shoved the gearshift back into drive. "Let's get closer."

They started down the valley road, and through intermittent stands of pine, Jane caught other views of the settlement, the destruction more appalling with every new glimpse. By now the sound of their vehicle had filtered down the slope, and the lone coyote fled toward the surrounding woods. As their SUV drew closer, Jane spotted dark lumps scattered across the nearby field of snow, and she realized that they, too, were coyotes. But they were lying motionless.

"Jesus, it looks like the whole pack was slaughtered," said Jane.

"Hunters."

"Why?"

"Coyotes aren't real popular in ranching country." Cathy pulled to a stop beside the first burned foundation, and they both stared across the field of dead animals. At the edge of the woods, the lone surviving coyote stood watching them, as though he, too, wanted answers.

"This is weird," murmured Jane. "I don't see blood anywhere. I'm not sure those animals were shot."

"Then how'd they die?"

Jane stepped out of the SUV and almost slipped on ice. Snowmelt from the fire had flash-frozen into a hard glaze that was now dusted with an inch of white powder. Everywhere she looked, she saw scavenger prints on that fine layer of snow. The destruction stunned her. She heard Cathy's boots crunch away across the ice, but Jane remained beside the vehicle, staring at the jumble of charred wood and metal, here and there spotting a recognizable object in the ruins. A shattered mirror, a scorched doorknob. A ceramic sink, filled with a miniature ice rink of frozen water. An entire village reduced to rubble and ashes.

The scream was piercing, every echo flying back from the mountains like shards of glass. Jane bolted straight in alarm and saw Cathy standing at the far edge of the ruins. Her gaze was fixed to the ground, her gloved hand clapped over her mouth. In jerky robotic steps she began to back away.

Jane started toward her. "What is it? Cathy?"

The other woman did not answer. She was still staring downward, still in a stumbling retreat. As Jane drew closer, she spied bits of color on the ground. A scrap of blue here, a fleck of pink there. Fragments of cloth, she realized, the edges shredded. As she moved beyond the last burned foundation, the snow became deep and more riddled with scavenger tracks. The prints were everywhere, as if coyotes had staged a hoedown.

"Cathy?"

At last the woman turned to her, and her face was drained of color. Unable to speak, all she could do was point to the ground, at one of the dead coyotes.

Only then did Jane realize that Cathy was not pointing at the animal, but at a pair of bones poking up like slender white stalks from the snow. They might have been the remains of wild animal prey, ripped apart and gnawed on by predators, except for one small detail. Encircling those bones was something that did not belong to any animal.

Jane crouched down and stared at the pink and purple beads strung on a loop of elastic. A child's bracelet.

Her heart was pounding as she rose back to her feet. She looked across the snowy expanse that stretched toward the trees, and saw craters in the snow where the coyotes had been digging for treasure, fresh meat on which they had begun to feast.

"They're still here," Cathy said softly. "The families, the children. The people in Kingdom Come never left." She stared down at the ground, as if seeing some new horror at her feet. "They're right *here*."

THIRTY

BY NIGHTFALL, THE CORONER'S RECOVERY TEAM had extracted the fifteenth body from the frozen ground. It had lain entangled with the other corpses, buried together in one communal pit, limbs mingled in a grotesque group hug. The grave had been shallow, covered with only a thin layer of soil, so thin that even through a foot and a half of snow scavengers had detected the trove of meat. Like the fourteen bodies before it, this corpse emerged from the pit with limbs frozen and rigid, eyelashes encrusted with ice. It was only an infant, about six months old, dressed in a long-sleeved cotton sleeper decorated with tiny airplanes. An indoor outfit. Like the other bodies, this one bore no marks of violence. Except for postmortem damage by carnivores, the cadavers were strangely, disturbingly perfect.

This baby was the most perfect of all, eyes closed as if in sleep, its skin as smooth and milky white as porcelain. *Just a doll* was what Jane had first thought when she'd glimpsed the tiny corpse in the pit. It's what she'd wanted to believe. But soon the truth was apparent as the coroner's team, biohazard garb covering their heavy winter clothes, gingerly freed the body from its grave.

Jane had watched the steady succession of cadavers emerge, and the infant was what upset her most, because it made her think of her own daughter. She tried to block out the image, but it had already sprung into her head: Regina's lifeless face, the skin feathered with frost.

Abruptly she turned away from the pit and walked back to where the vehicles were parked. Cathy was still huddled inside her SUV. Jane climbed in beside her and swung the door shut. The vehicle stank of smoke, and Jane saw that the ashtray was full. Hands shaking, Cathy lit yet another cigarette and took a trembling puff. The two women sat for a moment without speaking. Through the windshield, they watched a member of the recovery team place the pitifully small bundle inside the morgue vehicle and swing the door shut. There was too little daylight left. Tomorrow the digging would resume, and they would certainly find more bodies. At the bottom of the pit, workers had already glimpsed an adult's rigid limb.

"No knife wounds. No bullet holes," said Jane as she watched the morgue vehicle drive away. "They look like they just fell asleep. And died."

"Jonestown," murmured Cathy. "You remember that, don't you? The Reverend Jim Jones. He brought nearly a thousand followers from California to Guyana. Established his own colony. When U.S. authorities came to investigate, he ordered his followers to commit suicide. More than nine hundred people died."

"You think this was a mass suicide, too?"

"What else would it be?" Cathy stared out the window at the burial pit. "In Jonestown, they made the children drink first. Gave them cyanide mixed in sweet punch. Flavor Aid. Imagine doing that. Filling a bottle with poison. Picking up your own baby. Slipping the nipple in its mouth. Imagine watching him drink, knowing that it's the last time he'll ever look up at you and smile."

"No, I can't imagine that."

"But in Jonestown, they did it. They killed their own children, and then they killed themselves. All because some so-called *prophet* told them to." Cathy turned to her with a haunted face. The deepening shadows of the vehicle emphasized the hollows of her eyes. "Jeremiah Goode has the power to command them. He can make you surrender your possessions and turn your back on the world. He can make you give up your daughter and cast out your son. He can hand you a cup of poison, tell you to drink it, and you'd do it. You'd do it with a smile, because there's nothing as important as pleasing him."

"I asked you this question before. I think I know the answer. This *is* personal for you, isn't it?"

Jane's words, spoken so softly, seemed to stun

Cathy. She went very still as her cigarette slowly burned down to ash. Abruptly she stubbed it out and met Jane's gaze. "You better believe this is fucking personal," she said.

Jane asked no questions, made no comments. She was wise enough to give her the time and space to say more when she was ready.

Cathy broke off eye contact and stared out at the fading light. "Sixteen years ago," she said, "I lost my best friend to The Gathering. She and I were as close as sisters—even closer. Katie Sheldon lived next door to us, and I'd known her since we were two years old. Her father was a carpenter, unemployed a lot of the time. A nasty little man who lorded it over his family like a two-bit emperor. Her mother was a housewife. Such a blank personality, I hardly remember her. They were just the kind of family The Gathering seems to attract. People who have no other connections, who need a reason for existence in their purposeless lives. And Katie's father, he probably liked the idea of any religion that gave him full rein to lord it over his family. Not to mention the young girls he'd get to screw. Multiple wives, Armageddon, the end times—he happily embraced it all. All of Jeremiah's bullshit. So the family moved away from our neighborhood. To Plain of Angels.

"Katie and I promised to write each other. And I did. I wrote letter after letter, and never got anything back. But I never stopped thinking about her, wondering what became of her. Years later, I found out."

As Cathy took a calming breath, Jane remained silent, waiting to hear what by then she knew would be a tragic conclusion.

"I finished college," Cathy continued. "Got a job as a social worker in a hospital in Idaho Falls. One day, an emergency obstetrical case came in through the ER. A young woman who was hemorrhaging after giving birth in Plain of Angels. It was my friend Katie. She was only twenty-two when she died. Her mother was with her, and she happened to let slip the fact that Katie had five other children at home." Cathy's jaw tightened. "You do the math."

"The authorities must have been notified."

"Oh, they were. I made damn sure they were. The Idaho police went to Plain of Angels and asked questions. By then, The Gathering had their story worked out. No, I'd heard wrong, it was only her first child. There were no underage mothers. There was no sexual abuse of girls. They were merely a peaceful community where everyone was happy and healthy, a true nirvana. The police couldn't do a thing." Cathy stared at Jane. "It was too late to save my friend. But I thought I could help the others. All the girls trapped in The Gathering. That's when I became an activist.

"For years, I've collected information about Jeremiah and his followers. I've urged law enforcement to do its job and protect those girls. But there's no way to shut down The Gathering until they arrest Jeremiah. As long as he's alive and free, he controls them. He can issue orders and send his men after people who defy him. But if he's cornered, he'll become dangerous. Remember what happened in Jonestown. And with the Branch Davidians in Waco. When Jim Jones and David Koresh knew they were about to go down, they took everyone with them. Men, women, and children."

"But why now?" asked Jane. "What would make Jeremiah order a mass suicide at this particular time?"

"Maybe he thinks authorities are closing in on him. That it's just a matter of time before he's arrested. When you face decades behind bars for sex crimes, when you know you're going down, you don't care how many people you take with you. If you fall, so must your followers."

"There's a problem with that theory, Cathy."

"What problem?"

"These bodies were buried. Someone dragged them out into the field and dug a pit and tried to hide what happened. If Jeremiah talked them into committing mass suicide with him, then who was left behind to bury the bodies? Who burned down these houses?"

Cathy fell silent, thinking about this. Outside, members of the recovery team were returning to their vehicles. They looked like puffy Michelin men inside their biohazard suits. The light had faded, turning the landscape a wintry gray and white. Deep in the shadow of the surrounding woods, more scavengers surely lurked, waiting for another chance to feast on poisoned meat. Meat that had already killed their companions.

"They're not going to find Jeremiah's body here," said Jane.

Cathy looked at the burned remains of Kingdom Come. "You're right. He's alive. He must be."

A rap on Cathy's door made both women start in surprise. Through the glass, Jane recognized state detective Pasternak's pallid face peering in at them. As Cathy rolled down the window, he said: "Miss Weiss, I'm ready to hear whatever you have to say about The Gathering."

"So now you finally believe me."

"I'm only sorry no one's been listening." He gestured toward her backseat. "May I get in out of the wind and join you two?"

"I'll tell you everything I know. On one condition," said Cathy.

Pasternak slid into the back and pulled the door shut. "Yes?"

"You have to share some information with us."

"Like what?"

Jane turned in her seat and looked at him. "How about starting with what you know about Deputy Martineau? And where he got the money to buy a brand-new Harley and a shiny new truck."

Pasternak glanced back and forth at the two women gazing at him over the seats. "We're looking into that."

"Where is Jeremiah Goode?" said Cathy.

"We're looking into that, too."

Cathy shook her head. "You've got a mass grave here, and you know who's probably responsible for it. You must have some idea of where he is."

After a moment, Pasternak nodded. "We're in touch with Idaho law enforcement. They told me they already have a contact inside the Plain of Angels compound. He reports that Jeremiah Goode isn't there at this time."

"And you trust this contact?"

"They do."

Cathy gave a snort. "Then here's lesson number one, Detective. When it comes to The Gathering, trust no one."

"An arrest warrant's been issued for him. In the meantime, Plain of Angels is under surveillance."

"He has contacts everywhere. Safe houses where he can stay hidden for years."

"You know this for a fact?"

Cathy nodded. "He has both the followers and the money to stay untouchable. Enough money to bribe an army of Bobby Martineaus."

"We're following that money trail, believe me. A big infusion of cash showed up in Deputy Martineau's bank account about two weeks ago."

"From where?" said Jane.

"It came from an account registered to the Dahlia Group. Whatever that is."

"It has to be Jeremiah's," said Cathy.

"The trouble is, we can't find any link between the Dahlia Group and The Gathering. The account is in a Rockville, Maryland, bank."

Cathy frowned. "The Gathering has no Maryland connection. Not that I'm aware of."

"Dahlia appears to be a shell company. A front for whatever its real business is. Someone's gone to a lot of trouble to hide the money trail."

Jane stared at the grave site, where workers were placing heavy boards over the pit to protect it from further predation. And to protect the predators as well, against whatever poison had killed both the human victims and the animals that had feasted on their tainted flesh. "So this is why Martineau got paid off," she said. "To keep quiet about what happened here."

"It would be a secret worth keeping," said Pasternak. "Mass murder."

"Maybe this is why he was killed," said Jane. "Maybe the boy had nothing to do with it."

"I'm afraid Julian Perkins is the only one who can answer that question."

"And there's a posse of armed men ready to kill him." Jane looked toward the mountains. Toward the sky, which was already darkening into another frigid night. "If they do, we may lose our only witness."

THIRTY-ONE

BEAR HEARD IT FIRST.

For most of the morning, the dog had been trotting far ahead of them, as though he already knew the way, although the boy had never before brought him up this mountain. They had traveled for hours without speaking, conserving their breath during the climb, Maura trailing last behind the boy. Every step was a struggle for her to keep up. So when Bear suddenly halted on a ledge above them and gave a bark, she thought it was directed at her. A canine version of *Come on, lady! What's taking you so long?*

Until she heard the growl. Looking up, she saw he wasn't focused on her, but was staring east, toward the valley from which they had just ascended. Rat halted and turned to face the same direction. For a moment they were silent. Pine branches creaked. Snow swirled, stirred up by invisible fingers of wind.

Then they heard it: the distant baying of dogs.

"We have to move faster," said Rat.

"I can't go any faster."

"Yes you can." He reached out to her. "I'll help you."

She looked at his outstretched hand. Looked up into his face, filthy and haggard. He has kept me alive all these days, she thought. Now it's time for me to return the favor.

"You'll move faster without me," she said.

"I won't leave you behind."

"Yes you will. You're going to run, and I'm going to sit here and wait for them."

"You don't even know who *they* are."

"I'll tell them what happened to the deputy. I'll explain everything."

"Please don't do this. *Don't.*" She heard tears break through his voice. "Just come with me. We only have to get over the next mountain."

"And then what? Do we have to climb the next one, and the next?"

"It'll just take another day to get there."

"Get where?"

"Home. My grandpa's cabin."

The only safe place he has ever known, she thought. The only place where he's been loved.

He looked across the valley. There, on the snowy flank of the opposite hill, small dark shapes were moving. "I don't know where else to go," he said softly and wiped a filthy sleeve across his eyes. "We'll be okay there. I know we will."

It was magical thinking, nothing more, but it was

all he had left. Because nothing would ever be okay for him again.

She looked up toward the peak. It was at least half a day's climb to the top, but it would give them the high ground, if something went wrong. If they had to make a stand.

"Rat," she said, "if they get too close, if they catch up, you have to promise me one thing. You have to leave me behind. Let me talk to them."

"What if they don't want to talk?"

"They could be policemen."

"So was the last one."

"I can't outrun them, but you can. You can probably outrun us all. I'm just slowing you down. So I'll stay and speak to them. If nothing else, I can buy you enough time to escape."

He stared at her, dark eyes suddenly shimmering. "You'd really do that?" he asked. "For me?"

She touched a glove to his dirt-streaked face, smearing away tears. "Your mother was crazy," she said softly. "To ever give up a boy like you."

Bear gave an impatient *woof* and stared down at them with a look of *What are you two waiting for?*

She smiled at the boy. Then she forced her aching legs to move again, and they followed the dog up the mountain.

By late afternoon, they had climbed above the tree cover, and she had no doubt their pursuers could easily spot them, three dark figures moving up the stark white slope. They see us, just as we see them, she thought. Predator and prey, with only a valley separating us. And she was moving far too slowly, her right snowshoe wobbling on her boot, her lungs wheezing in the thin air. Their pursuers were steadily closing the gap. They weren't tired and tattered and hungry from days in the wilderness; they didn't have the body of a forty-two-year-old city woman whose idea of exercise was a leisurely walk in the park. How had it come down to this unlikely moment? Slogging up a mountain with a dog of uncertain breed and a cast-off boy who trusted no one, who had every reason not to. These were the only two she could count on out here, these two friends who had already proven themselves again and again.

She looked up the slope at Rat, moving tirelessly up the path ahead of her, and he seemed far younger than sixteen, just a frightened child, clambering up the hillside like a mountain goat. But she had reached the end of her endurance, and now she could scarcely move one foot in front of the other. She struggled up the trail, snowshoes creaking under her weight, her thoughts on the encounter to come. It would happen before nightfall. One way or the other, she thought, by tonight all will be decided. Glancing back, she saw that their pursuers were already emerging from the trees below. So close.

We'll soon be within their rifle range.

She looked up the mountain again, to the peak

still looming far ahead, and the last of her strength seemed to crumble and fall away like ashes.

"Come on!" Rat called down to her.

"I can't." She stopped, sagging against a massive boulder, and whispered, "I can't."

He scrambled back down to her, scattering powdery snow, and grabbed her arm. "You have to."

"It's time to do it," she said. "Time for you to leave me."

He pulled harder on her arm. "They'll kill you."

She took him by both shoulders and gave him a shake. "Rat, listen to me. It doesn't matter now what happens to me. I want *you* to live."

"No. I won't leave you." His voice cracked, shattered into a boy's sob, a boy's frantic appeal. "Please try. *Please*." He was begging now, his face streaked with tears. He would not stop tugging on her arm, hauling with such determination that she thought he would single-handedly drag her up the mountain, whether she cooperated or not. She let herself be pulled a few more steps up the slope.

Suddenly she heard the crack of wood, felt a bolt of pain shoot up her right ankle as the broken snowshoe collapsed under her weight. She toppled forward, arms splayed out to catch herself, and sank up to her elbows in snow. Spluttering, she struggled to rise, but her right foot would not move.

Rat wrapped an arm around her waist and tried to wrench her free.

"Stop!" she cried out. "My foot's stuck!"

He dropped to the ground and began tunneling into the snow. Bear stood by, looking bewildered as his master dug like a frenzied dog. "Your boot's wedged between boulders. I can't get it free!" He looked up at her, eyes lit with panic. "I'm going to pull. I might be able to get your foot out of the shoe. But it's going to hurt."

She looked down the mountain. Any moment, she thought, those men will be within rifle range, and they'd find her trapped like a staked goat. This was not the way she wanted to die. Exposed and helpless. She took a breath and nodded to Rat. "Do it."

He wrapped both hands around her ankle and began to pull. Pulled so hard that he groaned with the effort, so hard that she thought her foot would be torn apart. The pain ripped a cry from her throat. All at once her foot wrenched free of the boot and she sprawled backward onto the snow.

"I'm sorry, I'm sorry!" Rat cried. She smelled his sweat and fear, heard him wheezing in the cold as he grabbed her under the arms and hauled her up. Her right foot was clad only in a wool sock, and when she put her weight down on it, her leg sank knee-deep in snow.

"Lean on me. We'll get up the trail together." He draped her arm over his neck and grabbed her around the waist. "Come on," he urged. "You can make it. I know you can make it."

But can you? With every step they took together,

she could feel his muscles straining with the effort. If ever I had a son, she thought, this is the kind of boy I would want him to be. As loyal, as courageous, as Julian Perkins. She clutched him tighter, and the warmth of their bodies mingled as they fought their way up the mountain. This was the son she'd never had and probably never would have. Already they were bonded, their union forged in battle. *And I won't let them hurt him.*

Their snowshoes creaked in unison, and the steam from their breaths joined in a single cloud. Her exposed sock was soaked, her toes aching in the cold. Bear scrambled ahead of them, but they moved slowly, so slowly. Surely their pursuers could mark their quarry's progress up the barren slope.

She heard Bear growl, and she looked up the trail. The dog stood stock-still, his ears laid back. But he was not facing their pursuers in the valley; he was looking toward a plateau above them, where something dark was moving.

Gunfire cracked, echoing like thunder against the cliffs.

Maura felt Rat stumble against her. Suddenly the shoulder that had been supporting her collapsed and his arm slid away from her waist. As his knees buckled, she was the one trying to hold him up, but she wasn't strong enough. The best she could do was to break his fall as he sank to the ground. He fell beside a stand of boulders and lay on his back, as though to make a snow angel. He stared up at her with a look of astonishment. Only then did she notice the splatters of blood on the snow.

"No," she cried. "Oh God, *no.*"

"Go," he whispered.

"Rat. Honey," she murmured, fighting not to cry, to keep her voice steady. "You're going to be okay. I swear you're going to be okay, baby."

She unzipped his jacket and stared down in horror at the stain spreading across his shirt. She ripped the fabric apart and exposed the bullet wound that had punched into his chest. He was still breathing, but his jugular veins were distended, bulging like thick blue pipes. She touched his skin and felt the crackle of crepitus as air leaked from his chest and infiltrated the soft tissues, distorting his face, his neck. *Punctured right lung. Pneumothorax.*

Bear bounded back and licked Rat's face as the boy struggled to speak. Maura had to push the dog away so she could hear the boy's words.

"They're coming," he whispered. "Use the gun. Take it . . ."

She looked down at the deputy's weapon, which he'd pulled out of his jacket pocket. So this is how it's going to end, she thought. Their attackers had given them no warning, made no attempt to negotiate. The first shot had been meant to kill. There would be no chance to surrender; this was to be an execution.

And she was their next target.

Maura rose to a crouch to peer over the boulders.

A lone man was moving down the mountain toward them. He carried a rifle.

Bear gave a threatening bark, but before he could lunge from the cover of the boulders, Maura grabbed his collar and commanded: "Stay. *Stay.*"

Rat's lips had darkened to blue. With every breath he took, the punctured lung was leaking air into the chest cavity, where it was trapped, unable to escape. The pressure was building, squeezing that lung, shifting all the organs in his chest. If I don't act now, she thought, he will die.

She yanked open Rat's backpack and scrabbled through the contents for his knife. Sliding open the blade, she found it streaked with rust and dirt. To hell with sterility; he had only minutes left to live.

Bear barked again, a sound so frantic that she swung around to look at what had alarmed him. Now he was facing down the hill, where a dozen men were climbing toward them. *A man with a rifle above us. More armed men approaching from below us. We are trapped between them.*

She looked down at the gun, which had fallen in the snow beside Rat. The deputy's weapon. When this was over, when she and Rat were both dead, they would point to this gun as proof that they were cop-killers. No one would ever know the truth.

"Mommy." The word was barely a whisper. A child's plea from a young man's dying lips. "Mommy."

She bent close to the boy and touched his cheek.

Though he was looking straight at her, he seemed to be seeing someone else. Someone who made his lips slowly curve into a weak smile.

"I'm here, darling." She blinked as tears slid down her cheeks and chilled on her skin. "Your mommy will always be here."

The snap of a breaking branch made her stiffen. She raised her head to peer over the boulder and saw the lone rifleman just as he saw her.

He fired.

The bullet kicked snow into her eyes and she dropped back to the ground beside the dying boy.

No negotiations. No mercy.

I refuse to be slaughtered like an animal. She picked up the deputy's gun. Raising the barrel, she fired high into the air. A warning shot, to slow him down. To make him think.

Lower on the slope, dogs barked and men shouted. She saw the approaching posse scrambling up the mountain toward her. She had no cover against their gunfire. Crouching here beside Rat, she was exposed to the firing squad moving toward her.

"My name is Maura Isles!" she shouted. "I want to surrender! Please, let me surrender! My friend is hurt and he needs . . ." Her voice died as a shadow loomed above her. She looked up, into the barrel of a rifle.

The man holding it said, quietly: "Give me the gun."

"I want to give up," Maura pleaded. "My name is Maura Isles, and—"

"Just hand me that gun." He was an older man, with implacable eyes and authority in his voice. Though the words were spoken quietly, there was no compromise in that command. "Give it to me. Slowly."

Only as she started to obey him did she suddenly realize this move was wrong, all wrong. The gun in her grasp. Her arm lifting to hand it over. The men watching from below would not see a woman about to surrender; they would see a woman preparing to fire. Instantly she released her grip, letting the gun tumble from her fingers. But the man standing above her had already lifted his rifle to fire. His decision to kill her had been preordained.

The blast made her flinch. She fell to her knees, cowering in the snow beside Rat. Wondering why she felt no pain, saw no blood. *Why am I still alive?*

The man on the boulder above her gave a grunt of surprise as the rifle dropped from his hands. "Who's shooting at me?" he yelled.

"Back away from her, Loftus!" a voice commanded.

"She was gonna shoot me! I had to defend myself!"

"I said *back away.*"

I know that voice. It's Gabriel Dean.

Slowly Maura raised her head and saw not one,

but two familiar figures moving toward her. Gabriel kept his weapon aimed squarely at the man on the boulder, as Anthony Sansone ran to her side.

"Are you all right, Maura?" Sansone asked.

She had no time to waste on questions, no time to marvel over the miraculous appearance of these two men. "He's dying," she sobbed. "Help me save him."

Sansone dropped to his knees beside the boy. "Tell me what you want me to do."

"I'm going to decompress the chest. I need a chest tube. Anything hollow will work—even a ballpoint pen!"

She picked up Rat's knife and stared at the thin chest, at the ribs that stood out so starkly beneath the pale skin. Even on that frigid mountainside, her palm was sweating against the grip as she gathered the nerve to do what had to be done.

She found her landmark, pressed the blade against his skin, and sliced into the boy's chest.

THIRTY-TWO

HE WOULD HAVE KILLED ME," SAID MAURA. "IF
Gabriel and Sansone hadn't stopped him, that
man would have shot me in cold blood, the way he
shot Rat. No questions asked."

Jane glanced at her husband, who stood by the
window, looking out over the medical center parking lot. Gabriel neither contradicted nor confirmed
what Maura had said, but remained strangely un-
communicative, letting Maura tell the story. Except
for the murmur of the TV, its volume turned low, the
ICU visitors' lounge was quiet.

"There's something all wrong about what happened up there," Maura said. "Something that
doesn't make any sense. Why was he so determined
to kill us?" She looked up, and Jane scarcely recognized her friend in that gaunt and bruised face.
Maura's usually flawless skin was marred by
scratches that were now scabbing over. The new
sweater she wore hung far too loose on her frame,
and her collarbones stood out on the pitifully thin

chest. Without her stylish clothes, her makeup, Maura looked as vulnerable as any other woman, and that unsettled Jane. If even cool, confident Maura Isles could be reduced to this battered creature, then so could anyone. *Even me.*

"A deputy was killed," said Jane. "You know how things turn out whenever a cop goes down. Justice gets a little rough." Again she glanced at her husband, waiting for him to comment, but Gabriel just stared in silence at the glitteringly clear morning. Although he'd shaved and showered after his return from the mountain, he still looked exhausted and windburned, tired eyes squinting against the sunlight.

"No, he showed up there *intending* to kill us," said Maura. "Just like that deputy did, on Doyle Mountain. I think this is all about Kingdom Come. And what I wasn't supposed to see there."

"Well, we now know what that was," said Jane.

The day before, the last of forty-one bodies had been recovered from the burial pit. Twelve men, nineteen women, and ten children—most of them girls. The majority showed no signs of trauma, but Maura had seen enough in Kingdom Come to know the victims had surely been force-marched to their graves. The blood on the stairs, the abandoned meals, the pets left behind to starve—all pointed to mass murder.

"They couldn't let any of you live," said Jane. "Not after what you saw in that village."

"The day I hiked out, I heard a snowplow coming up the mountain," said Maura. "I thought they were finally there to rescue us. If I'd been there, with the others . . ."

"You would have ended up like them," said Jane. "With your skull fractured and your body burned up in the Suburban. All they had to do was roll it into the ravine, set it on fire, and that was the end of it. Just a group of unlucky tourists, dead in an accident, no questions asked." Jane paused. "I'm afraid I complicated things for you."

"How?"

"By insisting that you were still missing. I brought your clothes for the tracking dogs. I gave them everything they needed to hunt you down."

"I'd be dead now," said Maura softly. "If it weren't for the boy."

"Seems to me, you returned the favor." Jane reached out to take Maura's hand. It felt strange to do so, because Maura was not a woman who invited touches or hugs. But she did not flinch at Jane's touch; she seemed too weary to react at all.

"The case will all come together," said Jane. "It may take time, but I'm confident they'll find enough to tie it to The Gathering."

"And Jeremiah Goode."

Jane nodded. "It couldn't have happened unless he ordered it. But even if those people voluntarily drank poison, it's still mass murder. Because you're talking about children, who had no choice at all."

"Then the boy's mother. His sister . . ."

Jane shook her head. "If they were living in King-dom Come, they're probably among the dead. None of them have been identified yet. The first autopsy will be done today. Potassium cyanide is everyone's guess."

"Like Jonestown," said Maura softly.

Jane nodded. "Fast, effective, and available."

Maura looked up. "But they were his followers. The chosen ones. Why would he suddenly want them dead?"

"That's a question only Jeremiah can answer. And right now, no one knows where he is."

The door opened, and an ICU nurse stepped in. "Dr. Isles? The police have left, and the boy's ask-ing for you again."

"They should leave the poor kid alone," said Maura as she pushed herself out of the armchair. "I've already told them everything." For a moment she looked dangerously weak and wobbly, but she managed to regain her balance and followed the nurse out of the room.

Jane waited until the door swung shut again, then she looked at her husband. "Okay. Tell me what's bothering you."

He sighed. "Everything."

"Care to be more specific?"

He turned and faced her. "Maura's absolutely right. Montgomery Loftus fully intended to kill her and the boy. He didn't come with our search party.

He was canny enough to predict the boy would head for Absolem's cabin, and he hired a chopper to drop him off there. That's where he waited to ambush them. If we hadn't stopped him, he would have killed them both."

"What's his motive?"

"He claims he just wanted justice to be done. And no one around here is questioning that. After all, these are his friends and neighbors."

And we're just the meddlesome outsiders, thought Jane. She looked out the window at the parking lot, where Sansone was walking Bear. They made an odd couple, the wild-looking dog and the man in the cashmere coat. But Bear seemed to trust him, and willingly jumped into the car when Sansone opened the door for the drive back to the hotel.

"Martineau and Loftus," Jane said softly. "Is there a connection between them?"

"Maybe there's a money trail to follow. If Martineau got paid off by the Dahlia Group . . ."

She looked at Gabriel. "I've heard that Montgomery Loftus is having money trouble. He's barely hanging on to the Double L Ranch. He's ripe to be bought off, too."

"To kill Maura and a sixteen-year-old kid?" Gabriel shook his head. "He doesn't seem like a man you could buy off with money alone."

"Maybe it was a *lot* of money. If so, that's going to be hard to hide."

Gabriel glanced at his watch. "I think it's time I head to Denver."

"The Bureau field office?"

"We've got a mysterious shell company in Maryland. And large amounts of money being thrown around. This is starting to feel really big, Jane."

"Forty-one dead bodies isn't big enough?"

He gave a somber shake of the head. "That may be just the tip of the iceberg."

THIRTY-THREE

MAURA PAUSED IN THE ICU CUBICLE DOORWAY, unnerved by the sight of all the tubes and catheters and wires snaking around Rat's body, an invasion that no sixteen-year-old boy should ever have to endure. But the rhythm on the cardiac monitor was reassuringly steady, and he was now breathing on his own.

Sensing her presence, he opened his eyes and smiled. "Hey there, ma'am."

"Oh, Rat." She sighed. "Are you ever going to stop calling me that?"

"What should I call you?"

You called me Mommy once. She blinked away tears at the memory. The boy's real mother was almost certainly among the dead, but she did not have the heart to break the news to him. Instead she managed to return the boy's smile. "I give you permission to call me whatever you want. But my name is Maura."

She sat down in the chair beside his bed and

reached for his hand. Noticed how calloused and scabbed it was, the fingernails still stubbornly stained with dirt. She, who did not easily reach out to touch anyone, took that battered hand in hers, and took it without hesitation. It felt natural and right.

"How's Bear?" he asked.

She laughed. "You'll be changing his name to Pig when you see how much he's been eating."

"So he's okay?"

"My friends have been spoiling him rotten. And your foster family promised they'd look after him until you get home."

"Oh. Them." Rat's gaze drifted away from hers, and he looked up listlessly at the ceiling. "I guess I'll be going back there."

A place he clearly did not want to go. But what alternative could Maura offer him? A home with a divorced woman who knew nothing about raising children? A woman who was carrying on a furtive love affair with a man she could never acknowledge as her partner? She was a poor role model for a teenage boy, and her life was already troubled enough. Yet the offer trembled on her lips, an offer to take him in, to make him happy, to fix his life. To be his mother. Oh, how easy that offer was to make, and once made, how impossible to retract. Be sensible, Maura, she thought. You can't even keep a cat, much less raise a teenager on your own. No responsible authority would grant her custody. This boy had already known too much rejection, too many disappointments; it would be cruel to make promises she couldn't keep.

So she did not make any. She merely held his hand and stayed at his bedside as he drifted back to sleep. The nurse came in to change the IV bottle and whisked out again. But Maura remained, pondering the boy's future, and what part she could realistically hope to play in it. *I know this much: I won't abandon you. You'll always know that someone cares.*

A knock on the window made her turn, and she saw Jane beckoning to her.

Reluctantly Maura left the bedside and stepped out of the cubicle.

"They're about to start the first autopsy," Jane said.

"The Kingdom Come victims?"

Jane nodded. "The forensic pathologist just arrived from Colorado. He said he knows you, and he's wondering if you'd care to observe. He's doing it downstairs, in the hospital morgue."

Maura glanced through the window at Rat, and saw that he was peacefully sleeping. The lost boy, still waiting to be claimed. *I'll be back. I promise.*

She nodded to Jane, and they left the ICU.

When they arrived in the morgue, they found the anteroom crowded with observers, Sheriff Fahey and Detective Pasternak among them. The sheer number of victims had made this a high-profile case, and nearly a dozen law enforcement and state and county officials had gathered to witness the autopsy.

The pathologist saw Maura walk into the room and raised a beefy hand in greeting. Two summers ago, she'd met Dr. Fred Gruber at a forensic pathology conference in Maine, and he seemed pleased to spot a familiar face.

"Dr. Isles," he called out in his booming voice. "I could use another set of expert eyes. You want to gown up and join me in there?"

"I don't think that's appropriate," said Sheriff Fahey.

"Dr. Isles is a forensic pathologist."

"She doesn't work for the state of Wyoming. This case is going to be watched closely, and questions could be raised."

"Why would there be any questions?"

"Because she was in that valley. She's a witness, and there could be charges of tampering. Contamination."

Maura said, "I'm only here to observe, and I can do that perfectly well from this side of the window, with the rest of you. I assume we can watch it on that monitor?" She pointed to the TV screen mounted in the anteroom.

"I'll turn on the camera, so you'll all have a good view," said Dr. Gruber. "And I'm going to ask all the observers to remain in this room anyway, with

the door shut. Since there's a possibility we're dealing with cyanide poisoning."

"I thought you had to swallow the stuff to get
sick," one of the officials said.

"There's the chance of outgassing. The biggest
danger is when I cut into the stomach, because that's
when cyanide gas might be released. My assistant
and I will be wearing respirators, and I'll dissect the
stomach under the fume hood cabinet. We've also
brought a GasBadge sensor, which will immediately
alert us if it detects hydrogen cyanide. If it's negative,
I may be able to let some of you into the room. But
you'll have to wear gowns and masks."

Gruber donned dissection garb, including a respirator hood, and pushed through the door into the
autopsy lab. His assistant was already waiting,
similarly garbed. They turned on the camera, and on
the TV monitor, Maura could see the empty autopsy
table awaiting its subject. Gruber and his assistant
wheeled the plastic-shrouded body out of cold
storage and slid it onto the table.

Gruber unzipped the shroud.

On the video monitor, Maura could see that the
body was a young girl, only about twelve or thirteen.
Since the exhumation from the frozen ground, her
flesh had been allowed to thaw. Her face was ghostly
pale, her blond hair a crown of damp ringlets. Gruber and his assistant were quietly respectful as they
removed the garments. Off came a long cotton dress,

a knee-length slip, and modest white briefs. The corpse, now nude, was slender as a dancer's, and despite days of burial, she was still eerily beautiful, her flesh preserved by the valley's subfreezing temperatures.

The officials pressed in closer around the monitor. As Gruber collected blood, urine, and vitreous specimens for toxicology, the men's eyes took in what should never have been revealed to them. It was a violation of a young girl's modesty.

"The skin is markedly pale," they heard Gruber say over the intercom speaker. "I see absolutely no residual flush."

"Is that significant?" Detective Pasternak asked Maura.

"Cyanide poisoning can sometimes cause the skin to appear bright red," she answered. "But this body has been frozen for days, so I don't know if that would affect it."

"What else would you find in cyanide poisoning?"

"If it's ingested orally, it can corrode the mouth and lips. You'll see it in the mucous membranes."

Gruber had already slipped a gloved finger into the oral cavity and he peered inside. "Membranes are dry, but otherwise unremarkable." He glanced through the window at his audience. "You getting a good view of this on the monitor?"

Maura nodded at him. "There are no corrosive lesions?" she asked over the intercom.

"None."

Jane said, "Isn't cyanide supposed to smell like bitter almonds?"

"They're wearing respirators," said Maura. "They wouldn't be able to smell it."

Gruber carved the Y-incision and picked up the bone cutters. Over the intercom, they heard the *crack, crack* as he split the ribs, and Maura noticed several of the officials suddenly turn away and stare at the wall. Gruber lifted up the shield of sternum and ribs, exposing the chest cavity, and reached into the chest to resect the lungs. He lifted out one wet and dripping lobe. "Feels pretty heavy to me. And I'm seeing some pink froth here." He sliced into the organ, and fluid oozed out.

"Pulmonary edema," said Maura.

"What does that signify?" Pasternak asked her.

"It's a nonspecific finding, but it can be caused by a number of drugs and toxins."

As Gruber weighed the heart and lungs, the camera remained fixed on a static view of the torso, gaping open. No longer were they staring at a nubile young girl. What once might have titillated had been transformed to butchered flesh, a mere carcass of cold meat.

Gruber once again picked up his knife and his gloved hands reappeared on the monitor. "This damn face shield keeps fogging up," he complained. "I'll dissect the heart and lungs later. Right now, I'm most concerned about what we're going to find in the stomach."

"What is your sensor showing?" Maura asked.

The assistant glanced at the GasBadge monitor. "It's not registering anything. No cyanide detected yet."

Gruber said, "Okay, here's where things could get interesting." He looked through the window at his audience. "Because we could be dealing with cyanide, I'm going to proceed a little differently. Normally I'd just resect, weigh, and open up the abdominal organs. But this time I'm going clamp off the stomach first, before I resect it in toto."

"He'll place it under the fume hood before he slices it open," Maura explained to Jane. "Just to be safe."

"Is it really that dangerous?"

"When cyanide salts are exposed to gastric acid, they can form toxic gas. Open that stomach and you release the gas into the air. That's why they're wearing respirator hoods. And why he's not going to cut into that stomach until it's under a fume hood."

Through the window, they watched Gruber lift the clamped and resected stomach out of the abdomen. He carried it to the fume hood cabinet and glanced at his assistant.

"Anything showing up on the GasBadge?"

"Not a blip."

"Okay. Bring that monitor closer. Let's see what happens when I start cutting." Gruber paused, staring down at the glistening organ, as though bracing for the consequence of what he was about to do.

The fume hood blocked Maura's view of the actual incision. What she saw was Gruber's profile, his head craned forward, his shoulders hunched in concentration as he sliced. Abruptly he straightened and looked at his assistant.

"Well?"

"Nothing. It's not reading cyanide, chlorine, or ammonia gas."

Gruber turned to the window, his face obscured by the fogged mask. "There are no mucosal lesions, no corrosive changes in the stomach. I have to conclude that we're probably not dealing with cyanide poisoning."

"Then what killed her?" asked Pasternak.

"At this point, Detective, I'd be guessing. I suppose they could have ingested strychnine, but the body shows no lingering opisthotonos."

"What?"

"Abnormal arching and rigidity of the back."

"What about that other finding, in the lungs?"

"Her pulmonary edema could be due to anything from opiates to phosgene. I can't give you an answer. I'm afraid this is all going to come down to the tox screen." He pulled off his fogged respirator hood and heaved out a sigh, as though relieved to be free of that claustrophobic mask. "Right now, I'm thinking this is a pharmaceutical death. A drug of some kind."

"But the stomach's empty?" said Maura. "You didn't find any capsule remnants?"

"The drugs could have come in liquid form. Or

death could have been delayed. Sedation, followed by assisted asphyxiation."

"Heaven's Gate," Maura heard someone say behind her.

"Exactly. Like the Heaven's Gate mass suicide in San Diego," said Gruber. "They ingested phenobarbital and tied plastic bags over their heads. Then they went to sleep and never woke up." He turned back to the table. "Now that we've ruled out any danger of cyanide gas, I'm going to take my time. You'll all have to be patient. In fact, some of you may find the rest of this tedious, if you'd like to leave."

"Dr. Gruber," one of the officials said, "how long is this first autopsy going to take? There are forty other bodies waiting in the deep freeze."

"And I'm not thawing any more of them until I'm satisfied I've done justice to this young lady." He looked down at the girl's corpse, and his gaze was mournful. Entrails glistened in her gaping abdomen, and her freshly thawed flesh dripped pink icemelt into the table drain. But it was her face that seemed to hold his attention. Staring up at the monitor, Maura, too, was transfixed by the face, so pale, so innocent. A snow maiden, frozen on the threshold of womanhood.

"Dr. Gruber?" the assistant said. "Are you okay? Doctor?"

Maura's gaze shot back to the viewing window. Gruber swayed and put his hand out to catch himself against the table, but his legs seemed to dissolve away beneath him. A tray toppled and steel instruments clattered across the floor. Gruber collapsed, his body landing with a sickening thud.

"Oh my God!" The assistant knelt down beside the body. "I think he's having a seizure!"

Maura grabbed the nearest telephone and dialed the operator. "Code Blue, autopsy lab," she said. "We have a Code Blue!" As she hung up, she saw to her dismay that three observers had already pushed through the door into the lab. Jane was about to follow them when Maura grabbed her arm and stopped her.

"What the hell?" Jane said.

"You stay right here." Maura snatched an autopsy gown off a shelf and thrust her arms into heavy rubber dissecting gloves. "Don't let anyone else into that room."

"But the guy's having a seizure in there!"

"*After* he took off his hood." She glanced around frantically for another respirator, but she saw none in the anteroom. No other choice, she thought. I have to be quick. She washed out her lungs with three deep breaths and pushed through the door, into the lab. Gruber had left his respirator lying on the fume hood cabinet. She snatched it up and pulled it over her head. Heard a clang and turned to see one of the men sag against the sink.

"Everyone, get out of here!" she yelled as she grabbed the wobbling man and helped him toward the door. "This room is toxic!"

The morgue assistant shot her a stunned look through his mask. "I don't understand! The Gas-Badge monitor didn't register a thing!"

She bent down to grab Gruber under his arms, but he was too heavy, an immovable deadweight. "Take his feet!" she ordered.

Together she and the morgue assistant dragged Gruber away from the table and across a floor littered with instruments. By the time they pulled him into the anteroom, the Code Blue team had arrived and was strapping oxygen masks onto three pale-looking men.

Maura looked down at Gruber, whose face was tinged with blue. "This man's not breathing!" she yelled.

As the code team converged on the patient, Maura backed away to let them do their jobs. Within seconds they were forcing oxygen into his lungs, slapping cardiac leads on his chest. On the monitor, an EKG tracing appeared.

"He's got a sinus rhythm. Rate of fifty."

"I'm not getting a blood pressure. He's not perfusing."

"Start compressions!"

Maura said, "He was exposed to something. Something in that room."

But no one seemed to hear her through her respirator hood. Her head was pounding. She pulled off the hood and blinked against lights that suddenly seemed too bright. The medical team was in full

Code Blue mode now, and Fred Gruber's torso was completely bared, his bloated abdomen humiliatingly exposed and jiggling with each cardiac compression. The stench of urine rose from his soaked scrub pants.

"Do we have any history on this man?" the doctor called out. "What do we know about him?"

"He collapsed while doing an autopsy," Jane said.

"He looks about a hundred pounds overweight. I'm betting he had an MI."

"He wet himself," said Maura.

Again, her voice went ignored. She was like a ghost hovering at the periphery, unheard and unheeded. She pressed a hand to her head, which was pounding even worse, and struggled to think, to focus. Somehow she managed to push her way into the throng of personnel and kneel down near Gruber's head. Lifting one of his eyelids, she stared at the pupil.

It was barely a pinprick of black against the pale blue iris.

The stench of urine wafted up from his body, and she looked at his soaked scrub pants. Suddenly aware of the sound of retching, she glanced across the room and saw the morgue assistant was vomiting into a sink.

"Atropine," she said.

"I got the IV in!" a nurse called out.

"I'm still not getting a blood pressure."

"You want a dopamine drip?"

"He needs atropine," said Maura, louder.

For the first time, the doctor seemed to notice her. "Why? His heart rate's not that slow."

"He has pinpoint pupils. He's soaked with urine."

"He also had a seizure."

"We all got sick in that room." She pointed to the morgue assistant, who was still leaning over the sink. "Give him the atropine now, or you're going to lose him."

The doctor lifted Gruber's eyelid and stared at the constricted pupil. "Okay. Atropine, two milligrams," he ordered.

"And you need to seal that lab," said Maura. "We should all move into the hallway now, as far from that room as possible. They need to call in a hazmat team."

"What the hell is going on?" said Jane.

Maura turned to her, and just that sudden movement made the room seem to whirl. "They've got a chemical hazard in there."

"But the GasBadge readings were negative."

"Negative for what it was monitoring. But that's not what poisoned him."

"Then you know what it is? You know what killed all those people?"

Maura nodded. "I know exactly why they died."

THIRTY-FOUR

ORGANOPHOSPHATE COMPOUNDS ARE AMONG the most toxic of pesticides used in the agricultural industry," said Maura. "They can be absorbed by almost all routes, including through the skin and by inhalation. That's how Dr. Gruber probably got exposed in the autopsy room. When he removed his respirator and breathed in the fumes. Fortunately, he received the appropriate treatment in time, and he's going to recover." She looked around the table at the medical and law enforcement personnel who had gathered in the hospital conference room. She did not need to add the fact that she was the one who'd made the diagnosis and saved Gruber's life. They already knew it, and although she was an outsider, she heard a tone of respect when they addressed her.

"That alone can kill you?" said Detective Pasternak. "Just doing an autopsy on a poisoned corpse?"

"Potentially it can, if you're exposed to a lethal dose. Organophosphates work by inhibiting the enzyme that breaks down a neurotransmitter called acetylcholine. The result is that acetylcholine accumulates to dangerous levels. That causes nerve impulses to fire off like crazy throughout the parasympathetic nervous system. It's a synaptic storm. The patient sweats and salivates. He loses control of his bladder and bowels. His pupils constrict to pinpoints, and his lungs fill with fluid. Eventually, he'll start convulsing and lose consciousness."

"I don't understand something," said Sheriff Fahey. "Dr. Gruber got sick within half an hour of starting that autopsy. But the coroner's recovery team dug up forty-one of those corpses, put them in body bags, and moved them into an airport hangar. None of those workers ended up in the hospital."

Dr. Draper, the county coroner, spoke up. "I have a confession to make. It's a detail that was reported to me yesterday, but I didn't realize it was significant until now. Four members of our recovery team came down with the stomach flu. Or that's what they thought it was."

"But no one keeled over and died," said Fahey.

"Probably because they were working with frozen bodies. And they were wearing protective garb, plus heavy winter clothes. The body in the autopsy room was the first one to be thawed."

"Would that make a difference?" asked Pasternak. "Frozen versus a thawed corpse?"

Everyone looked at Maura, and she nodded. "At higher temperatures, toxic compounds are more likely to aerosolize. As that body defrosted, it started to release gases. Dr. Gruber probably sped up the process when he sliced it open, exposing body fluids and internal organs. He wouldn't be the first doctor to fall ill from exposure to toxins in a patient."

"Wait. This is starting to sound familiar," said Jane. "Wasn't there a case like this out in California?"

"I think you're referring to the Gloria Ramirez case, in the mid-1990s," said Maura. "That was discussed quite a bit at forensic pathology conferences."

"What happened in that case?" asked Pasternak.

"Gloria Ramirez was a cancer patient who came into the emergency room complaining of stomach pains. She suffered a cardiac arrest. As the medical team worked on her, they began to feel ill, and several of them collapsed."

"Was it due to this same pesticide?"

"That was the theory at the time," said Maura. "When they performed the autopsy, the pathologists donned full protective gear. They never did identify the toxin. But here's the interesting detail: The medical personnel who collapsed while treating her were successfully resuscitated with intravenous atropine."

"The same drug used to save Gruber."

"That's right."

Pasternak said, "How sure are you that this organophosphate stuff is what we're dealing with?"

"It will need to be confirmed by the tox report.

But the clinical picture is classic. Gruber responded to atropine. And a STAT blood test showed a significant drop in cholinesterase activity. Again, that's something you'd find with organophosphate poisoning."

"Is that enough to say it's a slam dunk?"

"It's pretty damn close to one." Maura looked at the faces around the table and wondered how many of these people, aside from Jane, were ready to trust her. Only days ago, she had been a possible suspect in the shooting of Deputy Martineau. Surely doubts about her still lingered in their minds, even if no one voiced them aloud. "The people who lived in Kingdom Come were most likely poisoned by an organophosphate pesticide," she said. "The question is, was it mass suicide? Homicide? Or an accident?"

That was met with a sound of disbelief from Cathy Weiss. The social worker had been sitting in the corner as if aware she was not fully accepted as a member of this team, although Detective Pasternak had invited her to attend the briefing.

"An accident?" Cathy said. "Forty-one people are dead because they were *ordered* to drink pesticide. When the Prophet tells his followers to jump, their only possible response is to ask *how high, sir?*"

"Or someone could have dumped it in their well water," said Dr. Draper. "Which makes it homicide."

"Whether it's homicide or mass suicide, I have no doubt it was the Prophet's decision," Cathy said.

"Anyone could have poisoned the water," pointed out Fahey. "It could have been a disgruntled follower. Hell, it could have been that Perkins boy."

"He'd never do that," said Maura.

"They kicked him out of the valley, didn't they? He had every reason to get back at them."

"Oh right," said Cathy, not bothering to hide her disdain of Fahey. "And then that lone sixteen-year-old boy single-handedly drags forty-one bodies into the field and buries them with a bulldozer?" She laughed.

Fahey looked back and forth at Maura and Cathy, and he gave a dismissive snort. "You ladies obviously don't know what sixteen-year-old boys are capable of."

"I know what Jeremiah Goode is capable of," Cathy shot back.

Pasternak's ringing cell phone cut off the conversation. He glanced at the number and quickly rose from his chair. "Excuse me," he said, and left the room.

For a moment there was silence, the tension from the last exchange still hanging in the air.

Then Jane said, "Whoever did it needed access to the pesticide. There must be a record of its purchase. Especially since we're talking about a large enough supply to kill an entire community."

"The Plain of Angels compound in Idaho grows its own food," said Cathy. "They're a completely self-sustaining community. It's likely they'd keep this pesticide on hand for farming."

"Doesn't prove they're guilty," said Fahey.

"They have the poison. They have access to Kingdom Come and its water supply."

"I'm still not hearing a motive. No reason why Jeremiah Goode would want forty-one of his own followers dead."

"For a motive, you'll have to ask *him*," snapped Cathy.

"Yeah, well, you tell us where to find him and we'll do that."

"Actually," said Pasternak, "we do know where to find him." The detective was standing in the doorway, cell phone in hand. "I just got a call from the Idaho State Police. Their contact inside The Gathering reports that Jeremiah Goode has just been spotted inside the Plain of Angels compound. Idaho's mobilizing for a raid at first light."

"That's at least seven hours from now," said Jane. "Why are they waiting so long to do it?"

"They need enough manpower. Not just law enforcement but also child protective services and social workers, to deal with the women and children. If they meet up with resistance, it could get dangerous." Pasternak looked at Cathy. "And that's where you come in, Ms. Weiss."

Cathy frowned. "What do you mean?"

"You seem to know more about The Gathering than anyone else does."

"And I've been trying to warn people about them for years."

"Well, now we're listening. I need to know how they might respond. Whether they'll react with violence. I need to know exactly what to expect." He glanced around the room. "Idaho is requesting our assistance. They want us to be mobilized before sunrise."

"I can be ready to leave within the hour," said Cathy.

"Good," said Pasternak. "You'll ride with me. Tonight, Ms. Weiss, you are my new best friend."

They drove through the night, Pasternak at the wheel, Cathy riding beside him. In the backseat, Jane sat alone. This was to be a police operation, one that Maura could not be part of, and Cathy was the only civilian invited to participate.

As they journeyed west, Cathy predicted what they would face at Plain of Angels. "The women won't talk to you. Nor will the children. They've been conditioned to be silent around outsiders. So don't expect cooperation from any of them, even when you get them away from the compound."

"What about the men?"

"They'll have designated spokesmen, handpicked

by Jeremiah to deal with the outside world. In return for their loyalty, they enjoy special privileges in the cult."

"Privileges?"

"Girls, Detective. The more trusted you are, the more young brides you get as your reward."

"Jesus."

"All cults work in similar ways. It's a system of reward and punishment. Make the Prophet happy, and he'll let you take another new wife. Piss him off, and you're banished from the sect. These spokesmen are men he trusts, and they're not stupid. They know the law, and they'll try to snow you with legalese. They'll hold us at the gate forever while they examine the warrant with a fine-tooth comb."

"Will they be armed?"

"Yes."

"And probably dangerous," Jane muttered in the backseat.

Cathy turned to look at her. "When they're facing years in prison for raping underage girls? Yeah, I'd say that makes them dangerous. So I hope you're all prepared."

"How big a team is moving in?" asked Jane.

Pasternak said, "Idaho's pulling in law enforcement from multiple jurisdictions, both state and federal. The team lead is Lieutenant David MacAfee, with the Idaho State Police. He guarantees there will be a massive show of force."

Cathy released a deep sigh. "Finally, it's going to end," she whispered.

"Sounds like you've been waiting for this a long time," observed Pasternak.

"Yes," Cathy said. "A very long time. I'm just glad I'll be there to see it happen."

"You do know, Ms. Weiss, that you're not to take an active role in this operation. I don't want you in danger." He glanced over his shoulder at Jane. "And it might be better if you remain an observer as well."

"But I'm law enforcement," said Jane.

"From Boston."

"I was working this case before you stepped in."

"Don't get all women's libber on me. I'm just saying this is Idaho's show. You've been invited to advise and assist where necessary. If they want to keep you on the sidelines, that's their decision. That's just the way it works, Rizzoli."

Jane sank back against the seat. "Okay. But just to let you know, I *am* carrying."

"Then keep it holstered. If this is handled right, there'll be no need for weapons. Our objective is to move the women and children into protective custody, and do it with a minimum of force."

"Wait. What about Jeremiah?" said Cathy. "If you find him, you *are* arresting him, aren't you?"

"At this point, it's just for questioning."

"Forty-one dead followers isn't enough to charge him?"

"We haven't proven that he's responsible for those deaths."

"Who else would be?"

"We need more than that. We need witnesses, someone who'll step forward and talk to us." He glanced at Cathy. "That's what I need you to do. Talk to those women. Convince them to cooperate."

"That won't be easy."

"Help them understand that they're victims."

"Remember Charles Manson's women? Even after years in prison, they were still Charlie's girls, still under his spell. You can't deprogram in a few days what's been pounded into your head for years. And if they insist on going back to the compound, you can't hold them indefinitely."

"Then do it another way," said Jane. "DNA tests on the babies. Find out which men are the fathers. Find out if the mothers were underage when they gave birth."

"That's like cutting the branches to kill a tree," said Cathy. "There's only one way to bring it crashing down. You have to destroy the root."

"Jeremiah," said Pasternak.

Cathy nodded. "Lock him up and throw away the key. Without the Prophet, the cult implodes. Because Jeremiah Goode *is* The Gathering."

THIRTY-FIVE

CLOAKED BY A VEIL OF FALLING SNOW, THE army stood assembled. Jane stamped her feet, trying to stay warm, but already her toes had gone numb and even the scalding cup of coffee she'd just gulped down could not ward off the bitter chill of that Idaho dawn. If she were a member of the strike team, the cold would not matter to her, because adrenaline made one immune to discomforts as minor as subzero temperatures. But on this morning, relegated to the status of mere observer and forced to stand idly by, she felt the chill gnaw deep into her bones. Cathy, standing beside her, seemed not to care at all about the weather. The woman was utterly still, her face heedlessly exposed to the wind. Jane heard the rising pitch in the voices around her, could feel the tension in the air, and she knew that action was imminent.

Pasternak came striding back from the huddle of command officers. He was carrying a two-way radio. "We're ready to move, as soon as they pull the gate down." He handed Jane the radio. "You stay with Cathy. We'll need her advice once we get in there, and you're her escort. So keep her safe."

As Jane clipped it to her belt, an alert came over the speaker.

"We have activity inside the compound. Looks like two men approaching."

Through the falling snow, Jane saw the figures walking closer, identically dressed in long black coats. They moved without hesitation, striding directly toward the lawmen. To Jane's surprise, one of the men produced a set of keys and unlocked the gate.

The law enforcement team leader stepped forward. "I'm Lieutenant MacAfee, Idaho State Police. We have a warrant to search the compound."

"There's no need for a warrant," the man with the keys answered. "You are welcome to enter. All of you." He swung the gate wide open.

MacAfee glanced at the other officers, clearly taken aback by the welcome.

The greeter beckoned the visitors forward. "We've gathered in the assembly hall, where there's room for everyone. We ask only that you keep your weapons holstered, for the safety of our women and children." He opened his arms wide, as though inviting in the whole world. "Please join us. You'll see that we have nothing to hide."

"They knew," Cathy muttered. "Goddamn it, they *knew* we were coming. They're prepared for this."

"How did they get word of it?" Jane asked.

"He can buy anything. Eyes, ears. A cop here, a politician there." She looked at Jane. "You see what the problem is? You see why he'll never have to face justice?"

"No man's untouchable, Cathy."

"*He* is. He always has been." Cathy's gaze returned to the open gate. The law enforcement team had already walked into the compound, their figures fading beyond the falling snow. Over the radio, Jane listened in on the chatter. Heard calm voices, matter-of-fact responses.

"First building checked and clear . . ."

"All clear in number three."

Cathy shook her head. "He'll outsmart them this time as well," she said. "They don't know what to look for. They can't see what's right in front of their goddamn eyes."

"No weapons. All clear . . ."

Cathy stared at the distant figures, now receding to little more than ghostly shapes. Without a word, she, too, walked through the open gate.

Jane followed her.

They moved between rows of buildings that stood silent and dark, following in the boot prints of the police team. Ahead, Jane saw candlelight glowing warmly in the assembly hall windows, and she heard music, the sound of many voices raised in song. It was a sweet and ethereal hymn that soared heavenward on notes sung by children. The scent of wood smoke, the promise of warmth and fellowship, beckoned them toward the building.

They stepped through the door, into the assembly hall.

Inside, a multitude of candles lit the soaring space. A congregation of hundreds filled gleaming wood pews. On one side of the aisle sat the women and girls in a sea of pastel dresses. On the other side were the men and boys, clad in white shirts and dark trousers. A dozen law enforcement officers had gathered at the rear of the hall, where they stood looking about uneasily, uncertain how to proceed in what was clearly a house of worship.

The hymn came to an end, and the final, thrilling notes faded. In the silence, a dark-haired man emerged onto the stage and calmly surveyed his congregation. He wore no priestly robes, no embroidered shawl, no ornaments that set him apart as different or special. Instead he stood before them garbed in the same clothes as his followers, but the sleeves of his white shirt were rolled up to the elbows, as though in preparation for a day's labors. He needed no costume, no eye-catching glitter to hold the crowd's attention. His gaze alone, so intense it seemed radioactive, riveted every pair of eyes in the hall.

So this is Jeremiah Goode, thought Jane. Though his hair was shot through with silver, it still looked like a young man's mane, thick and leonine, falling almost to his shoulders. On this gloomy winter's day, his presence seemed to give off as warm a glow as the flames leaping in the hall's enormous stone hearth. In silence, he surveyed the audience, and his gaze finally settled on the police officers standing at the rear of the hall.

"Dear friends, let us all rise to welcome our visitors," he said.

As if they were a single organism, the congregation rose in unison and turned to look at the strangers. "Welcome" came the chorus of greeting. Every face looked scrubbed and pink-cheeked, every gaze wide-eyed with innocence. *Wholesome and healthy* was the picture here, the portrait of a contented community united in purpose.

Again, in unison, they all sat down. It was an eerily choreographed movement that set off a simultaneous creak of benches.

Lieutenant MacAfee called out: "Jeremiah Goode?"

The man onstage gave a solemn nod. "I am Jeremiah."

"I'm Lieutenant David MacAfee, Idaho State Police. Would you come with us, sir?"

"May I ask why this show of force is necessary? Especially now, in our hour of distress?"

"Distress, Mr. Goode?"

"That is why you're here, isn't it? Because of the atrocities committed against our poor brethren in Kingdom Come?" Somberly, Jeremiah looked around at his congregation. "Yes, friends, we know, don't we? Word came to us yesterday, the terrible news of what was done to our followers. All because of who they were, and what they believed."

In the audience, there were nods and murmurs of sad agreement.

"Mr. Goode," said MacAfee, "I'm asking you again to come with us."

"Why?"

"To answer a few questions."

"Then ask them here and now, so that all may listen." Jeremiah held out his arms in an extravagant gesture toward his followers. This was grand theater, and he was center stage, with the hall's arches soaring above him, and the light from the windows beaming down on his face. "I keep no secrets from this congregation."

"This isn't a matter for a public forum," said MacAfee. "This is a criminal investigation."

"You think I don't understand that?" Jeremiah stared at him with a gaze that seemed to sear the air. "Our followers were *murdered* in that valley. *Executed* like sheep, and their bodies left to be torn and devoured by wild animals!"

"Is that what you heard?"

"Is it not the truth? That forty-one good people, including women and children, were martyred because of what they believed? And now you come here, invited through our gates. You men with your guns and your disdain for those who don't believe what you do."

MacAfee shifted uneasily. In the warmth of the hall, beads of sweat gleamed on his forehead. "I'll ask this one more time, Mr. Goode. Either you come with us willingly, or we'll be forced to arrest you."

"I *am* willing! Didn't I just say I would answer your questions? But ask them now, where these good people can hear you. Or are you afraid of the whole world learning the truth?" He looked around at his followers. "My friends, *you* are my protection. I call on you to bear witness."

A man in the congregation rose to his feet and called out: "What are the police afraid of? Ask your questions so we can hear, too!"

The crowd joined in. "Yes, ask now!"

"Ask him here!"

Benches creaked as the crowd grew agitated, as other men stood. The police officers glanced nervously around the room.

"Then you refuse to cooperate?" MacAfee said.

"I *am* cooperating. But if you're here to ask about Kingdom Come, I can't help you."

"You call this cooperation?"

"I have no answers for you. Because I wasn't witness to what happened."

"When were you last in Kingdom Come?"

"It was October. When I left them, they were thriving. Well provisioned for winter. Already digging the foundations for six more houses. That was the last time I laid eyes on the valley." He looked to his congregation for support. "Am I telling the truth? Is there anyone here who would contradict me?"

Dozens of voices took up his defense. "The Prophet doesn't lie!"

Jeremiah looked at MacAfee. "I think you have your answer, Lieutenant."

"Not by a long shot," MacAfee snapped.

"Do you see, my friends?" Jeremiah said, gazing around at his followers. "How they profane God's house with their army and their weapons?" He shook his head in pity. "This spectacle of force is a tactic of *small* men." He smiled at MacAfee. "Has it worked for you, Lieutenant? Do you feel *larger* now?"

This taunt was more than MacAfee could endure, and his spine stiffened at the challenge. "Jeremiah Goode, you are under arrest. And all these children are now in protective custody. They are to be escorted off this property, where buses are waiting for them."

A startled cry rose from the women, followed by a chorus of wails and sobs. The entire congregation surged to its feet in protest. In a matter of mere seconds, MacAfee had lost control of the room, and Jane saw officers' hands drop to their weapons. Instinctively, she reached for her own as the fury swelled, as violence seemed just one spark away.

"My friends! My friends!" Jeremiah called out.

"Please, let us have peace." He raised his arms and the room instantly hushed. "The world will know the truth soon enough," he proclaimed. "They'll see that we conducted ourselves with dignity and compassion. That when confronted by the brutal face of authority, we responded with grace and humility." He released a deep and mournful sigh. "My friends, we have no choice but to obey. And I have no choice but to submit to their will. I ask only that you remember what you witnessed here today. The injustice, the cruelty of families wrenched apart." He gazed upward, as though speaking directly to the heavens. Only then did Jane notice the congregant in the upper balcony, filming the entire speech. *This is all on camera. The video-taped martyrdom of Jeremiah Goode.* Once that footage was disseminated to the media, the whole world would know of this outrage against a peaceful community.

"Remember, friends!" commanded Jeremiah.

"Remember!" the congregation responded in unison.

He descended the steps from the stage and walked calmly toward the waiting police officers. As he moved up the aisle, past his stunned followers, the sound of weeping filled the hall. Yet Jeremiah's expression was not mournful; what Jane saw on his face was triumph. He had planned and orchestrated this confrontation, a scene that would be played and replayed on TVs across the country. The humble prophet walking with quiet dignity toward his tormentors. He's won this round, she thought. Maybe he's even won the war itself. How would a jury convict him when he was the one who looked like a victim?

He came to a stop in front of MacAfee and raised his hands, meekly offering up his wrists to be cuffed. The symbolism could not be more blatant. MacAfee obliged, and the clack of the metal was shockingly loud.

"Will you exterminate us all?" Jeremiah asked.

"Give it a rest," MacAfee retorted.

"You know very well I had nothing to do with what happened in Kingdom Come."

"That's what we'll find out."

"Will you? I don't think you want the truth. Because you've already chosen your villain." Head held high, Jeremiah walked the gauntlet of police officers. But as he neared the exit, he suddenly halted, his gaze riveted on Cathy Weiss. Slowly his lips curved into a smile of recognition. "Katie Sheldon," he said softly. "You've come back to us."

Jane frowned at Cathy, whose face had gone frighteningly pale. "But you told me Katie Sheldon was your friend," Jane said.

Cathy didn't seem to hear Jane, but kept her gaze on Jeremiah. "This time it ends," Cathy said softly.

"Ends?" He shook his head. "No, Katie, this only makes us stronger. In the eyes of the public, I'm a martyr." He regarded her windblown hair, her haggard face, and the look he gave her was almost pitying. "I see the world has not been kind to you. What a shame you ever left us." He smiled as he turned to leave. "But we must all move on."

"Jeremiah!" Cathy suddenly stepped behind him, her arms thrust out in front of her. Only then did Jane see what she was clutching in both hands.

"Cathy, no!" yelled Jane. In an instant she had her own weapon out. "Drop it. Drop the gun, Cathy!"

Jeremiah turned and calmly regarded the weapon that was now pointed at his chest. If he felt any fear at all, he did not show it. Through the pounding of her own heart, Jane heard gasps in the pews and frantic footsteps as the congregation scrambled for cover. She had no doubt that a dozen police weapons were now drawn and pointed as well. But Jane's gaze stayed glued on Cathy. On the raw, wind-chapped hands now clutching the gun. Though any cop in that room could have fired on her, no one did. They all stood paralyzed by the prospect of taking down this young woman. *We never imagined she'd be armed. Why would we?*

"Cathy, please," Jane said quietly. She was standing closest to the woman. Almost close enough to reach out and take the gun, if only Cathy would hand it to her. "This doesn't solve anything."

"But it does. This ends it."

"That's what the courts are for."

"The *courts*?" Cathy's laugh was bitter. "They won't touch him. They never have." Her grip tightened, and the barrel tilted higher, yet Jeremiah did not flinch. His gaze remained serene, almost amused.

"You see, my friends?" he called out. "This is what we face. Irrational anger and hatred." He gave a sad shake of the head and looked at Cathy. "I think it's clear to everyone here that you need help, Katie. I feel only love for you. That's all I've ever felt." Once again, he turned to leave.

"Love?" Cathy whispered. *"Love?"*

Jane saw the tendons in Cathy's wrist snap taut. Saw the woman's fingers tighten, yet her own reflexes refused to kick in. Her hands froze around her weapon.

The blast of Cathy's gun sent a bullet flying into Jeremiah's back. He lurched forward and stumbled to his knees.

The room exploded in gunfire. Cathy's body jerked and twitched as a hail of police bullets punched into her flesh. Her weapon thudded to the floor and she went sprawling. She landed facedown beside the body of Jeremiah Goode.

"Cease fire!" shouted MacAfee.

There were two final, stuttering shots, and then silence fell.

Jane dropped to her knees beside Cathy. From the congregation came a woman's wail, a high and eerie keening that did not even sound human. Now others joined in, a chorus of shrieks that soon became deafening as hundreds of voices cried out in grief for their fallen prophet. No one mourned Cathy Weiss. No one called out her name. Only Jane, kneeling on the bloody floor, was leaning in close enough to stare into the woman's eyes. Only Jane saw the light in those eyes fade out as her soul tumbled away.

"Murderer!" someone screamed. "She's a Judas!"

Jane looked at the body of Jeremiah Goode. Even in death, he was smiling.

THIRTY-SIX

HER BIRTH NAME WAS KATIE SHELDON," said Jane, as she and Maura drove toward Jackson. "At age thirteen, she became one of Jeremiah's so-called spiritual brides, expected to submit herself completely to his desires. For six years, she belonged to him. But somehow, she managed to pull together the courage to escape. And she fled The Gathering."

"That's when she changed her name?" asked Maura.

Jane nodded, but kept her eyes on her driving. "She became Catherine Sheldon Weiss. And she devoted her life to bringing down Jeremiah. The problem is, no one was listening to her. She was just a voice in the wilderness."

Maura stared ahead at what was now a familiar road, one she'd traveled every day to visit Rat at the hospital. This would be her last visit. Tomorrow, she was flying home to Boston, and she dreaded this goodbye. Dreaded it because she still did not know what kind of future she could offer him, what promises she could realistically keep. Little Katie Sheldon had been deeply poisoned by The Gathering; was Rat similarly damaged? Did Maura really want to take such a scarred creature into her home?

"At least this answers a few questions," said Jane.

Maura looked at her. "What questions?"

"About the double homicide at the Circle B Guest Ranch. The couple killed in their motel cabin. There was no forced entry. The killer simply walked in and proceeded to bash the husband's head, completely obliterating his face."

"A rage killing."

Jane nodded. "They found the murder weapon in Cathy's garage. A hammer."

"So there's no doubt she did it."

"It also explains another thing that puzzled me about that crime scene," said Jane. "There was a baby left alive in the crib. Not only was she unharmed, there were four empty bottles in the crib with her. The killer wanted that baby to survive. Even removed the DO NOT DISTURB sign, so housekeeping would be sure to come in and find the bodies." She glanced at Maura. "Sounds like someone who cares about kids, doesn't it?"

"A social worker."

"Cathy kept constant tabs on The Gathering. She knew when any of them showed up in town. Maybe she killed that couple out of fury. Or maybe she was just trying to save one baby girl." Jane gave a grim nod of approval. "In the end, she saved a lot of girls.

The kids are all in protective custody. And the women are starting to leave Plain of Angels. Just as Cathy predicted, the cult's collapsing without Jeremiah."

"But she had to kill him to make it happen."

"I'm not going to judge her. Think of how many lives he destroyed. Including the boy's."

"Rat has no one now," said Maura softly.

Jane looked at her. "You realize he comes with a big set of problems."

"I know."

"A juvenile record. Bounced around among foster homes. And now his mom and sister are dead."

"Why are you bringing this up, Jane?"

"Because I know you're thinking about adopting him."

"I want to do the right thing."

"You live alone. You have a demanding job."

"He saved my life. He deserves better than what he's got."

"And you're ready to be his mom? Ready to take on all his problems?"

"I don't know!" Maura sighed and looked out at snow-covered rooftops. "I just want to make a difference in his life."

"What about Daniel? How's the boy going to fit into that relationship?"

Maura didn't respond, because she herself didn't

know the answer. *What about Daniel? Where do we go from here?*

As they pulled into the hospital parking lot, Jane's cell phone rang. She glanced at the number and answered: "Hey, babe. What's up?"

Babe. The endearment slipped off Jane's lips so easily, so comfortably. This was how two people who shared both a bed and a life spoke to each other, no matter who was listening in. They didn't need to whisper, to slink off into the shadows. This was what love sounded like when it came out of the darkness and declared itself to the world.

"Is the lab absolutely certain about that result?" said Jane. "Maura's convinced otherwise."

Maura looked at her. "What result?"

"Yeah, I'll tell her. Maybe she can explain it. We'll see you guys at dinner." She hung up and looked at Maura. "Gabriel just spoke to the toxicology lab in Denver. They ran a STAT analysis of the girl's stomach contents."

"Did they find organophosphates?" asked Maura.

"No."

Maura shook her head in bewilderment. "But it was a classic case of organophosphate poisoning! All the clinical signs were there."

"She had no degradation products in her stomach. If she swallowed that pesticide, there should be some trace of it, right?"

"Yes, there should have been."

"Well, there was nothing," said Jane. "That's not what killed her."

Maura fell silent, unable to explain the results. "You can also absorb a fatal dose through the skin."

"Forty-one people got the stuff *splashed* on them? Does that sound likely?"

"The gastric analysis can't be right," said Maura.

"It's going to the FBI lab for further analysis. But right now, it looks like your diagnosis was wrong."

A medical supply truck rumbled into the parking lot and pulled up beside their vehicle. Maura struggled to concentrate as the truck's rear panel rattled open and two men began unloading oxygen tanks.

"Gruber had pinpoint pupils," said Maura. "And he definitely responded to that dose of atropine." She sat up straighter, more convinced than ever. "My diagnosis *has* to be correct."

"What else could cause those symptoms? Is there some other poison, something the lab might not have picked up?"

The noisy clang of metal made Maura glance out in annoyance at the two deliverymen. She focused on the oxygen tanks, lined up in the cart like green missiles, and a memory suddenly clicked into place. Something that she had seen in the valley of Kingdom Come, something she hadn't registered at the time. Like those oxygen tanks, it had been a cylinder, but it was gray and encrusted in snow. She thought of the Code Blue in the autopsy suite, remembering

Fred Gruber's pinpoint pupils and his response to atropine.

My diagnosis was almost right.

Almost.

Jane pushed open her car door and stepped out, but Maura didn't move from her seat. "Hey," said Jane, looking in at her. "Aren't we going in to visit the kid?"

Maura said, "We need to go to Kingdom Come."

"What?"

"There's only a few hours of daylight left. If we leave now, we can get there while it's still light. But we have to stop at a hardware store first."

"A hardware store? Why?"

"I want to buy a shovel."

"They've recovered all the bodies. There's nothing left to find there."

"Maybe there is." Maura waved Jane into the car. "Come on, let's go! We need to leave *now.*"

With a sigh, Jane climbed back behind the wheel. "This is going to make us late for dinner. And I haven't even started packing yet."

"It's our last chance to see the valley. Our last chance to understand what killed those people."

"I thought you had it all figured out."

Maura shook her head. "I was wrong."

Up the mountain road they drove, the same road that Maura had traveled on that unlucky day with Doug and Grace, Elaine and Arlo. She could still hear their voices arguing in the Suburban, could picture Grace's lips pursed into a sulk and Doug's unwavering cheerfulness as he insisted that everything would turn out okay, if you just trusted in the universe. Ghosts, she thought, and they still haunt this road. They still haunt me.

Today no snow was falling, and the road was plowed, but Maura could picture it as she'd seen it on that day, obscured by a blinding curtain of white. Here, at this bend, was the spot where they'd first talked about turning around. If only they had. How different everything would have come out if they had gone back down the mountain, if they had chosen, instead, to return to Jackson. They might have had lunch at a nice restaurant, said their goodbyes, and gone back to their lives. Perhaps, in some parallel universe, that was the choice they'd made, and in that universe Doug and Grace and Arlo and Elaine were still alive.

The PRIVATE ROAD sign loomed ahead. No snowdrifts, no chain or gate barred the way this time. Jane turned onto the road, and Maura remembered trudging past these same pine trees, Doug in the lead, Arlo dragging Elaine's roll-aboard suitcase. She remembered the sting of blowing snow and the darkness thickening around them.

The ghosts were here, too.

They passed the sign for Kingdom Come, and

as they started down the road into the valley,
Maura glimpsed charred foundations, and the ex-
cavated burial pit. Strands of discarded police
tape littered the field in bright slashes of color that
fluttered against the snow.

Jane's tires crunched over ice as they reached the
first ruined foundation.

"They found the bodies all buried together, over
there," said Jane, pointing to the pit that still gaped
in the snow. "If there's anything left to uncover
around here, it won't be obvious until spring."

Maura pushed open her door and stepped out.

"Where are you going?" Jane asked.

"For a walk." From the back, Maura pulled out
the shovel that she'd just purchased in the hardware store.

"I told you, they've already gone over this field."

"But did they search the woods?" Carrying the
shovel, Maura headed down the row of ruined
houses, the ice crackling beneath her boots. Everywhere, she saw evidence that law enforcement personnel had combed this site, from the trampled snow
to the multiple tire tracks to the cigarette butts and
scraps of paper fluttering across the snow. The sun
was sinking, taking with it the last daylight. She
strode more quickly now, leaving behind the burned
village, and started into the trees.

"Wait up!" Jane called.

She could not remember exactly where she and

Rat had entered the woods. Their snowshoe prints had since vanished under subsequent snowfall. She kept moving in the general direction in which they had fled from the men and the bloodhound. She had not brought snowshoes, and every step was hard work, through knee-high drifts. She heard Jane complaining loudly behind her, but Maura kept plowing ahead, dragging the shovel, her heart pounding from the effort. Had she gone too far into the woods? Had she missed the spot?

Then the trees opened up and the clearing stretched before her, the snow mounded over heaps of construction debris. The excavator was still parked at the far edge, and she saw the skeletal frames of new buildings, still awaiting completion. Here was the place where she had fallen, mired in a deep drift. Where she'd lain helplessly as the bloodhound closed in. She saw it all again, her pulse thudding at the memory. The bloodhound leaping toward her. His yelp of surprise as Bear intercepted him in midair.

All traces of the dogs' battle had vanished beneath fresh powder, but she could still make out the depression in the snow where she had fallen, could see the hilly contours of construction rubbish cloaked beneath white.

She sank her shovel into one of the mounds and flung aside a scoop of snow.

Jane finally caught up and trudged, panting, into the clearing. "Why are you digging in this spot?"

"I saw something here before. It might be nothing. It might be everything."

"Well, that sure answers my question."

Maura flung aside another scoop of snow. "I got only a glimpse of it. But if it's what I think it is . . ." Maura's shovel suddenly hit something solid. Something that gave off a muffled clang. "This could be it." She dropped to her knees and began scooping away the snow with her gloved hands.

Little by little the object emerged, smooth and curved. She could not pry it loose because it was solidly frozen to the mound of debris beneath it. She kept scooping away snow, but half of the object remained buried out of sight and encased in ice. What she'd exposed was one end of a gray metal cylinder. It was encircled by two painted stripes, one green and one yellow. Stamped on that cylinder was the code D568.

"What is that thing?" asked Jane.

Maura didn't answer. She just continued to scrape away snow and ice, exposing more and more of the cylinder. Jane knelt down to help her. New numbers appeared, stamped in green.

2011-42-114
155H
M12TAT

"You have any idea what these numbers mean?" Jane asked.

"I assume they're serial numbers of some kind."

"For what?"

A scrim of ice suddenly broke away, and Maura stared at the stenciled letters that she'd just revealed.

VX GAS

Jane frowned. "VX. Isn't that some kind of nerve gas?"

"That's exactly what it is," Maura said softly, and she rocked back on her knees, stunned. She stared across the clearing at the excavator. The settlers were putting up new buildings on this site, she thought. They'd cleared the trees and were digging foundations for more homes. Preparing the valley for new families who'd be moving into Kingdom Come.

Did they know that a time bomb lay buried in this soil, the soil they were digging into and churning up?

"A pesticide didn't kill these people," said Maura.

"But you said it matched the clinical picture."

"So does VX nerve gas. It kills in *exactly* the same way that organophosphates do. VX disrupts the same enzymes, causes the same symptoms, but it's far more potent. It's a chemical weapon designed to be dispersed through the air. If you release it in a low-lying area . . ." Maura looked at Jane. "It would turn this valley into a killing zone."

The growl of a truck engine made them both jump to their feet. *Our car is parked out in the open,* thought Maura. *Whoever has just arrived already knows we're here.*

"Are you carrying?" Maura asked. "Please tell me you're armed."

"I left it locked in the trunk."

"You have to get it."

"What the hell is going on?"

"*This* is what it's all about!" Maura pointed to the half buried canister of VX gas. "Not pesticides. Not mass suicide. It was an *accident*. These are chemical weapons, Jane. They should have been destroyed decades ago. They've probably been buried here for years."

"Then The Gathering—Jeremiah—"

"He had nothing to do with why these people died."

Jane looked around the clearing with growing comprehension. "The Dahlia Group—the fake company that paid off Martineau—it has something to do with them, doesn't it?"

They heard the snap of a breaking branch.

"*Hide!*" whispered Maura.

They both ducked into the woods just as Montgomery Loftus stepped into the clearing. He was carrying a rifle, but it was pointed at the ground, and he moved with the casual pace of a hunter who has not yet spotted his quarry. Their footprints were all over that clearing, and he could not miss the evidence of their presence. All he had to do was follow their tracks to where they both crouched among the pines. Yet he ignored the obvious and calmly approached the hole that Maura had just dug. He looked down at the exposed cylinder. At the shovel that Maura had left lying there.

"If you bury anything for thirty years, it'll eventually corrode," he said. "Metal gets brittle. Accidentally run over it with a bulldozer or crush it against a rock, and it'll fracture apart." He raised his voice, as though the trees themselves were his audience. "What do you think would happen if I fired a bullet at this right now?"

Only then did Maura realize that his rifle was pointing toward the canister. She remained frozen, afraid to make a sound. Out of the corner of her eye she noticed Jane slowly creep deeper into the woods, but Maura could not seem to move.

"VX gas doesn't take long to kill you," said Loftus. "That's what the contractor told me thirty years ago, when they paid me to dump it. Might take a little longer to disperse on a cold day like this. But on a warm day, it spreads fast. Blows on the wind, seeps through open windows. Into houses." He lifted his rifle and aimed at the canister.

Maura felt her heart lurch. One blast from that weapon would disperse a cloud of toxic gas that they could never hope to outrun. Just as the residents of Kingdom Come could not outrun it on that unseasonably warm November day, when they'd opened their windows and their lungs. Death had wafted in and swiftly claimed its victims: children at play, families gathered for meals. A woman on the stairs, whose dying tumble left her bleeding at the bottom.

"Don't!" Maura said. "Please." She stepped out from behind the tree. She could not see where Jane was; she knew only that Loftus was already aware of her presence, and she could not hope to outrun his bullet, either. But the rifle wasn't aimed at her; it remained pointed at the canister. "This is suicide," she said.

He gave her an ironic smile. "That is the general idea, ma'am. Since I can't see any way this is going to turn out right for me. Not now. Better this than prison." He looked off toward the destroyed village of Kingdom Come. "When they get back the final analysis on those bodies, they'll know what killed them. They'll be all over this valley, searching for what should've stayed buried. It won't take them long to come knocking on my door." He released a heavy sigh. "Thirty years ago, I never imagined . . ." The rifle drooped closer to the canister.

"You can make things right, Mr. Loftus," Maura said, struggling to keep her voice calm. Reasonable. "You can tell the authorities the truth."

"The truth?" He gave a grunt of self-disgust. "The truth is, I needed the goddamn money. The ranch needed it. And the contractor needed a cheap way to get rid of this."

"By turning the valley into a toxic dump?"

"We're the ones who paid to make these weapons. You and I and every other tax-paying American. But what do you do with chemical weapons when you can't use them anymore?"

"They should have been incinerated."

"You think government contractors actually built the fancy incinerators they promised? It was cheaper to haul this away and bury it." His gaze swept the clearing. "There was nothing here then, just an empty valley and a dirt road. I never thought there'd be families living here one day. They had no idea what was on their land. A single canister would've been enough to kill them all." He looked down, once again, at the cylinder. "When I found them, all I could think of was how to make those bodies go away."

"So you buried them."

"Contractor sent their own men to do it. But the blizzard moved in."

That's when we showed up. The unlucky tourists who stumbled into a ghost town. The same blinding snowstorm had stranded Maura and her party in Kingdom Come, where they saw too much, learned too much. *We would have revealed everything.*

Once again, Loftus lifted the rifle and aimed at the canister.

She took a panicked step toward him. "You could ask for immunity," she said.

"There's no immunity for killing innocent people."

"If you testify against the contractor—"

"They're the ones with the money. The lawyers."

"You can name names."

"I already have. There's an envelope in my truck. It has numbers, dates, names. Every detail I can remember. I hope it's enough to bring them down." His hand tightened around the rifle stock, and Maura's breath froze in her throat. *Where are you, Jane?*

The rustle of branches alerted Maura.

Loftus heard it, too. In that instant, whatever uncertainty had plagued him suddenly vanished. He looked down at the canister.

"This doesn't solve anything, Loftus," said Maura.

"It solves everything," he said.

Jane emerged from the woods, weapon clutched in both hands, barrel pointed at Loftus. "Drop the rifle," she said.

He looked at her with an expression that was strangely impassive. The face of a man who'd given up caring what happened next. "It's your move, Detective," he said. "Be a hero."

Jane took a step toward him, her weapon rocksteady. "It doesn't have to end this way."

"It's only a bullet," said Loftus. He turned toward the canister. Raised his rifle to fire.

The explosion sent a spray of blood across the white ground. For a second Loftus seemed to hang suspended, like a diver about to plunge into the ocean. The rifle dropped from his hand. Slowly, he collapsed forward, to sprawl facedown on the snow.

Jane lowered her weapon. "Jesus," she murmured. "He forced my hand!"

Maura dropped down beside Loftus and rolled him onto his back. Awareness had not yet left his gaze, and he stared up at her, as though memorizing her face. It was the last image he saw as the light left his eyes.

"I didn't have a choice," said Jane.

"No. You didn't. And he knew it." Slowly Maura rose to her feet and turned toward the vanished settlement of Kingdom Come. And she thought: They didn't have a choice, either, not those forty-one people who died here. Nor had Douglas and Grace, Elaine and Arlo. Most of us march through life never knowing how or when we'll die.

But Montgomery Loftus had made his choice. He had chosen today, by a cop's bullet, in this poisoned place.

Slowly she breathed out, and the white cloud from her breath curled into the twilight like one more untethered soul drifting into the valley of ghosts.

THIRTY-SEVEN

DANIEL WAS STANDING ON THE TARMAC, WAIT-
ing to greet them when Sansone's private jet
taxied to the executive air terminal. The same high
winds that had delayed their flight to Massachusetts
were now lashing Daniel's black coat and whipping
his hair, yet he stoically endured the gale's full force
as the jet came to a stop and the stairway was lowered.

Maura was first off the plane.

She walked down the steps, straight into his waiting arms. Only weeks ago, they would have greeted
each other with only a discreet peck on the cheek, a
chaste hug. They would have waited until they were
behind doors, the curtains drawn, before embracing.
But today was her homecoming, her return from the
dead, and he pulled her against him without hesitation.

Yet even as Daniel held her, joyfully murmuring
her name, pressing kisses to her face, her hair, she
was aware of her friends' eyes watching them.

Aware, too, of her own discomfort that what she had tried so long to conceal was now in the open.

It was not the biting wind, but her awareness of being watched that made her pull away from Daniel far too quickly. She glimpsed Sansone's darkly unreadable face, and she saw Jane awkwardly turn to avoid meeting her gaze. I may be back from the dead, she thought, but has anything really changed? I am still the same woman, and Daniel is the same man.

He was the one who drove her home.

In the darkness of her bedroom, they undressed each other, as they had so many times before. He kissed her bruises, her healing scratches. Caressed all the hollows, all the places where her bones were now far too prominent. My poor darling, you've lost so much weight, he told her. How he'd missed her. Mourned her.

It was not yet morning when she awakened. She sat in bed and watched him sleep as the night lifted outside the window, and she committed to memory his face, the sound of his breathing, the touch and the scent of him. Whenever he spent the night with her, dawn always brought sadness because it meant his leaving. On this morning, she felt it once again, and the association was so powerful that she wondered if she'd ever again be able to watch a sunrise without a stab of despair. You are both my love and my unhappiness, she thought. And I am yours.

She rose from bed, went into the kitchen, and made coffee. Stood at the window sipping it as daylight brightened, revealing a lawn laced with frost. She thought of those cold, silent mornings in Kingdom Come, where she had finally faced the truth about her own life. *I am trapped in my own snowbound valley. I am the only one who can rescue me.*

She finished her coffee and went back into her bedroom. Settling down beside Daniel, she watched him open his eyes and smile at her.

"I love you, Daniel," she said. "I will always love you. But it's time for us to say goodbye."

THIRTY-EIGHT

FOUR MONTHS LATER

J ULIAN PERKINS CARRIED HIS LUNCH TRAY FROM the high school cafeteria line and scanned the room for an empty table, but they were all occupied. He saw other students glance at him, and noticed how quickly they turned away, afraid that he might misconstrue their looks as invitations. He understood the meaning of those stubbornly hunched shoulders. He wasn't deaf to the snickers, the whispers.

God, he's weird.

The cult must've sucked out his brains.

My mom says he should be in juvie hall.

Julian finally spotted an available chair, and as he sat down, the other kids at the table quickly scooted away as though he were radioactive. Maybe he was. Maybe he emitted death rays that killed anyone he loved, anyone who loved *him*. He ate quickly, as he always did, like some feral animal afraid that his food would be snatched away, gulping down the turkey and rice in a few ravenous bites.

"Julian Perkins?" a teacher called out. "Is Julian Perkins in the cafeteria?"

The boy cringed as he felt everyone turn to look at him. He wanted to duck under the table where he could not be found. When a teacher yells your name in the cafeteria, it sure as hell isn't a good thing. The other students were gleefully pointing at him, and already Mr. Hazeldean was coming toward him, wearing his usual bow tie and scowl.

"Perkins."

Julian's head drooped. "Yes, sir," he mumbled.

"Principal wants you in his office."

"What did I do?"

"You probably know the answer to that one."

"No, sir, I don't."

"Then why don't you go and find out?"

Regretfully abandoning his uneaten chocolate pudding, Julian carried the tray to the dirty dishes window and started up the hallway toward Principal Gorchinski's office. Truly he did not know what he'd done wrong. All the other times, well, yeah. He should not have brought his hunting knife to school. He should not have borrowed Mrs. Pribble's car without her permission. But this time, he couldn't think of any infraction that would explain the summons.

When he reached Gorchinski's office, he had his all-purpose apology ready. *I knew it was stupid, sir.*

I'll never do it again, sir. Please don't call the police again, sir.

Principal G's secretary barely looked up as he walked in. "You can go straight into his office, Julian," she said. "They're waiting for you."

They. Plural. This was sounding worse and worse. The poker-faced secretary, as usual, gave nothing away—just kept tapping at her keyboard. Pausing outside Gorchinski's door, he prepared himself for whatever punishment was waiting. *I probably deserve it,* he thought, and stepped into the room.

"There you are, Julian. You have visitors," said Gorchinski. Smiling. This was new and different.

The boy looked at the three people who were seated across from Gorchinski. He already knew Beverly Cupido, his new caseworker, and she, too, was smiling. What was with all the friendly faces today? It made him nervous, because he knew that the cruelest of blows too often came with a smile.

"Julian," said Beverly, "I know it's been really rough for you this year. Losing your mother and sister. All those questions about the deputy. And I know you were disappointed that Dr. Isles wasn't approved as a foster parent."

"She wanted to have me," he said. "She said I could live with her in Boston."

"That wasn't an appropriate situation for you. For either one of you. We have to weigh the circumstances, and think about your welfare. Dr. Isles lives alone and she has a very demanding job, sometimes with night call. You'd be left alone far too much, without any supervision. It's not the sort of arrangement that a boy like you needs."

A boy who should be in juvie hall was what she meant.

"That's why these people have come to see you," said Beverly, gesturing to the man and woman who had risen from their chairs to greet him. "To offer you an alternative. They represent the Evensong School in Maine. A very good school, I might add."

Julian recognized the man as someone who had come to visit him while he was still in the hospital. That had been a confusing time, when he'd been foggy with pain meds, and there'd been detectives and nurses and social workers trooping through his hospital room. He didn't remember the man's name, but he definitely remembered those laser eyes, which were now fixed on him with such intensity that he felt all his secrets were suddenly laid bare. Discomfited by that gaze, Julian looked instead at the woman.

She was in her thirties, skinny, with shoulder-length brown hair. Although she was dressed conservatively in a gray skirt suit, there was no hiding the fact that she was pretty damn hot. The way she stood, one slim hip audaciously jutting out, head at a mischievous tilt, gave off a weird hint of street punk.

"Hello, Julian," the woman said. Smiling, she held out her hand to shake his, as if she were meeting an equal. An adult. "My name is Lily Saul. I teach the classics." She paused, noting his blank look. "Do you know what I mean by that?"

"I'm sorry, ma'am. No."

"It's history. The history of ancient Greece and Rome. Very fascinating stuff."

His head drooped. "I got a D in history."

"Maybe I can change that. Have you ever ridden a chariot, Julian? Swung a Spanish sword, the sword of the Roman army?"

"You do that at your school?"

"All that and more." She saw his chin suddenly tilt up in interest, and she laughed. "You see? History can be a lot more fun than you thought. Once you remember it's about people, and not just about boring dates and treaties. We're a very special school, in a very special setting. Lots of fields and woods, so you can even bring your dog if you'd like. I believe his name is Bear?"

"Yes, ma'am."

"We also have a library that any college would envy. And teachers who are among the best in their fields, from all around the world. It's a school for students who have special talents."

He didn't know what to say. He looked at Gorchinski and Beverly. They were both nodding approvingly.

"Does Evensong sound like a school that might interest you?" said Lily. "A place you might want to attend?"

"I'm sorry, ma'am," Julian said. "Are you sure you're talking to the right Perkins? There's a Billy Perkins in this school."

Amusement flickered in the woman's eyes. "I'm absolutely certain I have the right Perkins boy. Why would you think you're not the one we want?"

Julian sighed. "The truth is, my grades aren't all that good."

"I know. We've looked at your transcript."

Again he glanced at Beverly, wondering what the trick was. Why such a privilege was being offered to him.

"It's a great opportunity," said his caseworker. "A year-round boarding school with top academic standards. A full scholarship. They have only fifty students, so you'd get plenty of attention."

"Then why do they want *me*?"

His plaintive question hung for a moment unanswered. It was the man who finally spoke.

"Do you remember me, Julian?" he said. "We've met."

"Yes, sir." The boy found himself shrinking under the man's piercing gaze. "You came to see me at the hospital."

"I'm on the board of trustees at Evensong. It's a school I deeply believe in. A school for unique students. Young people who've proven themselves extraordinary in some way."

"Me?" The boy laughed in disbelief. "I'm a thief. They told you that, didn't they?"

"Yes, I know."

"I broke into houses. I stole stuff."

"I know."

"I killed a deputy. I shot him."

"To stay alive. It's a talent, you know. Just knowing how to survive."

Julian's gaze drifted to the window. Below was the school courtyard, where cliques of students were huddled together in the cold, laughing and gossiping. *I'll never be part of their world,* he thought. *I'll never be one of them. Is there anywhere in the world where I belong?*

"Ninety-nine percent of kids wouldn't have lived through what you did," said the man. "Because of you, my friend Maura is alive."

Julian looked at the man with sudden comprehension. "This is because of her, isn't it? Maura asked you to take me."

"Yes. But I'm also doing it for Evensong. Because I think you'll be an asset to us. An asset to . . ." He stopped. It was in that silence where the real answer lay. An answer that the man chose at that moment not to reveal. Instead, he smiled. "I'm sorry. I never properly introduced myself, did I? My name is Anthony Sansone." He extended his hand. "May we welcome you to Evensong, Julian?"

The boy stared at Sansone, trying to read his eyes. Trying to understand what was not being said. Principal Gorchinski and Beverly Cupido were both smiling cluelessly, oblivious to the strange current of tension in the room, a subaudible hum that told him there was more to the Evensong School than Lily Saul and Anthony Sansone were telling him. And that his life was about to change.

"Well, Julian?" said Sansone. His hand was still extended.

"My name is Rat," the boy said. And he took the man's hand.

ACKNOWLEDGMENTS

Writing is a lonely profession, but I am far from alone. I am fortunate to have the help and support of my husband, Jacob; my literary agent, Meg Ruley; and my editor, Linda Marrow. I owe thanks as well to Selina Walker at Transworld; to Brian McLendon, Libby McGuire, and Kim Hovey at Ballantine; and to the lively and wonderful crew at the Jane Rotrosen Agency.

Read on for an exciting preview
of Tess Gerritsen's next thrilling novel
featuring Maura Isles and Jane Rizzoli

THE SILENT GIRL

ONE

SAN FRANCISCO

ALL DAY, I HAVE BEEN WATCHING THE GIRL. She gives no indication that she's aware of me, although my rental car is within view of the street corner where she and the other teenagers have gathered this afternoon, doing whatever bored kids do to pass the time. She looks younger than the others, but perhaps it's because she's Asian and petite at seventeen, just a wisp of a girl. Her black hair is cropped as short as a boy's, and her blue jeans are ragged and torn. Not a fashion statement, I think, but a result of hard use and life on the streets. She puffs on a cigarette and exhales a cloud of smoke with the nonchalance of a street thug, an attitude that doesn't match her pale face and delicate Chinese features. She is pretty enough to attract the hungry stares of two men who pass by. The girl notices their gazes and looks straight back at them, unafraid. It's easy to be fearless when danger is merely an abstract concept. Faced with a real threat, how would this girl react? I wonder. Would she fight or would she crumble? I want to know, but I have yet to see her put to the test.

As evening falls, the teenagers on the corner begin to disband. First one and then another wanders away. In San Francisco, even summer nights are chilly, and those who remain huddle together in their sweaters and jackets, lighting one another's cigarettes, savoring the ephemeral heat of the flame. But cold and hunger eventually disperse the last of them, leaving only the girl, who has nowhere to go. She waves to her departing friends, and for a while lingers alone, as though waiting for someone. At last, with a shrug, she leaves the corner and walks in my direction, her hands thrust in her pockets. As she passes my car, she doesn't even glance at me, but looks straight ahead, her gaze focused and fierce, as if she's mentally churning over some dilemma. Perhaps she's thinking about where she's going to scavenge dinner tonight. Or perhaps it's something more consequential. Her future. Her survival.

She's probably unaware that two men are following her.

Seconds after she walks past my car, I spot the men emerging from an alley. I recognize them; it's the same pair who had stared at her earlier. As they move past my car, trailing her, one of the men looks at me through the windshield. It's just a quick glance to assess whether I am a threat. What he sees does not concern him in the least, and he and his companion keep walking. They move like the confident predators they are, stalking much weaker prey who cannot possibly fight them off.

I step out of my car and follow them. Just as they are following the girl.

She heads deep into the neighborhood south of Market Street, where too many buildings stand abandoned, where the sidewalks seem paved with broken bottles. The girl betrays no fear, no hesitation, as if this is familiar territory for her. Not once does she glance back, which tells me she is either foolhardy or clueless about the world and what it can do to girls like her. The men following her don't glance back either. Even if they did, which I do not allow, they would see nothing to fear. No one ever does.

A block ahead, the girl turns right, vanishing through a doorway.

I slip into the shadows and watch what happens next. The two men pause outside the building that the girl has entered, conferring over strategy. Then they too step inside.

From the sidewalk, I look up at the boarded-over windows. It is a vacant warehouse posted with a NO TRESPASSING notice. The door hangs ajar. I slip inside, into gloom so thick that I pause to let my eyes adjust as I rely on my other senses to take in what I cannot yet see. I hear the floor creaking. I smell burning candle wax. I see the faint glow of a doorway to my left. Pausing outside it, I peer into the room beyond.

The girl kneels before a makeshift table, her face lit by one flickering candle. Around her are signs of temporary habitation: a sleeping bag, tins of food, and a small camp stove. She is struggling with a balky can opener and is unaware of the two men closing in from behind.

Just as I draw in a breath to shout a warning, the girl whirls around to face the trespassers. All she has in her hand is the can opener, a meager weapon against two larger men.

"This is my home," she says. "Get out."

I had been prepared to intervene. Instead I pause where I am to watch what happens next. To see what the girl is made of.

One of the men laughs. "We're just visiting, honey."

"Did I invite you?"

"You look like you could use the company."

"You look like you could use a brain."

This, I think, is not a wise way to handle the situation. Now their lust is mingled with anger, a dangerous combination. Yet the girl stands perfectly still, perfectly calm, brandishing that pitiful kitchen utensil. As the men lunge, I am already on the balls of my feet, ready to spring.

The girl springs first. One leap and her foot thuds straight into the first man's sternum. It's an inelegant but effective blow and he staggers, gripping his chest as if he cannot breathe. Before the second man can react, she is already spinning toward him, and she slams the can opener against the side of his head. He howls and backs away.

This has turned interesting.

The first man has recovered and rushes at her, slamming her so hard that they both go sprawling onto the floor. She kicks and punches, and her fist cracks into his jaw. But fury has inured him to pain, and with a roar he rolls on top of her, immobilizing her with his weight.

Now the second man jumps back in. Grabbing her wrists, he pins them against the floor. Here is where youth and inexperience have landed her, in a calamity that she cannot possibly escape. As fierce as she is, the girl is green and untrained, and the inevitable is about to happen. Already the first man has unzipped her jeans and he yanks them down, past her skinny hips. His arousal is evident, his trousers bulging. Never is a man more vulnerable to attack.

He doesn't hear me coming. One moment he's unzipping his fly. The next, he's on the floor, his jaw shattered, loose teeth spilling from his mouth.

The second man barely has time to release the girl's hands and jump up, but he's not quick enough. I am the tiger and he is only a lumbering buffalo, stupid and helpless against my strike. With a shriek he drops to the ground, and judging by the grotesque angle of his arm, his bone has been snapped in two.

I grab the girl and yank her to her feet. "Are you un-hurt?"

She zips up her jeans and stares at me. "Who the hell are *you*?"

"That's for later. Now we go!" I bark.

"How did you do that? How did you bring them down so fast?"

"Do you want to learn?"

"Yes!"

I look at the two men groaning and writhing at our feet. "Then here is the first lesson: Know when to run." I give her a shove toward the door. "That time would be now."

I watch her eat. For such a small girl, she has the ap-petite of a wolf, and she devours three chicken tacos, a lake of refried beans, and a large glass of Coca-Cola. Mexican food was what she wanted, so we sit in a cafe where mariachi music plays and the walls are adorned with gaudy paintings of dancing señoritas. Though the girl's features are Chinese, she is clearly American, from her cropped hair to her tattered jeans. A crude and feral creature who noisily slurps up the last of her Coke and crunches loudly on the ice cubes.

I am beginning to doubt the wisdom of this venture. She is already too old to be taught, too wild to learn dis-cipline. I should simply release her back to the streets, if that's where she wants to go, and find another way. But then I notice the scars on her knuckles and remember how close she came to single-handedly taking down the two men. She has talent and she is fearless, and those are things that cannot be taught.

"Do you remember me?" I ask.

The girl sets down her glass and frowns. For an in-stant I think I see a flash of recognition, but then it's gone, and she shakes her head.

"It was a long time ago," I say. "Twelve years." An eternity for a girl so young. "You were small."

She shrugs. "Then no wonder I don't remember you." She reaches in her jacket, pulls out a cigarette, and starts to light it.

"You're polluting your body."

"It's my body," she retorts.

"Not if you wish to train." I reach across the table and snatch the cigarette from her lips. "If you want to learn, your attitude must change. You must show respect."

She snorts. "You sound like my mother."

"I knew your mother. In Boston."

"Well, she's dead."

"I know. She wrote me last month. She told me she was ill and had very little time left. That's why I'm here."

I'm surprised to see tears glisten in the girl's eyes, and she quickly turns away, as though ashamed to reveal weakness. But in that vulnerable instant, before she hides her eyes, she makes me think of my own daughter, who was younger than this girl's age when I lost her. I feel my own eyes sting with tears, but I don't try to hide them, because sorrow has made me who I am. It has been the refining fire that has honed my resolve and sharpened my purpose.

I need this girl. Clearly, she also needs me.

"It's taken me weeks to find you," I tell her.

"Foster home sucked. I'm better off on my own."

"If your mother saw you now, her heart would break."

"My mother never had time for me."

"Maybe because she was working two jobs, trying to keep you fed? Because she couldn't count on anyone but herself to do it?"

"She let the world walk all over her. Not once did I see her stand up for anything. Not even me."

"She was afraid."

"She was spineless."

I lean forward, suddenly enraged by this ungrateful brat. "Your poor mother suffered in ways you can't possibly imagine. Everything she did was for you." In disgust, I toss her cigarette back at her. She is not the girl I'd hoped to find. She may be strong and fearless, but no sense of filial duty binds her to her dead mother and father, no sense of family honor. Without those ties to our ancestors, we are lonely specks of dust, adrift and floating, attached to nothing and no one.

I pay the bill for her meal and stand. "Someday, I hope you find the wisdom to understand what your mother sacrificed for you."

"You're already leaving?"

"There's nothing I can teach you."

"Why would you want to, anyway? Why did you even come looking for me?"

"I thought I would find someone different. Someone I could teach. Someone who would help me."

"To do what?"

I don't know how to answer her question, and for a moment the only sound is the tinny mariachi music spilling from the restaurant speakers.

"Do you remember your father?" I ask. "Do you remember what happened to him?"

She stares back at me. "That's what this is all about, isn't it? That's why you came looking for me. Because my mother wrote you about him."

"I knew your father, too. He was a good man. He loved you, and you dishonor him. You dishonor both of them." I place a bundle of cash in front of her. "This is in their memory. Get off the street and go back to school. At least there, you won't have to fight off strange men." I turn and walk out of the restaurant.

In seconds she's out the door and running after me. "Wait," she calls. "Where are you going?"

"Back home to Boston."

"I do remember you. I think I know what you want."

I stop and face her. "It's what you should want, too."

"What do I have to do?"

I look her up and down. See scrawny shoulders and hips so narrow they barely hold up her blue jeans. "It's not what you need to do," I reply. "It's what you need to be."

Slowly I move toward her. Up till now she's seen no reason to fear me, and why should she? I am just a woman, the same age as her mother was. But something she now sees in my eyes makes her take a step back. For the first time she understands that this could be the beginning of her worst nightmare.

"Are you afraid?" I ask her softly.

Her chin juts up, and she says with foolish bravado, "No. I'm not."

"You should be."

TWO

SEVEN YEARS LATER

"MY NAME IS DR. MAURA ISLES, LAST NAME SPELLED I-S-L-E-S. I'm a forensic pathologist, employed by the medical examiner's office in the Commonwealth of Massachusetts."

"Please describe for the court your education and background, Dr. Isles," said the Suffolk County Assistant District Attorney, Carmela Aguilar.

Maura kept her gaze on the ADA as she answered the question. It was far easier to focus on Aguilar's neutral face than to see the glares coming from the defendant and his supporters, at least two dozen of whom had gathered in the courtroom. Aguilar did not seem to notice or care that she was arguing her case before a hostile audience, but Maura was acutely aware of it; a large segment of that audience was law enforcement officers and their friends. They were not going to like what Maura had to say.

The defendant was Boston PD Officer Wayne Brian Graff, square-jawed and broad-shouldered, the vision of an all-American hero. The room's sympathy was with Graff, not with the victim, a man who had ended up battered and broken on Maura's autopsy table six months ago. A man who'd been buried unmourned and unclaimed. A man who had, two hours before his death, committed the fatal sin of shooting and killing a police officer.

Maura felt all those courtroom gazes burning into her face, hot as laser points, as she recited her curriculum vitae.

"I graduated from Stanford University with a BA in Anthropology," she said. "I received my medical degree from the University of California in San Francisco, and went on to complete a five-year pathology residency at that same institution. I am certified in both anatomical and clinical pathology. I then completed a two-year fellowship in the subspecialty of forensic pathology, at the University of California, Los Angeles."

"And are you board certified in your field?"

"Yes, Ma'am. In both general and forensic pathology."

"And where have you worked prior to joining the M.E.'s office here in Boston?"

"For seven years, I was a pathologist with the M.E.'s office in San Francisco. I also served as a clinical professor of pathology at the University of California. I hold medical licenses in both the states of Massachusetts and California." It was more information than had been asked of her, and she could see Aguilar frown, because Maura had tripped up her planned sequence of questions. Maura had recited this information so many times before in court that she knew exactly what would be asked, and her responses were equally automatic. Where she'd trained, what her job required, and whether she was qualified to testify on this particular case.

Formalities completed, Aguilar finally got down to specifics. "Did you perform an autopsy on an individual named Fabian Dixon last October?"

"I did," answered Maura. A matter-of-fact response, yet she could feel the tension instantly ratchet up in the courtroom.

"Tell us how Mr. Dixon came to be a medical examiner's case." Aguilar stood with her gaze fixed on Maura's, as though to say: *Ignore everyone else in the room. Just look at me and state the facts.*

Maura straightened and began to speak, loudly enough for everyone in the courtroom to hear. "The decedent was a twenty-four-year-old man who was discovered unresponsive in the backseat of a Boston Police Department cruiser. This was approximately twenty minutes after his arrest. He was transported by ambulance to Massachusetts General Hospital, where he was pronounced dead on arrival in the emergency room."

"And that made him a medical examiner's case?"

"Yes, it did. He was subsequently transferred to our morgue."

"Describe for the court Mr. Dixon's appearance when you first saw him."

It didn't escape Maura's attention that Aguilar referred to the dead man by name. Not as *the body* or *the deceased*. It was her way of reminding the court that the victim had an identity. A name and a face and a life.

Maura responded likewise. "Mr. Dixon was a well-nourished man, of average height and weight, who arrived at our facility clothed only in cotton briefs and socks. His other clothing had been removed earlier during resuscitation attempts in the emergency room. EKG pads were still affixed to his chest, and an intravenous catheter remained in his left arm . . ." She paused. Here was where things got uncomfortable. Although she avoided looking at the audience and the defendant, she could feel their eyes on her.

"And the condition of his body? Would you describe it for us?" Aguilar prodded.

"There were multiple bruises over the chest, the left flank, and the upper abdomen. Both eyes were swollen shut, and there were lacerations of the lip and scalp.

Two of his teeth—the upper front incisors—were missing."

"Objection." The defense attorney stood. "There's no way of knowing when he lost those teeth. They could have been missing for years."

"One tooth showed up on X-ray. In his stomach," said Maura.

"The witness should refrain from commenting until I've ruled," the judge cut in severely. He looked at the defense attorney. "Objection overruled. Ms. Aguilar, proceed."

The ADA nodded, her lips twitching into a smile, and she refocused on Maura. "So Mr. Dixon was badly bruised, he had lacerations, and at least *one* of his teeth had recently been knocked out."

"Yes," said Maura. "As you'll see from the morgue photographs."

"If it please the court, we would like to show those morgue photos now," said Aguilar. "I should warn the audience, these are not pleasant to look at. If any visitors in the courtroom would prefer not to see them, I suggest they leave at this point." She paused and looked around.

No one left the room.

As the first slide went up, revealing Fabian Dixon's battered body, there were audible intakes of breath. Maura had kept her description of Dixon's bruises understated, because she knew the photos would tell the story better than she could. Photos couldn't be accused of taking sides or lying. And the truth staring from that image was obvious to all: Fabian Dixon had been savagely battered before being placed in the backseat of the police cruiser.

Other slides appeared as Maura described what she had found on autopsy. Multiple broken ribs. A swallowed tooth in the stomach. Aspirated blood in the lungs. And the cause of death: a splenic rupture, which had led to massive intraperitoneal hemorrhage.

"And what was the manner of Mr. Dixon's death, Dr. Isles?" Aguilar asked.

This was the key question, the one that she dreaded answering, because of the consequences that would follow.

"Homicide," said Maura. It was not her job to point out the guilty party. She restricted her answer to that one word, but she couldn't help glancing at Wayne Graff. The accused police officer sat motionless, his face as unreadable as granite. For more than a decade, he had served the city of Boston with distinction. A dozen character witnesses had stepped forward to tell the court how Officer Graff had courageously come to their aid. He was a hero, they said, and Maura believed them.

But on the night of October 31, the night that Fabian Dixon murdered a police officer, Wayne Graff and his partner had transformed into angels of vengeance. They'd made the arrest, and Dixon was in their custody when he died. *Subject was agitated and violent, as if under the influence of PCP or crack,* they wrote in their statement. They described Dixon's crazed resistance, his superhuman strength. It had taken both officers to wrestle the prisoner into the cruiser. *Controlling him required force, but he did not seem to notice pain. During this struggle, he was making grunts and animal sounds and trying to take off his clothes, even though it was forty degrees that night.* They had described, almost too perfectly, the known medical condition of excited delirium, which had killed other cocaine-addled prisoners.

But months later, the toxicology report showed only alcohol in Dixon's system. It left no doubt in Maura's mind that the manner of death was homicide. And one of the killers now sat at the defense table, staring at Maura.

"I have no further questions," said Aguilar and she sat down, looking confident that she had successfully made her case.

Morris Whaley, the defense attorney, rose for the

cross-examination, and Maura felt her muscles tense. Whaley appeared cordial enough as he approached the witness stand, as if he intended only to have a friendly chat. Had they met at a cocktail party, she might have found him pleasant company, an attractive enough man in his Brooks Brothers suit.

"I think we're all impressed by your credentials, Dr. Isles," he said. "So I won't take up any more of the court's time reviewing your academic achievements."

She said nothing, just stared at his smiling face, wondering from which direction the attack would come.

"I don't think anyone in this room doubts that you've worked hard to get where you are today," Whaley continued. "Especially taking into account some of the challenges you've faced in your personal life in the past few months."

"Objection." Aguilar heaved an exasperated sigh and stood. "This is not relevant."

"It is, your honor. It goes to the witness's judgment," said Whaley.

"How so?" the judge countered.

"Past experiences can affect how a witness interprets the evidence."

"What experiences are you referring to?"

"If you'll allow me to explore that issue, it will become apparent."

The judge stared hard at Whaley. "For the moment, I'll allow this line of questioning. But only for the moment."

Aguilar sat back down, scowling.

Whaley turned his attention back to Maura. "Dr. Isles, do you happen to recall the date that you examined the deceased?"

Maura paused, taken aback by the abrupt return to the topic of the autopsy. It did not slip past her that he'd avoided using the victim's name.

"You are referring to Mr. Dixon?" she said, and saw irritation flicker in his eyes.

"Yes."

"The date of the postmortem was November first of last year."

"And on that date, did you determine the cause of death?"

"Yes. As I said earlier, he died of massive internal hemorrhage secondary to a ruptured spleen."

"On that same date, did you also specify the manner of death?"

She hesitated. "No. At least, not a final—"

"Why not?"

She took a breath, aware of all the eyes watching her. "I wanted to wait for the results of the toxicology screen. To see whether Mr. Dixon was, in fact, under the influence of cocaine or other pharmaceuticals. I wanted to be cautious."

"As well you should. When your decision could destroy the careers, even the lives, of two dedicated peace officers."

"I don't concern myself with consequences, Mr. Whaley. I only concern myself with the facts. Wherever they may lead."

He didn't like that answer; she could see it in the twitch of his jaw muscle. All semblance of cordiality had vanished; this was now a battle.

"So you performed the autopsy on November first," he said.

"Yes."

"What happened after that?"

"I'm not sure what you're referring to."

"Did you take the weekend off? Did you spend the following week performing other autopsies?"

She stared at him, anxiety coiling like a serpent in her stomach. She didn't know where he was taking this, but she didn't like the direction. "I attended a pathology conference," she said.

"In Wyoming, I believe."

"Yes."

"Where you had something of a traumatic experience. You were assaulted by a rogue police officer."

Aguilar shot to her feet. "Objection! Not relevant!"

"Overruled," the judge said.

Whaley smiled, his path now cleared to ask the questions that Maura dreaded. "Is that correct, Dr. Isles?" Whaley asked. "Were you attacked by a police officer?"

"Yes," she whispered.

"I'm afraid I didn't hear that."

"Yes," she repeated, louder.

"And how did you survive that attack?"

The room was dead silent, waiting for her story. A story she didn't even want to think about, because it still gave her nightmares. She remembered the lonely hilltop in Wyoming. She remembered the thud of the deputy's vehicle door as it closed, trapping her in the backseat behind the prisoner gate. She remembered her panic as she'd futilely battered her hands against the window, trying to escape from a man she knew was about to kill her.

"Dr. Isles, how did you survive? Who came to your aid?"

She swallowed. "A boy."

"Julian Perkins, age sixteen, I believe. A young man who shot and killed that police officer."

"He had no choice!"

Whaley cocked his head. "You're defending a boy who killed a cop?"

"A *bad* cop!"

"And then you came home to Boston. And declared Mr. Dixon's death a homicide."

"Because it was."

"Or was it merely a tragic accident? The unavoidable

consequence after a violent prisoner fights back and has to be subdued?"

"You saw the morgue photos. The police used far more force than was necessary."

"So did that boy in Wyoming, Julian Perkins. He shot and killed a sheriff's deputy. Do you consider that justifiable force?"

"Objection," said Aguilar. "Dr. Isles isn't the one on trial here."

Whaley barreled ahead with the next question, his gaze fixed on Maura. "What happened out there in Wyoming, Dr. Isles? While you were fighting for your life, was there an epiphany? A sudden realization that cops are the enemy?"

"Objection!"

"Or have cops always been the enemy? Members of your own family seem to think so."

The gavel banged down. "Mr. Whaley, you will approach the bench *now.*"

Maura sat stunned as both attorneys huddled with the judge. So it had come to this, the dredging up of her family. Every cop in Boston probably knew about her mother, Amalthea, now serving a life sentence in a women's prison in Framingham. The monster who gave birth to me, she thought. Everyone who looks at me must wonder if the same evil has seeped into my blood as well. She saw that the defendant, Officer Graff, was staring at her. Their gazes locked, and a smile curled his lips. *Welcome to the consequences,* she read in his eyes. *This is what happens when you betray the thin blue line.*

"The court will take a recess," the judge announced. "We'll resume at two this afternoon."

As the jury filed out, Maura sagged back against the chair and didn't notice that Aguilar was standing beside her.

"That was dirty pool," said Aguilar. "It should never have been allowed."

"He made it all about me," said Maura.

"Yeah, well, that's all he has. Because the autopsy photos are pretty damn convincing." Aguilar looked hard at her. "Is there anything else I should know about you, Dr. Isles?"

"Other than the fact that my mother's a convicted murderer and I torture kittens for fun?"

"I'm not laughing."

"You said it earlier. I'm not the one on trial."

"No, but they'll try to make it about you. Whether you hate cops. Whether you have a hidden agenda. We could lose this case if that jury thinks you're not on the level. So tell me if there's anything else they might bring up. Any secrets that you haven't mentioned to me."

Maura considered the private embarrassments that she guarded. The illicit affair that she'd just ended. Her family's history of violence. "Everyone has secrets," she said. "Mine aren't relevant."

"Let's hope not," said Aguilar.